I0552460

DEDICATION AND ACKNOWLEDGEMENTS

This novel is dedicated to my lovely wife, Kat, and the many other wonderful people who made this book possible. Special thanks to Jim, Shana, Rakie, Matthew, Sonja, Bobbie, Devan, Tim, Joe, Thom, and everyone else.

C. T. Phipps

ELDRITCH OPS

BOOK 2 OF THE RED ROOM SERIES

BY C. T. PHIPPS

"I hate being a bureaucrat," I muttered, sitting at a table in the back of an Aspen ski lodge. I was in a large, log-cabin cafeteria by a window overlooking the slopes. It was a public place, filled with mundanes—the perfect place for a meeting between two groups of supernaturals who didn't trust one another. It was a hour past sunset and everyone was enjoying the brightly lit slopes.

"Oh, quit your bitching." Shannon O'Reilly's voice spoke through my concealed earpiece. "You're in Aspen on the House's dime. Stop acting like you're locked in the basement doing accounting reports."

Though we weren't partners anymore, Shannon usually accompanied me on my missions for the Committee. We'd been together over a year, and my succubus girlfriend made these little excursions much easier.

"You have me there. Still, I was useful in the field," I said, taking a sip of my hot cocoa. "The majority of my work now consists of signing off on other people's missions and coddling VIPs. That's not real spy work."

"Real spy work involves tapping phones, long hours in crappy hotels, and paying people to give us their boss's trash. I'm up for the more sedate life of a House politician. Twice the glamour and half the sleeping with loathsome targets."

"Point taken."

"Are you sure it's not who you're meeting with rather than why?"

"It's both. I've killed more vampires than any other field agent this century," I said, rolling my eyes. "This is like sending Jack the Ripper to negotiate with the International Union of Sex Workers."4

They even had a name for me: The Cleaver. I hated vampires because of what they'd done to my former partner, Christopher, and had done my best to enact a bloody vengeance on them with what influence I'd wielded in the House. I'd stopped that pursuit after ascending to the Committee. I had too much influence now to merrily plunge the House into war. Millions could die if I fumbled the ball here. But no pressure, eh?

PROLOGUE

Monsters are real. This is a fact I've lived with my entire life. I was born to it, you might say. My ancestors have been members of the House, the secret society that covers up the creepy-crawlies, since John Dee and Hiawatha. I was raised to know there was no other way to deal with the supernatural than a bullet to the head, which is awkward when your mother is a dragon.

I'm one hundred percent human (it's complicated), but that didn't keep me from realizing the House's worldview wasn't entirely accurate. It's gotten doubly complicated since I started dating a succubus full time. That doesn't mean the monsters aren't dangerous, mind you. The majority may not be any worse than regular humanity, but as history shows, that's still pretty damn evil. Also, some of the monsters really are soulless killing machines.

My name is Derek Hawthorne, and I am the youngest member of the House to ascend to membership in the Committee. I'm not very good at my job; I was raised to be an agent rather than a leader. Worse, I'm not entirely in step with the rest of my fellows. They're very much of the "the only good supernatural is a dead supernatural," bent and believe the supernatural should be covered up at all costs. That kind of attitude isn't an option anymore, though. In the age of social media, instant messengers, cellphone videos, and YouTube, it's only a matter of time before regular humanity learns it's not alone in the big scary world.

Recently, tensions have risen between the House and one of the more powerful supernatural factions. The Vampire Nation, an alliance of bloodsucking horrors the world over, has been implicated in a series of magical terrorist attacks worldwide. This is a direct violation of the many treaties it has signed with the House. The war hawks are itching for a fight against them, to prove we're still the biggest, baddest baddies on the block.

I've been sent to prevent that. To preserve the peace—even if I hate vampires for what they did to my partner. This is the story of how I failed.

CHAPTER ONE

"I hate being a bureaucrat," I muttered, sitting at a table in the back of an Aspen ski lodge. I was in a large, log-cabin cafeteria by a window overlooking the slopes. It was a public place, filled with mundanes—the perfect place for a meeting between two groups of supernaturals who didn't trust one another. It was a hour past sunset and everyone was enjoying the brightly lit slopes.

"Oh, quit your bitching." Shannon O'Reilly's voice spoke through my concealed earpiece. "You're in Aspen on the House's dime. Stop acting like you're locked in the basement doing accounting reports."

Though we weren't partners anymore, Shannon usually accompanied me on my missions for the Committee. We'd been together over a year, and my succubus girlfriend made these little excursions much easier.

"You have me there. Still, I was *useful* in the field," I said, taking a sip of my hot cocoa. "The majority of my work now consists of signing off on other people's missions and coddling VIPs. That's not real spy work."

"Real spy work involves tapping phones, long hours in crappy hotels, and paying people to give us their boss's trash. I'm up for the more sedate life of a House politician. Twice the glamour and half the sleeping with loathsome targets."

"Point taken."

"Are you sure it's not *who* you're meeting with rather than why?"

"It's both. I've killed more vampires than any other field agent this century," I said, rolling my eyes. "This is like sending Jack the Ripper to negotiate with the International Union of Sex Workers."

They even had a name for me: The Cleaver. I hated vampires because of what they'd done to my former partner, Christopher, and had done my best to enact a bloody vengeance on them with what influence I'd wielded in the House. I'd stopped that pursuit after ascending to the Committee. I had too much influence now to merrily plunge the House into war. Millions could die if I fumbled the ball here. But no pressure, eh?

"Actually, this is more like sending *me* to negotiate with the International Union of Sex Workers. I'm the one who kills people with a kiss," Shannon joked. "This? This makes perfect sense. You're a vicious killer; they're vicious killers. It's kismet."

"Are you in position?" I said, deciding to change the subject.

"Affirmative," Shannon replied. "Anyone tries to hit you from the right side and I've got you."

"I'm watching the left," I said, frowning. "We should have people covering all the exits and windows."

"Blame cutbacks," Shannon said, her voice serious. "Senior agents are spread very thin since the whole kerfuffle with Cassandra last year. We've got people covering potential sniper targets and other places, but we don't have enough people to cover a closer target."

"Do we even know who the ambassador is?"

"Nope."

"Great." I rubbed the bridge of my nose. "Listen, just keep me informed. These negotiations have to succeed. Open warfare is a real possibility."

Dozens of agents had been assassinated in recent memory, and several large-scale massacres of humans had been conducted, resulting in hundreds of deaths. The bodies had been mutilated badly and evidence left of vampirism. It was a deliberate challenge to the House's authority, even if it was also tremendously stupid. After all, the Vampire Nation had as much to lose as anyone if the truth came out.

"Do you really think they're responsible?" Shannon asked.

"No. It'd require too much courage to provoke us the way these incidents have. Vampires are scavengers, not genuine predators. They're a species of cowards and parasites that send others to die in their place. This is likely a group of extremists, but we need to force them to take care of the issue."

"Yes, I suppose you do," a voice said behind me. It was male, familiar, and tinged with a British accent. "Though I would argue that vampires are *very good* at making other people die in their place. Parasites and cowards, we may be, but we're hardly weak."

I stared, stunned. "You..."

"Me," the vampire said, sitting down across from me.

My third partner. Christopher Hang. The reason I hated the undead. Those bastards had turned him.

"Huh," I said, not sure what else to say.

Christopher didn't look a day older than thirty, appearing much as he did when he was dragged off during our battle with the Vampire Nation in New York. He had shining black hair that trailed down to his shoulders and model good looks. Christopher was dressed smartly, having traded his agent's business suit for a black winter coat and pants that cost more than a new car. I looked at him in sheer disbelief, unsure what to say to a man who had been my closest friend—now an enemy of the House.

"Should I say the obligatory 'You look like you've seen a ghost'?" Christopher said, smiling.

"A ghost would be less surprising," I said, stunned. "I'm sorry, Chris. I am. I didn't—"

Christopher raised his right palm. "No apologies necessary. You did everything you could. In fact, more than you should have. Did you actually kill the entire New York City agents by yourself?"

I looked away, feeling silly. "I wasn't alone. There were other guys with me."

Including my brother Alec's crew of mercenaries. I wasn't about to implicate them to the Vampire Nation, though, even if I wanted desperately to trust Christopher. Given the amount of brainwashing new recruits went through, it was entirely possible he wasn't the Christopher I once knew.

"You shouldn't have done that. Not all the people killed in your retaliation deserved to die."

I was surprised by my response. I wanted to defend my

actions but found myself unable to do so. Instead, I just said, "I wish I could have done more."

"You did what you could." Christopher gestured for a buxom, blonde-haired slope bunny, and she brought him a cup of hot cocoa without prompting. He smiled at her, and I suspected she would have offered her neck then and there if he'd asked. Instead, he gestured for her to depart and she did, leaving us alone again. "There's something you can do for me."

"What's that?" I asked, trying to recover my sense of decorum.

"We'll get to that," Christopher said.

Knowing Christopher was alive—unalive—whatever left me rattled even as I did my best not to show it. I'd been an agent for the House for over a decade, and much of that had been lonely bitter nights fighting monsters, not knowing who I could trust. At one point, Christopher had been the person I'd trusted most in the world. He was responsible for helping me get my fiancé out of the House and knew all my secrets.

While the emotional part of me was overjoyed he was in front of me, the more logical side started calculating just how much damage his being a vampire could do to us. How much had he told his fellows? What secrets had been compromised? Did he feel any loyalty to me, or had they managed to mesmerize it out of him? I wanted to believe my friend was the same person he'd been four years ago but that was unlikely.

"You look well, Derek," Christopher said, smiling. It seemed forced, somehow, as if it wasn't an action he was used to anymore. "Two eyes, too. I'd heard you lost one fighting the Wazir."

"In fact, it was the Committee who tore it out," I said.

Christopher's face remained impassive. "I see."

"The House has an excellent health plan, though." I tapped my left eye with my forefinger. "Got a magictech replacement in three weeks."

"Impressive," Christopher said, without emotion.

"Not really. So, you're my contact?" I asked, pushing that thought down. "How did you get on the Council of Ancients so fast? You've only been a vampire a short time. I mean, it's in the name: Council of Ancients. 1000+ years undead or bust. You're not even an Old One."

"I might ask you the same thing," Christopher said, stirring his cocoa with his long finger. "When I last knew you, you said everyone over the rank of senior agent was a horse's ass. How the hell did you become one of the Committee?"

"It's a long story," I said.

"Same here," Christopher said. "Let's just say I'm more their herald than an actual member, though. Even then, I had to pull a few strings to get assigned the job. They're the most trusting bunch of eldritch monsters."

I realized I wasn't going to get any more. "Consider the subject closed. I suppose we're here to negotiate a settlement."

Christopher reached under his coat, and I tensed up before I saw he was removing a folder similar to the ones I had. "Negotiating a settlement is easy enough. However, that is not why I brought you here."

"I will do anything I can." I paused. "Within reason."

"First, business." Christopher pulled out a manila envelope and slid it across the table. "This should be able to get your superiors off our backs."

"I only have equals and subordinates now."

"Does the rest of the Committee know that?"

It was a well-known fact the other members of the ruling commitee considered me a junior member at best. It was a fact he shouldn't know, though.

"They will soon," I said, my gaze darkening.

"If you say so."

Looking over my shoulder to make sure no one was paying attention, I took the envelope and opened it. Inside, I saw the detailed history and profile of a long-standing enemy of the Red Room: John Ruthford. He was a renegade Old One who was responsible for thousands of human deaths as well as the deaths of numerous agents.

The folder listed not just his safe houses, contacts, and bank accounts, but also his itinerary for the next few months. The Vampire Nation offering him up would go a long way to normalizing relations with the House. Mind you, we'd have to figure out a way to kill him permanently that would stick. Ruthven's group wasn't related to the more recent terrorist attacks, though, and made me wonder if this was some sort of dodge. If so, it was a good one.

"This is like giving me the Devil's GPS coordinates," I said, whistling. "How the hell did you get all this?"

"I called in every favor I could. It wasn't easy," Christopher said. "You have a lot of enemies."

"For what I did trying to avenge you," I said.

"I wasn't dead, Derek," Christopher said.

I glared. "*I didn't know that.* I've lost three partners over the years. Each time it's like being shot in the stomach."

"I'd like to believe we're still friends and partners." Christopher laughed. "The next question I'm going to ask you leans on our friendship."

"Are you the same man I knew?" I asked.

"Are you?" Christopher asked.

"Don't dodge the question," I said.

Christopher paused before responding. The resulting silence was oppressive and reminded me I was in the presence of a predator who considered my race food—no matter what he'd once been. "No, Derek, I'm not. My hands aren't clean. However, I am mostly me. I also think what I'm about to ask you is something I can only get from you and is the greatest favor I could ask."

"Is it for the Vampire Nation?" I asked.

"No," Christopher replied.

"Good." I paused, considering my answer. "I might do a favor for you. I'll never do one for an enemy state. Tell me what I can help you with."

Christopher's expression became serious. "Protocol Zero."

I stared at him, shaking my head. "Sorry, never heard of it."

"Come on, Derek." There was a hint of anger in his face before he clenched his fists. It was uncharacteristic behavior from my usually cool and confident friend. Then again, that had been before he became a bloodsucking creature of the night.

"This is one of those situations where the answer would be the same whether I knew anything or not. If you have any trust in me, please understand I've never heard of a Protocol Zero," I said.

Christopher's shoulders deflated. "This is personal for me. Have you, at least, heard about Protocol Ten?"

I reluctantly nodded. "It was a plan by the Red Room to inoculate most of the world with a dangerous anti-vampire viral toxin. One of the so-called Black Protocols. Over a course of three to eight months, it would kill every single vampire who fed on the vaccinated subjects. It was the hope of the Committee they could wipe out the majority of the world's undead without war. The program to develop the serum was started in 1983 and lasted until 2013 when—"

"You shut it down," Christopher interrupted. "A curious response from an avowed vampire hater."

"Just because I think vampirism is a curse rather than a blessing doesn't mean I'm comfortable massacring everyone who suffers from it."

"Not everyone feels like you do."

I stared at him. "I've questioned my beliefs. Sometimes, the behavior of the Vampire Nation makes me think you are all evil. That doesn't mean I'm going to act as judge, jury, and executioner without having all the facts."

"Admirable," Christopher said, almost as if he was mocking me.

I didn't like that and stared. Was he making fun of me? Was the monster still my friend at all? I couldn't tell.

"I mean that sincerely," Christopher said, placing a hand over his heart. "I've heard about your efforts to integrate supernaturals into the House."

Thanks to my efforts, the first supernatural agents had been accepted into the Red Room's ranks. We'd gotten more intelligence from those who hated their own kind in the past three months than we'd gotten in the past ten years from other sources.

I wasn't going to let myself get distracted by flattery. "Tell me about this Protocol Zero and what you think it is."

Christopher tapped the folder he'd laid before me. "I believe Protocol Zero, a phrase we've heard from a number of resources but in very hushed tones with no reliable first source, is a project based out of the Red Room. It is based around kidnapping supernaturals, brainwashing them, and turning them into sleeper agents. They're responsible for the recent disasters."

"And your evidence for this is?" I asked.

"Suicide attacks, assassinations, sabotage, and out-of-character actions from numerous sources. There's been several kidnappings we've started to develop a pattern for. People go off the grid for months at a time before reappearing."

"So, you have no evidence for this," I said dryly.

"One of the ones who has disappeared is my wife." Christopher looked straight into my eyes. "I need you to find her. Please."

I stared at him, unsure how to respond. On one hand, a man I once considered my best friend was asking me to find his wife. On the other, he was accusing the Red Room of being responsible. My organization could do what he was describing, but I would know if they were—and they weren't. Yet how could I tell him that he was barking up the wrong tree? I'd hold onto any hope if the person I loved was in danger. "I don't—"

Shannon interrupted me, shouting over the earpiece so I could hear her. "Derek, get down!"

I didn't hesitate, throwing myself to the floor.

Above me, the window shattered, and the air filled with bullets.

CHAPTER TWO

Glass rained down onto my shoulders as bullets whizzed through the air above my head. Thankfully, the gunfire missed all the ski lodge's patrons. That didn't prevent all-out pandemonium from ensuing. People screamed, ran in every direction, and threw themselves to the ground, unaware who was attacking them or why.

A smart assassin would have continued firing until we were dead or have used something more precise than random gunfire, but no second burst emerged, probably because he was waiting to confirm our deaths.

I hated amateurs.

Christopher was clutching his shoulder. The vampire's left side had taken an orihalcum bullet and the magical metal was burning inside him, causing a sickening odor to emanate from the wound where it poisoned his insides. The bullet wasn't deep, however, and Christopher jammed a metal fork in, prying it out.

"Are you all right?" I asked.

"Just kill that bastard!" Christopher hissed.

"All right."

Above our heads, I heard the sound of a snowmobile revving up. Risking looking up over the window's edge, I saw a single red jumpsuit-wearing figure in a helmet on a black snowmobile. He had a Jupiter-82 submachine gun he was holding like he'd only had a little practice with it. Our attacker fired a couple of more rounds against the side of the building while I ducked below the table to avoid being hit. I heard him drive off a few seconds later. Rising, I was tempted to put a bullet in the back of the figure's head, but as much as I wanted to, I needed to know who he was and whether he was working for anyone. I shielded my face with my arm and smashed through the remains of the window.

Running across the snow, I saw an abandoned still-running blue snowmobile owned by the lodge ski patrol and commandeered it. Squeezing on the accelerator, I took off after my rapidly disappearing assailant. He was heading down one of the bunny slopes and would get away if I didn't get to him quickly.

"Derek, I need an update!" I heard Shannon's voice coming from my earpiece.

"The assailant has orihalcum-based weaponry. Christopher is down but not out. In pursuit," I said, feeling bits of snow splatter against my face. "I need you to check on Hang. It's possible this was a distraction to get me away from him, so they can assassinate one or both of us."

"Copy," Shannon said. "Good luck."

I smiled. "He'll need it more than I will."

If I'd been thinking like a Committee member rather than an agent, I would have focused on getting myself to safety. I was, after all, a VIP and one of the most important assets of the House. Unfortunately, a year hadn't dulled the fact that I'd been one of the House's best wetworks men, and it wasn't until later that I realized chasing down an assassin via snowmobile just made me a bigger target.

Old habits die hard.

"Come on, you bastard," I muttered, the icy wind blasting against my face as I sped up.

The distance between my assailant and I diminished until we were only a few yards apart. That was when I saw him make a turn over a plastic sign planted into the snow that folded underneath his vehicle, which soon went under me as well. The sign said "DANGER - SLOPE CLOSED DUE TO SEVERE CONDITIONS." The side of the mountain gave way to a massive obstacle course of ice and rocks. A severe storm had covered the place in a landslide that seemed almost tailor-made for killing us.

Seeing it was entirely likely they'd used a witch to conjure it for that very purpose, I thought about my options. I needed to get within enough range to tackle the son of a bitch and disable him. Hopefully, he was human and wouldn't rip my arm off, but those were the dangers you dealt with as a Red Room agent.

If not? Well, life was short anyway.

I was within striking distance when the amateur took one arm off the wheel and grabbed his submachine gun, trying to take me out. Seizing that opportunity, I leapt forward and knocked him off his vehicle. The two of us slammed against the ground, with me using my assailant as a cushion. I'd misjudged our speed and the hardness of our landing. It hurt like hell, tearing up my knee and banging up my right arm. That was going to require some magic, possibly surgery, to fix.

I grunted, rolling over the figure underneath me and lifting him up to my face. "Who sent you?!"

My assailant turned out to be a dull-eyed blond man in his mid-forties with a stubble beard and vacant expression. He tried to hike his submachine gun, but I slammed my head into his, giving me a serious headache and knocking my opponent out. One look at him told me he'd been mesmerized.

Mesmerism wasn't an accurate term for the use of psychic abilities to brainwash people, but it'd fallen into Red Room jargon anyway. You couldn't mind control someone to love you or even to be your friend, but it could turn even strong-willed individuals into sleeper agents. I was dealing with nothing more than a patsy. No wonder he'd attacked so amateurishly.

"Christopher, I hope you're not responsible for this ..." I muttered. It was hard to suspect Christopher, but mesmerism was one of the chief tools of the vampire.

My thoughts were interrupted by the sound of four more snowmobiles coming my way. Looking up at the top of the closed slope, I saw a quartet of men in red jumpsuits riding on snowmobiles identical to my attacker's. They were carrying A-17 sniper rifles, far superior to J-82 for the terrain. They also carried themselves differently from their colleague. No, as they began aiming at me, I realized I was dealing with professionals. Dammit.

I threw myself behind a nearby rocky outcropping for

cover. A second after I did so, I heard a cartridge ricochet. I was trapped now, my enemies possessing a substantial advantage in terms of range as well as hardware.

Taking a deep breath as more shots whizzed into the side of the rock, I contemplated my options. I could call for backup, I could try and engage them by magically pulling a gun to me Jedi-style, or I could try to pull a rabbit out of my hat with my magic. Which was option one too now that I thought about it. Knowing Shannon would never let me down and not wanting to wait for her arrival, I decided to try for option three.

I rubbed the silver ring on my left hand. I'd spent most of my life without magic but I'd recently had awakened to it and done my best to learn as much as I could. I wasn't as good at sorcery as as my twin sister Penny had been when she was fourteen, but I was still able to pull off the occasional trick— especially with my power object.

Magic didn't work the same way as it did in the movies with wands, staves, and chants—though they were damn useful (we called them enhancers). You had to want something so badly that you were capable of imposing your will on the nature of reality, bringing your desires about. That required emotional energy dwarfing what most people felt in their lifetime.

My wedding ring was one of the few items I possessed capable of serving as a channel for my emotions, though not for the reasons you'd expect. My ex-wife, Cassandra, never loved me. She'd been brainwashed by her father into thinking she did. My feelings regarding our marriage were a mixture of guilt, shame, anger, and pain. Emotions I could harness to fuel my sorcery.

Channeling those feelings into my right hand, I slammed down my fist into the ice. All four of the assassins fell to the ground and slid down the slope. I couldn't shake the mountain, not at my level, but I was certainly able to make them *feel* like I could. Adjusting the flow of ki, or life-force, into my body, I increased my natural balance before moving to the next stage of my half-formed plan.

"Let's hope this works," I said. Reaching my right hand into my jacket, I pulled out my Pantheon .50 pistol and stood up, before starting to run. I was severely injured but I could control my ki enough to compensate—though that was probably just going to injure me further. Still, I was going to die unless I moved, and I could depend on the House's magic and advanced medicine to fix me if I survived.

A big "if."

I had just enough time to cross the distance and get into range to fire, shooting two of my assailants on the ground before they could get at their rifles. A third lifted his, only for me to throw myself on the ground and put a bullet through his head.

Which left one.

"Surrender!" I shouted, watching the final member of the team crawl behind a snowmobile with his weapon.

"No! God wills it!" the last remaining assailant shouted.

"God wills what?" I snapped.

His snowmobile and the ones around it exploded. I covered my face as sparks and bits of burning metal flew through the air and dropped down alongside me. The last of my attackers had possessed a grenade.

Climbing to my feet, I stared. "What the fuckity-fuck?"

Contrary to what *Doctor No* might tell you, people committing suicide to avoid being captured was pretty rare in the spy game. I'd seen it a total of twice before, and both situations were specifically the result of mental compulsion. A guy doing the whole "kill himself because God commands him to" thing was a new experience.

"Derek!" Shannon called, not on my earpiece but nearby.

I looked over to see Shannon coming over the side of the mountaintop, using skis like a pro and wearing a bright blue jumpsuit that contrasted with her long, dyed red hair. Shannon was a beautiful woman, unearthly so, the product of a union between a lilin and a normal woman. A succubus. I was glad she was on our side, having chosen to work with the Red Room even before nonhumans had been allowed membership.

Sliding and slipping down the sheet of ice, I saw the figure of Christopher Hang follow with unnatural steps. As a vampire, he didn't need skis to traverse snow. Vampires were powerful psychics who could practice levitation and flight. Vampires didn't so much move across the ground as glide, and it was somewhat unsettling to see my old friend move like he was no longer of this Earth. Which he wasn't, of course. To add to the odd juxtaposition, he was holding a seventeenth-century cutlass stained with blood.

I raised my hand, waving to them. "Nothing to see here, guys. Just four corpses. Everything's fine."

"I fear the number of bodies is going to get much larger before this ends," Christopher said, walking to me. "We were ambushed by a dozen gun-wielding men almost as soon as you left. This is going to be a rather bloody mess for you and your organization to clean up."

"You killed a dozen humans?" I asked, staring at my friend.

"I killed six," Shannon said, looking hurt.

I bit my lip, realizing my hypocrisy. I couldn't worry about my friend being a monster when the woman I loved was one too. Also, it was a trifle hypocritical when I was standing over the charred remains of four people I'd killed myself. Gods and immortals, sixteen people killed in the United States? Christopher was right—the clean-up crews were going to be apoplectic.

"Do you believe me now?" Christopher said, looking at the bloody remains with a longing look.

"I never said I didn't believe you." I pulled out my cellphone and dialed a special number. "I'm going to need your help in covering this up."

"Just as long as I don't have to be here when the Red Room's agents show up. I suspect the majority of them won't be as accommodating as you," Christopher said, putting on a pair of sunglasses to protect him from the sun's glare off the snow.

"I'm not accommodating. Working with vampire agents and traitors has increased the effectiveness of the Red Room's response against the Vampire Nation by twenty-one percent."

"It's closer to fifteen percent. Quite a few of those guys are working for us, working for you, working for us."

Shannon shook her head in dismay. "Spywork."

Looking at Shannon, I wondered what she thought of

Christopher and whether he could be trusted. She'd probably tell me to stake him and forget all thoughts of peace, let alone do him a favor. Casting aside those thoughts, I dialed the closest Red Room sub-station capable of dealing with our shootout's aftermath. Once I heard someone pick up the other line, I said, "This is Redwood-1. Authorization Code –Sigma-Alpha-Charlie. There's a Type-3 class cover-up needed at the Hopeview Lodge and Resort. We need all of the calls redirected, psychics for reprogramming, counselors, and a cover story. There's over a dozen bodies, so we should mesmerize people into thinking there's just a single body." I noticed Christopher was listening in. "I also will need our codes changed since this line isn't secure."

Christopher shrugged. "You can't blame a guy for trying."

"I can and I will."

I was answered on the other line by a man with a French accent. "Affirmative, Counselor. Estimation for arrival in thirty-two minutes."

"Make it twenty," I said, closing my cellphone.

"Do you believe me now?" Christopher asked, sticking his bloody sword into the ice.

Shannon answered for me. "A group of assassins after you doesn't indicate this is the work of your mythical conspiracy. Botched attempts to kill Derek are a weekly event. Tuesday, we had someone planning a car bomb. The Wednesday before that he had a Hoodoo curse for him to die of syphilis."

"It's been a rough year." I smiled. "Who knew so many people wanted to kill a member of the Committee."

"Everybody?" Shannon said.

"That's only because they all want to do it. Everyone wants a crack at the big dogs."

Christopher shook his head and handed me his sword. "Take this. It'll lead you to everything I've learned so far. If you're not convinced, I'll trust you'll be able to find out what is going on by yourself. I want to know if my wife is still alive, or whatever passes for it amongst our kind, and if not—who I have to kill to avenge her. You're the one person in the world I know who can make it happen." Christopher's expression didn't change as he spoke. His face no longer had automatic tics with his feelings, but his emotions required conscious effort to display. It was unsettling on a familiar face.

"Thank you," I said, taking the blade. It was heavy but otherwise felt like cold steel. There was none of the supernatural "aura" I felt from most artifacts. "Wait, *will* lead me? You can't just tell me?"

Christopher shrugged. "When you're immortal, whimsy becomes one of your last resorts."

Without speaking further, my ex-partner transformed into a shadow and vanished from sight. I wasn't sure if he could shape-shift, a rare gift amongst the undead, or whether it was just a trick of the mind. It didn't matter either way but reminded me my friend had changed beyond recognition.

Shannon looked at the burning corpses around me. "Do you think there's anything to his claims?"

"The last of them said 'God wills it' before he died. It could have been an attempt to throw us off track, but somehow, I doubt it. The Red Room has been secular since the twelfth century, so I'm inclined to think this is a group of God botherers."

Countless religious groups with supernatural agendas existed alongside the House. Most of these groups didn't last very long but included bodies like the True Rosicrucians, the Holy Hand of Allah, the Defenders of Judea, and the Poor Knights of Saint Peter. Vampires were hated by the majority of said groups. One of the few areas where I agreed with them. I was religious, myself, but felt I needed to keep a secular view of the supernatural.

"You remember I'm Catholic, right?" Shannon said, her expression chiding.

"I don't hold it against you," I said, smirking. "I'm religious myself, but I'm not the type to believe in fanaticism like blowing yourself up."

"You just believe it's right to kill and die for the House— which is worse than any three major religions combined."

"I'm not going to argue because I might sound unconvincing."

Shannon rolled her eyes. Then she took a deep breath. "I know I set up the meeting, but the circumstances of this attack were pretty suspicious. Do you believe Christopher?"

I shook my head. "Becoming a vampire changes you on a fundamental level. Vampires are known to brainwash their creations into becoming their slaves. Then there's the whole marriage thing."

Shannon placed a hand on my shoulder. "Love can change even the strongest beliefs."

"Love can destroy someone or raise them to godhood," I said, reciting one of my father's favorite quotes. "If anyone asks, I'm going to be investigating this because he provided that information on Ruthford. It's a pragmatic arrangement between two hostile foreign powers, nothing more."

"And in reality?"

"You have to ask?" I looked at her, disappointed. "I protect my friends, even if they're monsters."

Gods and immortals help me, I'd made my choice.

"I'm counting on that." Shannon said.

In the distance, I saw the movement of black unmarked helicopters—the standardized transports of the Red Room. They were arriving fast, which meant that either someone had taken my request seriously or they'd been waiting in the wings the entire time. My money was on the latter. There was just one man in the Red Room with that kind of pull who also had it in for me.

I was going to have to have a talk with the Professor.

CHAPTER THREE

A Type-Three cover-up was what happened when something nasty occurred in public involving Red Room agents. In today's age of cellphones, texts, and ubiquitous internet access, any witnessed incident could blow up into a major crisis for the Red Room's security. Thankfully, this hadn't involved anything overtly supernatural and merely looked like an old-fashioned shootout.

I used to take it for granted how much effort went into covering up the supernatural. Ironic, given my job. But watching the Red Room set up hundreds of relief tents and trauma counselors while sending fake police officers throughout the area—well, I had to say I was impressed.

Wandering through the junior agents and other people involved in the cover-up with my cutlass in hand, I came upon the sight of a tall, balding, African-American man in a jet-black suit. He looked like hundreds of bureaucrats who worked in Washington, D.C., only distinct now because he was standing outside a ski lodge looking pensive.

The Professor was a former CIA agent brought into the fold by my father. As a result, he was used to a certain way of doing things that often conflicted with the old boy network the House ran. That effect was doubled when he dealt with how I did things. He'd described it as "when cowboy agents meet gross insanity."

Several times, the Professor had threatened to have me sanctioned, which was Red Room speak for "shot in the back of the head and dumped in a back alley." I'm not sure he would have been wrong, either. After my second partner's death, I'd played it close to the edge and may have been daring him to make the call. I wouldn't say I'd developed a death wish, but having killed and lied for a decade, I was sick of the Great Game and wanted out. Things had changed in the past year, however, not the least thing being I was now his superior rather than his subordinate. Being on the other side of the desk made me appreciate more what his job entailed.

I still thought he was a prick.

"Hello, Professor. How's Mary Ann?" I said, striding up to his side and smiling in the most insincere manner possible.

"How long have you been saving that one?" The Professor said, unimpressed.

"About ten years," I said. "Now I can say it to your face, though. Why were you having me followed?"

"I don't know what you mean."

"This entire set-up would take eight or nine hours. You had it ready to move within five minutes."

"You're a member of the Committee, it falls onto the Red Room to guarantee your safety. I was preparing for your meeting with the Vampire Nation's representative to go south in the way your meetings with supernatural representatives tend to go."

"Funny, I'm pretty sure you're supposed to inform me of these sorts of maneuvers beforehand. Otherwise, it'll feel like you were doing this sort of shit behind my back."

"I wouldn't *need* to do this sort of thing behind your back if I didn't think, instead of having an evacuation plan, you'd choose to get into a gunfight with five Teutonic Knights."

"What?" I was shocked by my attackers' identity. "*Those guys?*"

"The Order of Brothers of the German House of Saint Mary, yes," the Professor said, sighing. "They were almost eradicated by Napoleon Bonaparte but went underground, passing along membership through the paternal lineage as secret societies are wont to do. We thought their last Grandmaster died in Heinrich Himmler's dungeons, but it appears we were wrong. The Teutonics direct their focus on destroying the undead and guarding profane relics. Assuming any remain after you and your partner killed an entire chapter."

"They started shooting first." It was a weak excuse. Truth

be told, I should have evacuated rather than attempt to engage them myself.

But I was in charge, so I did what I wanted.

The Professor wasn't impressed with my defense. "If we'd lost you, the treaty with the Vampire Nation would have fallen through. Despite the way you choose to act and my own personal feelings, you are not expendable."

"The hit was on Christopher Hang, not me."

The Professor stared at me, surprised. It was the first time I'd ever seen him that way. "They turned him?"

"A full one-eighty degrees. It's Rambo putting on a furry hat and waving around a hammer and sickle. We can presume anything he knew about the House and its structures is now known to the Vampire Nation."

The Professor looked at me sideways "You're not going to say he'd never betray us or something equally maudlin?"

"He was my best friend. I'm not so new to the Great Game that I don't realize he may not be the man I thought he was, either."

"Or even the man he claims to be. He could be a shape-shifter or someone they've altered to resemble him."

That was an angle I hadn't considered. "That's an awfully large amount of trouble to mess with me."

The professor snorted. "After Agent Hang was killed, you led the most ruthless suppression of vampires in modern history. It was one of the few times I considered your over-the-top antics to be justified, as it instilled fear and respect into the undead. Fear and respect that guards our agents' lives when they're compromised in the field. Your death would be an excellent way to demoralize the Red Room if they intended to go to war."

"If they were going to kill me, they would have used a better agent. These guys were strictly karaoke night."

"Like an agent shaped like your old partner?"

He had me there. "Point taken. Still, it was Christopher Hang. I know it. You can't fake some things."

The Professor shook his head. "There's no way of proving that without a DNA test and a series of divinations."

"Let's move on, shall we? Have you checked out those

documents he gave us?" I asked, making it a command. Rank had its privileges.

The Professor sighed. "About Ruthford, yes. Do I have your permission to make a strike?"

"Hit the bastard's location so hard not even necromancy will be able to raise him. Maybe throw some holy wafers and garlic over the ashes to be sure. That's not what I want to talk about, though," I said.

"What is?" the Professor said.

"We need to speak in private."

"Why do I always get the impression you're plotting against our organization whenever you say things like that?"

"Because intra-office politics kills half as many agents as the supernatural?"

"Touché."

The Professor moved down the hall as he started discussing risk management in allowing the patrons to leave for the next few days. When we were walking on the snow outside, he adjusted the Ring of Veritas on his right finger before I did the same. They were standard issue for Red Room agents and only other members of the organization could understand conversations, except for the ones owned by executives.

"All right, we can talk freely," the Professor said.

"What do you know about Protocol Zero?"

"Is that what Christopher Hang was asking about?"

"Let's say it was."

"It doesn't exist."

"Doesn't exist, or it exists but you're denying it exists?" I asked, serious despite my wordplay. The Professor had insight into the Red Room's operations that I didn't, even if he'd been born outside of it.

"It's a vampire conspiracy theory about the House. Anti-supernatural protocols one through seventeen all exist or existed, but zero was just the imaginings of paranoid bloodsuckers playing with half-truths and misinformation. It's the equivalent of the moon landing being faked." The Professor paused in mid-step. "I mean, yes, we removed the castles and so on from the photos, but we visited."

I didn't know how to respond to that.

The Professor pointed at my chest. "See? That's how irritating your jokes are."

"I'd never joke about the moon landing. Some things are sacred," I said, sighing. "Okay, say just for the sake of argument that Christopher thinks there's more to this program than meets the eye and believes it's responsible for his wife's disappearance."

"Why are we doing favors for vampires?" the Professor asked. "I mean, you hate them more than I do, and I approve of poisoning the lot of them like Blade."

I raised an eyebrow.

The Professor shrugged. "What? Wesley Snipes is a god."

"We're doing this favor because Christopher's provided us valuable intelligence that may lead to the destruction of one of the most important vampire terrorists in the world. If we can cultivate him as an asset within the Vampire Nation, it could be a serious boon to our intelligence efforts and lead to a demobilization of our resources against the undead."

"Peace with vampires is like peace with Nazis. I don't care what one hundred years of romantic fiction says."

I wasn't sure I disagreed. "Freeing up resources used to monitor and contain groups we have treaties with will allow us to eliminate esoterrorist groups we're just managing to hold our own against. We took a serious hit from Cassandra, and even the death of the Wazir and the majority of the Emerald Eye hasn't allowed—"

The Professor raised his right hand. "You don't have to justify yourself to me, Derek. That's what being on the Committee means. I may disagree with your choice of actions, but it's my job to support you when you make your decisions. That's what being part of an organization means."

"No wonder I hate it."

The Professor glared. "You should take whatever evidence you've compiled to Doctor Danvers-Hawthorne. If it *is* Christopher Hang you met with, it must have been some pretty compelling evidence to convince him a nonexistent branch of the House is behind his wife's kidnapping. He was not a stupid agent, even if he had a little too much of your paranoia."

"You're not paranoid if they're out to get you."

The Professor smiled and turned to me. "But which they?"

I smirked. "I see. You think this is a setup."

"Obviously," the Professor said.

"The Teutonic Knights?" I suggested.

"No, they're too straight-forward for this sort of action. More likely, they were manipulated into this by a third party. Given they were willing to risk eliminating leaders from both the Red Room and Vampire Nation's leadership, whoever is responsible is either desperate or confident enough he can deal with the retaliation by both."

I nodded. "So, someone powerful or too arrogant to realize how dangerous this is."

"Which can go hand in hand. Should I bother warning you this is too dangerous for you to investigate personally?" The Professor crossed his arms.

"Probably not. If I die, the rest of the Committee will have you promoted before my body is cold."

"I'd feel guilty about that. For at least an hour," the professor said.

I was starting to like the Professor. I'd have to nip that in the bud. "Thank you for your advice. I'll get Lucy right on the cutlass."

"I was wondering why you were carrying that." The Professor turned to the rest of the group. "Then I realized I didn't care. Is there anything else, or can I get back to the job of covering up your little shootout?"

I wasn't about to mention I'd agreed to look into this for Christopher. "No, I'm fine."

"Then Godspeed." The Professor departed.

Turning around and walking over to a series of crimson tents set up far from the rest of the lodge, I saw the White Room lab junkies sorting through the remains of the snowmobiles and the deceased Teutonic Knights. In a few hours, they'd be transferred to the laboratories back in D.C. for further examination, but I didn't expect much information to be obtained.

In the central tent, I saw Shannon talking to my sister-in-law,

Lucy. Lucy Danvers-Hawthorne was a year younger than me with long black hair she kept tied in a ponytail. She had pale skin and was on the short side, coming up to my chin. Today, she was bundled up in thick blue winter clothing and earmuffs with a white scarf around her neck.

Lucy was the smartest person I'd ever known, a polymath among polymaths, but was far too nice for the work she'd been called upon to do. If not for my sister's relationship with her, I'd suspect she'd have gone crazy long ago. Hell, since their marriage, Lucy had gotten much better mentally. The very fact she was outside of the Division One laboratories was a vast improvement on her previous behavior. Until last year, when we'd been forced out by an esoterrorist threat, she hadn't been off-site in a decade.

"The Teutonic Knights' bodies were damaged by the grenade blast, but I'm inclined to think they may not have been operating on their free will any more than the individual Derek incapacitated," Lucy said, talking to Shannon as I approached. Neither seemed to notice me, but I didn't think I could sneak up on Shannon in the middle of the night during a bombing run.

"Have you had a chance to investigate him? Was it vampire mesmerism?" Shannon asked, her arms folded across his chest.

"No," Lucy said, frowning. "That's the weird part. It appears to be something similar to vampire mesmerism but induced through a mixture of light-to-retinal manipulation and subliminal suggestion. Replicating that sort of mind control is possible with the House's resources, implying Protocol Zero exists, but that's adjusting evidence to fit theories rather than adjusting theories to fit evidence."

Brainwashing and mesmerism were the one area the Red Room had a strict rule against. On my watch, the rules had been relaxed to help provide alternatives to dealing with witnesses to supernatural activity. There was less need to kill someone for knowing too much if you could just remove their memories of an event, after all. I still debated if revoking the ban was the right decision. I suppressed those thoughts for the time being. "Interesting."

"I got that from *Sherlock*," Lucy said, sticking up her thumbs. "Love that show."

"So, we're dealing with non-magical mind controlled Teutonic Knights trying to kill me at a ski lodge?" I shook my head, calling attention to myself. "Only in America."

"Actually, the technology is in prototype form in Japan. Nothing concrete, but enough certain parties could reverse—" Lucy started to say.

"We'll follow up on that," I interrupted her, waving my sword at her. "I was curious if you might do me a favor and examine something."

"Oh, can I!?" Lucy said, clapping her hands. "I've always wanted to examine a real V.N. leader's blade!"

I tossed it to her, hilt first, only for her to miss it with her gloved hands. The blade landed in the snow at her feet.

Lucy looked down at the blade. "Fudge."

"Derek, I think we should talk about Christopher," Shannon said, crossing her arms. "I think your feelings may be compromised on this."

"Later," I said, not really interested in getting into a debate on it.

"Derek—"

"Later, please."

Shannon looked unhappy but nodded.

Lucy picked up the sword between her hands and started examining the blade. Her eyes widened as if she realized she were holding plutonium. "Um, Derek, I think you should return this to the Vampire Nation. Like now."

"Excuse me?' I asked, doing a double take. "Why would I do that?"

Lucy looked at me frantic. "Otherwise, I think you're going to start a war."

CHAPTER FOUR

I turned to Lucy, stunned by her statement. "Would you mind repeating that?"

Lucy took a deep breath, lifting the cutlass. "I think this is the Bloodsword. *The* Bloodsword."

"Aside from the sword having a generic yet badass name, does that mean something?" Shannon pointed a gloved finger at the blade.

"The Bloodsword is the symbol of office for the Vampire Nation's military commander." I stared at the blade. "It's one of the most powerful enhancers in the world and said to be indestructible. Lucy, are you sure it's not a replica?"

"I'd need to run some tests, but it bears all the outside markers. I can also feel the magic woven into this thing," Lucy said, waving it around a bit. "I think this is the real McCoy."

"There's no way the Warlord of the Vampire Nation would part with it," I said, wondering why I hadn't felt anything from the weapon.

"Who?" Shannon said, surprising me with her ignorance.

"Dracula," I said. "I thought you destroyed him once."

Dracula, as a vampire Old One, was almost impossible to kill. When most agents found out the Vampire Nation's most prominent member Dracula, they tended to react with laughter rather than horror. The truth was, though, Bram Stoker's book had been published by him to build his legend and manipulate the public's perception of vampires. It had mostly created a legion of amateur vampire hunters who got themselves killed as well as hundreds of glory-seeking undead eager to get their story translated to books or film. Dracula, himself, was supposedly a very different figure from the creepy aristocrat depicted in the book and had tried several times to kill Stoker for it. The Red Room had protected him, though, because it irritated the hell out of our primary foes.

"I ripped his head off in my succubus form. Not exactly a situation useful for chatting," Shannon said. "I haven't really immersed myself in vampire lore."

"Ooo, a chance for exposition," Lucy said, clapping her hands. "Derek, do you want to handle this?"

"Certainly," I said, amusing myself. I was still mad at her, but I couldn't help teasing her over this. "After the whole Turk slaughter and first death thing, Dracula turned pirate. That was when the Vampire Nation was formed by an alliance of the Council of Ancients with all the local *voivodes*. Strangely, the treaty was signed in Nassau."

The sea was a surprisingly good environment for the undead, food issues aside. Contrary to popular perception, vampires weren't very social creatures. They tended to freak out normal people and draw unnecessary attention with their inability to control their feeding. Plenty of ships believed to be shipwrecked or lost in storms were, in fact, depopulated by the undead. Nowadays, they simply made people disappear who wouldn't be missed. And there were a lot in the modern world.

"I'm not surprised you don't know," Lucy said, looking excited at a chance to explain. She started twirling around the sword for emphasis. "Only a few House leaders know the true history of the Vampire Nation. A lot of our current information was acquired by Derek during his murder-hobo spree."

"Murder-hobo?" I asked.

Lucy grimaced. "You were kind of in a bad place for a few months. They should have pulled you off that assignment and got you counselling immediately."

"The Committee wanted to make a statement. I made one." It was amazing that war hadn't happened, but the Vampire Nation had disavowed the actions of Elizabeth Bathory and her entire bloodline. The destruction of the New York City crew had also been one of the biggest non-war victories the House had achieved until shutting down the Emerald Eye last year. My part in both was one of the few reasons anyone in the

Committee paid any attention to my suggestions. That and all the blackmail material I'd managed to assemble in addition to the Wazir's old files.

Shannon looked between us, pointing. "Okay, give me the Cliff Notes version of vampire history. I have a feeling I'm going to need to know this."

Lucy grinned. "Can I do the rest of the explanation, Derek? Pleeeeease."

"Knock yourself out, Mrs. Wizard."

Lucy looked ecstatic. "Up until the Information Sharing Act of six months ago, a lot of divisions kept their files separate, so individual agents had varying degrees of knowledge regarding the supernatural in the House. They believed vampires were a form of hungry ghost like the jiang Shi or draugr. Flesh-hungry zombies just better preserved and not on a liquid diet. In fact, vampires aren't even undead."

"They aren't?" I asked, surprised. "I'm pretty sure they're dead. At least they don't bleed when you chop off their limbs."

"Ewwww," Lucy said, grimacing.

"Ha! I'm not the only one here with stuff to learn," Shannon said, letting out a short laugh.

Lucy recovered herself. "They have a deathly countenance, but that's different from being undead. Otherwise, they wouldn't be able to sire children or make others of their kind. Well, at least without significant scientific alterations like Cassandra made to the draugr. Vampires are the mystical descendants of the demon queen Lamia, who was cursed by the Creator to crave the blood of her children."

I frowned, regretting opening this can of worms. "Cut to the chase, Lucy."

"I'm getting there." Lucy shook her hands in frustration. "Well, the undead species for the most part, but Dracula changed this when he moved vampires from their traditional Babylonian paganism to a form of Satanism. Even so, vampires didn't have any real culture or government until Dracula created their first real society based on the republican ideals of the Nassau Pirates. Every vampire had rights even if it was all controlled by an oligarchy of the oldest and strongest. Like the pirates did there."

"Republican . . . pirates," Shannon said, as if the two words were contradictory.

Lucy continued, ignoring my desire for a swift explanation. "The majority of pirates during their heyday in the Caribbean were just out-of-work sailors after Queen Anne's War. People like Blackbeard didn't kill all that many people. They relied, instead, on their reputation to intimidate people into submitting. Besides, they were mostly robbing people who profited from the slave trade. Vampire pirates? They were the exception. They cut a bloody swath across the ocean and left nightmares in their wake."

"The more you know," Shannon said, looking more confused than enlightened. "Why the Caribbean?"

"Dracula was fleeing the House," Lucy explained. "They'd gotten sick of the chaos he'd sown in Eastern Europe and chased him to England and beyond by the end of the sixteenth century. He murdered a slave trader named Jack Standington and assumed his identity. Later, he'd go by the alias 'Red Jack.' The House reported killing him sixteen times both before and after this event. It's believed Tiamat-Abaddon's pact with Dracula granted him true immortality."

Tiamat-Abaddon was the name of the monster that supposedly ruled hell. Apparently, Lucifer had been overthrown by his daughter with an unknown mother. Tiamat-Abaddon was the inspiration for monsters like Judaism's Lilith and the Gaia who birthed the giants in Greek Mythology. She was the Mother of All Monsters and the person who created most of the supernatural races thousands of years ago.

"Most Old Ones are only killable only by other vampires," Lucy said. "Holy magic can get around that and pure sorcery but it's very hard to kill a centuries-old vampire permanently. Dracula is even harder to kill than most. His demon-worshiping followers have been known to resurrect him with necromancy."

"Nothing is immortal," I said. "Not even him."

"The Bloodsword was Jack's blade." Lucy handed me back the cutlass. "Which means, in addition to being a famous pirate sword, it's also the symbol of Dracula's authority. According to legend, it was given to him by Tiamat-Abaddon as a symbol of their bargain."

"So, Christopher stole the vampire crown jewels?" Shannon asked.

"So it seems," I said, staring at the blade now in my hands. "In between Dracula's resurrections, whoever holds the Bloodsword is ruler of the Vampire Nation. By presenting this weapon to me, he's given me an immense amount of leverage to play with."

Lucy stared, reminding me I hadn't told her. "Wait, Christopher is alive? Christopher Hang? As a vampire? Awesome!"

I narrowed my eyes.

Lucy cringed. "Or not? Maybe? Sort of?"

"Derek, I don't mean to rain on your paradise, but combined with Ruthford's location, this is starting to seem a little too good to be true. This is sounding less and less like a deal than full-blown treason on his behalf." Shannon stuck her hands in her pocket, obviously more concerned than she was letting on.

"If you've got something to say, you should probably say it."

"This seems like a trap."

"You think they turned Christopher into a vampire, brainwashed him, and sent him back to me with a sob story about his wife plus the Bloodsword, in order to make me trust him. All the while actually planning to turn me against the House by concocting a crazy story about how there's a conspiracy within it against vampires."

Shannon blinked. "Yeah, that's exactly what I was thinking."

"If it's a plan, it's an extremely good one."

"I actually think it's kind of obvious," Lucy said, surprising me. "Basic spycraft 101 is to play on relationships you've developed and present yourself as the good guy. I mean, sure, money is the reason a lot of people turned on the West during the Cold War, but you also want to—"

I glared at Lucy.

"Right, shutting up now."

"That's assuming he's Christopher at all," Shannon said.

I blinked. "What do you mean?"

"Derek, you know as well as anyone that there's plenty of shapeshifters out there. People who could adopt Christopher's form and voice, and then play on your emotions."

"He's a vampire."

"Vampire shape-shifting to that level is a very rare talent but not an unknown one," Lucy said.

I frowned. "That is a definite possibility."

"Even if he is Christopher, the fact is he's an enemy agent now," Shannon said. "The Vampire Nation traffics in slaves, arms, and drugs across six continents. Whoever he was before, he's no longer one of our people, and the very fact that he's working for them means he's a traitor. You can't do any favors for him, let alone investigate the House."

"Ashley Morgan," I said, staring at her.

"What?"

I'd been in love with three women in my life: Ashley Morgan, my ex-wife Cassandra, and Shannon. Ashley had been my first partner and a woman who was everything Shannon was in some ways—noble and courageous—while also things she wasn't, like determined to stop the injustices of the House. The official story was I'd killed her after she'd tried to betray the House. It was an event that had permanently vilified me in the eyes of my fellow agents as well as endeared me to the soulless bastards in charge of the House.

The truth was, she was still alive.

Free from the House.

Christopher had helped.

"If Christopher wanted to ruin me or destroy me, then he has a way of doing so," I said, frowning.

"Fuck," Shannon said, looking away. "How bad is it?"

"Pretty bad," Lucy said, suddenly uncomfortable.

"You know?" Shannon asked.

"I know all of Derek's secrets."

"Don't mention that to other people, or you may end up water-boarded by some of my rivals in the Committee."

"Hehe, yeah," Lucy said, not realizing I was serious.

"There's more," I said, looking out onto the snowy mountains. "I need to know just how much the Committee is doing behind my back. I've been trying to solidify my place there for the better part of a year, but I'm out of my depth and they know it. They're using me as the friendly liberal face of the House to deal with all the various Eso-Nations, but I'm locked out of the loop for a lot of shit. If I don't know what the hell is going on, I'm going to become nothing more than a puppet they use and discard."

"So, you what—want to investigate Protocol Zero to get some more blackmail material on them?" Shannon asked.

"Yeah," I said, taking a deep breath. "The thought had occurred to me. Also, if Christopher is sincere, then I might be able to leverage his wife's return to turn him. I can get him to betray the Vampire Nation; then I can use that as blackmail material on him. Having a member of the Council of Ancients in my pocket could be the key to forcing the Committee to take me seriously."

"Jesus, Derek." Shannon shook her head.

"You were worried about me being played," I said, sighing. "You don't have to worry about that. I'm willing to do whatever is necessary to try and reform the House. Even if it means betraying my friends."

Shannon stared at me, then walked past.

"What?" I asked, watching her leave. "I thought she was upset with me for letting Christopher get to me," I added, turning to Lucy.

"She was," Lucy said. "Now she's upset at you for something else."

I sighed. "Show me more about the Bloodsword. If this is the real McCoy, it can be another tool for leveraging the vampirates." I was unsure why Christopher had given me such an important relic. It made sense if he was trying to turn me, but something about that didn't feel right. I recalled he used to pass messages in plain sight by using artifacts and items that were important for other reasons. It gave me an idea.

"All right." Lucy pointed to a series of runes engraved on the side. "Take a look at this. The enchantments woven into its blade are based on a mixture of sanguimancy and ki-based enhancers. An obvious answer is there's knowledge stored in the weapon mystically, possibly a message, so—"

"So, feed it blood. Gotcha." I cut the tip of my thumb with the blade and let my blood drip on the blade. It mixed with the blood already on the blade and caused it to shimmer.

"—we should analyze it in a lab *under controlled conditions*," Lucy said, staring at me in horror. "What the hell are you doing?!"

"I made a judgment call," I said, watching the blood on the blade disappear into the steel of the weapon.

"When your judgment is impaired!"

"Dial it down. I'm sure whatever happens will—" I didn't get to finish my statement because I was knocked on my ass. I started shaking and foaming at the mouth, and my soul left my body.

Whoops.

CHAPTER FIVE

M y entire body felt like it was on fire, and for a moment, I thought I was going to die. Much to my surprise, I found myself on the deck of a late seventeenth-century galleon surrounded by a fog-covered ocean of blood. Storm clouds filled the sky and lightning struck the waves every few seconds.

The vessel's sails were tattered and ragged with holes every few feet, the result of cannon fire and storm damage. I knew, instantly, I was subject to a messenger spell. It was a way for wizards to communicate that was long on theatrics and light on practicality. On the plus side, though, it was untraceable.

Turning around, I saw there was no crew, only the singular figure of my ex-partner standing behind me. Christopher was dressed in a business suit like the one he'd worn when we were both senior agents of the Red Room, but the Bloodsword was strapped to his side with a belt and scabbard.

Christopher glanced over the side of the ship before turning back to me. "I hope you don't mind the surroundings. The screensavers for the Bloodsword's mind-to-mind messages range from the psychotically disturbing to the just plain silly."

"I think I would have preferred silly. Is this actually you or a recording?"

"A little bit of both," Christopher said, giving a brief shrug. "What we need to talk about can't be shared with anyone else."

"Which is why you're using the vampire Excalibur to do a video conference."

"I went to a lot of trouble to acquire the Bloodsword for you. Dracula's minions won't kill you as long as you wield that weapon," Christopher said, looking surprisingly calm despite our surroundings. "I learned that from marrying one of the Warlord's daughters."

I tried to hide my distaste for his revelation. Not only was Christopher a member of the Vampire Nation, but he was intimately tied to Dracula's bloodline.

"Congratulations," I said sarcastically. "I notice I wasn't invited to the wedding."

"Your invitation was lost in the mail. Feel free to send a late gift."

I tried not to smile. "Who's the lucky lady?"

"A long time ago she was known as Annabelle Jones."

"The Pirate Queen?" I asked.

Annabelle Jones had been one of Red Jack's female accomplices, right up there with Elizabeth Cambridge, a.k.a Black Beth. The three of them slaughtered slave ships and merchantmen until the British Navy (with the assistance of the Caribbean Red Room) captured their ship during the day. They'd spared themselves execution by claiming pregnancy before Dracula broke them out and transformed them.

"She's a lot nicer than her sister. I work my hardest to keep her satisfied, and we have a good relationship," Christopher said, smiling. "A happy wife makes for a happy life.."

"We're not married," I said.

"Perhaps you should be," Christopher said.

"Stay out of my personal life." I didn't like that Christopher had used Shannon against me, however innocently.

"As you wish." Christopher nodded. "Partners shouldn't lie to one another."

"You always were an asshole, Christopher. Undeath hasn't improved your attitude."

"But you will help me," Christopher said.

"Yes." I didn't let him know it was for reasons other than our friendship. I wished it could have been solely because we'd been friends, but we'd both changed too much for that.

Christopher reached into his suit and removed a scroll-case. "Take this and memorize the contents."

I took the scroll case, unscrewed the end, and pulled out the yellowed parchment inside. "A treasure map?"

Christopher shrugged. "Forgive me. You hang around the Council of Ancients long enough and you start thinking like Long John Silver. I'm lucky I don't speak in a Somerset accent with lots of *arrs* and *ahoys*."

"Perish the thought," I said, looking at the document. It showed the location of a Nassau bank with a safety deposit box code written above it. There was also a list of names on the back, including several Red Room agents the Vampire Nation had killed. "I take it these are your suspected Protocol Zero members?"

Christopher's voice lowered, becoming almost somber. "Those are the names of people who caused those terrorist attacks against the House."

"Excuse me?"

"A false flag operation. House agents assassinated by other House agents, then the blame laid at the feet of vampires. These attacks have been conducted against other Eso-Nations as well. Someone is attempting to turn the entire supernatural world against my kind. They're doing a very good job of it, too."

I looked at the names again. "These agents are dead."

"Are they?"

"You're saying the House is faking the deaths of agents to give them ease of movement."

"Like James Bond in *You Only Live Twice*."

"Not the time, Christopher."

Christopher balled his hands into fists. "It's larger than just a few renegade agents. I've been investigating this for years. Sleeper agents, millions of diverted funds, secret construction projects, and hundreds of supernaturals kidnapped only to emerge later as enemy agents."

"Enemies of the Vampire Nation. Not the House." My friend was sounding less and less rational and more like a paranoid lunatic. Which required a lot of effort when your listener knew for a fact the Illuminati, UFOs, and the supernatural were real.

Christopher frowned. "Yes."

"You think it's this Protocol Zero," I said.

"A House within the House, yes," Christopher said.

"Do you have any evidence?" I asked.

Christopher stared at me. "It's all in that safety deposit box. Everything I've managed to gather."

"Why not give it here?" I asked.

"I'm being followed by the Council of Ancients. There are people involved in it who don't want this to be a renegade offshoot. Friends of John Ruthford who want to start an open war with the House."

"This is starting to look like you're leaving a trail of breadcrumbs for me to follow. Breadcrumbs that will end in a witch's house in the woods," I said.

"Are you doing anything more important?" Christopher asked.

I shook my head. "I've been hanging around with the Fairy Affairs Department. There was a nymph porn ring we were debating shutting down and they wanted my opinion on whether it was better to monitor it or not. Personally, I think they just wanted an excuse to spend months watching the stuff on the House's dime."

That was another area the House had been shuffling me off into: useless cases and pointless busy work. Since I'd ascended to the Committee, I'd been deluged with diplomatic missions and supervisory positions with no real power or importance. They took my advice to liberalize and thaw relationships with the other Eso-Nations under advisement, but genuine reform had been illusionary.

For every step forward in reforming the House, we took another step back and then one to the side. I hadn't even warranted decent attempts to manipulate me, as they'd just sent a bunch of women to seduce me, cash payments, and gifts of property.

It was insulting, really.

How much of my desire to help Christopher investigate this was out of a need to prove myself actually worthy of a position on the Committee? I couldn't say, and that was a dangerous attitude to have when you were a spy, let alone a leader of spies. The first thing everyone in espionage needed to remember was the old maxim: know thyself. If you ever forgot who you were, then you were doomed.

I wasn't going to betray the House the way Christopher had. Willingly or not.

"Nymph porn stars, eh? To think we could have been on that mission together," Christopher said, showing a flash of fang. He looked positively hungry. "I don't know who is responsible for this group, Derek, but you're the only one I can trust."

I was not particularly concerned with the Vampire Nation's continued survival. "I'm not someone anyone should trust. I'm willing to investigate this, though. The question is whether or not you're trying to destroy the House."

"You think so little of me," Christopher said.

"I don't know who you are anymore," I said.

"Did we ever know each other?" Christopher asked.

I frowned, contemplatively. "I like to think we did. It's going to take a lot more than a magic sword and talk of old times to get me to trust you, though."

"Then trust my reasoning." Christopher walked around me, his steps never quite reaching the ground. "A war would destroy both our factions and lead to millions of human deaths, possibly billions, as humanity tears itself apart trying to figure out who is a monster amongst them."

"Or worse," I said.

"Or worse. Anyway, you don't have to fear me leading you into a trap." Christopher spread his arms out as if he was going to hug me.

I asked, suddenly suspicious. "How so?"

"Because I've already done so." Christopher clasped his hands together, stepping back. "I was the one who sent the Teutonic knights to kill you."

I blinked. "If this is a convoluted plan to gain my trust, you're doing a shit job of it."

"Protocol Zero has my wife, Derek. I am under their control. I have to follow their instructions, and that included hiring killers to attack you. They knew of our meeting almost as soon as I arranged it. I coordinated the attack, so you'd have a chance of fighting your way out while making it look like the Teutonic Knights broke their conditioning and went after us both. I killed a lot of them trying to protect you. Now we have breathing room until they plot their next move against you."

"You're saying the reason I should trust you is not because you're my former partner but because you've already tried to kill me but did a deliberately crap job."

Christopher paused. "Yes?"

"I'm rethinking staking you."

"Orihalcum bullets are more effective." Christopher was nonplussed. "For whatever reason, Protocol Zero thinks you're a threat. That means we have an advantage."

"I'm flattered you think so," I said.

Christopher shook his head. "You should be. I need to know who's behind Protocol Zero. They communicate with me using artificially disguised voices, and all the divination magic I use is blocked by powerful wards. Whoever they are, they're good and have access to vast amounts of both technology and magic. I need to know who is threatening not only my wife but the world as a whole."

If he was telling the truth, the most likely answer was a Committee member. Arranging wars and starting conflicts between various supernatural factions was what the Committee did before I arrived, and probably still did. If they were behind it, they wouldn't let it escalate to the level Christopher feared. Precious comfort to the victims caught up in the crossfire as such may be. I wasn't about to let Christopher off the hook, though. "You killed sixteen innocent people and brainwashed another to provide a distraction."

"Vampire hunters aren't innocent to me, not anymore. I'm a child of the Dragon now. I won't try and paint my people as innocent, but they *are* my people now. I'll protect them against those who would destroy them."

"Even me?" Christopher asked.

"Don't make me make that choice," I said. "King David loved Jonathan less than I love you, but he still killed him."

"Yeah, well there's a lot of messed up stuff in the Bible."

"Sorry. I'm a vampire. Flourishes come naturally to us," Christopher laughed, stretching out his arms. "You're my only hope."

"Don't quote *Star Wars* at me."

"Is *The Princess Bride* all right?"

"Yeah."

"Then I need a miracle."

I shook my head, no longer sure Christopher was remotely the man I once knew. The man I knew wouldn't try to manipulate me like this. He certainly wouldn't have tried to kill me. Maybe the Professor was right, and this was just an imposter. Rubbing my temples, I made my decision. "I said I'd help you and I meant it. However, if you try and kill me again or hurt anyone I know, I'll track down your entire bloodline and exterminate it. Are we clear?"

"Like the sea air." Christopher put his arm over his chest. "Godspeed, my ungentle prince."

"Right back at you."

With that, I woke up on the snow, an oxygen mask on my face as a group of EMTs were about to inject adrenaline into my bloodstream. The scroll case was now in my hands, existing alongside the Bloodsword.

That was weird.

CHAPTER SIX

It took a half hour to convince Lucy I was fit for duty and another two hours to convince the Professor to let me go. I could have overruled them, but I didn't want to get in their faces about another stupid decision I'd made. I wanted to talk to Shannon about all this, but she'd decided to go investigate Christopher's claims on her own—while I was unconscious.

Shannon left me a note encouraging me not to contact her, at least not for a few days. It was an overreaction to our conversation, and I privately suspected she'd gone off to investigate Christopher for me. If so, I wished her Godspeed. I needed a fresh pair of eyes on this, even if I would have welcomed her aid during my trip to Nassau.

Calling for a private jet to be fueled at a nearby airport, I sent feelers to individuals I knew I could trust in the analysis branches. If I was going to find out what was going on, I needed to follow up on the list of names Christopher supplied as to whether there was any truth to the allegations he'd made.

I needed to retrieve whatever was in the Caribbean safety deposit box and examine its contents. Back when I was a senior agent, I'd have gone "off the grid" and done my best to sneak in before picking up my package there. That wasn't an option anymore. Since joining the Committee, my every movement was tracked by hundreds of people both friendly and otherwise.

In a normal, trustworthy organization, I'd just pass along the job to my subordinates. However, Christopher's accusations meant I couldn't trust anyone with the whole story. That meant I had to change the rules of the game so a member of the Committee doing this made sense.

Driving along the icy roads of Aspen in a borrowed black

Cadillac SRX, I tried explaining my plan to my sister.

"Are you fucking insane?" Penny Hawthorne asked, her disdain carrying through my cellphone earpiece. She was my twin, half-human half-dragon, and the single person who still talked to me as if nothing had changed with my elevation to the Committee.

I shrugged and responded to my sister's accusation. "Well, my psychological profile does say I possess a mild case of megalomania and incipient sex addiction, but I think that comes with the territory."

"Uh-huh," Penny said, annoyed. "You want us to meet with representatives of the Council of Ancients in Nassau—while you're investigating them."

"More like while I'm planning to put one over on them. Make all the arrangements. Tell them how furious I am about the attack but confirm my commitment to peace and how I'm willing to meet with them at a non-neutral location. That way I can slip my way into the bank and get whatever Christopher was hiding from his fellows."

"That is the dumbest plan I have heard from you, which is saying something. Nassau is the capital of the Vampire Nation. You're going to be watched from the moment you step off your jet. Assuming they don't just blow it up once it touches the ground."

"They won't," I said, with all due confidence.

"Why?"

"It'd be too easy," I said, shaking my head. "Vampires smell weakness but flee from strength. If I come into their territory throwing my weight around, they're going to be cautious and wary. They won't attack until they're certain this isn't a trick."

"I'm coming down there."

"No, that's a bad idea," I said, not bothering to explain it was because I was only half sure this plan would work.

"Someone needs to protect you from you."

"Usually, that's Shannon," I said, regretting it the instant the words left my mouth.

"You're too close to this, Derek, on every conceivable level. You need to stick other agents on it and resolve it from a distance."

"I'm a rogue agent who doesn't play by the rules. See Derek Hawthorne in *Eldritch Ops*, coming to a theater near you."

"Ha ha," my sister said, without a trace of amusement. "Christopher has already admitted to trying to kill you. I say track the bastard down, stab him, cut off his head, and hang it from the nearest sailing mast like Robert Maynard did Blackbeard."

"A very appropriate reference," I said. "You think he can't be trusted."

"*He tried to kill you.* Fuck him and the coffin he sleeps in. The undead asshole can't be trusted."

"You know, Lucy says vampires aren't undead."

"With all due respect to my wife, who gives a shit? They're still untrustworthy inhuman bastards."

I wanted to say Shannon wasn't human either and neither was our mother, but I wasn't sure I could convince myself with such an argument. Shannon would always put the House before me, and my mother abandoned me and Penny at birth in our all-too-inattentive father's care.

Instead, I said, "A deal is a deal. Has the Ruthford situation got any news?"

Penny was silent.

"Penny?"

"Yeah, there's news."

It wasn't like my sister to hesitate. "What happened?"

"There was an emergency session of the Committee as soon as the Professor sent his location up the food chain. They all voted to attack at once. They used their contacts in the CIA and Pentagon to have the *U.S.S Van Buren* launch a trio of *Crazy Horse*-class missiles onto Ruthford's Maghreb-era estate."

"And?" I asked.

"The entire place is ashes. Division Eighteen got infrared satellite footage that puts almost two dozen mobile body-heat neutral figures within the compound when it hit. Analysis thinks they managed to get Ruthford's entire inner circle. They sent in a SEAL team to gather the ashes in special funeral urns so no one resurrect."

"Ruthford wasn't there?" I asked.

"No," Penny said. "He posted a threatening video on YouTube a half hour ago. I'm surprised no one's contacted you about it."

"Well, I'm talking with you," I said. "Admittedly, it's a big oversight."

The Committee considered me a probationary member at best, often ignoring my advice and rarely contacting me for my vote. This wasn't an example of such, though I wished it were. The Committee hadn't tried to remove me—yet—and until they did, they insisted on me being treated by others as a full-fledged member.

Penny kept talking about the strike. "There was a big cost in terms of collateral too. That plantation had a hundred regular humans living on it. That's not counting each vampire's entourage of dhampyr and Bloodslaves."

I didn't know how to respond to that. I'd killed dozens of monsters over the years, maybe as many as two hundred, but with the passing of a file I'd killed just as many innocent people. Even if it was justified by destroying one of the most ruthless vampire terrorist organizations in the world, that was a lot of blood on my hands.

You'd think having been raised in the Red Room, I would have a casual reaction to collateral damage. The fact was, I didn't. I'd seen up close the aftermath of drone strikes, bombings, and indiscriminate fire. Part of the reason why I preferred to be an assassin rather than the guy ordering the killings was I'd always been very good at hitting my targets and no one else. I hadn't always succeeded.

Hell, the Red Room had sent me after people I'd found out only later were innocent of any crime but standing in their way. But I'd done my best not to kill the innocent. It was stupid idealism, according to my father, who himself was the nicest member of the Committee, but I felt it was all that kept me from becoming a monster.

I wasn't sure I could make that claim anymore.

Is being a monster so bad? I heard a female voice whisper in my ear. For a second, I could have sworn it came from the Bloodsword.

Then, strangely, the thought left my mind. Shaking my head, I said, "I see. Thank you for relaying that."

I should have been there for making that decision. Instead, I was off preparing to do some work far less experienced agents could handle.

"That's a lot of lives," I finally said.

"They were doomed the moment you passed along that information, Derek. Even if you'd been there, they wouldn't have voted to wait for a more precise strike."

"I still would have said not to do it."

"Yeah, which is why they didn't wait for your vote."

I gave my vote, I wanted to say. *I just told the Professor to relay it without thinking about the consequences or specifics.* Instead, I said, "I don't think the vampires are going to much care for me after this. It makes the meeting I want to set up all the more important."

"I'll see you in Nassau."

"Penny—"

I didn't have much of a chance to respond further, because as I turned a corner, my car slammed into a pair of trees overturned in the road. The airbag activated and prevented me from smashing my face into the steering wheel as my body thrown against the seatbelt around my waist.

Disoriented, I looked around and saw there were several figures standing perfectly still on both sides of the road. They were beautiful, elegant, and dressed in clothes every bit as fine as Christopher's own. The clothes were inappropriate for the weather, though—a mixture of trench coats and suits with the occasional evening dress. None of them showed any sign of discomfort, however, looking at me with the same sort of gaze an owl might give a mouse.

Vampires. Shit.

The furthest one to the left moved so fast it seemed like he was teleporting, ripping off the car door before tearing out my seatbelt. He was six feet tall with skin like ivory and a spherical bald head. The vampire grabbed me by the neck, either to crush it or pull me out.

I didn't have much time to figure out my next course of

action because unlike what you saw in the movies, humans were pretty much helpless in personal combat with vampires. Even the lowest member of the undead possessed enough power to tear a man apart like wet tissue paper.

I'd slain more vampires than anybody else alive, but I'd done so with equipment designed for fighting them. By the time I drew my gun, the vampire holding my throat would have time to crush it a dozen times over. Instinct guided my next actions as I refused to be captured by the Vampire Nation.

Even if they intended to take me alive, my hatred for their parasitic race trumped any predisposition toward self-preservation. The discovery of Christopher's survival had dulled none of my rage. I summoned all my ki into my fists, feeling the swift and powerful flow of life energy through my body. It was difficult to strengthen myself because I was already going unconscious. The bald vampire had pulled me out of my car and was lifting me up by its right hand, giving the barest of squeezes but enough to strangle me. So, I knocked his head clean off with a kick of my left foot. I didn't mean this figuratively, either. I struck out with a ki-enhanced blow and decapitated the vampire. Its head traveled off its neck like a football, causing us both fall to fall to the ground. I'm not sure which of us was more shocked by the action.

Lying down in the snow next to my ruined car, I felt a surge in mystical energy. It was not clean energy, either, but the life-force of the slain vampire. A hateful mass of hunger and blood passed from the dead vampire on the ground to me. In an instant, the Bloodsword passed from the passenger's seat of the car to my right hand. Remembering cutting my hand on the weapon, I realized I'd consecrated the weapon to myself. I was a blood magician now.

The other vampires didn't hesitate to take advantage of my shock, three of them raising a pair of Uzis at me before firing. Time seemed to slow down, and I saw the bullets explode out of their weapons' barrels, moving in slow motion like I was in a Hong Kong action movie.

Falling backwards, I rolled on the ground and pulled out my pistol with my left hand. I fired at the vampires, striking all three of them in the skull. My aim was perfect despite the fact that I was firing with my oft-hand. Even more so, my weapon moved faster than their own, although vampires possessed unnatural speed.

With most of the monsters sent to hell, I felt another surge of alien power as the sword in my right hand took on a red-black hue. The black ki running through my body was incredible, giving me a rush greater than any of the drugs I'd taken undercover. I felt strong and invincible, as if the remaining three vampires before me were helpless. I lost all sense and found myself casting aside my gun. I burst forward at an inhuman speed, launching myself at the nearest vampire, driving the Bloodsword into the side of its chest and through its heart.

The vampire, a man with long black hair and crystal blue eyes, stared at me in disbelief. I witnessed rapid decay start to set in as his eyes sunk into the back of his head. His skin began to wrinkle and then crumbled to dust. The power that passed from the deceased vampire was ecstatic, and I wanted to sink my teeth into the side of the creature and drink its blood. However, there was none left after a moment. The creature was nothing more than powder and clothes falling before me. Even so, I felt charged. The Bloodsword felt like an extension of my body and I hacked into the closest of my assailants with wild abandon, severing chunks of its body away like I was slicing cheese. Blackish-red ichor flew from the creature's body in slow motion, the Bloodsword absorbing it and passing on a portion of the strength to me.

I felt like a god.

Yes, the female voice from earlier whispered. *We are gods.*

My sole remaining attacker stared at me, looking nonplussed by the hideous slaying of her fellow vampires. She was quite the contrast to her fellows, standing five foot nine and looking like a statue with short, bright red hair and crystal blue eyes. Unlike the others, who were dressed for a night on the town, the survivor had a goth flavor to her attire. One that reminded me of my sister's friends. She was wearing tight black leather pants, a Sisters of Mercy jacket, and a snug red halter top that contrasted with the snow around her.

The Bloodsword enhanced the urges that were pushing me forth in a berserk fury. I wanted to kill her, to chop her up into little pieces and drain the energy from her body. Years of training let me recognize this was an unnatural desire, but barely. Disgusted by myself, I forced those thoughts back into the recesses of my skull and did my best to assert my dominance over the sword's will. I wanted to cast aside the blade, but somehow, it managed to stick to my hand regardless.

"You have no right to that weapon," the woman said, her accent a strange mix of Bahamian and London English.

I coughed, trying to cleanse my throat of the taste of blood. I hadn't drunk from any of my victims, but it somehow felt like I had. "You have no right to take my life or any of the others you've slain."

"Do you assume all vampires are murderers?"

"Am I wrong to?" I spit on the ground.

"Perhaps not. Yet if we are all killers, then you are one too, Cleaver. The Warlord wishes to speak with you, and the deaths of my colleagues will stop me from bringing you to him."

I didn't hesitate with my response. "Not a chance."

"You were already trying to set up a meeting with us."

I wondered how she'd heard that. "A meeting between equals is different from being ambushed and captured."

"No one is equal in this world. My orders are to bring you in alive. Note, they did not say unharmed. I desire to hurt you a great deal for my fallen comrades."

"Then you shouldn't have tried to kill me."

"You fired first. The Bloodsword is empowered now and an extreme amount of damage can be done to your body without being fatal."

"Bring it, girl."

The woman narrowed her eyes. "The name is Elizabeth Cambridge. You can call me Black Beth."

She lifted her right hand and closed it. Seconds later, a sniper shot me in the chest. The Bloodsword fell from my grip and I bled in the snow, losing myself to darkness.

CHAPTER SEVEN

Despite the vampiress' statement about the Bloodsword being able to heal me, I was surprised to wake up. The first thing I noticed was I felt like shit. The second was that I had a pounding headache. And the third was that I was handcuffed to my chair. I opened my eyes to the dimly lit interior of a private jet.

It was extremely upscale, with black shag carpet, fine oak furniture, and a fifty-thousand-dollar entertainment center. The jet had no windows, but I could hear the whine of engines, telling me we were in the air. There were a number of figures moving around the jet's main cabin, all dressed similar to the vampires who'd attacked me, but no sign of Elizabeth Cambridge. I was woozy from being shot, as well as the frenzy the Bloodsword had pushed me into. Leaning forward, I felt a stab of pain in my chest and knew whatever healing was occurring wasn't complete.

Looking to my seat, I saw it was a black leather recliner, very expensive, with elaborate magical runes sewn into the lining. I didn't recognize their purpose but suspected they were designed to suppress what little magic I commanded. Given how much of a boost I'd received from the Bloodsword while fighting that vampire hit squad, I had to assume the only reason I wasn't healed was because the runes were keeping me from accessing its power.

Great.

Blood magic had made me powerful but turned me into a fool, leaving me vulnerable to enemy counterattack. Spotting the Bloodsword propped up against another chair, I wondered if Christopher had planned for the weapon to betray me. I shook that thought away. The vampires had me dead-to-rights, and if not for the aid of the Bloodsword, I would have been taken down much faster. The fact that the weapon had opened up my mind to a forbidden form of magic I'd been able to use instinctually should have disturbed me. But as a prisoner of the Vampire Nation, I couldn't help but wish I had access to a little more now.

"I don't suppose I could get a cup of coffee?" I called out, rattling my handcuffs for emphasis.

God, you are an asshole, the female voice from earlier whispered in my head. *I like that.*

Who's there? I asked, projecting my thoughts inward.

A friend.

Friends can speak to me face to face, I replied.

Soon, the voice cooed.

One of the vampires, a tall, leggy, brunette, walked over and smacked me across the face. It was all I could do not to slip back into unconsciousness. Say what you will about the walking parasites, but they were strong.

"Now, Minka, is that any way to treat our guest?" a deep, Ben Kingsley-like voice came from the back of the plane.

Looking over my shoulder, I saw a figure enter the cabin like he was stepping onto a stage. He was tall. Taller than me, with a short, well-trimmed goatee and flowing black hair trailing down over his shoulders. His mustache was anachronistic, large and waxed with the points coming out to both ends.

The rest of his attire was custom-tailored, with a long coat over an Italian suit that probably cost as much as my car. The coat was so large, it hung from him almost like a cape. There was a timelessness about the look that made it somehow fashionable, even if it was reminiscent of a seventeenth-century swashbuckler.

Behind the figure was Elizabeth Cambridge, still dressed like she was going clubbing, and glowering at me. I didn't blame her. I had killed six of her associates, after all, but there was something else I noticed in her posture. She was worried about something, or someone.

"Welcome, Cleaver," the man in the Italian suit said. "You

have no idea how much trouble you've caused me."

I looked up to the man, unimpressed. "I like to think I have a good idea how much trouble I cause the monsters of the world."

His smile took on a cold edge. "You have no idea who I am, do you?"

I cocked my head to one side. "A guy who needs to shave off that mustache. Who are you supposed to be? The Dread Pirate Burt Reynolds?" I knew who he was, of course, but I didn't appreciate being kidnapped.

All of the other vampires on the plane stiffened, as if I'd insulted the Pope about his hat. The one exception was Elizabeth, who gave a half smile to my statement. Right before returning to her previous scowl.

The mustached man gave a low dark chuckle, the laughter not reaching his eyes. "Let me show you who I am."

He grabbed me by my throat and made me meet his gaze. I didn't have time to shut my eyes before I was forced into his crystal blue ones. They were the sign of Christopher's vampire lineage, but purer and more hypnotic than all the others. That was when the vampire shoved centuries of horror into my skull.

I saw thousands of Turks impaled on wooden poles, their blood slowly draining to the ground, followed by a rampage of murder across Europe. I saw slave ships, their prisoners chained like animals, ripped apart like pigs for slaughter. I saw the streets of Victorian London, plied by broken women, stalked by a murderous madman with a knife.

My nose started to bleed as my mind rebelled against the atrocities I witnessed. The vampire continued to hold my throat, however, keeping me steady as he continued to show me sights that equaled or surpassed any I'd seen in the Red Room. Only his grip kept me from biting off my tongue, the horror too much for my brain. As I suspected, I was face to face with Dracula, Warlord of the Vampire Nation.

"Show respect," Dracula commanded, putting his will in my mind.

What followed was an overwhelming urge to love and obey him. The vision had weakened my will, and I was bombarded with affectionate feelings. Dracula was like Elvis, Jesus, Christ, and Buddha all wrapped into one. I wanted to get down on my knees and worship him. His power was stripping away all of my free will, leaving me nothing more than an obedient husk to do with as he saw fit.

"Now do you know who I am?" Dracula asked, his voice echoing in my mind. He wanted me to grovel.

To kneel.

And I wanted to.

But the memory of the horrible things he'd done to men, women, and children kept me from doing so.

Focus, I commanded myself, struggling to resist his command. I was not going to be a vampire's puppet. Not Christopher's, not Dracula's, not fucking Count Chocula's.

No one's.

"You're a guy with a shitty mustache." I laughed, grinning. It took every ounce of willpower in my body.

"I'm impressed." Dracula let go of my throat, letting me collapse back into my chair. "It's nice to meet someone who is deserving of their reputation. I expected my power to liquefy your mind. You must be one of those rare individuals who can resist mesmerism."

"And what if I couldn't?" I said, racked by a violent fit of coughs. Throwing off Dracula's influence had taken every bit of my will, and I wasn't sure if I could do it again. At least I had the small blessing that mesmerism grew more difficult once you'd failed against a subject.

"I'd have sent you back to your family to rape your siblings, kill your father, and then slit your wrists after confessing to it all on paper. Thankfully, that won't be necessary."

Some of the vampires laughed at Dracula's statement, while others looked uncomfortable. I had no doubt he was serious about his threat and wondered how many others had suffered such a fate.

I clenched my fists, trying to raise my head up from where I'd collapsed. "That would . . . lead to war with the Red Room."

The threat against my family infuriated me and allowed me to regain a bit of my strength. I didn't mind if he killed me— that was a danger of the Game—but bringing my brothers and sisters into this was a bridge too far. I wanted to reach up and rip the immortal's black heart out. The urge felt natural and pure.

What had the Bloodsword done to me?

Made you strong, the woman's voice spoke. *I am tired of vampires.*

Was it the Bloodsword? Oh crap, it was.

"I was under the impression we already were at war, my dear Cleaver." Dracula sat down in the chair across from me and gestured to Minka. Frowning, as if insulted by the request, she poured him a glass of blood from a decanter on a nearby table and brought it to him. "Or do I misinterpret the situation?"

I thought of the terrible casualties I'd inflicted on Ruthford's plantation. "Ruthford and his men have been at war with the House for a long time. As for the ones I just killed, they ambushed me. It was self-defense."

"You lying sack of—" Elizabeth stepped forward.

Dracula raised a hand, silencing her. "I do not speak of these things. Annabelle created Ruthford two centuries ago and it was his stupidity to believe your organization could be destroyed outright. The Wise will always compete with the Damned for domination of lesser beings. As for Elizabeth's team, they were expendable."

Elizabeth glared at her master. "The Blackguard served you well, Master."

"And they died. Therefore, they are irrelevant." Dracula's tone was beyond dismissive, more like angry that she would even bring up their losses in my presence. His gaze on me intensified, making my headache worse. "As for you, Cleaver, this war is your fault for other reasons. Your treasonous plotting with the recently discharged herald Christopher Hang. The two of you unleashing all manner of chaos on the Vampire Nation and her allies. Tsk-tsk, very naughty. Between you two, we were jumping at shadows."

I paused, processing that. "Wait. You think Christopher and I are trying to *start* a war?"

"Do you deny it?" Elizabeth pointed at me, hissing.

"We're trying to *prevent* a war!" I snapped, not caring that I was surrounded by psychopathic monsters.

Dracula took a sip from his glass. "I find that very difficult to believe. You do have a certain reputation."

A black man near the back, who was of medium height but very muscular, sneered at me. "Allow me to be the one to kill him, Warlord. I have spilled the blood of his line before."

I mentally filed that statement away for future reference.

"Later, Joshua," Dracula said. "I am interested in what the Cleaver has to say."

This was all a big game to Dracula, and there was no way to talk my way out of this. But if he didn't want a war with the House, I needed to do everything in my power to prevent one. I didn't know what Christopher's position was in the Vampire Nation right now, but I suspected it wasn't good. Given I'd met with him under the auspices of his being a representative of the Council of Ancients, I wished I could conjure him up and punch him. I hated being hustled.

Still, I wasn't about to let Christopher plunge the House and its hundred thousand employees into a battle with the nebulous numbers of the Vampire Nation. If Dracula didn't want a war, I had to play on those feelings. Christopher's quest to recover his wife and unearth his phantom conspiracy took a secondary priority, if it was anything more than a ruse.

"We met as part of an attempt to work out a truce between our two factions." I took a deep breath. It was painful due to the half-healed wound in my chest. "He told me there's a cabal of individuals who kidnapped his wife and have been manipulating events across the globe in order to start a war between the Vampire Nation and the House."

I wasn't happy revealing so much, but my situation wasn't secure. I needed to somehow turn Dracula into my ally, even if I found him loathsome. If I couldn't, I needed to get him to lower his guard so I could escape. From there, I could work on this problem from the outside. I swear, it was like playing chess without being able to see your opponent's pieces.

Elizabeth, much to my surprise, responded first. Her posture shifted from suspicious to concerned. "Annabelle has been kidnapped?"

"So he says. I'm trying to find her. Well, I would be if I hadn't been interrupted."

That little dig caused her to lose all sympathy. "You little beater."

Beater was a vampire slur for humans, coming from the fact that our hearts, well, beat. Personally, I preferred the human equivalent of bastard.

"What do you expect? He is a leader of the House," Joshua said, crossing his arms. "They lie like they breathe."

Dracula finished his drink, putting the glass to the side of his chair. "No, he's telling the truth, at least as far as he knows it. Mortals give off certain smells when they lie. I have spoken to enough Committee members over the centuries to know which ones are capable of fooling a vampire's nose. The Cleaver is not one of them."

That was a backhanded compliment if I'd ever heard one. "Christopher came to me with the information that our recent troubles were being manufactured by a third party. I take it he doesn't represent the Council of Ancients in this matter?"

Elizabeth snorted. "No matter his bloodline, he is unworthy of being a herald. Christopher Hang murdered and slept his way to the top of our organization. He would not be fit to be a voivode's *bellidix* if not for his marriage to Annabelle."

Which wasn't an answer. That's how everyone got their position in supernatural circles. Hell, a lot of regular circles as well. My father used to say more boardroom appointments were made with hookers and blow than PowerPoint presentations.

Dracula narrowed his eyes at me. "Christopher Hang *was* a member of the Council of Ancient's staff. That was before he stole my sword and killed a dozen associates of mine on his way out. Forgivable crimes, if not for the fact that he was collaborating with your organization. Perhaps he is the individual behind all of our mutual troubles."

"That makes no sense," I said, wondering whether Dracula would tolerate being corrected. "I wouldn't even know about the possibility of an agent provocateur if not for Christopher meeting with me."

Agent provocateurs were the black sheep of the intelligence

community. The worst of an already duplicitous bunch. They were the covert operatives whose job it was to incite rebellion, entice defectors, or goad enemies into making mistakes. Sometimes, they were involved in "false flag" operations, where they could pretend to be on one side, usually opposing, in order to get their enemies to fight one another.

I'd run dozens of these sorts of operations, but Christopher had always made it a point to avoid that sort of work. I would have discounted Dracula's words—they came from the mouth of a madman, after all—but for the fact that Christopher used the Teutonic Knights as a catspaw. Then there was the fact that he was using me, after trying to kill me, no less.

He'd changed.

He wasn't my friend anymore.

So why did I feel an obligation to him?

"Warlord, we need to investigate the possibility of Annabelle being in danger. You know what happened the last time she had one of her ... spells," Elizabeth said, her voice low and clear but holding an undeniable sense of panic. I wondered what sort of relationship she had to Christopher's wife.

"We lost Western Europe," Joshua said. "She should have been destroyed long ago."

Dracula looked irritated, perhaps because he wasn't used to being interrupted. Everyone in this plane was upset though, whether because of Christopher's betrayal or the men I'd killed. It made me wonder if the so-called Warlord's position wasn't as secure as he pretended. "If Annabelle has gotten herself into trouble, Elizabeth, it is because of her choice to associate with questionable company."

"But—"

"This discussion is finished!" Dracula hissed, burying his fingernails into his chair's armrests. "I have indulged you far too much, daughter. Say anything further and I will have your head cut off and suspended from the bowsprit like Thatch."

Elizabeth went silent, but I could see hatred burning in her eyes. Whoever Annabelle was to her, she was important enough that Elizabeth was willing to defy Dracula. Another useful piece of information to remember.

"Christopher isn't on my side and he's not on yours I bet, either," I said, struggling to take control over my heartbeat and body. I was sweating like I was coming down from a high or an extensive workout.

The combination of the Bloodsword's healing and Dracula's mindfuckery had left me a mess. It was no wonder he could tell whether I was lying or not. I needed to relax if I was going to get through this conversation alive.

Dracula released his fingers from the chair and pressed them together. All trace of his earlier anger disappeared. His mood changed on a dime, and I wondered if he was putting on an act or he was genuinely insane. "You'll forgive me if I don't take your endorsement as meaning much."

I cleared my head and stared at Dracula, risking eye contact. "I think Christopher's a monster whom I want to kill. He betrayed the Red Room, betrayed the House, and is nothing more than a blood-sucking leech like the rest of you. He gave me the Bloodsword and Ruthford's location because he wants to save your pack of murderers and scum. I don't want war with you. It makes me sick that he's fallen so low."

It was ninety percent bullshit, but for the duration of the statement, I forced myself to believe it. I took up every bit of anger at his betrayal, his manipulations, and the attack to obliterate any positive feelings I had remaining. I gritted my teeth and projected more hate than I'd felt for anyone else before. I wanted him to believe Christopher was loyal, regardless of whatever crimes he'd committed. That was the only way we were going to prevent a war.

Dracula looked at me, pausing to rub his goatee. "You know, I think I believe you. Tell me, who does our erstwhile traitor think is manipulating events?"

"Protocol Zero."

The weight of the words hung in the air for a second, no one reacting. Then Dracula burst out laughing.

"Is something funny?" I asked.

"Oh, my dear boy, you are out of your depth, aren't you?"

"Excuse me?" I asked, tugging on my handcuffs. They

were tied to the metal underneath the arm rest, but it wasn't very well screwed in.

Dracula clasped his hands together across his chest. "Protocol Zero was one of the original thirteen Black Protocols drafted in 1948 by the Red Room and Harry S. Truman. It was created during the beginnings of the Cold War under the assumption that after the Black Sun was defeated, the greatest threat to the human race would be a secret takeover by vampires."

I bit my lip. It wasn't good when your enemy knew more about your organization than you. "Sounds ... reasonable. If you were plotting that, I mean."

"Ha!" Dracula laughed, the disdain thick in his voice. "As if I didn't have better things to do than manage the affairs of cattle. A vampire exists to hunt mortals, not ranch them. Such a plan would also bring down the wrath of humanity's gods."

I raised an eyebrow. "They didn't intervene during the last couple of Great Wars."

"You'd be surprised," Dracula said, looking as if he'd tasted something foul. "Protocol Zero authorized research and operations illegal under the House's own laws. Its ultimate aim was to use sleepers and agent provocateurs across the world to trigger a war between supernatural factions, which would exterminate vampires worldwide."

"Harry Truman was a cold son of a bitch, wasn't he?"

"Better dead than undead," Elizabeth said, her voice like ice. "Truman was a smart man. Enough so that he saw Pantheon Corp as a threat to the United States's security, and the possibility of it taking over the democratic process—as it has."

Pantheon Corp, my ex-wife's company, was the world's biggest manufacturer of everything. It was also a backer for the House, providing the vast majority of funds for our operations in exchange for access to magic, intelligence, and "favors" that were best not thought about too deeply. It was one of the few groups in the world that could match the influence of the House or Vampire Nation.

"Your father is a majority shareholder in Pantheon Corp, is he not?" Dracula asked, raising an eyebrow.

"Why do you ask?" I said, wondering what Dracula's point

was. My father, Nathan Hawthorne, had semi-retired from the Committee after my ascension. He still voted on the board but now served as the Red Room's liaison to Pantheon Corp. It came with enough money that his previous billions were chump change.

"Because, Mister Hawthorne, if Protocol Zero were responsible for these events, then you'd know. It was your father who drafted it."

CHAPTER EIGHT

I sat there, my mouth agape. The idea of my father being involved in this should have been ridiculous, but it wasn't. Still, something wasn't right. It wasn't that I doubted my father was capable of planning vampire genocide, let alone sending in agents to brainwash or assassinate the Vampire Nation's members. Every dirty trick I knew, I'd learned from him, and I had limits he didn't possess. No, it was a matter of timing.

Thanks to the miracles of sorcery, my father was still a youthful-looking middle-aged man despite being a veteran of World War 2. He'd been a young man then, fighting the Japanese Imperialists alongside my mother (a dragon) and Frankenstein's monster. Which, by the description, you should realize meant the Red Room hadn't always been the stuffy backstabbing group of bastards it was today. My father had been an impressive agent back then, but that was all he'd been. He was eventually a friend of presidents, but it wasn't until the Seventies when he worked as Nixon's liaison to the Red Room, taking care of the things he didn't need to know about.

Narrowing my eyes, I pushed my willpower forward and once more felt Dracula's impressive mind bearing down upon me. After his blunt force attack on my sanity, he was trying something subtler. The old monster was enhancing my paranoia and suspicions about my superiors, particularly my father, in hopes of turning me against them. It was possible Dracula knew about my longstanding antipathy toward my father. I had barely spoken to Nathan Hawthorne since Ashley's "death," only involving him in my business when the entire world was at stake. Some crimes could never be forgiven. But was he responsible for what Dracula was claiming? Not a chance.

"Nice try," I said, waving my hand in front of my face. "I almost bought it."

"It would have gone better for you if you had," Dracula said, shaking his head. "Now, we're going to have to kill you."

"You can try," I said, concentrating and causing the handcuffs to disintegrate into powder. About the limit of my power but something I still had enough juice to pull off. I was about to bolt, but I noticed none of the vampires were moving to attack. My instincts told me now wasn't the time to move, despite the threat, so I stayed in my chair.

"Those were enchanted," Dracula said, smirking. "Designed to suppress the powers of a wizard many times your skill level."

"You should ask for your money back."

Dracula surprised me by saying, "No, I think they were working quite well. Relax, Mister Hawthorne, I am not going to kill you now. Just ... eventually. There may even be an alternative to your death."

Despite my little trick with the handcuffs, I wasn't up for fighting a single vampire, let alone the nine I counted on board this flight—one of whom was the most powerful bloodsucker alive. A part of me was seriously considering using everything I had to smash a hole in the plane. That way I'd have the comfort of taking out everyone else on board. Dracula and the other eldest would survive, but they'd spend the next few years regenerating.

"Tell me, Derek, what does the Bloodsword feel like to you?" Dracula said, interrupting my thoughts.

"Father?" Elizabeth said, dropping her earlier attitude problem to Dracula. Her tone was now affectionate and confused.

"It felt like someone mixed acid and LSD, and then poured it on my brain," I said, wondering what the hell he was getting at.

I didn't think he was trying to distract me so his men could jump me. They could get at me without difficulty. Then again, they probably had thought the same thing before I killed six of their operatives.

"The Bloodsword is a relic I have tied my essence to. Thanks to my pact with Tiamat-Abaddon, if people fear me, I can regenerate when fools like you try and destroy me. It is an indestructible item, so I have no fear telling you this. Nothing can scare a man who has nothing to fear from death. It is why I have allowed myself to become so famous."

I snorted, realizing he wasn't going to kill me just yet. No, he was going to bore me to death with a speech first. "Okay, Sauron, I'm sure the ego boost had nothing to do with it."

Dracula made a dismissive wave of his hand. "There is that benefit, true. My point is, the Bloodsword is a symbol of my power, but I do not have to be the one to wield it. Our link transcends such foolishness. In the past, I have chosen others to serve as its wielder. As my champion. The position is now open."

He is not my master, merely a wielder, the Bloodsword spoke. *I choose who controls me.*

Who are you? I asked. *Why do I interest you?*

You will know soon.

I forced myself to concentrate on Dracula's words. "What? So, you can't control me and were going to kill me, but now are going to offer me a job?"

"I can feel you drawing on its power even now," Dracula said, stroking his goatee. "The sacrifices you offered the blade are very strong, and that magic is now flowing through you. If you agree to serve as my proxy in the matter of resolving this Protocol Zero business, I'll bestow upon you the Bloodsword and significant rewards."

"If I cared about money, I'd kiss up to my father," I said.

Dracula snorted. "I'm not talking about money, Mister Hawthorne. You're a poor wizard. My spies witnessed your rather pathetic performance against the Teutonic Knights earlier today. Your powers didn't even awaken until last year when you defeated the Wazir. I believe it is because you are suppressing your true potential. Blood magic seems to be your forte. With the proper focus and training, you could learn to dominate your fellow Committee members. I can also introduce you to such pleasures as you would not believe."

This time, Dracula filled my mind with a different set of images, far more pleasant ones. I felt power at my fingertips like

I'd never experienced. I saw the Committee rotting in the ground, the entire House subservient to me, and my father hanging from a gallows. Life, centuries of life, was at my disposal, and I didn't even have to become a vampire to enjoy it. The blood magic would keep me young and vital. There were salacious images too, Shannon and other women all turned into obedient slaves. Dracula oversold his pitch, though, since I had no interest in becoming a blood-obsessed, mind controlling rapist.

Feeling my chest wound heal over, I stared at my opponent. I felt strong now, stronger than I'd felt in—well, ever. "You're not my type."

Dracula just stared at me. "Three times you have defied me, Cleaver. That is the limit of my power. I can no more influence you now than the God I have forsaken. Unfortunate for us both."

Things were starting to click into place. "You let Christopher take the Bloodsword. You let him set up the meeting with me. Hell, you might even be behind the kidnapping of his wife. Was all of this to ambush me so you could get a member of the Committee under your thumb, or are you a hell of a lot more scared of what Christopher was predicting than you've been letting on?"

"That, Mister Hawthorne, is something you'll never find out." Dracula waved his hand. "Dump him out the side of the plane."

Elizabeth was the first to move, being the strongest and fastest of Dracula's minions. She was almost on me, but my strength had returned, and I grabbed hold of my seat, only to give her a double kick into Dracula and two vampires behind her. Minka drew a pistol from a holster underneath her dress and began firing indiscriminately, shooting out one of the windows and causing a depressurization of the cabin.

I was grabbed from behind by Joshua as the large vampire began to pull on my shoulders so hard it felt like he was going to rip them out. Channeling my ki into the back of my skull, I slammed it backwards and crushed the front of the vampire's face. Joshua let out a primordial scream, slackening his grip, which allowed me to give a judo throw into the rest of the bloodsucking horde coming at me.

I didn't have time to think of why I felt so strong or what was going on. Instead, I went for the Bloodsword lying a few feet away against the front of the cabin. Wrapping my hands around the weapon, I felt the killing urge within me double, and then triple. It was ecstasy to hold the weapon again, and while it had betrayed me down on the ground, I knew it was my only chance of getting out of here.

A long-haired Chinese man launched himself at me, his hands having grown bear-like claws and his face a contorted parody of a human's. He showed far too many teeth and all of them were razor-sharp. He was faster than the others of his kind, but to me was moving in slow motion.

I laughed at his assault, slashing through both of his arms before bisecting him with the Bloodsword. The vampire had recently fed, so it was like popping a balloon, all of the blood inside him exploding outward in a violent spray.

I drew power from the spilled blood on the ground and stared at the vampires before me, no longer thinking of escape but of feeding. There was a hunger in my chest, almost sexual in nature, driving me to kill them all. I was barely aware of the low oxygen around us and how the plane was rocking from its disrupted atmosphere.

Elizabeth and Minka aimed their pistols at my chest, taking position in front of the other vampires. I felt like I could tear the guns apart with my mind, but I rebelled against that thought. The confidence generated by the sword was a false one, luring me into believing I could fight my opponents one-on-many.

I needed to find a way to escape.

"Impressive," Dracula said, stepping in front of the two vampire women. "But you forget who is the master."

I charged at Dracula, but he just raised his right hand and snapped his fingers. All of the blood on the ground flew upwards and became like pieces of broken glass. I felt cuts all across my legs, chest, shoulders, and arms. Dracula stretched out his hand and my blood started to boil, the cuts giving him an in to manipulate me.

I fell to my knees, feeling pain like I'd never felt before in my life. It was as if my insides were on fire, the pain moving through every nerve ending and then somehow doubling back stronger than before. I could feel the pain intensify to the point where I was ready to black out, but couldn't. Dracula was going to kill me with pain, and I could see the joy in his eyes as he did so.

If he had been trying to kill any other agent in the House, I suspect his plan would have worked. The problem was that I wasn't a good wizard—I was a pretty terrible one, in fact—but I was a pretty damn good martial artist. I used it to supplement my magic, and one of the first things I'd picked up was how to push aside pain. Suppressing the pain, I cleared my head enough to do a single spell and drew on the Bloodsword's power to do so, channeling everything I had into a single drop of blood in my right hand that I hurled with my fingertips towards the emergency exit.

I underestimated the power of the magic flowing through me, because as I watched the little droplet fly through the air, it glowed with an ever-expanding aura of energy that exploded when it struck the door.

I'm not speaking figuratively. Half of the plane detonated in an explosion of white light, and every individual inside, myself included, was sucked out into the wild blue yonder. It was a level of magic I'd never had to deal with, and the fact that I wasn't killed stunned me. Unfortunately, I was still flying through the air with no parachute and saw the blue waters of the Caribbean stretched out before me in every direction.

I said the first word that came to mind. "SHIIIIIIIIIIIT!"

I was about twelve thousand feet in the air—not a high distance, but still enough to flatten me when I struck the waves below. It was beautiful seeing the ocean reflected against the setting sun. I was hurtling free-form and couldn't think of a way to prevent my death. Still, I struggled to slow my descent with magic, covered myself in protective spells, and prayed to all my gods for salvation. In the end, I struck the water, and everything went black. My last thoughts? That this was a crappy way to end my life story.

CHAPTER NINE

I wasn't aware of whether I lived or died for some time thereafter. You might find this strange but knowing there was an afterlife meant I was prepared to spend days, if not weeks, in the limbo between life and death. What does one do in this state? I'm sorry to say reminiscing about life is about it. Memories are the sum of who we are. Daoism teaches that it's the present that matters rather than the past, but we are the products of our past interacting with the now. That, if I may take a moment to go all Yoda on you, is what shapes our future.

Too often, we let our imagination fill in the gaps and alter our pasts to live with ourselves. We remember ourselves being bullied when we, ourselves, bullied others. We remember the past better than it was. We even forget important details because they're too painful. When you were an agent of the Red Room, you didn't have that luxury.

As a spy, memories are doubly important because you must remember things *exactly* as they are on missions. The truth is often painful, humiliating, and ambiguous. We rarely know why people do things, so we fill in the blanks with stories to make sense of it all. That man killed his wife because she was cheating on him, or that woman stole from her employer because she needed the money for drugs. Many times, things just happen, and we never know the whys or the how.

In my case, I didn't have many happy memories as an adult. I didn't have a troubled childhood. I was a spoiled little shit if you must know the truth, but I'd more than made up for it upon graduating the Black Room's field academy. Aside from some brief moments of happiness with Cassandra, Ashley, Christopher, my family, and Shannon, my life was a series of traumatic events interrupted only by the dull tedium of office work. I'd been an agent of the Red Room since I was twenty-one, and it appalled me to realize the past thirteen years of my life had been about 80% filing reports. Gods and immortals, no wonder I hated being a Committee member.

I tried to hang on to the good memories, so I kept reliving them: my wedding with Cassandra, my trip to the Hollow Earth with Shannon, the Vegas mission, when I first told Ashley I loved her, and volunteer work with Christopher at the House's summer camp for superhuman children. But the dark ones sneaked past. I saw a blood-splattered school lunchroom, Cassandra's dead body leaking out brain matter on the ground, and Christopher being dragged away. The worst memory, though, was when I realized I could never escape the House. That I was a prisoner by choice.

That memory I experienced as if it were happening anew. It was All Hallows Eve on an unusually busy night. Halloween was typically a dull time for monster hunters. Why? I dunno. The lab guys might have a specific reason, but I guessed it was because most of the creepy crawlies considered it too gauche to menace people on the supposedly most haunted night of the year. Despite this, I'd come back to the family mansion with my first partner after a case. She was upstairs getting changed while I was playing pool with my father in the billiard room. We'd put down a banshee at Chicago Stadium, but it hadn't darkened our mood for revelry.

Yes, billiard room. Hawthorne House was large enough that it had all the rooms from the *Clue* game, and then some. I once made a joke that the place had its own phone extension, only to find out it did. Despite my present modest means, I came from money. The kind people used to buy and sell islands with. That night was the night I broke with my father and all his wealth.

That night was the event that changed everything.

Nathan Hawthorne was not what most people pictured when they imagined the most powerful wizard on Earth. He was handsome, looking no older than his late forties, with a strong resemblance to Robert Redford in his prime. I'd long suspected my father, not content with being a master magus and richer than God, had used magic to adjust his appearance.

This night, he was dressed in an all-black business suit with a small white handkerchief in his left front pocket. It was a stark contrast to me, wearing a ball cap, blue jeans, and a loose t-shirt. Neither of us were dressed for a party, perhaps because my father never bothered to relax unless it was to indulge himself with his latest mistress or his rampant Sinophilia.

"I need you to kill Ashley Brea Morgan," my father said, having gotten us alone in my family's sprawling mansion.

"If you were anyone else, I'd put a bullet in your head right this second," I said, narrowing my eyes.

How did one react when a loved one, the man you admired most in the world, threatened the person you cared for the most deeply? For me, I was confused and on the verge of violence. If it had been anyone else, I'd have thought it a sick joke. But my father never joked about work, not when it involved murder.

"I'm not the one who ordered her death," Nathan Hawthorne said, picking a pool cue off the wall rack before chalking the end. "This is an order that comes straight from the Chairman. I said I'd handle it and I wanted to bring it to you first."

I looked to the doorway, knowing Ashley was waiting upstairs for me. "I brought her here to meet the family. I intend to marry her. You know I'm going to do everything in my power to protect her."

I'd been a solo agent for much of my career, the Black Room's teachers determining I didn't work well with others. That had changed when I recruited Ashley, training her even as she taught me a great deal about how the outside world functioned.

My father rolled his eyes and placed the cue ball to break. "Don't be so melodramatic, Derek."

"Melodramatic? What is wrong with you!" I slammed my fists down on the other end of the pool table. If I'd known magic, I would have shattered it.

I was young and idealistic back then. Despite being a secret agent who'd killed over a dozen people, I still had delusions of being the good guy. I pretended the monsters didn't have human feelings, the Red Room was all about protecting humanity, and we were there for one another. How wrong I was.

"She contacted a reporter," Nathan said, not showing the slightest bit of remorse or sympathy. He took a shot and half a dozen striped balls went into three different pockets. "Several, in fact. My agents managed to squash any hint of a story, but not without considerable time and expense. Things they wouldn't have needed to do if you'd kept watch over her. She's your partner, your responsibility."

My blood ran cold. "You're lying. Ashley knows better than that. She wouldn't . . ."

But I knew she would. Ashley loved me, but she *hated* the House. Ashley hated the lies, the murders, the blackmail, and the constant fear-mongering that allowed us to stay one step ahead of the supernatural races. She was too honest for spy work, let alone what we did, and would live openly as a psychic if she could.

"Wouldn't she?" Nathan said, ignoring my trailing off. He went around the table and put billiard ball after billiard ball into the nearest pockets. His voice rose with each one he sunk. "When did you start sleeping with her?"

"That's none of your damn business," I said.

"Michaelson Peak, six months after your separation from Cassandra," Nathan said, taking a deep breath. "It's in your files. Everything you do is monitored by the Blue Room. You were a fool to think you were being discreet."

I bit my lip. "We weren't—*aren't*—doing anything wrong."

"Oh, but you were. How long has she hated us?"

"Always. You recruited her at gunpoint," I said, taking off my hat and wiping the sweat caused by the hot lamps above me.

"*You* recruited her at gunpoint," Nathan said, reminding me of how we'd met. "She was seeking out others of her kind when you found her—a Morgan family psychic of immense potential. It was a choice of joining the Red Room or removing her abilities with surgery. You made the judgment call she could be made to fit in."

"She's done excellent work."

"Because she's in love with you," Nathan corrected, once more reminding me of the real issue at stake. "That doesn't mean she's fitting in. If I weren't your father, you'd both have had bullets put in the backs of your heads by now."

"Listen—"

"She loathes everything we stand for. She's a risk to every man, woman, and child on this Earth."

"You're exaggerating."

"Am I? The Truth must be suppressed. The reason people are able to live normal lives in this world, Derek, is because they do not know how much danger they are in!" Nathan finished knocking in the last ball into the corner pocket. He was apparently not actually playing pool but just distracting himself. He proceeded to conjure Ashley's file into his right hand. He tossed it into the air, the document opening and hovering over the pool table. It was her psychology report, and I had no doubt it contained damning testimony.

"You can't tell everything about a person from reports," I said, biting my lip. I was ready to beg now, plead with him to use his influence to make this right. "Father—"

"Shows an unwillingness to use violence against supernatural and human opponents, questions the necessity of hiding the Truth from the masses, shows unnecessary sympathy to nonhumans, has an insubordinate attitude regarding superiors—"

"We can't all be as loyal as me," I said, shrugging my shoulders. The irony was, before that night, I'd been a company man through and though. People had praised me for my willingness to obey orders without question. Ashley's family had a long history with the Red Room but not all of its members were happy with it. Quite a few had been sanctioned or died under questionable circumstances over the years.

"My enemies are going to discredit you with this," Nathan said, looking up from the pool table. "Discredit me. Discredit your siblings."

I felt sick. "Is that what this is about, your damn position?"

"*You* brought her into the House, you convinced Penny to pass her on in the Black Room, and you insisted on partnering with her. You've been holding her hand the entire way—"

"And?" I said, gritting my teeth.

"And they will bury you with her," Nathan said, tossing his

pool cue to the side. "If you're not the one to pull the trigger, they'll have enough evidence to kill you next. Nothing will save you. You're too good of an agent to lose."

I had one last card to play, an appeal to the heart. "What would you do if they asked you to kill my mother?"

"Who's to say I didn't?" Nathan said, shattering any trust I had in the man.

That allowed my emotions to come together with my conscious mind, letting me know what I had to do. "I understand."

"You do?" my father asked, his voice skeptical.

"I'll take care of it. Tonight." My mouth was dry, but I no longer felt any reservations about my situation.

"Of course," Nathan said, taking a deep breath. "It's for the best, Derek. Millions benefit every year from the House's acti—"

"Don't speak to me," I said, my voice cold and empty. "Ever again."

"Derek—"

"No," I said, closing my eyes and sucking in a steadying breath before opening them. "As far as I'm concerned, any relationship we had is gone. You're not my father and I don't want anything from you. Not your money, not your support in the House. I'll make my own way from now on."

"Derek—" Nathan said, looking annoyed rather than hurt.

I walked out the door and slammed it behind me.

For a second, I saw a glimpse into the future. There was a beautiful redhead, myself, and my uncle Talbot. I saw a rotund white-bearded man with one eye grinning at me. Cassandra had a smoking gun pointed at my bleeding arm. There were also other images of Washington burning, two versions of me staring at each other, my hands wrapped around the world, a little white-haired girl about twelve years old, and my body twisting to become a metal dragon with glowing eyes. Not being a wizard yet, I dismissed it as random imagery and shook it away. You got used to strange images when you were a Red Room agent.

Heading up the stairs of the palatial estate, I went to my old room and knocked on the door. Whereas once Hawthorne

House had felt like home, it now felt like a gaudy prison. Whereas I'd once seen just the excess, I now saw how much good could have been done with the money instead. It was shameful, in retrospect, to have all of these revelations come out of a reaction to my father's words, but they'd shaken me to the core.

"Come in," Ashley's deeply Southern-accented voice spoke on the other side of the door.

Moving my hand to the bronze knocker, I turned it and headed on in. I wasn't the agent I'd become in later years, but I wasn't stupid, either. Looking down at the floor, I reached into my pocket and clicked the end of a mechanical pen I'd outfitted with an illegally-modified Ring of Veritas. Everything that happened in this room would be blinded to both mundane and mystical monitoring techniques.

In my head, I was already working out how to fool the Red Room into believing Ashley was dead. I also was questioning how many friends and colleagues I would be willing to murder to keep her safe. The answer? As many as it took. I was surprisingly calm about it. I knew what I was willing to do and had no regrets about it. In a weird way, this was the moment I became the agent I'd always wanted to be.

"How do I look?" Ashley spoke, drawing my eyes up at her.

Ashley was a tall, curvaceous woman with shoulder-length brown hair. She wasn't traditionally beautiful, her gray eyes too large and her frame more muscular than Hollywood said was allowed. However, looking back, I could honestly say until Shannon I had never thought anyone as beautiful. Tonight, she was wearing a bright yellow spandex outfit with a white strip in her hair. "I love the outfit," I said, my breath running away from me. How was I going to tell her? How was I going to do this? "Rogue from the X-men?"

"Pre-Anna Paquin," Ashley said, smirking. "I have your Gambit costume over there."

I frowned. "I'm sorry to say I'm not in the mood to play dress-up."

"I figured since we managed to put that poor woman's ghost down—" Ashley looked to the ground.

"It was a banshee," I corrected her. "She, it, wasn't a woman anymore. It never was. It was the ghost of a dead fairy with neither human values nor attitudes."

"Whatever. What I was saying is …" Ashley trailed off before wrinkling her brow. "Wait, you're going to fake my death?!"

"What?" I said, looking over my shoulder. *"No, I'm not."*

"I'm a psychic, dammit!" Ashley said, appalled. "What the hell is going on?"

"No way to do this easily then," I said, pressing two fingers into the side of her neck and hitting a spot where the ki centers of her aura intersected. I was never happier to be a student of Vibrating Palm martial arts.

Ashley crumbled to the ground unconscious. It was a good thing she was surprised by my thoughts; otherwise she would have been able to order me to stop or blab out everything I'd been told downstairs.

"Man, she is going to be pissed when she wakes up," I muttered, throwing her over my shoulder and heading to the window.

CHAPTER TEN

I'm not sure what it says about the Red Room that, in a mansion of super spies, not a single person noticed me climbing out a window on the side of the house with an unconscious woman over my shoulders. Of course, the way my father talked, most of them probably knew I was supposed to kill Ashley. That thought smothered any remaining loyalty I felt to my employers. Once you started doubting the motives of the people controlling you, you couldn't stop, and it became an avalanche of suspicions and recriminations.

Carrying Ashley to a grey Cadillac CTS I'd bought that year, I opened the door and slipped her in the side passenger's door before shutting it and getting in on the other side. It was a cool night, and the stars were visible over the Massachusetts estate.

Pulling out my cellphone, I debated who I could trust in this sort of situation. I wasn't going to kill Ashley—I'd rather die—but trying to fool the Red Room was near unthinkable. They had hundreds of agents, every bit as talented as I was, and an entire army of scientists whose job was to make sure no detail escaped them. Not to mention magic.

My first thought was to ditch the whole "fake her death" plan and try to make a run for it. There were a few places in the world where the Red Room didn't have any power. They were in countries where you didn't want to settle down, but they existed. There was also the option for full-scale treason and seeking refuge with one of the major factions who opposed the House. I dismissed that last idea, since not only was I not a traitor, but I'd also done plenty of missions to find these individuals and kill them.

I was the weak link in all this. My father was a new member of the Committee, possessed of more resources than the president. If I betrayed the Red Room, he'd track us down across the globe not just to protect his own position, but also to defend his other children. He had several other kids by various mistresses, and while he tended to favor Penny and me, I didn't doubt his love for them. Nor did I doubt the Red Room's willingness to take their revenge on my family if I betrayed them. How had I ever deluded myself into believing the House had any kind of moral superiority?

"Derek?" Penny said, opening the driver's side backdoor and sliding on in behind me.

"Ah!" I said, almost jumping out of my seat. I hadn't yet developed the kind of ice-cold emotional control that would make me a great agent.

Turning my head around, I saw the purple-haired figure of my sister. Her lip, nose, and ear were pierced, while her eyes were enchanted to appear a bright shade of purple. Penny Hawthorne had never left her high school goth phase, and tonight she was dressed in a black corset with nothing over it and a black ballerina's dress, complete with tights. It was her way of rebelling against the stuffiness of her upbringing. Beside her was a twisted white oak staff covered in Iroquois symbols, Penny's first attempt to create an enhancer.

"What the hell are you doing here?!" I asked, overreacting to the situation.

"Hoping my brother's girlfriend just had one too many," Penny said, staring at me. "However, I know you're panicking, which is disturbing since you've killed like a dozen people without any significant reaction. Have you considered seeing a psychologist?"

"Monsters aren't people," I said, my hands shaking. "Nor are the humans who serve them."

How wrong I was. There were beings like Dracula who could kill entire countries without feeling an ounce of remorse, and entities whose moral superiority shamed the saintliest humans. It wasn't their species which determined such, though. No, the monster that lay in all of us was made visible only by fangs and claws. After all, many supernaturals used stories of me to scare each other.

"What's wrong?" Penny asked, shaking me from my fugue. "I'm picking up a galaxy-level freak-out from you."

I frowned at her. "Don't read my mind, sis."

"We're twins, Derek. The Son and Daughter of the Dragon. You may not choose to express your magical potential, but that doesn't mean it's nonexistent. When you stub your toe, I get a sense of it."

"That's…creepy," I said, really hoping she was joking.

"Think how I feel when you're having sex," Penny said. "But no, I just saw you come out here holding Ashley and figured something had gone sideways."

I grimaced. "Too much information." I closed my eyes, on the verge of tears. It was a sign of weakness I never would have shown normally. "Dad—no, *Committee member Hawthorne*—has ordered that Ashley be killed. I'm trying to figure out how to save her."

Penny took a second to respond. "Jesus."

"I *know*," I snapped.

Penny stretched her hand out and placed it on my shoulder. "I know what to do."

"Do you?"

Penny nodded. "I do. There's a man who does what you want to do for Ashley. He's good enough to fool the Blue Room."

I raised an eyebrow. "It sounds like a trap. You know, let people know there's a way out of the Red Room only to shoot them when they try."

Again, I was self-deluded about the Red Room. In retrospect, it was amazing it took me this long to realize we weren't the forces of justice and nobility my superiors claimed us to be.

"It's legitimate," Penny said. "I can confirm it."

"How?" I asked, looking at her with desperation in my eyes.

Penny bit her lip. There were no secrets between us. I'd die before betraying her, and I knew the feeling was mutual. The only thing we'd ever disagreed upon in our lives was her decision to go looking for our mother.

"Because I've helped other agents, or would-be agents, leave the House," Penny said, admitting to treason almost as bad as Ashley's.

"Excuse me?" I said, staring at her.

Penny shook her head. "I'm an instructor at the Black Room, Derek. I teach kids, sixteen-year-olds, and sometimes younger, how to be soldiers in an eternal war against monsters. I know the ones who aren't going to pass. Some of them can be sent for retraining, but others are just not capable of shouldering the burden the House puts on them. Do you think I just mark them for death?"

I stared at my sister, wondering how long she'd held these views and why I hadn't picked up on them. "Penny, do you know what kind of danger you're—"

Penny raised an eyebrow, an identical gesture to my own signature look.

"Okay, point taken," I said, looking over at Ashley. She was still sleeping, the ki strike I'd hit her with working better than chloroform. "People in glass towers shouldn't use rocket launchers."

"Do you love her?" Penny asked, causing me to do a double take.

"What?"

"I'm about to help my obsessive brother go against every principle he's spouted since the day he graduated. Predictably, it's over a woman, so I figured I'd ask if he loved her or if this was just because you knocked boots after Cassandra dumped you. A quality, I would remind you, she shares with half the female staff of Division One including the Madison—"

"I love her," I interrupted. "She's the only genuinely good person I know."

"Gee, thanks."

"You know what I mean," I said, sighing. "I've done a lot of things for the greater good over the years. Questionable things. The problem is, I'm starting to realize the lesser evil might still be evil. There's no Diet Coke when it comes to what we do."

Later, I'd find out the Committee lied about a lot of my mission details. Why tell an agent the person they're going to assassinate is just going to do an exposé on Red Room corruption of Capital Hill politicians when you can say he's a magically enhanced pedophile serial killer wearing the skin of a previous victim? Even then, though, it wasn't always possible to reconcile the decisions I made in the field. Innocents died, good men's lives were ruined, and the bad guys were sometimes allowed to continue operating if it meant they were now your bad guys.

I took a deep breath. "On one of our first cases together, we were called to upstate New York to deal with a Carrie."

A Carrie was a psychic or magician—the difference was academic, really—with little to no control over their abilities.

I continued. "He was a fourteen-year-old boy not so dissimilar to Ashley when we first met, only younger and a lot more traumatized. He'd already killed his abusive stepfather, mother, and a couple of neighbors with his powers. The boy had telekinesis, pyrokinesis, and a couple of other kineses capable of tearing through a small town like it was wet tissue paper. Our orders were to defuse the situation, but it was pretty clear the reason we were given leeway to take him alive was for the possibility of weaponization."

I could remember that mission as vividly as my past self. Ashley was still uncomfortable with me, having just finished six months of retraining her powers, and more than a little repulsed by our organization's draconian methods. The two of us couldn't have been more different. Whereas she saw a scared and lost little boy, I saw the charred and burned bodies that would only multiply as the local authorities antagonized something they didn't understand.

"So, what happened?" Penny asked, probably wondering why I hadn't shared this story before.

"Ashley found a way to talk him down. Even better, she helped the boy remove the worst of the pain from his mind. His powers even shifted to healing and biomancy. It wasn't the last time Ashley found a peaceful solution when my training told me to shoot first."

"You're not the kind of guy who kills kids, Derek."

"The Red Room wants me to be."

Penny looked down. "Are you going with her?"

"Yeah, are you?" Ashley said, waking up.

"Ah crap," I said, shaking my head. "I am sucking at my job tonight."

Ashley stared at me. "Yes, yes you are. So the real question is whether I should alter your brain to become obsessed with the works of Liberace."

"Touch my brother's brains and I swear I will find a way to damn your soul to the furthest reaches of hell." My sister narrowed her eyes and lowered her voice an octave.

Ashley didn't react well to threats. "You'd have to cast a spell before I wiped—"

I raised my hands in the air as if surrendering. "Let's remember who the enemy is here, people. Me."

"You'll never be my enemy, Derek," Ashley said, staring at me. "Even if I want to telekinetically hurl a car at you right now."

"Can she do that?" Penny asked, surprised.

I shrugged, not caring to satiate my sister's curiosity about Ashley's power level. "Magicians can do more, psychics hit harder. That's what I learned in the academy."

"Except for our father, who can hit harder and do more than anybody," Penny said, defending the family's honor. "Not that I suspect you're in the mood to defend our father right now. Also, Comic Con cosplayer is not the best look for escaping the House."

"Look who's talking, Carmilla."

I put my face in my hands, counting to ten. "So, you heard everything we were talking about."

"Yeah, I did," Ashley said, turning to stare out into the night. "You didn't answer my question, though."

It was a harder question than she imagined. I loved Ashley, more than any other woman I'd ever met. I had trained my entire life to be an agent of the Red Room, and despite all the ethical questions I'd faced, I still believed it was a necessary evil. Without the House to stand between humanity and the forces of the supernatural, the world would eat itself within weeks.

That didn't require me, though.

Really, the choice was simple. Did I value my continued service to a group that would ask me to kill someone I loved more than I valued the person I loved? If I said yes, then I couldn't claim to love that person at all. Love was something you either possessed absolutely or not at all. My mother abandoned both my sister and me, leaving behind my father. I didn't think she loved us. If she did, she never would have left.

And I wasn't my mother.

"I want to come with you," I said, taking a deep breath. "I want it more than anything."

Ashley looked at me, probably not too pleased with the amount of doubt she'd sensed within me. "Derek—"

"You realize, we're never going to see each other again if you leave, right?" Penny said in the back. Her voice was quivering. I don't think she expected me to choose Ashley over her. I wished I could reassure her I wasn't.

But I was.

I lowered my head, unable to respond to my twin. Strange. For a decision that was supposed to be romantic, I felt sickened.

"Your brother loves you, Penelope. He's—" Ashley started speaking for me, reaching over to put her hand on my shoulder.

Penny cut her off. "I don't need you to tell me what my brother thinks of me. I'll make the phone call. He was going to be coming here anyway."

I looked back at her. "Why?"

Penny didn't answer. Only later did I have the sense to realize she'd been intending to leave too.

CHAPTER ELEVEN

We drove for about three hours until we reached a small village on the coast. I didn't bother to learn its name, but it was the kind of place that didn't lock its doors or believe in evolution. The buildings downtown were all one story, and the only major franchise I saw was a McDonalds that looked like it hadn't been updated since the eighties.

All the lights were off, and the streets were empty, leaving me both relieved and unnerved. This was the place we were supposed to meet with Penny's contact, a man she knew as the Cuckoo. Parking the car in front of an old-time department store, I turned the engine off and waited for him to show. I wasn't sure I trusted Penny's contact. This was all a bit too coincidental for my tastes, but our options were limited.

"I wish we had time to change clothes." Ashley crossed her arms. "This is an awkward outfit to die in."

"That's assuming we're going to die tonight. We may have to go into hiding for a while," I said, thinking about the kind of preparations necessary to fake someone's death well enough to fool the Red Room.

They boggled the mind.

You had to overcome magic, science, a veritable army of investigators, and a spy network larger than anything but the United States. Hell, they had access to the spy network of the United States, too. I'd spent months infiltrated into the CIA, copying all of the agency's files on supernatural happenings, with no one the wiser. It made me wonder if I should try to do this on my own. I shook my head of the thought. I trusted Penny. If she said this person could be trusted, I believed her. Even if it was hard to do so.

"I've worked with the Cuckoo three times," Penny interrupted, sensing my doubts. She'd been silent during the trip here. "He's very effective at pulling off these missions and has ties to the Blue Room. If anyone is capable of getting you out of the House's sights, it's him."

I wasn't so sure and hated feeling that way, since Ashley would pick up on my emotional state. I'd spent my entire life training to be a part of the House's elite, and the idea of leaving said life behind was difficult. I also knew what they were capable of. Even if we managed to get away, it'd be years before I stopped looking over my shoulder.

"We should go to India," Ashley said, picking up on my distress. "A billion people is a large crowd to get lost in."

"Says the neon-dressed white girl," Penny rolled her eyes.

"Says the neon-dressed Irish girl," Ashley corrected. "If you're going to poke holes in my suggestion, then at least do them right."

"We'll have to change our appearances," I said, sighing. "Mannerisms, names, and habits. No use of credit cards, just cash, and it'll be best if we avoided being out in the open as well. The Cuckoo will probably provide us existing identities, but I won't feel comfortable until we disappear again after that."

"If only one of us were trained as a covert operative of some kind," Ashley said, staring out the window. "But where would we find someone with that sort of training? I mean, you'd have to be some sort of *spy*."

I rolled my eyes. "Very funny."

"I remind you, India is where Marie got killed in the *The Bourne Supremacy*, so don't get too comfortable." Penny leaned over the side of Ashley's seat to glare at her. "I'd rather my brother didn't have to fish you out of some river after Karl Urban kills you. Not that I don't think you'd deserved it."

"That movie is hardly what I'd call a classic," I said. "You should stick with better references."

"Excuse me?" Ashley said, turning to her.

"It isn't a classic?" I asked.

"I meant the 'deserve it' part," Ashley said, slapping me across the shoulder.

Penny returned to her seat in the back. "I'm sorry. I love my brother and I'm not happy I'm about to be separated from him forever. I'd like to know just what the hell you did to warrant being killed by the Red Room."

"Penny—" I started to say.

"Maybe I looked at someone the wrong way. People get killed for no reason in the Red Room." Ashley could barely hold back the venom in her voice.

"The Red Room has done more good for this world than any other body in the history of ever. Do you like the idea of being born and raised in blood camps? Because that's what would have happened if not for our parents and Uncle Talbot. It's been doing it for millennium. Let me tell you about the Nephilim's reign in the Pre-Babylonian Era which—" Penny started to speak before I raised my hand.

"It doesn't matter," I said, interrupting. "What matters is I'm willing to follow her into hell."

I hope our escape is a little better than hell, Ashley said in my mind. *I never meant for you to become involved in this.*

I wasn't psychic, but I'd learned how to communicate with her once she opened the channel between us. It was useful on missions and helped with everything from sex to resolving arguments. *What did you think was going to happen when you went to the media?*

I dunno. Ashley shifted in her seat. *I guess I wanted to try and change the world.*

No one can change the world without bloodshed, I thought back to her. *Martin Luther King never would have made it half as far without Malcolm X. Gandhi's martyrdom was the shock India needed to institute his changes. Selfishness and insanity seem too ingrained to remove with anything but a scalpel. I didn't like it, but it was the way I perceived the world.*

I don't believe that, Ashley said. *Not for a second. I know what people are like under their stated opinions. Almost everyone wants peace. It's only fear that keeps them going for their weapons first.* Ashley looked down to her lap. *Aren't you sick of the lying? The violence? Derek, you're one of the most peaceful men I know. I can't understand how you murder people so effortlessly.*

Practice, I responded.

And you wonder why you sometimes scare me, I said.

Are you? I asked, hurt.

Ashley didn't respond.

Around us, a storm broke and a torrent of rain began pouring down. It made the atmosphere much more morbid and depressing. The air felt charged, as if everything were generating static electricity. Thunder clapped, and dozens of lightning strikes filled the skyline.

I stared at the sudden weather change. "That's not normal."

"It's the Cuckoo. He uses storm elementals and cloud cover to block divination as well as remote viewing," Penny explained, looking up into the sky. "Like I said, he's very good at what he does."

"Have you ever checked up on what happened to these people after he helps them escape?" I asked, uneasy.

Penny shrugged. "No, of course not. That would defeat the whole purpose."

"Great," I said, imagining this Cuckoo shooting his clients in the back of the head and leaving them in a ditch.

"He's not like that," Penny said, waving her hand. "He's a good man."

I shrugged. "Trust no one. The Dao of Fox Mulder."

"You realize if we were on that show we'd be the bad guys, right?" Penny pointed at me, no longer focused on Ashley. I hated leaving her behind. We'd been through so much together, from the womb to Black Room graduation. It would be like cutting my own arm off to never see her again.

I forced that thought away, focusing instead on my love for Ashley. "I thought you wanted to leave the Red Room, P? Why don't you join us?"

Penny shook her head. "There's no way anyone would believe all three of us died together. I'll stay to cover your escape and provide you a cover story. I believe in the Red Room. I just don't believe I can keep killing children for it. Maybe I'll ask for a transfer to field work after this."

I could tell she was thinking about our father.

"Can you stomach killing children, Derek?" Ashley asked, teaming up with Penny. She was trying to make me feel better about leaving my job behind.

I thought of demonic possession, psychic parasites, and other conditions that could turn the innocent into monsters. "It depends on how many children I save by doing so."

My statement ended all conversation in the car, creeping out Penny and Ashley. I was grateful for the silence because another car had driven up. It was a black Jeep Grand Cherokee, the kind of car that wouldn't stand out in this environment at all. The car flashed its headlights twice, signaling he was our man. Glad this ordeal was coming to its climax, I unbuckled my seatbelt and opened the driver's side door.

"Let me talk to him," Penny said.

"No, I want to size this guy up," I said, shaking my head. "Just for my peace of mind."

"Also, he's still filled with doubt," Ashley added, turning her head to me. "I'm just surprised it's not about me."

I didn't bother thinking about what Ashley was saying, which was a shame since it might have clued me into what would turn into a central problem for the next part of my life— my inability to separate myself from my family's vocation. Ashley knew what I didn't back then. She knew I was a killer and did what I did because I was good at it.

I didn't enjoy murder, but it didn't affect me as it did other people. I'd say it was the dragon blood, but my mother was the noblest warrior my father had met. Somehow, somewhere along the way, I'd changed from being a normal person into a weapon that had no use when it wasn't pointed at someone.

Walking through the rain, I reached the jeep and knocked on the driver's side window. I couldn't quite make out the figure inside but got the message when the backseat door to my side opened. Sliding on in, I saw a handsome Chinese man with long black hair wearing a turtleneck sweater in the driver's seat.

I recognized him. "Christopher Hang."

I'd met Christopher Hang during one of my information-sharing missions to Division Sixteen in Hong Kong. The Red Room was divided into a hundred and twelve regional branches, and rarely did agents get along, but we still lent each other assistance on a regular basis. We were, after all, on the same side.

Theoretically.

I didn't know the man well, but he'd been one of the rising stars of the agency when I'd first graduated. Unlike most agents, who were sensible enough to engage our enemies only when they had overwhelming force backing them up (and still suffered horrific casualties), Christopher took risks. Lots of risks. Risks that had paid off. That was, of course, true right up until my second year of service, when he'd gotten a fellow senior agent killed and was transferred to the Blue Room to keep him out of trouble.

"Well, this is awkward," Christopher said. "I expected to be meeting with your sister, Mister Hawthorne."

"There's been a slight complication," I said, shutting the door behind him.

"You want to help Ashley Morgan escape."

I stared. "You know about that?"

"Everyone in the Blue Room knows," Christopher said, adjusting his rear-view mirror to look at me. It was unnecessary given that we were alone, but I appreciated the nod to classic spy work. Too many people didn't even bother these days. "Your father is targeting her to get to you. You realize this, right? If she's taken out of the game, then you'll be forced to stay, and your sister won't abandon you. It's genius, albeit evil."

I processed his statement and nodded. It sounded like the kind of thing Nathan would do. "I take it you're not going to help me leave with Ashley."

"I was going to tell your sister this plan wasn't going to work. I'm very good at helping low-level initiates and burnouts to escape, but your sister and you are House royalty. I'd have an easier time helping the president's kids disappear."

I didn't miss a beat. "What about Ashley?"

Neither did Christopher. "Her, I can help."

"Tonight?"

"Yes."

I paused, taking in the monumental nature of all this. I'd

just agreed to abandon my old life and start a new one with Ashley, only to find out that wasn't an option anymore. "I don't suppose there's any way I could track her down after this?"

"If you want to kill her, yeah." Christopher snorted. "Listen, I'm good at my job. I make people disappear. When I'm done with Ashley, she will register as dead to everything from divination spells to the county coroner. I have a blood magic spell capable of turning a corpse into a perfect replica of someone, right down to the DNA. That's not even covering the bribes, mind-magic, and new identities I'm capable of providing. Believe me, when I say I can make her disappear, I mean she will never be seen again—by you, or me."

"That sounds suspicious, if you don't mind me saying."

Christopher raised three fingers and crossed them. "I swear on my true name and the Five Powers what I'm saying is true."

I paused. "You're a wizard?"

Christopher lifted his right hand and conjured a tiny ball of free-floating electricity before making it disappear. "More than you, less than your father."

I nodded. "All right, I believe you. No magician would risk his soul like that if he wasn't telling the truth."

Christopher shrugged, not turning back to look at me. "I know a few. They're all dead, though."

"Now for the real question, how much?" I asked, wondering what sort of payment was required for a man to betray the House.

"Money is something I have enough of, and I never thought I'd say that. The House doesn't care if you siphon funds from the monsters' accounts as long as they get their cut. I don't charge for this service I provide here. I do, however, rely on favors. You could offer me a pretty big favor."

"You overestimate me. My position in the House wasn't able to save Ashley, and I just broke ties with my father."

"I want back in."

"You help people escape the House and yet your requested fee is being put back in the field?"

"One out of three agents die in the field and another gets out as quickly as possible. It's not a business for the faint at heart. I'm good at it, though. I know how the monsters think. Vampires, jiang shi, lycanthropes, and pro-supernatural politicians. They're my tableau. Given the number of guys you've taken down, I'd think you'd understand."

"Reports of my viciousness are exaggerated."

"If you say so, chief."

Against my better instincts, this was when I started to like Christopher Hang. He was a proactive sort in an organization that was determined to keep everyone under its thumb. I believed him when he said he was doing this for reasons other than money, not the least because my father also made himself rich by exploiting the House's resources.

It would take all of my pull, but what Christopher was asking wasn't impossible. Assuming the Committee believed I'd killed Ashley, they would grant me any favor I wanted. An easy and understandable one would be to request my next partner. I wasn't sure I wanted to spend the rest of my career with this guy, but I could do what he asked.

I made my decision. "Can you guarantee me she'll have a happy life?"

"No one can guarantee that."

I sighed. "All right. Do it."

CHAPTER TWELVE

I sat there in the back of the jeep for a few minutes. I couldn't help but wonder how I'd arrived at this position. I'd come here to try and make sure I wouldn't be separated from Ashley but ended up guaranteeing it would happen.

"Are you okay?" Christopher asked, surprising me. I hadn't expected the so-called Cuckoo to care.

"Not really, no."

"It's not too late to call it off."

"It is if I want her to live."

Christopher looked back over his shoulder. "Love is a crazy thing. We always hurt those we care about most."

He sounded like he spoke from experience. I didn't care about that, though. All I wanted to do was finish up this farce. Tomorrow, I would have to go back to an organization I now hated and continue work for people I loathed, but at least Ashley would be safe.

I stared at him and said, "Show up Monday morning. We've got a backlog of cases. The number of rogue monsters has increased. There's also a serious question whether someone is trying to organize them."

"Someone is always trying to organize them. Emerald Eye, the Invisible Court, the Doomsday Brotherhood, the Fifth Column, the Human League, the Daughters of Bachuus—"

"Point taken."

Christopher surprised me with his next words. "I've helped almost two dozen operatives and would-be operatives escape the House. I got into this business as a favor to a friend and it's sort of grown from there. There's something you need to understand, though. A quality that will either make you feel better about this or break you."

"I don't think I'm going to feel better about this."

"Not now, no. I've parted husbands from wives and fathers from children. The thing you have to understand is the House is a burden born by killers. Once you pull the trigger, you either know you're one or not. If you are one, you wouldn't be able to survive out there. You'd see a kid torn up by an animal and know, yeah, that was a Rakshasa, or someone's suicide you pick up is because someone's had their happiness stolen by fae."

"I know how to keep cover."

"Does Ashley?" I asked.

"Ashley helps people. She doesn't kill them."

"Then she'd be able to find another way to live. I can set her up as a psychiatrist to heal damaged minds or whatever else her abilities would help. I can't help killers, though. The only one I helped became a vampire hunter within a month. I had to track down his body and melt it in acid when I found out he'd gotten himself killed."

"I am a killer, but I could have found peace with her."

Christopher didn't address that. "You're not the first person to lose someone you loved to the job, one way or the other. My recommendation is for you to focus on the rage, pain, and hatred you feel and turn it into a weapon against the monsters. Not so much you'll become reckless, but enough you'll be able to forget."

"Sounds like pretty stupid advice."

"It's worked for me."

The impulse to lose myself in my job was a strong one. I couldn't imagine moving on from this point and ironically didn't want to think about serving the Red Room's agenda anymore. If I was a weapon, maybe I should just be one and forget all about the politics. A part of me wanted to die for this betrayal, but it was a fleeting emotion. No—if I was honest, I wanted to make other people die for tearing me away from the woman I loved.

"Maybe you're right."

Christopher didn't know about my inner struggle, though. He just smiled and tried to reassure me. "I have a lot to show you, my friend. I think we'll work well together."

"Maybe," I said.

Christopher and I would prove to be a formidable pair and he was just the sort of guy to distract me from Ashley's loss. Hell, he even liked paperwork—a kind of nasty mutation which must have come from his huji jing ancestry. In the coming years, I'd come to rely on him as someone who had my back no matter the circumstances. He taught me a lot, showing me how to exploit the monsters' blind spots and act unpredictably.

Unfortunately, I knew what lay next in my vision. The next part of my flashback was almost too painful to relive. It was a moment of pure unadulterated heartbreak. I'd killed, lied, cheated, stole, blackmailed, and engaged in all manner of espionage over the years. I'd plumbed the innermost secrets of over a thousand individuals and written papers on how to destroy someone's life, so the Red Room could pick up the pieces. This was my moment, the event that turned mid-level agent Derek Hawthorne into someone who didn't care whether he lived or died.

"Are you okay?" Christopher asked, watching me hesitate as I stared out at the window to my side.

"No," I said, opening the rear passenger door and stepping out into the night. The rain had stopped and there was now just a trickle, the storm clouds rumbling overhead. Ashley was standing in front of me, her clothes drenched, and arms crossed. One only had to look at her face to know she knew everything I'd said to Christopher. That she wouldn't be escaping out into the Big Beautiful World with her lover. No, she'd be going alone, and there wasn't a damn thing either of us could do about it. Ashley looked devastated, raindrops mixing with tears. I felt her pain, knowing it reflected my own.

"Why?" Ashley asked, her voice quivering.

"I'd rather be miserable and you safe than you dead."

A nearby streetlamp exploded as she narrowed her eyes, fury replacing sorrow. The air became filled with static and I felt an immeasurable power building within her.

Ashley's abilities were off the scale, and if she'd possessed the slightest inclination to mastering her power, she might have become the psychic Mozart. The Red Room taught psychics how to conquer and destroy to the exclusion of other disciplines. That wasn't Ashley, and the House hadn't forced the issue. They preferred having a level-five psychic capable of levitating cars that tolerated them than a level-ten capable of leveling mountains that hated them. Right now, I wasn't sure if Ashley had been holding back during those tests.

"Don't you dare try to say this is for me," Ashley whispered, her words hanging in the air as her powers burned them into my mind.

Not far away, I saw Penny get out of the car, and I made a slight gesture with my fingers. I didn't want my sister getting involved with this mess any more than she was. Christopher had the good sense to stay in the car.

"Who else would it be for?" I said, calm and without malice.

Ashley walked over, each step feeling like a small earthquake as her emotions enhanced the telekinetic fury raging within her. More streetlights exploded, and trash cans moved across the street, dragged by her building energy. Cars nearby, including the jeep, moved a few feet forward even though they were in park.

It was a visual representation of how we both felt.

"I love you," I said, unable to say anything more.

I'd said those words before, but there had always been a caveat. The words spoken to Ashley just now, though, felt right. Truer than anything I'd experienced with my wife. Why now, though, when we were about to be separated forever?

"We can't be together," Ashley said, staring down. "Because of your father."

"Believe me, if my father were the only thing standing between us, I'd have killed him back at the mansion."

"You shouldn't say things like that."

"You know I would, though."

"I know." Ashley bit her lip. "And that's what frightens me."

I snorted. "The people you love shouldn't scare you."

"The people you love are the scariest people in the world," Ashley said, looking up into my eyes.

I was crying now. I couldn't remember the last time I'd done so. "Promise me you're going to live the life you deserve. Have children. Just be happy."

Ashley reached over and put her hand against my face. It was warm in the freezing cold. "I wanted to have children with you."

"I can't have kids. It's something magical," I said, not yet knowing the source of my ailment. "Besides, we could never bring them up in this environment."

Ashley looked like she wanted to tell me something, reveal some fact of life that would change everything. Instead, she closed her eyes. "You would have made a great father."

"It'd be hard to be worse than my dad."

Ashley leaned in and pressed her lips against mine. There was an immediate spark and everything felt topsy-turvy. My vision grew blurry and I pulled away, unsteady on my feet. It was not the reaction I expected.

"What was that?" I said, feeling like I could collapse at any second.

"I closed away the parts of your mind that contain our feelings and built a barrier. No one will be able to read your mind about tonight or influence you to forget. We'll always be linked, Derek Hawthorne, and I want you to be as happy as me."

"I can't be happy without you," I whispered.

"You will be."

I don't recall much of what happened thereafter, but Penny drove me home and I spent the next few days in bed. My father pretended to be fooled that I'd executed Ashley in cold blood and everyone outside of my family started treating me like I was evil incarnate.

Christopher was a comfort, and I learned the value of friends lay not in quantity but in quality. I renewed my relationship with Lucy, Sakura my secretary, and a half-dozen other people who served me better than the dozens I'd thought I could rely on. I'd had one other partner than Christopher and Ashley Morgan, but the less said about Solomon the better. I shit you not, he died getting gored by a unicorn. I mean, it shouldn't be funny, but it was.

With Christopher, I took my revenge out on the supernatural world. We became one of the most effective pairs of agents in the

House as well as the most ruthless. I needed to hit something to make myself feel better and Christopher needed kills to improve his position. We both got what we wanted and became infamous for the damage we did to enemy plans—sometimes when softer approaches would have worked better. The images of the carnage, bloodshed, and mayhem threatened to drown me. I'd gone mad after Christopher's disappearance, and it took Penny to draw me back. I realized I couldn't count the number of people I'd killed. Human and monster.

Four hundred thirty-seven, a spectral voice whispered in my ear. *Those are the ones you've killed personally. The number is much higher incorporating those you've killed indirectly, via orders, or as part of a group.*

It sounded . . . approving.

437? Holy shit.

That was insane. That meant I'd killed more than four people a month. I didn't want to calculate an exact figure, lest it expose just what sort of fucked-up psychopath I'd allowed myself to become.

Not a psychopath, a warrior, the spectral voice whispered. *The Wrath of God on a fallen world.*

I tried to regain some sense of control over my body, but it was like I was trapped underwater, my body moving of its own volition.

Who are you? I asked, speaking inside myself.

A friend, the voice said, its tone now feminine and seductive.

I don't have any friends who like murder, I spoke back to the voice.

My dearest Derek, Son of the Morning, Child of the Dragon, those are the only friends you have, it whispered.

My eyes burned as a sudden brightness washed over them and I found my body rising out of the water I'd felt myself drowning in. As my eyes adjusted to the light, I saw I was stepping onto one of the beaches of Nassau. Its beautiful hotels were visible just off from the sandbar and I was getting stared at by a dozen people getting tans with their families.

I was soaked to the bone with seawater, my trench coat

hanging off me like a shroud. The sun was shining bright in the sky and I wondered if I'd swum for an entire day. I didn't feel tired, though. More like numb. Even more troubling, I saw my right hand was clenching the handle of the Bloodsword. The accursed artifact seemed welded to my fingers, my tight grip around its steel something I could no more influence than the movement of the Earth around the sun. The Bloodsword looked different now, no longer a cutlass but a Chinese *jian* or longsword. Its seductive power was unmistakable, though.

The weapon had bestowed upon me the physical strength to survive falling out of a plane, had pushed my body to be able to travel to land, and had kept my arms and legs going while distracting my conscious mind. These acts had drained it of its immense mystical strength and left a raw overpowering hunger for more bloodshed. It needed to be fed.

You, I thought to it.

Yes, the Bloodsword whispered. *I am at your command.*

Let go, I commanded, feeling my body continue to walk to the roads beyond the beach. A spell washed out from my body, causing everyone around me to go back to their vacations as if a man rising from the sea were a commonplace occurrence.

Soon, the Bloodsword said. *We both need to feed first.*

"No," I muttered, shaking my head.

Yes, the Bloodsword said. *Sleep, my Angel of Death. I will handle everything.*

I tried to resist, tried to draw on my Red Room training, but it seemed a poor defense against the power inside the sword. I was exhausted both in mind and body. I found myself falling asleep as the weapon hijacked my body. A flood of pleasant images from the romances of my life drowned my attempts to fight back.

Everything went black again.

The Bloodsword was in command now.

Fuck.

CHAPTER THIRTEEN

I regained control of my body days later, possessing only the vaguest sense of what had happened in the meantime. I sensed darkness, violence, magic, and death. Waking up was simultaneously refreshing and disgusting. The disgusting part coming from the fact that I awoke coughing up blood into the sink of a bathroom. I was naked except for a pair of expensive new black silk boxer shorts, the kind with pockets. My head hurt worse than when Dracula messed with it.

The bathroom had a black marble floor, six different kinds of towel, and walls decorated in heraldry-covered green wallpaper. I was in a hotel. A high class one, too. It was the kind of place I'd used to stay in when I was richer than God and not on a mission. I didn't miss those days, but it made me wonder what I'd been up to.

Looking up into the mirror, I saw my bare chest was sporting a number of new tattoos. Representations of the twelve animals of the Chinese Zodiac were across my chest, arms, and legs in a dizzyingly beautiful intertwined pattern. I could feel mystical power buried within the ink. *Corrupt* mystical power.

Even the dragon tattoo on my back I'd had before my blackout felt like it had been redone. Reaching out with my limited sixth sense to touch the tattoos, I could hear screams of those whose blood had gone into creating them. Someone, probably me, had killed people in order to harness their life energy. It was extra disturbing because I could feel *a lot* more power running through my ki centers, or chakras. My entire adult life, I'd struggled to do even the simplest spells compared to my father and siblings. Last year, I'd had a breakthrough, but even then, I lagged behind them by decades. Now I felt *strong*.

I was never going to be the kind of magical big-wig my father was, nor would I ever use the kind of power my sister, who was more Billy Joel, wielded. I thought I'd come to terms with it but I hadn't. Here, covered in black magic-enhanced tattoos forbidden by the Red Room for centuries, it would have been a lie to say I wasn't the least bit excited. I coughed a bit more and ran the water in the sink to wash away the blood. It didn't feel like I'd done so out of disease or injury. No, it felt more like I was spitting up something I *drank*.

Shaking my head, I muttered, "Man, I am messed up."

In the mirror, my reflection took on a life of its own and crossed its arms. "Well, we knew that. The big question is what we are going to do about it?"

Normally, a person might find this sight unsettling, but my mirror reflection was quite chatty. One of the consequences of my awakening was that my soul was capable of communicating with me whenever it wasn't pleased.

Which was most days.

"What the hell is going on?" I asked, hoping my reflection knew more about what had happened during my blackout.

My soul frowned, shaking his head. "Perhaps you should look in the bedroom for answers."

"This is going to be bad, isn't it?"

"Yes."

"Great."

Taking a deep breath, I turned around and walked to the wooden door of the bathroom. Reaching down, I turned the door handle and opened the door. On the other side was an abattoir.

The walls were covered in crimson mystical sigils and there was a lovely dark-haired woman, with her heart missing, laid out on the bed. She was not wearing any clothes, and it didn't take Sherlock Holmes to piece together what had happened.

Turning my head, I saw the Bloodsword resting on top of a corrupted Daoist shrine built on my dresser. It had incense burning in front of a trio of pictures. Computer printouts of Ashley, Penny, and Shannon's images formed a trinity in the shrine's center.

The room looked like the home of an occult serial killer.

Which, I suppose, it was.

Unable to say a word, I walked over to the woman's corpse and placed my hand to her neck. It wasn't to check her pulse—I wasn't stupid—but the act somehow made it real that I could have done something like this. Touching her skin, I remembered driving the Bloodsword through her chest while holding her down.

I also remembered the woman flashing her fangs at me.

"She was a vampire," I said, taking a deep breath.

Palpable relief flooded me.

"Does that make a difference?" my soul said, stepping out of the bathroom mirror and walking into the room behind me.

"Honestly? Yes. Yes, it does."

My soul glared at me.

"What the hell happened to me during this time?" I asked, looking around and trying to figure what the hell sort of magic I'd been working around here. Blood magic wasn't forbidden by the Red Room, but I didn't know how to cast even a tenth of the magic worked here.

There was a lot more sorcery worked into these walls than could have come from a single blood sacrifice either, even if the victim were a vampire and had much more magical oomph inside her. No, someone had done multiple kills here.

Treating the whole thing like a crime scene—ignoring the fact that I, having been mind controlled by a magical sword, was the perpetrator—made me less inclined to flip out. And I was on the verge of a flip-out.

"You've been exterminating Nassau's vampire population for the past seven days. Together, we have killed sixteen Old Ones in their organization." A female voice came from the foot of the bed and I turned my head.

Sitting on the edge of the bed was a woman wearing grease-paint, her red hair in girlish braids like Lucy, a blood-red corset like my sister favored, and a pair of black leather pants with a Little Red Riding Hood-like cape around her back. Her eyes were a beautiful shade of blue, similar to Shannon's. There was something both unsettling and familiar about her, as if she combined a dozen people I knew into a single entity who looked like all but none of them.

"Oh great, it's you," my soul said, rolling its eyes. "I was hoping you'd taken the night off."

Reaching out to sense what sort of being she was, I pulled back as I detected the largest concentration of dark magic I'd ever felt in my life.

"You're a demon," I said, scared I'd sacrificed my soul and sanity by using the weapon.

"A mortal term," the woman said, shrugging her dainty shoulders. "I'm not a fallen angel, just a spirit of bloodshed and murder."

"Oh, my mistake," I said, faking shock at my faux pas. "Clearly, I misjudged you as someone evil."

She smiled with blood-red lips. "I was created when Cain first killed Abel."

"I'm pretty sure cavemen were killing each other well before Aaron wrote down that parable. There's no Garden of Eden, Cain and Abel, or Eve in my beliefs. Just evolution and hominids smacking each other around."

The creature turned to me as her eyes glowed bright green. "Most stories have a grain of truth to them. There *was* an Adam, and an Eve, and they had children in Eden. It was just in a different place than the world you know."

My soul snorted. "And demons never lie."

"You assume angels always tell the truth," the demon snipped at my soul.

"Admittedly, true. What should I call you?"

"Bloody Mary," the demon said. "One of my previous masters had an obsession for sending me to kill foolish boys and girls who spoke my name in front of mirrors. I found it tiresome and demeaning work."

"Killing children usually is."

"I agree," the demon said, smiling. "We already have something in common."

"Derek, this is dangerous," my soul said behind me. "Don't engage this monster. I've been trying to fight her off this entire week."

"And what a bang-up job you've been doing." I turned back to our new guest. "What do you want?"

"To help you, my love."

"Sorry, Mary, I don't date demons."

Bloody Mary stood up and walked over to the altar, where she looked at the Bloodsword. "You kill with me, though, and that's what I want. It's why I left Dracula's service for yours."

I was having a conversation with the One Ring. That was how I felt right now. "I'm pretty sure Dracula has killed more people than me."

"He preys on the weak. You prey on the strong. It has been centuries since a true warrior's hands have held my grip." Bloody Mary's tone made that sound dirty.

"So, you expect me to believe the Bloodsword has decided to serve a guy who wants to bring peace to the world," my soul said behind me. "No matter how violent he is."

"Hey," I snapped at my soul. "I get enough of that shit from other people. I don't need my conscience nagging me."

"That's what I'm *for*," my soul pointed out.

Okay, he had me there.

"I come bearing gifts," Bloody Mary said, aiming her fingers at my boxer shorts. "Look at your ring."

I reached into my boxer shorts' right pocket and found my wedding band there. I hadn't worn the ring in years, but there it was. The ring's golden color had been replaced with a beautiful black sheen. It also felt heavier. I touched it with my extra-normal senses and was bombarded with nightmarish images. They were familiar images, too. I saw the Wazir, the vampires I cut to pieces, and two hundred other victims—all mine. The power in the ring was tremendous. The tattoos were one thing, but the magic in the ring was even more powerful. I could be a real wizard now.

Bloody Mary seemed amused by my reaction. "Magic begins in belief and emotion. However, the most powerful sorcery is born from two acts—the giving and taking of life. Men have always feared and coveted the former power when wielded by women. They have always wielded the latter, though. You are an exquisite murderer, Derek Hawthorne, and I would like to see you reach your full potential."

"Men are involved in the life-giving process too," I said, avoiding her question. The magic available to me was clouding my judgment.

"Which is why your father has sired so many children and keeps them so close. His seed so freely spread has given him great power that he's turned against his enemies. I could reveal more of his secrets."

Ripping my ring off, I tossed it against the wall. Holding my hands to my head, I focused on positive feelings and tried to summon the necessary energy to banish the darkness before me.

I failed.

Bloody Mary narrowed her eyes, not even looking like she felt it. "Thinking me away won't work, Derek. You have far too much imbalance in your soul. If you want to be alone, though, you only had to ask."

The demon disappeared, leaving me alone with my soul.

"We are so fucked," I said, rubbing my temples.

"Technically, there's no 'we,'" my soul said. "You're going to have to clean this up."

"I'm a little more worried about the fact that I'm Jack the Ripper," I said, disgusted at all the carnage surrounding me.

"If it's any consolation, I think you only lured her here with the promise of sex. Also, she was going to kill you anyway."

"It's really not." I took a moment to try and gather my wits. "So, we're on the verge of war with the Vampire Nation, Shannon is close to breaking up with me, there's a possible conspiracy within the Red Room, and I'm possessed."

"I'm glad you have your priorities straight," my soul snarked. "I'm sorry about this, Derek. We should have more mental resistance to Bloody Mary. It's just—"

"I used the weapon's power a half-dozen times, which in terms of magical law is an invitation for the demon to possess me."

"Yes."

"Fucking Christopher," I grunted. "Why did I ever trust him?"

"Because he's your friend." My soul took an oddly reassuring stance. "The weapon seems to want to help you. You were close to death when you emerged from the ocean. Every bone in your body was broken and your organs near-liquefied when you hit the water. The Bloodsword and its power kept you going, and these sacrifices repaired your body. The Vampire Nation is on the run. Nassau has been their American capitol for centuries, and half the undead population has fled. They aren't used to being hunted in their home territory."

"Which isn't going to help prevent a war," I said, looking at him.

"It might, actually." My soul paused. "You know, if the Red Room decided to turn you over to them in exchange for peace."

I stared at him. "Is it wrong knowing that helps relax me? That I *won't* be responsible for things going completely to shit?"

"Quite the opposite," my soul answered. "I know you love peace more than anyone. It's just you're not very good at it."

I closed my eyes and cleared my mind. "We have to handle this one thing at a time. What is the Vampire Nation's likely response to my actions here?"

"I imagine they're combing Nassau. The police, local agents, and every blood slave they have will be on the lookout for you. The Bloodsword has the ability to thwart perception and allowed you to move around undisturbed."

"Like invisibility? It *is* the One Ring."

"More like being unnoticed. Which, when you think about it, is superior to invisibility."

"Well, that's not an option anymore. I need to continue with my mission and find out what's in the safety deposit box Christopher lured me here with."

"Given that I'm you, it's redundant for me to point out how stupid that is."

"Someone is trying to manipulate me, and I'm going to find out who."

"I believe it's obvious Christopher is behind this. Whatever affection he once had for you is gone. He's attempting to use you as a weapon against someone. You should count yourself lucky you survived Dracula. You need to return to the Red Room, report your findings, and get a dozen well-qualified exorcists to do an industrial-strength cleansing."

Tempting as that was, I was sick of following everyone's lead. I needed to get ahead of this. Reliving my experience with Ashley strengthened my convictions. I'd made a decision that night to never be anyone else's pawn again, and if Christopher was behind all this, I was going to make him regret it.

"I—"

"I know. There was never any doubt you would choose otherwise. I just held out hope you might surprise me."

I walked over to the bed and pulled the sheet up over my last victim. I didn't have much sympathy for vampires as a general rule. I didn't think they were people. At least, not people who didn't suffer a need to devour the living and a psychotic break from their conscience. I didn't know this person, either, but I'd moved past the period where I killed monsters just because they were monsters. I couldn't say whether she'd deserved to die or whether she'd been a one-in-a-million vampire who gave a shit about others.

Hell, where did I get off judging anyway? What I did know was everyone deserved a dignified death, and this wasn't anything close to one. Bloody Mary had decided I wanted to kill vampires—or maybe she sensed I had a lot of lingering anger toward them and used that as an excuse to start killing them. Maybe she thought I'd mind less than slicing up a bunch of innocents. She was right, but that didn't mean I was going to let her hang around my head, giving me advice and occasionally taking over. I needed to figure out a way to stop her and get her out of my body.

"Suggestions?" I asked, knowing my soul would know what I was talking about.

My soul crossed his arms. "She's enhanced your ability to work sorcery by several orders of magnitude. I wouldn't be surprised if your gross power output rivals Penny. You can make use of that and other blood magic rituals to drive her away if she makes another appearance."

"Isn't that like using laughing gas to fight the Joker?"

My soul gave me a dry look. "Really?"

"Sorry. I didn't want to keep making references to the One Ring and Sauron."

"Derek, you're thirty-two years old and a spy. We need to talk about your obsession with pop culture."

"I'm pretty much a wizard cyborg dragon James Bond who knows kung fu. Allow me one vice."

"I allow you about fifty. That includes being an asshole. We're getting off topic, though."

"Let's just focus on the situation," I said, wondering how else I could oppose Mary. "Are there any other methods we can use to fight her?"

"You realize you're talking to yourself. Right?"

"I'm in a room that couldn't be shown in a slasher movie for how much gore is on the walls. I think we're past the point of me being worried about looking crazy."

My soul paused, leaning up against the wall. "According to most sources, blood magic draws its power from death and destruction. That's the theme park version of it, though. Blood magic also draws life from healing and sacrifice. At the risk of blaspheming your old faith, Rabbi Joshua Ben Joseph changed the Roman Empire with his crucifixion."

"Let's hold off on comparisons to Jesus, okay?"

"I'm saying love and self-sacrifice fights violence and hate. It's why kisses break curses and true love can overthrow gods. It's also why betrayal brings down the wrath of the gods. White magic and black magic are two sides of the same coin."

"Let's also avoid fairy tales as guides for fighting demons."

My soul rolled his eyes. "Fine. Summon Bloody Mary with magic, force her to manifest, and kill her."

"Now we're talking!"

My soul sighed and vanished, leaving me alone in the room. Taking in all of the sigils, I sighed. It would be no use leaving all of this mess for the rest of Nassau to find. Worse, I had no idea what sort of DNA or trace evidence I'd left behind for them to track me with.

In normal situations, I'd call the Red Room to clean this up, but they didn't have any influence on Nassau. The Vampire

Nation had claimed it and killed any agent who arrived without strict diplomatic endorsement from three levels above them.

Lifting up my hands, I channeled the Bloodsword. I drew every drop of blood in the room into my body, feeling the power in the walls fade away as it became a part of me. I got a sense of the spells, which were divinatory in nature. Bloody Mary had been using me to cast *haruspex* or entrails-reading magic.

What had she wanted to find out?

I didn't have time to find out. In the pristine room, only the bloodless corpse of the vampire remained. I placed my hand on top of her covered form and muttered a spell I'd never had the power to perform before. In an instant, her body crumbled to dust, and I disposed of the remains in a trash bag.

Finding a set of clean clothes in the dresser, I changed into them, and departed into the night.

I had to find my sister.

CHAPTER FOURTEEN

Nassau was a beautiful city. Too bad it was a city living under a curse. Founded on New Providence Island by the British, taken over by pirates, and retaken by the British, Nassau had been living with the aftermath of those decisions ever since. Nassau's population included the descendants of British loyalists resettled there after the Revolutionary War and Africans taken off slave ships when human trafficking was outlawed. It was also the heart of the Vampire Nation.

I was walking down a street filled with tourists milling about, passing under the shadow of several massive hotels and resorts. It was nighttime, so the beaches were closed, but the Vampire Nation made sure there were countless entertainments to be had to keep the transient population out and about. Before they'd taken over Nassau's tourist industry, the city hadn't had much nightlife, but now it was one of the most entertaining cities in the world after dark.

Just off Cable Beach was Night Row, where there were nightclubs, casinos, carnivals, restaurants, and more adult entertainments behind the businesses meant for families. All of them were designed as feeding grounds for the undead. They didn't want to scare off the tourists, so the number of visitors who died was low. No, the Vampire Nation wanted things kept neat and tidy. They drank, instead, from many victims. A tourist was more likely to die from drinking too much alcohol than blood loss. That didn't keep people from dying, though. Surveying the crowds of tourists debating whether to go to the pirate museum or buy tacky gifts, I thought of the people who got imported here for feeding purposes.

The Red Room kept a count of individuals from Haiti,

Cuba, and even the United States who were offered jobs here on Nassau by shady businesspeople. Of them, only a fraction didn't disappear without a trace. The vampires of Nassau didn't have to kill in order to feed themselves, but the data spoke of dozens going missing every month. The Red Slave Trade was a means of showing Dracula's largess. You didn't have to moderate your feeding habits if he was leader. Just follow the rules of who, what, when, and where to eat. The Red Room considered these victims to be acceptable collateral damage in order to keep the Vampire Nation in check.

Bastards.

I was presently reading a stolen Pantheon e-tablet containing several thousand names. I was attempting to narrow down Penny's location by going through her favorite aliases (Ann Millions, Molly Gables, Dorothy Liddell, and Alice Gale). I'd tried calling her on a cellphone I'd stolen, but her number had been disconnected. This might have been cause for alarm, but I thought otherwise. Penny had a keen insight for when her phone was being tapped and changed her number on a regular basis.

I could have called other individuals in the House, but there were only a few friendly assets on Nassau and I wasn't about to compromise them. Instead, I'd gone to a clothing store, bought myself a disguise, worked a little magic so I wouldn't be recognized, and pretended to be a blood slave. It said everything you needed to know about the Vampire Nation's level of control that every hotel I'd visited handed over their guest lists once I indicated I worked for the Council of Ancients.

Unfortunately, after four hours of work, I was getting nowhere. She was supposed to be here negotiating with the Vampire Nation, but there was no sign of her. I'd hoped luck and my bond with my twin would give me a lead, but so far, I had nothing. I didn't even know what was going on between the House and the Vampire Nation. I needed information and couldn't contact the Red Room. At the very least, they would want to pull me out, which would prevent me from finding out what was really going on.

"I need a new strategy," I said, sighing.

Looking at a particularly obnoxious-looking tourist who was yelling at his family, an idea came to me. "If the mountain won't come to Muhammad, then Muhammad must go to the mountain."

Walking by and lifting his cellphone, I cycled through it and dialed the number written on the side of a dark and energetic-looking dance club across the street. The neon graffiti called it "Club Ecstasy," and something about it just screamed vampire-owned business.

"Hello?" a woman's voice on the other end asked, techno playing in the background.

"Yeah, I think Derek Hawthorne is in front of the Seven Heavens Hotel and Casino parking lot."

"Who?"

"Just tell your boss. I work for the Vampire Nation."

"Um, okay."

About sixty minutes later, enough time for the club's owner to contact his master and probably his master to contact his, I saw a plain white van pull up on the sidewalk and six well-muscled individuals get out. They were armed, but their weapons were concealed, avoiding terrifying the tourists around us. It was a pity for them, because if they'd just been willing to do a drive-by or shoot me, they might have ended my threat right there. Which was what I was counting on. If they were professionals, they'd make my snatch and grab look like they were hustling me away. Really, I was surprised they didn't show up in a cop car.

I'd removed my disguise and dismissed the magic protecting my identity. It was far less powerful than whatever the Bloodsword had been using anyway, so there could be no doubt I was the person they were looking for. The blade was sheathed in a mystical hidden leather compartment woven into my coat, another of Bloody Mary's gifts, allowing me reasonable certainty they'd fail to find it.

Walking up to me, two of the group grabbed me by the arms, and a third shoved a black bag over my head before zip-tying my hands. I revised my mental opinion of them when the tourists around me screamed, and one of my kidnappers fired a gun in the air to scare the crowds away. These guys were very stupid.

Blinded and bound, I was shoved in the back of the van and felt it pull away. I didn't expect anyone to respond to the shooting, and I was right. We drove for about forty minutes, stopping numerous times, before the engine was turned off. My captors were silent the entire time, but I could tell they were nervous. They just gave off a vibe I could feel in the air. Capturing one of the Committee was well above these guys' pay grade, and I suspected they knew something was wrong with how easily I'd gone down.

"So, guys. We here?" I asked, smiling under my bag.

I was rewarded with someone pistol whipping me, which sent me to the floor. Seconds later, the doors to the van were pulled open behind me, and I was dragged off again. I ended up being carried up a flight of stairs and dumped in a metal chair before being handcuffed to it by both wrists. Only then was the bag removed from my head.

The room I was located in had seen better days. It was the former upstairs bathroom of a middle-class house that had seen better days. The bathtub had been ripped out along with the sink, leaving a lot of extra space and a large drain in the floor.

Five of my captors stood around me. Pipes above our heads leaked. There was a single bare bulb, and the windows were boarded over and covered with a faded white curtain, with sound-proofing material between them. The interiors of the bathroom's walls were lined with it too, and the door had a mattress nailed to it. It looked like they'd knocked out the wall to the next room, giving more space for their torture. In one corner, I saw a shelf filled with bindings and pharmaceuticals while in another, there was a man-sized steel cage.

A tray of surgical equipment stood next to a chair on top of a metal stand. The stand's second and third layers contained other notable items: a garden hose, a set of pliers, a car battery with copper wire on top, and a couple of objects used for sex but which I suspected my captors used for "enhanced interrogation techniques." What we in the spy business knew as torture.

It was all amateur-hour stuff, and I hoped this was all for

show. Not because I was afraid of anything they could do to me, but because torture was a shit way of getting information. As they explained to us on the first day of training, nothing prevents a person being subjected to torture from lying to his captor. If you don't know there's a bomb on a plane, waterboarding the guy who does isn't going to make him want to tell the truth. He could say the bomb was in the president's bathroom or nonexistent just as easily. Cash, magic, and forming friendships worked much better. Somehow, I doubted these guys wanted to win me over.

"We should kill him now," a Caucasian man with a thick red beard and glasses wearing a loud Bahamian shirt said. "If this guy's the Cleaver, then he let us bring him here."

Their leader, I presumed, was a black man in cargo pants and a red t-shirt. "Don't be stupid. If we killed him and he turns out to be the Cleaver, then the Ancients will have our heads."

"And your families' heads," I said, leaning back in his chair. "Probably your girlfriends', boyfriends', and pets', too."

The leader kicked me in the chest with a big, heavy boot. Were I not prepared for, it would have broken three ribs. "Shut the fuck up, Nat. We drink the blood. We have the power. We're *immune.*"

Nat, short for natural, was a derogatory term used by vampire henchmen for people who didn't drink vampire blood. It was their way of pretending they weren't human anymore and were somehow more than junkies.

"Great, Bloodslaves," I said, rolling my eyes. "I was hoping someone important would be capturing me."

As I planned, the leader pulled out a Glock 41 and pointed it at my head. "What did you call me, Conchy Joe?"

"Conchy Joe" was Bahamian slang for a white man. I could see the frustrated intelligence behind the man's eyes. He'd no doubt had to struggle for everything in his life up until this point, and the height of his achievement so far was to become a vampire's errand boy. He probably thought he was going to become a vampire himself, but the system didn't work like that. Bloodslaves were rarely turned. Vampire hemoglobin eroded the mind and made you a psychopath after too many uses. People never stopped using it, though, because it gave an amazing rush and cured all but the nastiest wounds. In simple terms, vampires turned people they considered peers and had no respect for their slaves—especially blood addicted slaves.

"I'm about as white as you, chief," I said, undisturbed by the gun being pointed in my face. These guys weren't going to kill me without their masters' say-so. "Mom's human form was Chinese, and Dad's mother was a Cayuga Indian. She was a doctor in 1911, you know. Quite the accomplishment. The House is progressive that way. Dad dyes his hair, though, so you can't tell—"

The leader pulled back on his gun and put a bullet in the chamber. "You just keep talking."

"You're the boss," I said.

Those words caused the leader to relax. "Yeah, you're right. I *am* the boss. You're our ticket to the big time, biggity. We gon' all cross over when we deliver you to Mister Fangs. Each one of us is going to be living forever when you are purged."

I felt bad for the guy, I did. No matter the fact he was probably mesmerized, high as a kite on vampire blood, and party to no end of crimes—he didn't deserve what was about to happen to him.

Another Caucasian blood-slave walked in, carrying a cellphone, and shut the door behind him. "Quartermaster, we got order from Mister Fangs. We to put a hex on the biggity, no argie, before he jams things up."

"Dead book?" the leader asked.

"Double time," the other man said.

That was my cue.

The handcuffs popped open, responding to my mental commands in a way my magic had never worked before, and I moved like lightning past the group to the light switch. Turning it off, I grabbed the nearest blood-slave and slammed him into the wall with enough force to liquefy a normal man. Two of the four remaining individuals pulled out guns and started shooting, but I was already on the ground. Then, tackling another, I broke his jaw with a ki-enhanced strike.

The next thirty seconds were a collection of screams followed by gunshots, punches, and attempts by the Bloodslaves to turn back on the lights. It was futile, though, and when I flipped the switch, all six men were lying out on the ground prostrate. Even the leader, who had put up a better resistance than all of his men together, was clutching three broken ribs and looking on the verge of unconsciousness.

I picked up all their guns, sorted through them, and chose the one I liked best. The Glock 41 wasn't a gun I swore by, but it would get the job done. I checked the ammo and noted it wasn't orihalcum, enchanted, or even silver. No, it was plain ordinary rounds—which might as well have been papier-mâché when used against vampires.

"Well, shit," I muttered.

You should kill them, Bloody Mary's voice whispered in my ear. *They are evil men and will threaten innocents in the future.*

"Fuck off."

One is bleeding from where he attracted friendly fire. He will die unless he is given the proper medical attention. You are not avoiding taking any more lives, Bloody Mary's voice chided. *You will need all the strength you can get to face Dracula again.*

I walked over to the leader, delivered a Vibrating Palm strike to his neck, and took his cellphone. Sitting up, I said, "You guys can tell your bosses I turned out to be someone disguised as Derek Hawthorne, some guy I cast an illusion over maybe, and avoid retaliation, or you can tell them you lost me. Up to you. I'm going to be using your equipment, though, and walking out the front door. Either way, you were out of your league."

They will betray you. Their loyalty to their masters is strong, Bloody Mary hissed.

I walked over and zip-tied their arms and legs from a box of ties on a shelf in the corner. None of them resisted, though a few were still conscious.

"Maybe," I said, shrugging. "On the other hand, it annoys you and that's a big plus."

Bloody Mary was silent, but I gathered she wasn't happy with my actions.

Good.

Lifting up my gun, I proceeded to open the door to the bathroom and saw an ordinary-looking middle-class house's interior. The paint on the walls was an eggshell white and the carpet was a fluffy shade of dark, perhaps to hide any blood that might be tracked in. A staircase led downstairs from where I could hear a humming noise.

Dracula's actions had left me bereft of resources, contacts, and information in what might as well have been a hostile foreign nation, for how much influence the Vampire Nation could exert. The Vampire Nation kept dozens of sub-stations across the island so they could monitor tourists and conduct business deals. They were usually filled with all manner of equipment, records, and stores of blood to accommodate their masters' needs.

Creeping down the stairs with my gun raised, I searched for any sign of other personnel in the sub-station. Once I reached the bottom, I saw that the first floor was clean and well-maintained. It could have looked like the home of any normal suburban family if not for three facts. The first was the windows were boarded up, soundproofed, and curtained like the upstairs. The next was that all the furniture had plastic wrap around it. I suppose it was intended to show consideration for guests with messy eating habits. Third, the living room had a massive computer station set up in its center.

Dozens of cables were on the ground, hooked into sixteen separate government-grade Pantheon Corp CPUs that had been modified to work together. These were plugged into a desk that sported a collection of more than a dozen monitors. They were all wired together like a government security room, giving live feeds from businesses around the city (and a few homes).

Sitting at the desk, surrounded by a dozen empty Mountain Dew cans and with a copy of the novel *Agent G: Infiltrator* was a dreadlocked black man in his mid-thirties. He had a pair of headphones on from which, even from ten feet away, I could hear Coldplay's "Hurts Like Heaven" playing. The man had a Batman t-shirt on, ripped blue jeans, and a pair of flip-flops that made him look less than intimidating.

Crouching down so he couldn't see me approach in the

monitor's glare, I came up behind him and put my gun to the back of his head. Pulling his headphones off, I said, "All right, jackass, we're going to have a conversation. Your answers better be good."

That was when he turned into a werewolf.

CHAPTER FIFTEEN

Well, shit.

In the few seconds I had before the giant wolf tore my throat, I thought about the oddity of my situation. Vampires and werewolves *hated* each other. It was a feud stretching back centuries when Dracula's predecessor, the Shadow Queen, had kept most of their race as mind controlled slaves. Why the hell was one working for the Vampire Nation?

It didn't matter, though—I was screwed either way. Without the Bloodsword drawn or orichalcum ammunition, my chance of defeating one was slim. Werewolves were strong, fast, twice as durable as vampires, could change in an instant, and were capable of healing any wound no matter what form they took. Only magic could kill one forever, and I wasn't sure I had enough in me after my slaughter of the others.

Watching the massive warg-like monster spring from its chair, I refused to buckle under its attack and grabbed its paws in midair before using my legs to boost the monster over my head. I had to throw my ki into my limbs for enough strength, the wolf weighing about three hundred pounds, but I managed to send it over my head.

The massive red-furred thing slammed against the wall behind me and let out a surprised yelp, allowing me to aim my gun at it. I didn't hesitate to put about six rounds inside the creature's chest, inflicting pain if not lasting damage. I was about to put more when I caught the wolf's yellow-eyed gaze. I'd pissed it off now.

I can help you. Bloody Mary's voice was like ice against a fever. Soothing and relieving. *Just will the sword into my hands and let me drink of the monster's blood. You have no need to worry about killing anyone you would not normally.*

"You possessed me!" I hissed. "I'm not trusting you with anything."

Is this because of your brother, Stephen?

I didn't answer. Backing away toward the door, I continued firing, watching the werewolf change again. This time, it took a few seconds because eight or nine rounds were being forced out of its chest, but the being became a seven-foot-tall, fur-covered monstrosity that wasn't too far removed from the creature from John Landis's *American Werewolf in London*.

Realizing there was no chance of fleeing, as a werewolf could outrun some cars, I had the choice of wielding the Bloodsword again or dying. So, I made my choice.

I was nobody's bitch.

Dropping the gun and clenching my fists, I raised them up and prepared to give as good a fight as I could. Even with magic-enhanced martial arts, I suspected it would last about five seconds, and that's because I didn't think the werewolf would knock my head off with the first blow. No, the snarling monster before me looked like it wanted to savor the kill. I was terrified, my knees shaking, and my breath coming in short ragged breaths, but I stood my ground.

Oh, for the Dark Mother's sake, Bloody Mary muttered.

The demon washed over my mind, and I found myself unable to resist her commands. She animated my jaw, and words came out of my mouth I didn't speak. "Malcolm, it's me. I'm sorry for the shooting."

The werewolf was just a few feet away and lifted claws the size of switchblades to tear out my throat. Then it paused before speaking in a thick, guttural growl, "Derek? Derek Hawthorne?"

What in hell? How did it recognize me?

Exactly, Bloody Mary muttered in my mind. *You would do well to submit yourself to my guidance. So many unpleasant misunderstandings could be—*

Shut.the.hell.up, I thought back at her.

"Uh, yeah, it's me," I said, raising my hands in surrender. "Oops?"

The seven-foot-tall werewolf transformed back into the five-foot-five geek I'd seen before. His clothes looked unchanged, another sign of the magical heritage that allowed their species to move instantly from form to form.

"Why you shoot me, D-man?" Malcolm said, rubbing his stomach. "I thought weres and the House being friends?"

"A misunderstanding." It was a good thing I was an incredible liar. "I took care of the yokels upstairs and wanted to make sure it was you. Then you went all Warren Zevon on me."

"I almost went a lot worse," Malcolm said, pointing at me. "Your undercover?"

"Yes," I said, projecting calm and authority. I also slipped in a slight bit of magic into my voice to accentuate my next words. "Your help has been appreciated through all this. You should tell me it all, so I don't forget how much I owe you."

"The Pact doesn't like the House, but you kill vampires and don't bring down the law. The Father and Mother of my pack say you good. So, I slip you names and addresses. Might as well give you the whole thing, though. This role busted. Time to take a new skin and look the part of someone else."

I almost laughed. Malcolm here was a mole in the Vampire Nation's organization. The Pact was an alliance of the Western Hemisphere's shapechangers. They enforced the Truth's suppression almost as vigorously as the House, leading the two powers to maintain an uneasy neutrality with one another. I'd actually been at the treaty renewal in Bright Falls, Michigan last year.

"Good luck with that," I said, looking at the computers. Thankfully, they were still intact. "I need some help, though, before we head off."

"About getting that demon out of you or finding that safety deposit box?"

"Err . . ." I trailed off.

Inside me, I swore Bloody Mary felt surprised.

"Werewolves see the other side," Malcolm said. "You a horse for a bad spirit."

"Yeah, I sort of noticed." I then wrinkled my brow. "Is that a problem?"

"Possessed or not, you are killing vampires. No skin off my nose."

"Good," I said. "I have it under control."

I was lying but hopefully he'd accept that. It wasn't like Pact members cared much about what happened to House personnel. I was annoyed he recognized me, though, which meant that supernaturals were passing around my picture. James Bond being the world's most famous secret agent in the movies meant he was terrible at his job. Then again, I wasn't a secret agent anymore, was I?

"Gotcha. You kill a lot of leeches and make my job much easier," Malcolm said, shrugging. "Mister Fangs be running scared."

"Your accent is very...unique," I said.

Malcolm shrugged. "Pack lingo, Nassau streets, blood slave impersonation, television, and MIT. You pick up the lingo where you go. No different from how you say things like 'collateral' and 'sanctioning' when you mean dead innocents and murder."

"Point taken." I was starting to like this guy. "I don't suppose you know what's going on in the Red Room right now?"

"Only an outsider's perspective, yo. The Red Room and the Vampire Nation are both ready for war. They say you dead, which I know is wrong, and you killed the Dracula. Did you?"

"Nothing that will stick."

"Pity. He needed killing since he was a wee tot in Transylvania."

"Wallachia."

"Don't give a shit."

I took a deep breath. "I need your help, Malcolm. I need everything you know about Christopher Hang, his wife, any abductions involving vampires, and the United National Interests and Trusts bank. The latter is where the safety deposit box is located."

"Asked and answered. You sure you don't want to ask your Dark Rider what's what?"

"Very much so."

I could feel Bloody Mary giving a Cheshire cat grin inside the back of my head. She was powerful and had the ability to influence me.

I *really* needed to get her out of my head.

Malcolm walked over to his computers and inserted a flash drive into the closest console. "Then I'll tell you what I know. Christopher Hang is bad magic. He's a cannibal of his own kind, drinking the blood of the older ones and absorbing their power. He lies, manipulates, and kills—growing ever stronger in the Vampire Nation until he was as high as a newborn can go. Then he got a little higher."

"Sounds like him. What about Annabelle Jones?"

"Deadeye Ann?" Malcolm raised an eyebrow.

"Everybody in this town has a nickname, it seems."

"Says the Cleaver." Malcolm shrugged.

"What's she like?" I needed to understand how Christopher had come to have these sorts of feelings for a woman.

"Insane," Malcolm said, looking up at the stairs as if expecting the rest of his group to come down. "Deadeye Ann and Black Beth were the two right hands of Dracula, but the former was far more terrifying to vampires. According to legend, she ran away from Dracula after her change and lived a mortal life for decades before he tracked her down. He slew her husband, children, and everyone she knew as a lesson."

"Sounds like Dracula all right."

"That's not where the story ends, though. He locked her up in a coffin for a decade, and when she got out—she exterminated every vampire in Europe."

"That can't be right."

"She had the help of the Red Room and my kind, biggity. Still, the legends tell she was a powerful sorceress before she was turned and beloved of the Hebrew god. His angels led her to hundreds of resting places and turned the Old Country into a tinderbox. Bonapartists blamed English, English blamed Bonapartists, nobles blamed peasants, and peasants got screwed. Same as it always was, just the names are changed."

I'd been raised on the Red Room's history since I was able to walk, and I'd never heard anything about Annabelle Jones outside of some dry historical details. I was familiar with the Napoleonic Wars, however, and how said conflict served as a cover for the largest mass destruction of supernaturals in human history—at least until the Great Wars. It wouldn't surprise me in the slightest to find the House had gotten creative in recording its history and edited out Annabelle Jones's role in order to make it look like they'd carried out these purges on their own.

I wasn't sure how a renegade vampire fit into all of this, though. "So how the hell did she end up back in the Vampire Nation?"

"No idea. Some say it was love for Elizabeth, others say it was because Dracula put her under his mind control, and others still say she renounced the God of Israel when his angels tried to stop her carnage."

"So, a girl who doesn't really much care for vampires."

"Yeah," Malcolm said, scratching the back of his neck. "I dunno what she saw in Christopher, though. Seems a mismatch made in hell."

"What about United National?"

"You'd have an easier time breaking into Fort Knox."

"I did, once, with Shannon. We just needed some uniforms, a few fake ID's, and a bit of magic. We made off with a private who was infected with a kind of extra-dimensional parasite. Very *Aliens*."

"This will be a little harder. United National is the piggy bank for all the Mister Fangs. Digitized magical surveillance, wards, body-heat sensors, lethal countermeasures, and a bunch of Bloodslaves with demon-possessed dogs. No human customers, either. All business gets done by the leeches themselves or electronically."

"What about employees?"

"Dracula's handpicked minions serve as the management. Bred like animals to be more susceptible to his mesmerism than others and addicted to the blood from birth. Everyone else is mesmerized to the point they need to be told to use the crapper over loudspeakers."

"It's increasingly apparent Christopher didn't do me any favors assigning me this job."

"You think, yo?"

"I don't suppose you could give me any insights into its interior?" I asked, going for a shot in the dark.

Malcolm smiled, turning around to tap on the keyboard

behind him. "You be lucky you dealing with the master of math-magic, my friend. It take long to replace one of these poor fools as their computer guy. Took much longer to get a backdoor in there. Had to take the skins of many an employee and make it look like the vamps' idea."

All the monitors started showing security footage from inside a gray and colorless building. There was something oppressive about the place, even just looking at it. The guards were mean and vicious-looking, while the employees worked with blank stares on their faces. It reminded me of some of the human slavery rings I'd investigated stateside. It also gave me a rough idea about the layout, security, and how to breach it.

"Malcolm, you are a genius."

"Tell me something I don't know."

"Don't trust me. I'm a danger to us both."

"I said something I *don't know*, D."

I smirked. "Thank you. This information will be an immeasurable help."

"Still suicide to go in."

"I've gotten into better-guarded places."

"I don't believe you."

He was right not to. Every system had a weakness. As long as there were people behind them, they could be shut down or subverted. That didn't mean I was capable of pulling it off, especially by myself with minimal resources. Subtlety might be the worst option here. A better one would be to blow a hole in the building, run in with some hired goons, and grab the material within.

No, it would never work. Argh.

It would with me. Give me your consent and I will return the box and its contents to you within the hour. All that is required is a blood sacrifice of someone who deserves to—

Go away. I gritted my teeth. *Leave me alone.*

Feed my hunger, warrior, or I will make you. Bloody Mary caused my right hand and the muscles in my arm to clench. In an instant, she could make me strike at Malcolm and attack him with the intent to kill. I'd either kill him quickly, the demon turning my fists into weapons that could harm a werewolf, or he'd kill me. I could see it all in my mind, shown in vivid detail by the demon's power, with the implicit statement she was being polite for only if it suited her purposes.

Please, I begged, willing my hand to open and getting nowhere.

Because you asked so nicely.

My hand opened.

"She's got her hooks into you deep, doesn't she?" Malcolm said, looking at me with pity in his eyes.

"So it would seem."

"Spirits of violence feed on the dark and hate in one's soul. You need to let go of it to starve them out."

That wasn't going to happen. Violence and death were such an ingrained part of my life, I couldn't imagine living without them. Indeed, if not for my natural contrariness, I doubt I even would have minded Bloody Mary's presence. How fucked up was that?

I was about to bid my farewells to Malcolm when I saw something on the monitors. Shannon O'Reilly, my girlfriend, walking down the hall in a red trench coat, black pants, and silk shirt. Beside her was a plain blonde-haired woman with glasses who was talking at length, though I couldn't make out the words.

"Ah, crap. Is this live?"

"As live as you or me."

"I have to get down to the United National building right now. I think a friend of mine is about to get in over her head."

"Biggity, you crazy."

"Yeah, I am, but I've—"

That was when I heard a vehicle squeal onto the road, and hit the ground out of instinct. Seconds later, the boarded-up windows and walls exploded with hundreds of bullets intended to kill us. It looked like someone higher up in the Vampire Nation had gotten wind of my presence and decided the local goon squad was an insufficient response.

Lying down next to Malcolm's shredded body, I started crawling away, deciding to take the better part of valor. The door was breached seconds later and a squadron of armored militia men wielding assault rifles burst in.

CHAPTER SIXTEEN

I was having a bad week. Crawling on the broken-glass-and-splinter-covered ground, I felt half a dozen cuts open up across my body.

Concentrating, I somehow willed the attackers not to notice me. Bloody Mary may have had something to do with that because I was able to reach a nearby closet, turn the door knob, open the door, and slide in before anyone noticed me. Not that my situation had improved all that much. I was now trapped in a closet, in the dark, with six armed men outside.

If they were men at all.

I'd gotten a semi-decent look at my attackers after they'd burst through the door, and they didn't look anything like the yahoos who'd kidnapped me off Night Row. They were paramilitary types with urban gray and white camouflage pants, ski masks, black berets, and Pantheon Corp-manufactured M90s.

It was possible they were Bloodslaves, but somehow, I doubted it. These felt like the kind of assassins I'd encountered on my way to the airport. Unlike Black Squadron, these guys seemed to shoot first and ask questions later.

They are Skull Squadron, a group of loyal dhampir whom the Vampire Nation uses to fight the Nassau wizards and hunters who seek to liberate their land. Their father is leading them tonight. Bloody Mary's voice was excited, like she was at a football game. Though there were hints of something more sexual to her anticipation.

Great. Just once I'd like to meet some nice vampires, I thought, hearing them search the rooms around me. Upstairs, there was the sound of shouting, followed by gunfire. Skull Squadron didn't seem to be pleased with the performance of my captors. I closed my eyes. *I just need to focus on keeping myself hidden.*

I feel that's not an option, my dear Derek, Bloody Mary said. *The only reason you were able to get here was because I helped with your rather pathetic attempts at a cloaking spell. You are going to be found as soon as I drop it.*

I gritted my teeth. "I see."

You are going to fight against these fool half-breeds, are you not? Bloody Mary asked.

Speaking as a foolish half-breed, yes. My fists clenched while I tried to figure a way to take down a bunch of superhumans with assault rifles.

Then allow me to level the playing field. I believe we have gotten off on the wrong foot. Bloody Mary surprised me by sounding apologetic. *I have no wish to control your mind; I swear this on every god and demon in the astral plane. I admire your beauty, your ability to kill, and the grace of your planning. Let me help you achieve your potential as a warrior.*

"No," I muttered, knowing I was outmatched.

Even if Shannon and others die because of your foolishness? Your sister is still out there too, Derek. Bloody Mary sounded unconvinced.

They're pretty good at taking care of themselves. No damsels in distress on this train wreck I call life, I said.

Can you take the risk of them screwing up your investigation? Bloody Mary said. *You are far too arrogant to trust even the people you love most with your actions.*

She had me. "Help me."

Outside the closet, I could hear the movement of a man as he overturned computers and other objects around the room. It was strange behavior if he was looking for me, but consistent with that of a man who was under a spell. Bloody Mary was protecting me, even if I didn't want her to.

Reach into your pocket, Bloody Mary cooed. *There you will find your salvation.*

Against my better judgment, I reached in and found my fingers wrapping around a ring. Pulling it out, I saw the cursed artifact that I'd thrown away in my bedroom. My wedding ring shined despite the blackness of my surroundings.

"I am not calling it my precious," I said, no longer concerned about them hearing me.

I'm surprised you haven't made any Stormbringer jokes, Bloody Mary joked.

"What?" I asked, confused.

Michael Moorcock? Elric Saga? Evil magic sword? Bloody Mary asked.

"Is it a fantasy series?" I asked, not knowing what she was talking about.

You should duck now, Mary said.

"What?" I repeated, looking through the keyhole and seeing the dhampir outside aiming his M90.

"Oh shit," I said, hitting the ground.

Covering my ears, I was deafened by the sound of bullets exploding through the wooden door in front of me and tearing through the clothes above my head. A patch of light was opened as the rounds punched a hole and tore through the other side of the closet. Skull Squadron didn't take any chances. But then again, neither did I.

Drawing on my hatred, rage, and despair, I poured my power through the ring and threw it outward. It was unlike any other sorcery I'd ever worked before and left me feeling changed. All the darkness around me swirled into a wave and lashed out, eating the light in the air before blasting through the closet door and decapitating the dhampir on the other side.

The light bulbs in the computer room exploded and all the power in the house went off, plunging it into darkness. I felt the black all round me like it was a comforting cloak. The shadows were at my command, and they had a tangible substance. Somehow, I had become a master of obscuromancy, or shadow magic. It was wizardry associated with hell and evil.

I didn't care.

Skull Squadron wasn't made of amateurs, though, and immediately turned on night-vision goggles before unloading with their M90s at me. I created a shield of darkness in front of me, solidifying it to something harder than steel. Hundreds of rounds disappeared into the solidified blackness as I felt immense power within my ring.

Kill them, my love, Bloody Mary whispered.

"*Yes,*" I muttered, feeling stronger than I had ever felt before. *This* was what a wizard was supposed to be.

I lashed out, and horrific alien tentacles composed of Stygian darkness exploded through the chests of four Skull Squadron members, the otherworldly tendrils ripping them apart in a spectacularly gory fashion. I could feel the Bloodsword grow stronger as it fed on the blood I spilled and the lives around me being snuffed. A part of that power passed to me, increasing the mystical power at my disposal.

I exalted in the ecstasy of it all, right before I was smashed in the back of the head and thrown through an open door onto the house's dining room table. All the black tendrils and mystical darkness I'd summoned vanished into the ether.

Lying in the broken remains of the dining room table, I found myself picked up by a member of the Skulls who removed his night vision to reveal a man with olive skin and piercing blue eyes. His fangs were extended, and I realized he wasn't a dhampir but a full-fledged vampire. Perhaps the father of the unfortunates I'd just killed.

I didn't get a chance to say anything to the enraged father because he threw me against the wall, grabbed me with his super speed before I hit the ground, and threw me against the wall again. He then took me by the throat and smashed my head through the plaster of the wall. I felt the magic within me weaken and suspected I'd be dead if not for the magic I'd absorbed from those I'd killed.

The vampire pulled me out and started punching me in the chest. All the magic I'd gained from the ring seemed to vanish, abandoning me at a critical moment. I wasn't going to let that setback stop me. Throwing every bit of life I had left in me into my fists, I slammed them into the side of the vampire's head.

He screamed, blackish energy surrounding his head and my hands. This aura seemed to burn him like sunlight. I slammed my forehead into his, causing the vampire to grab his injured face. Delivering a series of punches to his skull, I leapt into the air and spin-kicked him through the dining room window. I shouldn't have been able to do it, but it seemed like my body no longer functioned like a normal human's.

So, this was what it felt like to be one of the monsters.

I didn't get a second to rest before a flock of ravens exploded through the shattered window, swarming me and pecking me dozens of times with knife-like beaks. The vampire had transformed into a murder of crows and was going to kill me one bite at a time.

I screamed, throwing out countless knives of living shadow from my body. Every single crow was impaled and when the shadows vanished, their bodies fell to the ground, where they turned into ashes.

I fell to the ground, beaten and broken. The initial rush from using so much magic had passed, and I felt like an addict who'd been denied his fix. Blood poured from my wounds on the ground, and I didn't know whether I was going to live or die.

Magnificent, Bloody Mary said. *Your control over your shadow power is crude but effective. I knew you could kill the Father.*

"Screw . . . you," I said, spitting up blood. I wondered if the vampire's beating had punctured a lung. I couldn't go to a hospital and wondered if I didn't deserve to die for abandoning my moral principles like I had. I'd given into the allure of black magic and had added to my already horrific body count.

You overestimate your wounds, Bloody Mary said. *You also complain about things you have already chosen to do. Why waste time on regret? You would do the same if given a choice between yourself and another killer again.*

"I am not like that," I lied.

Oh Derek, you amuse me so, Bloody Mary said.

I had no response for that.

This is going to hurt, Bloody Mary said.

Pain like I'd never felt filled my body. I screamed in agony as my bones knit themselves into place, tissue healed, and muscle regrew. Magic that would have normally taken days worked in the span of minutes, but these were some of the most painful of my life. In the end, I was nothing more than a quivering mass on the ground.

Such a complainer, Bloody Mary said. *Women used to go through more pain during childbirth and did so for much of human history. It's the problem with you male champions. You're such whiners. I don't know why I keep choosing you.*

I climbed to my feet, tears falling from my right eye. My right eye could see through walls and half a dozen other tricks but couldn't shed tears. I needed to make this right, no matter the cost.

Stumbling over my own legs, I maneuvered to the living room where Malcolm's body was lying on the ground, riddled with bullet wounds. Unlike the ones I'd shot him with earlier, these didn't appear to be the kind he could regenerate from. Either they'd overloaded his immune system, or the bullets were made of a metal a lycanthrope was vulnerable to, like silver or orihalcum.

Blood-magic enhanced, Bloody Mary corrected. *After learning how to manipulate the essence of life from me, he passed it along to their followers. You could learn how to use it in such a manner too if you'd just let me teach you.*

"I want you to help him," I said, looking down at Malcolm's cold, dead eyes.

He's dead, Bloody Mary said.

"There's varying levels of dead," I said, breathing hard. "His brain is intact, he's only recently been shot all to hell, and I know you can do this. He's just some dead, not all dead."

Quoting The Princess Bride doesn't change anything, Bloody Mary said, surprising me again with her depth of pop culture knowledge. *Still, I will try. You realize you will have to draw on depths of power you have never imagined probing.*

"I just killed a bunch of guys. How much more bloody do I have to make things?"

Somewhere between the Aztecs and the Assyrians, Bloody Mary said, making a joke. *For a proper resurrection that doesn't turn your associate into a cannibalistic monster, you will need to focus on positive emotions. I'm not sure there's enough good in your life to raise a man from the dead.*

I paused, thinking about her words. "How many people would I have to kill to do it the Assyrian way?"

Too many before the body got cold, Bloody Mary said, making a tsk-tsk noise. *Come on, Derek. It's worth a try. I'm eager to see whether you can succeed or fail.*

"I thought a demon wouldn't want me to heal someone," I said, pulling out the Bloodsword from its sheath.

That shows how much you know, Bloody Mary said.

Kneeling with the weapon lifted in the air, I tried to concentrate, struggling to keep my eyes open. I wasn't sure if it was the aftereffects of Bloody Mary's healing magic or whether I'd sustained a concussion.

Six of twelve, half a dozen of another. Even I have difficulty tampering with human brains. You should be fine in a couple of hours.

I ignored Bloody Mary as I tried to find a memory that was good enough to satisfy the needs of the spell. I had no idea where to begin. I had plenty of good memories, but they all felt shallow to the needs of a spell to restore the dead.

Indeed, I felt guilty about the fact I'd gotten Malcolm killed trying to get access to this safe house. Aside from discovering where Shannon was right now—inside the place I needed to get into—all I'd accomplished was getting the computers shot up and a bunch of Vampire Nation's foot soldiers killed.

This was a disaster, and it was my fault.

I needed to think positive emotions, though, or this would fail. If his body got any colder, there was no way this sort of magic would work. There were sorcerers who could resurrect the dead, manifested gods too, but this was more like plugging a magical defibrillator into him. If I could draw away the blood magic from the bullets and restart his regeneration, I could bring him back.

Yeah, I had to think this was easy even if it was a load of crap. Otherwise, the magic wouldn't work. I searched for a memory pure enough to serve as a focus for my magic. My marriage had ended tragically, my childhood had been spent in preparation of Red Room service, my relationship with Ashley had ended poorly (to say the least), Shannon and I were stalled in a state of kinda-together, and even my time with my sister was tainted with the knowledge we were both going to die in the Red Room's service. The past seemed a dead end, tainted by the compromises necessary to survive.

Outside I heard a thunderclap, and it was like a bolt of lightning had struck my mind. The past would always be tainted because we were always dealing with mistakes, compromises, and regret. We could romanticize it and whitewash it, but the past would never be as perfect as we wanted it to be. The future, though, was always open to possibilities. Someday, I could get Penny and me out of the Red Room's service. We could work to bring an end to the endless Cold War between the House and other factions. I could forge a future with Shannon. I believed in possibilities. I hoped for the future.

Concentrating on these feelings, I imagined a world where there was at last peace between the supernatural and the mundane. A world where the House was torn down and all of its secrets exposed, showing the Truth to humanity. I saw a world where humanity had matured to the point where it no longer needed a secret society to protect it with lies and misdirection.

I saw a world with no need for people like me.

Interesting, Bloody Mary observed.

The Bloodsword glowed with a soft white light and enough magical power flowed from the room around me to cause the bullets inside Malcolm to force themselves out. His heart began beating again and his regeneration kicked in. Even so, it took about ten minutes of me pouring magical energy into him to stabilize him. If I hadn't killed five or six supernatural beings, I doubted there would have been enough ambient power to restore him. Yay for black magic used in the service of good.

Malcolm choked, and the werewolf lay still for another twenty minutes. I wanted to pick him up and take him out to the car, so I could get out of this place and go after Shannon, but moving him at such a critical juncture might defeat the resurrection.

And no one died for me. Not again.

The complete absence of cops or reinforcements to Skull Squadron told me that things were hectic in Nassau right now. Either the vampires trusted Skull Squadron to take care of me or they'd degenerated to the point that no one was watching out for each other. I didn't care which.

Finally, Malcolm's breathing steadied. "D, I think I am going to avoid associating with you in the future."

I laughed and helped him up. "That's probably a good idea. We might want to get out of here, though."

"No kidding."

It occurred to me I had no idea how to navigate Nassau's supernatural quarters. "Despite that, would you like to help me out?"

"Not at all. But if I do, just for the sake of argument, will we kill vampires?"

I had to wonder just how long the natives of Nassau, werewolf or otherwise, had been fighting the Vampire Nation. If Dracula really had come over with the early pirate settlers, it made me think their struggle was centuries old. Combine it with the werewolves' historical antipathy to the undead, and I'd probably stumbled upon the only supernatural group in the world that might view the Cleaver as an ally.

I still felt guilty when I said, "I just killed Skull Squadron. Their leader is currently spread out over the dining room floor."

Malcolm's eyes widened before he pulled himself up. "D, I believe this is going to be the start of a beautiful friendship."

Or an alliance of convenience.

CHAPTER SEVENTEEN

Malcolm and I left the Vampire Nation safe house and hijacked the Hummer that Skull Squadron had left outside the residence. We ditched that at a run-down motel before boosting a 1986 Chevrolet, which could barely run and smelled like someone's personal pot farm but allowed us to get where we needed to go.

We stopped at a twenty-four-hour internet cafe and printed up a few dozen pages from Malcolm's files, giving me all his data on the United National bank and the vampire's defenses of it. From there, we did an hour-long survey of the building. I admit, it was because I hoped I would see Shannon come out. Instead, all I saw was the heart of Nassau in all of its vampire-run glory.

Downtown Nassau was a different sort of beast from Cable Beach and Night Row. The latter were designed for the consumption of visitors to Nassau. My father had taken me, Tessa, and our half-brothers Alec and Stephen on vacation here. Back when the vampires had been less solid in their control, downtown had been a beautiful mix of local culture and modern business from Junkanoo Beach to East Bay.

While the local culture still existed in landmarks like the Vendue House and Christ Church Cathedral, they were overshadowed with the Vampire Nation's recent constructions. In addition to the United National Interests and Trust Bank, there were a dozen more skyscrapers that dotted the skyline with their ugly black mirrored windows. All of them were owned by vampires and represented the personal holdings of the undead who laundered their fortunes through the bank we were circling.

It was past two in the morning when we came to a stop and parked outside of the building's western corner. Malcolm hadn't been exaggerating—the United National Interests and Trust bank was a fortress. Even with all the supernatural powers I'd gained from my association with Bloody Mary, there was no way of sneaking in. At least not before morning, when the bank opened for business. A frontal assault, despite my bravado, was out of the question because it had hundreds of private military contractors guarding it.

"This is going to be difficult," I said, looking through the papers Malcolm had assembled in hopes of finding a weakness to the building's security.

"Try impossible, D. You should call your people and have them bring in the Marines."

"I don't try and involve my quote-unquote people in this sort of thing unless it's necessary."

Malcolm looked at me. "That fits with what I've heard, but I didn't believe it."

I looked up. "What do you mean?"

"They say you Che," Malcolm said.

"Excuse me?" I asked.

Malcolm snorted. "Che Guevara. The Revolutionary."

I frowned. "I know who Che Guevara is. I can't say it's a flattering comparison."

"That's because you're American," Malcolm said.

"Che wasn't too nice to the homosexuals and I have two gay siblings. Then there was his desire to nuke non-socialist nations. The whole Butcher of La Cabaña thing. I could go on," I said.

"Abraham Lincoln said he would preserve the Union by freeing no slaves if he could. You dislike Honest Abe, too?" Malcolm shrugged.

I realized this line of conversation was going nowhere. "History has a way of exposing the contradictions that lie in all men. Why are people comparing me to Che Guevara? Are they putting me on t-shirts?"

"They say you're a reactionary pro-supernatural Committee member and the only reason they haven't killed you yet is because you are too ornery to die."

"That's quite flattering. I'm not that reactionary, though," I said.

"You want to kill all supernaturals?" Malcolm asked.

"No," I said.

Malcolm laughed. "Then you might as well be waving the sickle and hammer in Ronald Reagan's Cabinet as far as the Pact is concerned. Everyone knows the Pyramid-Heads want to kill us all and have done a damn good job of keeping us on the defensive all these years. Then you come along and say we should all play nice-nice."

I wanted to ask any number of questions regarding his statement. Instead, I just said, "Pyramid Heads?"

"You guys rule everything from the top of the pyramid. The eye on the back of the dollar bill. The House, man. It's all Illuminati bullshit."

"The Eye of Providence is a Christian symbol representing the Trinity, dating back to at least the fifteenth century. It's featured in the work of Jacopo Carucci and numerous other artists."

"Yeah, yeah," Malcolm said, raising his hand. "I just wanted to know how you really get along with the House. You seem like a nice guy, but I lost my dad to House hunters. They lured him out with his human sister and then put a bullet through his eye. I was ready to help you just to get back at the vampires who sold them the information, but you don't act like one of them."

"You've known me all of three hours, Malcolm."

"You're sitting here, in a car with a werewolf, trying to rescue your succubus girlfriend. Plus, the Network says you're not to be targeted."

I hadn't been aware of that last fact. "Oh?"

Malcolm realized he'd said too much. "I want to know what you believe, D. I owe you my life and would be very disappointed to find out you're a genocidal ass hat like the rest of your group."

I ruffled the papers a second and closed my eyes. I should have been focused on figuring out a way to get Shannon, but I'd need time to work this out in my head. Until then, I just had to trust that Shannon knew what she was doing and had managed to infiltrate the bank with a plan. It was difficult, though. I wanted to be there for her. Unfortunately, I'd driven her away. With her help, I might have avoided this lengthy comedy of errors.

"I believe the only differences between vampires, humans, shape-shifters, and dragons are biological. In their heart, everyone is the same," I said, lying. I kind of hated vampires, no matter how much I still felt for Christopher.

Malcolm snorted. "That's stupid."

"Is it?" I asked.

Malcolm stared forward. "I've never met a vampire who I didn't want to kill, a rakshasa who belonged in this world, or a human who wasn't secretly an asshole. Likewise, having met the spirits, I can tell you they don't think anything like us."

"I was just saying what I believe," I said, continuing to lie.

"Hey, don't let me get you down. I think it's admirable, even if stupid. As much as I hate the vampires and the Raks, they're a part of this world. Destroying them all is a decision that's way above my pay grade. Likewise, you can respect something even if it's different from you."

"Afterschool specials aren't really my thing. Yeah, I don't like the fact the House treats all supernaturals as inherently dangerous regardless of whether they pose a risk to civilians. I also don't like the way the House exploits its power to enrich its leaders and control the minds of others. I don't even like its suppression of science and magical study in the interests of keeping a monopoly, and I sure as hell don't care for forcing every human with magic to join."

"Man, why are you *with* the House then?"

"If you can't be with the group you love, love the group you're born in."

"Ah."

"I have real power in the organization for the first time. I can't change everything on my own, but the world itself is changing, so that gives weight to my words. If we can broker a lasting peace between the various factions, then when the regular humans of the world find out that they're not alone— well, it won't end in a bloodbath."

It wasn't the first time I'd articulated my philosophy and motivations, but it was the first time I'd said them to someone who wasn't human. Until my reliving of my experience with Ashley, I'd never thought about how much she'd influenced my worldview.

However, as much as I respected her views, I didn't hold to them. The Red Room was necessary to keep the worst of the worst in line. In a world where people lied, cheated, murdered, and stole, you had to be better at it than them all in order to make sure the world didn't come crashing down.

Malcolm looked at me, pity in his eyes. "D, I don't mean to bring you down, but for every dollar you guys spend on saving the world, you spend a hundred on being at the top of the food chain. I've been in your files. The Red Room manufactures bombs, backs up dictators, and puts addictive stuff in cookies to keep their foot on the neck of regular humans. You may not rule the world, but you own a big-ass chunk of it. People like that aren't going to be interested in peace."

I thought about revealing my investigation of Protocol Zero. I decided against it. Malcolm was my ally today, but tomorrow, anything I told him could end up killing my fellow agents. "War is not what television depicts it as. My favorite books, *The Lord of the Rings*, are about good versus evil as well as the temptations thereof. The thing is, though, there's no such thing as a good war. If I'm going to bring peace, I'm going to have to bury a few bodies and enrich a bunch of already wealthy reprehensible movers and shakers. If it keeps this world from spilling into chaos, though, it's worth it. The eternal conflict between the supernatural races and the House has to end."

"Then why you killing so many vampires?"

"Because I am shit at peace-making."

Malcolm laughed aloud, but it wasn't all that funny. I'd spent the past year trying to build up a détente with the other supernatural factions. I'd blackmailed, bribed, seduced, made reparations, and signed off on murder in order to try and make things better. Relations with the other powers had been softening since World War 2, perhaps because of the realization that regular humanity had the power to destroy the world.

The only difference between my actions now and the ones when I was a junior agent were the fact that I was choosing what I did now and why. God, Jesus, Shang-Di, Lao-Tzu, and the Son of Skywalker help me, but I'd probably started a war. If the Vampire Nation and the House came to blows, there was no way the Truth wouldn't come out.

The world would burn.

You must find these agitators and destroy them, Bloody Mary whispered in my mind. To achieve a greater peace, you must accept a little war.

I pushed Bloody Mary away from my mind and rubbed my temples. Things were getting out of hand, and there wasn't a damn thing I could do about it. I needed information, and the only way that was going to happen was getting it from the source. This was a stupid idea, and I should never have come to Nassau. Christopher was worse than dead and could not be trusted. I needed to return to friendly territory and come up with a new plan.

"Ahem," Shannon said, knocking on the window.

Shannon was still wearing the same clothes she'd worn in the live feed. The difference was she was now holding a flash drive in her right hand that was a good three times the size of a normal one. She looked less than pleased at my presence.

I did a double take. "Well, that was convenient timing."

Rolling down the window, I saw Shannon glaring at me.

"Where the hell have you been for the past week? The entire House thinks you're dead, a prisoner, or AWOL."

Malcolm leaned over and spoke to Shannon for me. "He's been possessed by a demon for the past week, one that has the hots for him and has been using him to kill vampires. He just resumed control and killed a ton of dhampir back at my place. Oh, and the leader of Skull Squadron. D was coming here to rescue you."

Some of that he shouldn't have known.

"Rescue me?" Shannon's incredulity couldn't be understated.

"That's what you focused on?" I asked, looking between them.

"Everything else could be called Thursday for us," Shannon

said, shrugging. "I got the information from the safety deposit box."

"Really? How?"

"My powers work on the majority of men and a minority of women," Shannon said, waving the flash drive around. "I can even press it to work on all of them if I don't mind burning out their minds. Anyway, Penny sent me to do an infiltration and recover the safety deposit box's contents. Dracula had the whole thing watched, but I was able to distract the guards. Come on, Derek, we need to get out of here before they clue in."

I looked over at Malcolm. "Is there any way to get in touch with you after this?"

Malcolm produced a card between his fingers like a stage magician. "My phone number. Useful for those in dire need of help."

I took it. "You run a tech support service?"

"We all got to eat. I'm going to tell the Elders about you, D. Be warned, they may order me to kill you."

"Would you?"

"No, but I wouldn't stand in the way when they send someone else. I owe you, but the Pact's members are my brothers."

"Good luck, my friend," I said, giving him the car keys. "I'm sorry we didn't meet under different circumstances."

"I'm not. I would have killed you."

I smirked. "Probably."

Opening the door, I stepped on out and shut it behind me, looking at Shannon. "How much time do we have before they catch on to you?"

"The vampires have been trying to cover the entirety of the island in CCTV cameras. I managed to disable quite a few of them before going in, but I'm pretty sure the ones in the United National building were still watching me. It won't take them long to figure out who I was."

"I suspect I may have distracted them."

Shannon nodded. "That doesn't make up for you being a complete bastard to me back in Aspen."

"What?"

"You tried to shut me out of your plans."

"I don't seem to recall it that way."

"Men."

"Sorry?"

Shannon rolled her eyes. "Whatever."

My, my, she's attractive. Bloody Mary purred in my mind.

You've already seen my memories, I said.

The real thing is different, Bloody Mary replied.

I didn't argue with Bloody Mary. I was too focused on Shannon and the fact that she was there, in front of me. "I've been going through hell the past week and need to talk with you about a lot of things."

"Word on the street is you killed Dracula."

"No, I just blew up the plane we were on."

Shannon sighed. "This seems like a story I need to hear."

Malcolm started the car behind us and pulled out.

"It is," I said, sucking in my breath. "Is Penny here?"

"She's moving back and forth as developments with the Committee spiral out of control. The Vampire Nation is on DEFCON 1, and the House is talking with a half-dozen other major powers for a joint strike."

I stared at her. "Other groups are talking about allying with us?"

Shannon nodded. "The fruits of a year of extending olive branches. A bunch of supernatural nations are interested in joining forces with the House to crush the weakened Vampire Nation. By the end of the week, you may have just laid the groundwork for the genocide of the vampire race."

I stared at her. "I don't know how I feel about that."

"Neither do I. Come, let's get on my bike." Shannon grabbed me by the arm and led me off.

CHAPTER EIGHTEEN

Shannon had managed to appropriate a 2012 Hayabusa motorcycle, which she drove, and I rode on the back. We took a circular route through the city streets, weaving past several dead cameras before heading into the countryside. I welcomed a chance to ponder the weight of my situation in relative peace.

Genocide.

Is it accurate to call it that when your enemies are already dead? Of course, I couldn't use that excuse with Lucy's research. Even if that were true, I already knew they were thinking and feeling beings. The Vampire Nation might be corrupt, but human history was littered with evil governments and cultures that went on to become decent ones.

What would human history have looked like if aliens had come down to the Earth during the Roman Empire or the Confederacy, and judged everyone worthy of death? The Council of Ancients was composed of ruthless evil beings, but was the average vampire complicit in their crimes? The fact that I didn't know made me sick.

You sympathize with supernatural beings that prey on your race, Bloody Mary said in my mind. *I do not understand.*

I thought about how best to express my feelings. *William Blackstone said in the seventeenth century, "It is better that ten guilty persons escape than that one innocent suffers." I happen to agree with him. If one vampire is innocent of murder and destruction, then the destruction of their race is not warranted.*

Even if those guilty parties go on to kill hundreds of innocents? Bloody Mary asked. *You have a strange morality.*

I closed my eyes, shaking my head. *It's pretty much the same morality from the Old Testament, Ms. Cain and Abel.*

I didn't say I found the Creator's morality comprehensible either, Bloody Mary said.

"Where are we going?" I shouted to Shannon as the wind washed against my face. We were passing a bunch of low-income houses within spitting distance of ones that cost over a million for just the property.

"Saunders Beach!" Shannon said. "A vampire I killed while trying to find you owned it. It's where I've been squatting."

"Is that wise?" I asked.

"No, but it's an awesome house!" Shannon said, her enthusiasm infectious. I ended up thinking no thoughts at all as I clung to Shannon, enjoying the ride until we arrived at a beautiful beach house with red tile roofing and white walls. Its lawn was well tended and there were even a couple of pink flamingos standing on the front. It was the opposite of the sort of place you'd expect a vampire to live, yet I could remember slaughtering its owner here, along with all her bodyguards.

The monster you killed here deserved to die, Bloody Mary whispered. *As did her slaves for protecting her.*

You'll forgive me if I don't trust your standards, I said.

I used your standards to judge her, Bloody Mary said.

That makes it worse, I thought.

Shannon pulled her motorcycle to a stop and let me off before rolling it into the beach house's garage. "We'll be safe here until we can figure out our next move."

"I thought you said it wasn't safe," I said.

"I was joking. Penny set up about a hundred wards over this place to make sure the vampires don't come looking for it." Shannon walked out of the garage, closing it behind her.

"I'll take your word on that." I sighed, looking up to the sky. It was gray, with signs of a storm coming. "Do we have a computer, so we can upload the flash drive's contents?"

"It's the twenty-first century and I'm a spy, so yes," I said.

I almost asked her not to be snide, but that seemed like an elephant telling a cheetah to lose some weight. "Thank you, Shannon. This means a lot."

She looked at me, noticing perhaps for the first time how

exhausted I was. "You look like you could use some sleep, Derek. By the way, where did you get all those tattoos? Get drunk and decide to make some poor life choices?"

"Sure, let's go with that. As for sleep? I'll sleep when I'm dead. Probably not even then."

Shannon looked down at the ground. "I'm sorry about keeping my relationship with Christopher a secret."

"How much of a relationship was it?" I asked, wondering how to ask what was on my mind.

Shannon raised an eyebrow. "Do you want to go there?"

"Yeah, I know, this is an odd time to be jealous. I still want to know."

"Well, it was a long time ago. Christopher was doing something I'm not comfortable talking about. It's something that would put you in an awkward position."

"You mean smuggling people out of the House?"

"You *knew* about that?" Shannon asked.

"I *am* sort of a spy." I stuck my tongue out halfway. It was a childish gesture, but childishness was about the only thing that got me through some days.

"Yeah, but you're kind of a crap one." Shannon smirked. "You're sort of the 'shoot-up places and sneak in to strangle people' sort of spy. Really more of an assassin."

"I'm wounded."

"Twenty-four times, according to your files. Seriously, though, Derek. The only reason I wasn't worried about you is you've survived almost a ridiculous number of insane situations."

"True." I took a deep breath. "Could you tell me why you chose to keep Christopher's survival a secret from me?"

Shannon looked away. "I admitted I was wrong. Isn't that enough?"

"We promised we'd never keep secrets from each other." I didn't want to push Shannon, but this was a non-negotiable point of our relationship. I was comfortable with just sex and friendship, but if that was the extent of our relationship, I wanted to know.

Shannon crossed her arms and turned back to me. She

pointed at my chest. "What you're asking is harder than it sounds. I've got a lot of ugly in my past I don't want you to see."

I knew enough of what she was talking about to be sympathetic. "Believe me, I know, but I tell you everything. Including stuff that should never be shared with anyone and inflicts insanity just looking at it."

"The sad fact is, I believe you," Shannon said, looking guilty. "You're the person I trust the most in this world. If I didn't have a good reason for holding back the truth, I wouldn't have. I swear by God, the saints, and on my mother."

Now I was starting to get irritated. "You still haven't answered my question."

Shannon looked down at her feet. "Okay, fine. I thought you might hunt him down and drive a stake through his heart. He's a friend of mine, no matter what he's done, and I'd rather you not do that."

"As someone informed me, I'd have better luck killing him with an orihalcum bullet."

"Not funny."

"It's not meant to be," I said, kicking one of the lawn flamingoes. Shannon's reaction perplexed me, and it took me a minute to realize what she was worried about. "Wait a second— you thought my reaction to discovering my old friend was still alive would be to track him down and execute him? Just because he was a vampire? That's how little you think of me?" This conversation had a lot of subtext and it wasn't all about Christopher.

Shannon frowned. "Not just because he was a vampire. I figured you'd take it personally that he's probably turned over all sorts of information on the House."

"I'm not enthusiastic about the fact that he's a traitor, no. I would have thought the past year would have taught you I want peace with the other supernatural factions, though."

"You kill monsters, Derek. That's what my past year with you taught me. You're just better at differentiating among them than the rest of the Committee, except with me."

It was times like this I remembered how much Shannon hated being lilin. It was the reason the House had accepted her as a member. That and divine intervention. Shannon believed with all her heart the lilin were evil and deserved to be destroyed. Ninety-nine percent of the time, at least. Other times she thought of herself as the beautiful and wonderful woman she was. No matter how often I tried to increase the number of times she thought that, I could never get over the rage she felt against the supernatural blood in her veins.

"I don't think of you as a monster, Shannon."

"That's the problem. I've killed more people than you. You think two hundred is bad? I've killed twice that."

I paused, processing that information. Her file had listed only the kills she'd committed as a member of the Red Room. "That's quite—"

"Mostly people who didn't deserve it."

I snorted at the idea that all of my kills were deserved. "I dropped a missile strike on a vampire plantation earlier this week, Shannon. Old men, housekeepers, children, and habitual victims of the vampires died by the dozens. All because of a careless comment I made and the job I've done."

"It's not the same."

"Isn't it?"

Shannon sighed, looking more guilty than combative. "I wasn't prepared to find out that Christopher, someone I knew as a human, had become one of the monsters. He was a good man, someone who could be trusted. He helped a lot of people get away from the Red Room who couldn't survive the life we led. When he said he wanted to talk with you and make peace between our factions, I was torn. I wanted to believe that even though he'd become a Fang, he was still the good person I remembered. I spent months doing check-ups on his past and giving him tests to prove his decency."

"You could have just come to me."

"The only thing that scared me more than the possibility that Christopher had become an irredeemable monster, Derek, was that he was sincere. Then I knew you'd do everything in your power to prevent him from dying. I didn't want you risking your life trying to protect the vampire race from a war with the House."

"The vampire race isn't synonymous with the Vampire Nation, at least not to me. Have you had a chance to look at the flash drive?"

Shannon pulled it out of her pocket and lifted it up between us. "No. This was it in the safety deposit box. Well, this and a note saying that you shouldn't use the Bloodsword to kill anyone because it'll link you to a demon inside."

"Something he could have told me earlier."

Oh, like you haven't benefited from our association, Bloody Mary muttered. *I should take away the power I have given you just to show you how much you need me.*

And statements like that are why I don't trust you, I said. *That and the demon thing.*

Racist, Bloody Mary said.

Shannon held the flash drive tight. "At this point, I don't care what's in this. I see you out there breaking all the rules and doing your own thing knowing that the consequences won't affect you. Either that or not caring. I don't work like that, though. I need the rules to keep me sane."

"What are you saying?" I asked.

Shannon shook her head. "I'm saying I need to choose who I am loyal to through all this. It's not Christopher, it's not the Committee, it's you."

It wasn't the sort of promise Shannon made casually. "All right, then. I promise to never do anything as a Committee member to make you compromise yourself. I will instead ask you to do the right thing. As difficult as that may be to figure out in a world where Sumerian gods can be summoned by morons at any given time."

Shannon looked up to me. "Thank you."

I smirked. "Though I am going to look forward to ordering you to do some things."

She rolled her eyes. "In that place we're going to remain equals. Actually, scratch that— whenever it's about our relationship, I'm in charge."

"Yes, mistress."

I walked over to her and took her by the hands, looking into her eyes as a light rain began to pour down on us. Shannon was beautiful. The most beautiful woman I'd ever seen. It wasn't her features that made her gorgeous in my mind. No, it was the fact that I loved her. It had been a long time since I'd felt that sort of feeling and even now, I felt like it could go away at any moment. This moment, though, was ours. All that mattered was there was one person on this blood-soaked, violent, war-torn hellhole of a planet who I wanted to be with.

"We're going to get through this," I said. "We'll stop this war and Dracula, and discover whatever Christopher was trying to bring to my attention."

"The fact is, I don't care. It just matters if it's with you."

"The same."

I put my hands on her cheeks and kissed her. Shannon pulled me closer and deepened the kiss. We made love that night, a distraction from the creeping darkness that seemed to pervade everything. Unfortunately, my dreams were no longer my own.

As I lay with Shannon, exhausted from our passion, Bloody Mary made me once more relive the worst night of my life.

CHAPTER NINETEEN

The blackness parted, and I was in a metropolis I'd never much cared for: New York City. Plenty of local agents and non-House personnel would hang me from my toes for suggesting it wasn't the greatest place on Earth, but that didn't change how I felt. There was just something about the Big Apple that left me feeling cramped and paranoid.

I blamed it on the fact that I was used to looking at everyone as a potential threat, be they disguised monsters or humans who'd somehow decided today was the day they'd take me out. Being in the city with a million stories, I felt like I was surrounded by twelve million potential attackers. Either that, or it was because I was from Massachusetts.

Yet it was New York City I was assigned to. One didn't get to choose where one was sent on a job when one was a newly promoted senior agent. Besides, Christopher seemed to love the place, and his presence helped take the edge off.

The two of us were eating hot dogs in a subway station the House had cordoned off for repairs. It was a cold day in late December, and the two of us were wearing winter coats, gloves, and scarves while we waited for our contact to arrive.

"So, you want to pick up a couple of hookers after this?" Christopher said, taking a bite out of his hot dog.

"Thank you, but no. I've never felt the need to pay for my company." I looked at my hot dog, disgusted with its taste.

"I don't need to pay either, but it's a service like any other. It cuts down on the hassle of who, what, when, where, and calls," Christopher said.

"You'll forgive me if I still decline. I've seen too many rings of mesmerized girls and boys to trust anything is consensual."

I threw my hotdog into a nearby wastepaper basket before changing the subject. "I'm sorry, but I don't know how you can eat those things."

Christopher rolled his eyes. "I'm sorry they didn't have tofu dogs, Mister Daoist."

"Please don't mock my religion," I said.

"I'm just saying you kill people," Christopher said. "A lot of people. Daoism is a passive, life-affirming religion. You're not going to balance your chi or whatever by not eating meat when you carry around a sniper rifle in your luggage."

"The sniper rifles are usually provided for me on site," I said.

"It's a metaphor, Derek," Christopher said.

I snorted. "It's a poor one. I choose clean living as part of a larger attempt to bring myself in harmony with the universe. The Dao is individualistic and cannot be defined, my path being different from everyone else's."

"Says the white man to the Chinese guy," Christopher said.

I frowned. "That joke would be hilarious if the kids in the Hamptons didn't call me and my sister the Mutt twins."

"That joke is hilarious because you grew up in the Hamptons," Christopher said.

He had me there. "Do we have any idea when our contact is going to be arriving?"

Christopher smirked. "Should be any minute now. You've been on edge since we got here. Do you have a problem with the mission, or is it just my rousing rendition of 'New York, New York'?"

"A little of both. You need singing lessons," I said.

Christopher placed a hand on his heart. "I was trying to imitate the Kurgen from the movie *Highlander*."

I rolled my eyes. "I'm just not comfortable with missions that take us against the Network."

The Network was a new organization, having sprung up in the past couple of years and uniting several previous smaller organizations. Its stated ethos was to passively resist the House in all things. It attempted to smuggle magic users away from the House's recruiters, disseminate the Truth to people who might believe whenever possible, and distribute free knowledge of magic (particularly spells designed to thwart the Red Room's monitoring systems). Rumors attested it had the assistance of groups like the Hand of Allah, Righteous Defenders of Judaea, and other religious groups.

The Red Room had thankfully not overreacted to their presence. Aside from a few near-misses with WikiLeaks and other internet news agencies, they hadn't done much to damage our cause. I'd argued cracking down with maximum force would just turn it into a group of martyrs. For once, my superiors had listened to me. As a result, we were still gathering information. It was my hope to discredit the group rather than send in a bunch of commandos.

"Feeling a wee bit sympathetic to the poor distressed multitudes of lesser, witches, and psychics?"

"A little bit, yes."

"I don't."

"How . . . ironic." I didn't bring up the fact that Christopher used to be a smuggler. I didn't have to.

"If they were just trying to organize so they could avoid being drafted, I wouldn't mind. However, they're against the Great Lie, and that could lead to some serious shit."

"How much damage could a bunch of hackers and activists do?"

"I'm not sure whether you're being sarcastic or just ignorant." Christopher raised his ring hand and lifted his thumb and pinky.

Electricity flowed through the two like an open circuit, creating a tiny lightshow. "Besides, they're not just hackers. They're magicians just like you and—"

"Actually, just you."

"Sorry, I keep forgetting you're our Muggle senior agent."

"I don't read children's books."

Christopher snorted. "How did it end up skipping a generation, anyway? Your sister is one of the toughest witches I know. Shouldn't you have some sort of magic power that doubles when you touch each other?"

"We're not the Superfriends," I said.

"Ah-ha!" Christopher exclaimed.

"I said I don't read children's books," I backtracked. "Not watch cartoons."

"That's worse," Christopher said.

I smirked. Christopher always won our arguments. "I dunno, it just passed me over. Most of the other members of the family can work magic, big or small. I just don't have the knack."

Christopher shook his head. "It's a skill, Derek, not a mutation. Even if you don't have the same level of aptitude as the rest of your family, you should be able to learn ritual magic, if not sorcery. If the House was so inclined, we could be teaching it in schools like algebra."

I smiled. "I didn't pay much attention to my algebra teacher, either."

Back then, I still had my mental block on the practice of magic. As Christopher indicated, it wasn't something that was inborn, but learned. The difference was certain bloodlines had access to more magical "oomph" than other people. If you were related to a god, a demon, or a fairy, or had practiced inbreeding with other magical bloodlines (always a bad idea), then you probably could channel more power than the quote-unquote normal people of the world.

The thing was, there were ways around that for both regular humans and those who already had access to power. Saints and sinners could exalt or deform their souls while others crafted enhancers to channel their magic for them. My grandmother, Anne, kept a familiar in the form of a falcon. Even if you couldn't do sorcery or magic on the fly, everyone could do a well-prepared magical ritual if they believed in it enough. I just...couldn't.

"I could try and show you." Christopher dismissed his electrical trick. "We just need to find your knack."

"My father tried to show me how to manipulate minds like he could while Penny almost burned the house down demonstrating her skill. Believe me, everyone has tried to show me how to do it. I just don't get the symbolism."

"Ah. Well, there's your problem. Magic is all about the

symbolism. It's a language born from emotion, and you need to understand before you can speak."

"Thank you, Mace Windu. I am so enlightened."

"Please. I'm the hot and sexy Obi-Wan."

We were spared further discussion by the arrival of someone who seemed to warp my memory around her. Whereas everything else felt bland, dull, and colorless in my memory, the newcomer was a vivid and sharp presence.

She was beautiful, surpassing everyone I'd ever seen in my life, save possibly Shannon. Each step she made wearing an ordinary black sweater and dress with stylish heels was like a note of music to my brain. Her cheek bones were finely cut and her eyes were the color of emeralds. A ponytail of blood-red hair hung over her shoulders. By the way Christopher showed no reaction and a vague awareness of how wrong this was, I made the mental conclusion this was *not* the person I met all those years ago.

I found myself entranced and remembered encountering a fallen angel when tracking my renegade brother Stephen. I'd had to have months of psych evaluation, drugs, and low-level brainwashing to erase the mind-numbing beauty from my mind. Sometimes, even today, I had dreams of the demon's glorious wings and his terrifying eyes.

The woman smiled, almost as if she could hear my thoughts. She extended her hand, shaking it. "Evan."

I tried to remember who I'd met with that night. I seemed to recall it had been a semi-frantic overweight man in his forties. However, that memory was a distant second to the vision I was having now. Evan, whatever her real name was, was the woman in my dreams. The fact that this vision came so soon after making love to Shannon left me feeling unclean. Indeed, the features of the woman reminded me of Shannon and Cassandra with little touches of Ashley here and there.

Remember, a voice whispered in my ear. *Remember this night.*

Evan extended her hand and I took it. "It is an honor to meet you, Derek Hawthorne."

Christopher frowned and said, "And what am I, chopped liver?"

"You have a certain reputation as well, Agent Hang."

"Nothing good, I hope." Christopher gave a mischievous smile.

"Then you're in luck." Evan fluttered her eyelids. "Because none of it is."

"How cold," Christopher said. "You have information on the Network?"

Evan said, "Yes, though not perhaps information you'll find useful."

Christopher frowned. "That sounds very much like an excuse. You're getting paid to provide actionable intelligence."

"The Network has been running an underground railroad—"

"Can we not compare the Red Room's monitoring of psychics and magicians to slavery?" I asked, frowning at the comparison.

Evan batted her eyelashes in a way that was identical to Cassandra. "Would you prefer I compare it to the other people who have been driven into hiding out of fear for their families?"

I gritted my teeth. "Go on."

"They've set up an underground railroad through New York. They provide psychic and sorcery-talented human beings with new identities, passports, and even new features or memories if the magic is available. They've established collaborators with the House as well."

"Can you confirm the latter?" I asked, not liking this. If I reported the latter, people would die. We had to nip this in the bud, though, or the House would come down even harder.

"Yes," Evan said. "But the network in New York is no longer going to be of any concern."

"How's that?" Christopher said, tossing his hot dog away. "Are they shutting down? If so, we'll need to know where they're moving."

"The vampires have taken them."

"Excuse me?" I asked, a chill running down my spine. "The Vampire Nation has found a bunch of unprotected supernatural humans?"

Christopher looked disgusted. "That's one way of dealing with a problem like that."

"Dozens," Evan said, shaking her head. "Their leader has been monitoring the situation for some time. Since these individuals aren't under the protection of the House and are in defiance of it, there's no violation of treaty to take them."

I felt sick to my stomach. It was one of the policies of the House to inhibit vampires from taking people who had magical potential into their ranks. Vampires could learn sorcery, but for whatever reason, they weren't able to learn much more than they'd understood in life—blood magic and obscuromancy exempted. Forty or so humans with magical potential they could turn into mystical agents meant a substantial shift in the power balance, like North Korea gaining a truckload of ICBMs.

"Shit," I said, disgusted. "Do you know where they're being held?"

"Yes, a dockside warehouse owned by a Vampire Nation shell corporation," Evan said, lifting a Pantheon Corp tablet. "I was able to assemble a good deal of information on the situation."

"Tragic," Christopher said. "We should report this and await further instructions."

"We need to rescue them," I said flatly.

"Excuse me?" Christopher asked, doing a double take.

I took the tablet from Evan and started looking through her notes. "There are six vampires and a dozen Bloodslaves guarding this facility. It looks like they're keeping their subjects drugged up and held in shipping containers. Basic human trafficking stuff. We can assemble a team, hit them, and recover the hostages before the Vampire Nation knows what hit them."

It was exceeding our orders, but that was one of the benefits of being a senior agent. You were trusted enough in the field not to be micromanaged and had broad latitude to make decisions based on your perception of the situation. The Vampire Nation and the House had been longtime enemies, so while it was better to seek permission, striking at them in a way that couldn't be traced back would be considered worthy of a medal rather than recrimination.

"Derek, can I talk to you in private?" Christopher asked, gesturing behind us.

"Could you hold on a minute, Evan?" I asked, handing her back her tablet. I'd already memorized everything inside.

Going to a nearby corner, Christopher and I pulled out our Rings of Veritas and put them on. It would be impossible for our contact to know what we were talking about now.

I started speaking first. "I know what you're going to say. You don't think it's wise to waste the lives of operatives on traitors."

"Actually, no. I'm all for rescuing the poor unwashed masses from being mind-raped, actually raped, and then turned into bloodsucking monsters. You know they mesmerize every new member, so their loyalty is to the Vampire Nation?"

"I think that's a rumor."

"Trust me, it's true."

"So, what is your problem, then?"

"What do we do with them after we rescue them?" Christopher said, pointing at my chest. "The best-case scenario is they get shifted off to Division Zero for brainwashing."

"Division Zero is a myth."

Division Zero was a supposed multi-room black site that existed as a prison camp for agents, scientists, and assets of the House that were too valuable to kill outright. It was also a place that monsters were taken for experimentation or interrogation. It was an urban legend as far as I was concerned, as freedom from brainwashing was one of the perks of being a House member. Likewise, there was no one too valuable to kill outright. Having grown up the son of a Committee member, I was pretty sure if Division Zero existed, I would know about it.

"Now who's being naive?" Christopher rolled his eyes. "The fact is these people have been running from the Red Room's recruiters and are attempting to join an organization designed to overthrow us. Nothing good will come to them, especially if we bring a bunch of Red Room heavies to back us up."

I thought about what he said, looking over at Evan. "You're right. I need to make a few phone calls. I think I can set us up with a group that's willing to keep this off the books."

"Mercenaries?" Christopher raised an eyebrow.

"Mercenaries." I nodded.

"Things just got a lot more complicated," Christopher said, smirking. "The vampires won't know what hit 'em."

Neither would we, in the end.

CHAPTER TWENTY

Once my call was made, it took twenty minutes for a black SUV to arrive outside the subway station and five of the most dangerous people in the world to step out. As Evan and Christopher stood behind me underneath a street light, I looked the newcomers over.

The four behind the group's leader were a mix of eccentric-looking individuals. The first were two women, one brown-haired and one platinum, dressed in white camouflage pants and gray jackets. Beside them was a seven–foot-tall black man who was made of muscle and whose eyes glowed in a way that wasn't human. To the right was a five-foot-tall white-haired boy, seventeen if that, but whose eyes were void of any human emotion.

The leader of the group was a beret-wearing man a few inches shorter than me with a goatee and small glasses—a very deliberate attempt to emanate Johnny Depp in looks. Unfortunately, for him, he was achieving French communist terrorist more than the star of my sister's favorite movie (she was a Christina Ricci fan).

He was dressed in a long-sleeved sweater and beige pants and had one of those new electronic cigarettes in his right hand. Underneath his sweater, I could tell he was wearing Kevlar armor, and the bracelets under his sleeve were transmorphic items capable of becoming all manner of weapons.

This was Alec Hawthorne, my younger half-brother and the child of my father's first affair after my mother's disappearance. He was also one of the most dangerous men alive. Unlike myself, he'd been found to be too brutal and rebellious to serve as an agent, but had survived by becoming a contractor for missions the Red Room didn't want linked to themselves.

"Hey, Alec, did no one tell you electronic cigarettes combine the unhealthiness of smoking with the taint of neo-yuppie?" I said, offering my hand to my brother. I'd never been as close to my half siblings as I was to my twin but tried to maintain cordial relations with them. It wasn't their fault our father was a sociopath.

"You have a funny way of asking for a favor." Alec took my hand and shook it, speaking while sucking on his cigarette. "My associates and I were planning an operation."

"It pays a million dollars."

Christopher coughed. "Excuse me?"

"I have a black card. It was a gift last Christmas from my father. He can't buy me, but it might as well see some use."

"And you let me pay for half our meals?" Christopher said, horrified.

"Those are comped by the Red Room and you know it," I said, wondering what the problem was.

"Not the good ones!" Christopher said, shaking his head. "For shame."

"That'll cover most ops," Alec said. "What's the target?"

"Vampires," I said, saying the word like I was cursing. "They're smuggling people out of New York City harbor. We're going to hit the warehouse, get the people out, and transport them to a secure location. Killing the undead is a bonus but unnecessary."

"We'll need to leave no witnesses," Christopher corrected.

"Fine," I said, handing over the information to Alec.

Alec looked at the tablet, memorizing the information. "I don't like messing around in the politics of the Vampire Nation, but this is the kind of mission my Raptors are made for."

"Raptors? Like in *Jurassic Park*?" I asked.

"More like birds of prey," Alec said, not missing a beat. "Not everything needs to be a pop culture reference."

"How's the rest of the clan?" I asked, changing the subject.

Alec didn't bother looking up from his tablet. "You could find out if you just dropped by to visit every once in a while."

"You know that's not going to happen. Nathan Hawthorne and I aren't going to reconcile."

Alec sighed. "Gerald is still in the accounting offices, showing no sign of magic, like you, but smart enough to stay out of danger. Rebecca just finished her Doctorate in neuroscience. Her thesis was about mesmerism—"

"Isn't she like twelve?"

"Nineteen, which you know," Alec said, frowning. "You should come to visit her in Georgetown. She idolizes you."

"I'll see about dropping by," I said, wondering if I would. The rest of my family idolized Nathan, and it was difficult to listen to them try and convince me to reconcile with him as they had for the past few years. Penny was the only one I could stand to hear it from, and only because we'd shared a womb.

Alec continued. "Hoshi is working in the White Room on nanotechnology. I'm quite worried she'll destroy the world."

I smiled.

"And the kids are fine. None of them have shown any sign of magic yet, but there's still time."

"What about Stephen?" I asked, addressing the black sheep of our bloodline.

"Still crazy," Alec said. "Possession will do that."

Stephen Hawthorne was another reason I'd come to loathe my father. The third-eldest Hawthorne brother had wanted to impress Nathan by following in his footsteps. He'd done everything he could to try and surpass me. Last year, when he was twenty-eight, he'd gone after a demon.

He'd ended up possessed.

Stephen killed a shopping center full of tourists in Dubai, then went on a seven-country killing spree. Marcus and Gwen, the other Hawthorne Red Room agents, had gotten themselves killed trying to bring him in—along with eleven other agents. In the end, Christopher and I had managed to bring him back alive.

The problem was, by that time, he'd merged with the demon. No psychologist or demonologist could figure out where my brother ended and the monster within began. His demon had been the fallen angel I'd found so beautiful, and I still remembered its loveliness when I'd somehow managed to force it back into its host. The Red Room should have killed Stephen, but my father refused.

He didn't want to damn one of his children to hell. Like the shit we did for a living wasn't going to. So, Stephen languished in an institute, gloating over all the horrors he'd committed. I couldn't prove it, but I knew my brother had made a pact with the monster inside him. He'd willingly become a partner to the murder of his siblings and the deaths of thousands. Someday, I intended to figure out a way to banish the demon and make sure Stephen faced justice.

Bastard.

"Yeah, sure," I said, wondering how much my belief in Stephen's guilt played a role in my alienation from the rest of the siblings. Hating our shared father was bad, but believing your brother practiced infernalism was worse.

"How many brothers and sisters does he have?" Evan asked Christopher.

"A lot," Christopher said. "It's like the Brady Bunch except they're multiracial spies."

I decided to get this show on the road. "Alec, do your people know the strengths and weaknesses of vampires? Not the stuff the Vampire Nation distributes through the media, but their actual capabilities."

"Old Ones and Ancients are irritated by sunlight but don't suffer injury from it while younger ones will explode. Blessed and enchanted items from any religion but Satanism will hurt them. Regular bullets and injuries will just hurt like hell and be healed by their next feeding. Fire, decapitation, orihalcum, and destruction of the heart will kill young ones. Old Ones, though, will resurrect unless you place holy items on their corpse and burn the bodies to ashes. With some, like Dracula, even that won't work, and you'll have to break whatever pact they've made with Tiamat-Abaddon. Blood Servants are always a pain being humans with half a vampire's strength. They can also mentally control draugr so vampires who don't mind cannibal corpses in their homes keep them as guard dogs."

I nodded, just making sure to dot all our i's and cross our t's. I'd learned everything I knew about vampires from Alec. "All accurate, but I don't think we're going to be facing any Elders. This is just a group of slavers. The eldest of them is less than a century old. We should take precautions, but I don't think he'll be a problem."

Alec said, "You should also keep two Greek funerary coins on your person at all times."

"What does that do?" I asked.

Alec shrugged. "Fucks with vampire mesmerism and their ability to create illusions. It won't help you too much, Derek, because you're a trained resistor. I have enough for my people and your friend, though, if he's not been cleared."

"I'm up to level six in mental conditioning," Christopher said.

"Derek's a level ten," Alec said.

Christopher stared at me. "Jesus, did your father water-board you as a child? How the hell did you get a level ten?"

Alec shrugged. "Beats me. I'm the biggest hardass I know, and I rate a level eight. Dracula's the only monster I wager who could bend Derek's mind. Him or Big Daddy Hawthorne."

"Don't even think about it," I said. "We don't need to invoke trouble by mentioning his name."

"I killed Dracula once," the brown-haired girl in the back said.

"Quiet, Shannon," Alec said. "Humans are talking."

The girl in the back gave him the finger. I, of course, didn't know until much later that she was my future lover in one of her shape-shifted forms. It amused me that Shannon and I had crossed paths before "officially" meeting, but that just went to show you how small the intelligence community was.

"What about physical capacities?" I said, making sure everything was set.

"Vampires move at three times a normal human's speed on average and are about as strong. Bloodslaves tend to be as strong as an Olympian but aren't superhuman. Thankfully, I've got the red, white, and blue pills for my team."

"You're juicing?" I asked, surprised.

The White Room was always experimenting with combining magic and medicine. There were plenty of ancient potions left over from Viking, Han Dynasty, and Roman times to give soldiers a boost in battle. The White Room thought these could be mass produced and improved on with SCIENCE, but the results were unpredictable. Everyone reacted differently when magic was involved, and it remained a case of "let the user beware."

"Some of my crew aren't human, but for the ones who are, I don't want them getting caught with their pants down by the monsters. I recommended to the Committee all strike teams should be on the pills. The occasional freakout and collateral is less of a problem than the casualties we suffer every year."

I rolled my eyes. "And people wonder why you're not a registered agent anymore."

"Because my dad is on the Committee so they couldn't kill me, but I'm not willing to drink the Kool-Aid and say they have our best interests at heart."

I chuckled. "It's good to see you, Alec."

Alec sucked on his electronic cigarette before responding. "It's good to see you, too. So, we steal a transport for them to evacuate in and dump them somewhere where they can get picked up by the Red Room?"

"Yes, and that's classified."

"Sure it is." My brother snorted. "Okay, let's do this."

What happened next was everything became like television static. I saw the next few hours in scattered images, like an old VHS tape that had been damaged and played anyway.

It was weird, but I could see past the veil of reality during this horrific moment. There, I saw Evan's true visage, that of a woman with long crimson tresses whose face was obscured by a horrific head injury. But it looked so familiar to me I could almost whisper her name into the air.

What followed were a series of mind-twisting images as I struggled to remember an event I'd repressed. Years later, I couldn't recall what happened in the warehouse the night Christopher was taken away by the vampires and half of Alec's team were killed. It had been a trap, of course, a trail of breadcrumbs left by the Vampire Nation to lure Red Room agents to their doom. All the Network members had already been turned into draugr, unintelligent zombies who feasted on the flesh of the living, while almost thirty vampires awaited us.

The images that remained were a collection of stills, frozen in time. I tried to sort them into a coherent narrative, but it was difficult—almost impossible.

Alec throwing a phosphorous grenade at a group of draugr.

Shannon turning into a bat-winged creature with horns and claws, tearing through the vampires.

A dozen vampire corpses, their heads and hearts shot once each, surrounding me in a circle. I held Christopher's gun in one hand and my own in another, having achieved a Zen-like state of battle.

Christopher disappearing into the shadows as an obscuromancer pulled him into the darkness.

The Raptors leaving me behind on my own request as the roof collapsed in the flames.

An Elder vampire screaming as I tore his limbs off and drank his blood to give me the strength to crawl my way through the fire and collapse at the foot of the ambulance people.

Dracula, dressed in plain clothes, looking down at me and letting me survive. I daresay he'd been impressed with my capacity for horror and will to survive.

The horrific vengeance I'd taken on the vampires of New York City thereafter.

I felt ill.

I found myself in a reproduction of my apartment in Boston, a luxurious penthouse I'd once shared with my wife. It had a widescreen television set, a white-cushioned couch, and a fabulous view of the harbor with more causal wealth on display than I could remember having since. In the right corner of the room was a painting worth over a million and a half dollars, which Cassandra had gotten me for our first wedding anniversary. I remembered it because I hated it but couldn't sell it without hurting her.

The world shifted for a second, and I saw a brief flash of red and gore with images of Cassandra being shot by Shannon, the destruction of an island in the South Pacific, and a blood ritual between a robed woman and a one-eyed man with a staff.

When the false apartment returned to "normal," I saw Evan lying on the couch.

Naked.

Well, almost naked. She was wearing a ruby necklace which lay between her breasts in a rather transparent attempt to draw attention to them. While noticing the almost supernaturally attractive woman, it wasn't enough to distract me from the horrible images I'd just been exposed to, or how obvious her identity was.

"Hello, Mary," I said, keeping my eyes on her face. "Done poking around in my memories?"

"Oh, Derek, I haven't even begun." Bloody Mary purred. "You cut open a vampire's throat to drink his blood in order to survive. You were able to tap into ancient warrior magic to slay dozens of beings far stronger than you. Indeed, you saved your brother and partner's life."

"My partner died," I said, my voice cold and unfeeling. "As for the rest, I don't remember it very well. I was happy just having scattered images."

"No one remembers it very well when they awaken to their power. You thought it was facing the Wazir, but it was far earlier. Yet you tried to suppress your insights and strengths. Why?" Bloody Mary asked.

"Because my power came during a traumatic and horrifying mission?" I snarked.

Bloody Mary chuckled. "Perhaps. Yet that environment is where you thrive. If you had been born to different parents in different circumstances, you might have been a detective or a soldier or perhaps an investigator for the FBI who specialized in serial killers. Something that would take you to the darkness."

"First, never suggest I'd work for the FBI again. I hate those people. Worst infiltration of my life. Second, I don't want you creeping around in my head ever again. There's a difference between exorcising you from my body and destroying you outright."

"Tsk-tsk," Bloody Mary said, looking at me. "What a pity. I can feel there's a part of you that hungers for bloodshed . . . and me. One can feed the other."

"I love Shannon," I said.

"So? I like her. Her lust for murder and sex is almost as great as my own." Bloody Mary sounded bored.

I could feel tendrils of darkness creeping in my mind, trying to force me to abandon myself to darker impulses. To take Bloody Mary in my arms and have the same sort of rough, intense, passion-driven sex I'd just had with Shannon. Closing my eyes, I drew on those intense feelings and snapped my fingers. There was a scream as I banished Mary to the dark recesses of my soul, leaving my consciousness my own for the next few hours.

Then I woke up.

CHAPTER TWENTY-ONE

I woke up with a monstrous headache. The air smelled acidic and my lungs burned. Above my head, the smoke alarm was beeping. My eyes stung, and I had to blink them several times in order to see straight. Great. The house was on fire.

Unconcerned save in the most general sense, I slipped into my boxer shorts and walked to the kitchen. It had been demolished. The refrigerator looked like someone had thrown a giant rock into it, spilling all its contents onto the floor, and the countertop was crushed. The cabinets had been seared as if hit by a flamethrower, charred black but not burning, the heat having been too hot to start a fire.

No, the smoke came from somewhere else.

Carefully stepping through the kitchen, I saw the living room was demolished as well, and a Middle Eastern man's upper torso lay face down in the middle of a shattered coffee table. His lower body was missing and there was a faint aroma of sulfur and brimstone to the air, the smoke that triggered the alarm from here. There were burn marks across the couch and carpet.

Shannon was cleaning up the broken glass from the coffee table with a broom and a dustpan, wearing a pair of green camouflage pants with a green camo top. It was obviously something she'd just thrown on. Either that or she had some very strange taste in battle attire, possible given her skin was harder than Kevlar.

Shaking my head, I said, "Should I even ask?"

"Do you like false reassurance?" Shannon asked.

"Yes," I said.

"Then no, everything's fine," Shannon said.

I rubbed my eyes before sighing. "What happened?"

"Dracula sent a djinn after us," Shannon said.

Djinn, the inspiration for genies, were the Arabic peninsula's equivalent of fairies. A collection of pre-Islamic gods and spirits, their power ranged from the omnipotent to no stronger than human wizards. They were a race born from smoke and fire who could transform into both at will. Like the rakshasas, they were one of the few supernatural races to have formed an empire as strong as the Red Room.

Leaning down, I turned over the dead body and checked the face of the dead man. Much to my surprise, I recognized him from the thousands of POI (Person of Interest) photographs I'd been required to memorize. It was Ali al-Fariq, the Living Smoke Which Kills. He was one of the many djinn imprisoned by angels in inanimate objects for crimes against humanity. Unlike the genie of the lamp, he didn't grant wishes (which wasn't what he did in *Arabian Nights* anyway). Ali murdered people his ring desired dead.

Dracula had acquired the Living Smoke Which Kills after killing a Turkish General who bargained it for his life (and was cheated) when the vampire was still Vlad III of Wallachia. The Vampire King had used it less than a dozen times across history, killing Committee members, heroes, and rivals with its power. The fact that he'd chosen to use it against us showed he was getting desperate. It also proved he'd not only survived the plane's destruction but also was awake and active.

"You know this guy?" Shannon asked, looking down.

"It's Dracula's favorite hatchet man."

"Score one for Team Living, then."

"If you want to look at it that way," I said. "We need to leave."

"I wouldn't worry about it," Shannon said, surprising me. "It came through my dreams. I was able to force it to manifest. If Dracula's goons were capable of following it, they would have been here an hour ago."

"It's been dead for over an hour?" I asked, surprised.

"Yeah, you slept like you were dead. I thought you were under a curse."

"I was, after a fashion." I stopped in mid-sentence. This next bit of conversation was going to be awkward.

"Derek ..."

"Yeah," I said, taking a deep breath. There was no way around this and it was better to just fess up while I still could. "Bloody Mary tried to seduce me last night."

Shannon looked between us. "Excuse me? When? Did she sneak in while I was asleep? Because I'm usually not a light sleeper. Especially for sex."

"In my dreams."

"Uh-huh," Shannon said. "So, did you get . . . seduced?"

"No," I said, sighing. "I pushed her away."

"Why?"

I wondered if she was playing with me. "Most girlfriends wouldn't be asking that. They'd either be upset with me because no one likes to think about their partner cheating, even if they turn down the opportunity, or happy I told you about it. You seem curious."

Shannon put her hands on her hips. "Derek, we've both slept with other people since we started our relationship."

"Yes, for business."

"I'm going to question that. I've seen some of the girls you've hooked up with for business. You're telling me you wouldn't sleep with Ashley if you ever saw her again?"

"This conversation is going in a very strange direction."

"I just want to know where we stand. Last year you wanted to start a relationship knowing I was a succubus and our jobs wouldn't allow us to have a traditional heteronormative single-partner relationship."

I realized what she was asking. "You want to know where we stand."

"Do I?" Shannon said. "Maybe I was just trying to say I don't care if you boff the demon."

"Boff?" I asked.

"Shut up, it's a real word."

"I don't believe you don't care," I said, getting up and walking toward her. "I think you care a great deal."

"What I feel and what I don't doesn't matter much, does it? The same for you. Derek, if you have a demon in your head that wants to bang you and it'll keep you alive against Dracula, I'm all for you taking her against the metaphysical table. Anything that prevents you from getting yourself killed out there."

"I love you, Shannon. I don't want to be with anyone else."

Shannon snorted.

"Okay, now this is getting insulting."

Shannon looked over her shoulder. "I'm not trying to insult you. It's just we've both been forced to listen to the other person have sex over the past year. We've had to use every resource at our disposal to try and bring peace. That's not going to change. Plus, you've got a bunch of girlfriends in your past. I've got a bunch of lovers, too. They're going to come up. Love like they talk about in movies just isn't in the cards."

I tried to figure out a good response. I came up blank. "You know, Hollywood has a lot to answer for. Movies never depict romantic conversations going this way. They've never depicted a realistic marriage or long-term relationship."

"Are we getting married?" Shannon asked, looking panicked.

"Would you—" I started to ask.

"Don't." Shannon pointed at my chest. "Don't ask me that. *Don't even think it.* Backpedal like Godzilla is coming after us and we can't turn around."

"What an odd metaphor," I said.

Shannon slumped her shoulders, defeated. "Derek, have I told you about my past?"

"Yes, though you've lied about it constantly."

"Only about my appearance, where I was from, and the fact that I was a supernatural sex monster."

"You're not a monster."

"I am," Shannon said, giving a sad smile. "I was raised by my mother until I hit puberty. I was always special. People, especially men, paid an inordinate amount of attention to me. My mother was able to protect me from anything . . . untoward . . . happening, but it wasn't much of a danger anyway. Even if they were attracted to me, most men aren't rapists waiting to pounce."

"I'll inform the media."

Shannon glared at me. "When I was twelve, my father came back for me. As far as my mother knew, he was just some guy she'd shacked up with for a feverish week of booze and sex. He was an incubus, though, and I was a succubus coming into my power. Do you know what happened?"

I did. I'd read her file just as she'd read mine. "I have a suspicion. I know this isn't a comfortable topic for you."

Shannon snorted. "Comfortable isn't the right word for it, no. He showed me how to kill. When you're young, moral frameworks like religion or law are ephemeral things compared to sex and pleasure. At that age, my hormones and the rush from feeding made me think my father's words were right. How could there be anything wrong with killing and rape when they felt so good?"

"While not one to cast stones, perhaps this isn't the best conversation to be had after my confession of eternal love," I said.

Shannon stared at me, her eyes full of long-repressed sadness. "It's the perfect time to have this conversation. I did unforgivable things, Derek, and I did them for years."

"You were a child," I said. "Titus is responsible for all that you did. Not you."

I'd done research on Shannon's father, one of the last pure-blooded lilin left on Earth. According to rumor, Titus was the son of Tiamat-Abaddon and Lucifer himself, though I suspected that was hyperbole. All the Red Room could say for certain was he'd shown up in the sixteenth century and had been fathering lilin ever since. It was his modus apparandi to corrupt them to Satanism (and not the Anton Lavey kind) before unleashing them on the rest of the world's peoples for shit and giggles.

Shannon looked down at the floor. "That's not his real name, you know. It's just the one he chose to go by. God, what a pretentious fuck."

"You killed him, though," I said.

"Yeah, maybe." Shannon didn't sound sure.

"Maybe?" That was a surprise to me. Shannon had never indicated in any of our conversations her father might still be around.

"My father was a master of lies. When he finally asked me to do too much, when the weight of all my sins started registering, I turned on him and broke his neck before leaving him in a burning church to die. The fact is, there's no telling what I remember happening actually happened. He had the power to manipulate my mind."

"But incubi can only manipulate the minds of those they—oh," I said.

"Yeah," Shannon said.

"Then you . . ." I trailed off.

"Do you want to go there?" Shannon asked.

I did not. "Not in the slightest. In fact, I'd like to drive a screwdriver in my head and pour bleach down the hole to burn away the image. I'd also like to find him, dead or alive, and put him in a wood chipper. Alive, if possible."

"Thank you. That's kind of sweet," Shannon said.

"Well, I am odd, and sometimes I've been known to be sweet," I said, paraphrasing Bill from *Kill Bill*.

Shannon snorted. "Says the guy who swears by video games he watches on the internet."

"It's a new medium for art," I said. "It's going to be huge eventually. We need to get in on the ground floor of this."

Shannon rolled her eyes. "Derek!"

I raised my hands in surrender. "Sorry for digressing. So, what you're saying is you don't think you deserve to be loved."

"I'm saying I have issues, and maybe you should look elsewhere if you want the white picket fence," Shannon said.

"Yes, because the possessed spy with an evil sword is the white picket fence type," I said.

Shannon frowned. "You can drive out the demon and get rid of the sword. I can't get rid of the fact that I'm a demonic—"

"You're who I want." I got up and took her by the hands. "I've been with a lot of people over the years. My psychotic ex-wife, Ashley, and you are the only ones who have meant anything to me. In the end, I have a chance of being happy with you. I'm never going to let you go of you, past actions or not."

"Even if we have . . . complications in the future," Shannon said.

"You're not just talking about having sex with one of your old lovers or to get intelligence, are you?" I asked.

Shannon had done so six times in the past year. I'd done it five. I'd been more surprised by my lack of jealousy than anything else. Indeed, I was bothered by how little the whole thing had troubled me and was concerned at how little she seemed disturbed by my sleeping around—even for a good cause. It had been the cause of at least three of our fights last year. Whatever we were, however much I loved Shannon, we were not a normal couple.

"No," Shannon said. "There're other reasons I'm not comfortable with total intimacy."

"Well, I can't have kids and you don't want any," I said, having been cursed by my ex-wife. It might have been broken or it might not have been. I hadn't bothered to check under the circumstances.

Shannon sighed. "I'm talking about the fact that we're both murderers. Do we deserve to be happy?"

I paused. "That's a question I can't answer. I know it's not our place to judge whether we can be happy, though, merely to experience it."

"There's also the fact that either of us could die at any given time. You're a Committee member, but you're no safer now than when you were a field agent. I'm not the type to hang up my catsuit and pistols either."

"I don't want a housewife who looks like a model. I want you."

Shannon raised an eyebrow. "Wait, are you saying I look like a model or are you saying I don't?"

"Shannon …"

She grinned. "'Cause I'm saying I'm far better built than the majority of those twigs. I admit, I may use my shape-shifting to pad out a few areas, but—"

"You're not going to derail this conversation."

"I don't want you to get killed, Derek."

"I don't want you to get killed, either. The best way to do that is to make sure the two of us always have each other's back."

"After this, we're going to find an island somewhere, get drunk, and have a ton of sex."

"It sounds like a plan. Thankfully, we're in the Caribbean already."

Shannon wrapped her arms around me and the two of us shared another passionate kiss. We probably would have had sex again if there hadn't been a dead body lying three feet away. Bloody Mary had tried to entice me with those kinds of images, but I wasn't a sadistic sociopath turned on by bloodshed.

Yet.

Pulling away, I instead focused on something else. Something we needed to do. "Let's check what's on the flash drive."

Shannon looked disappointed but nodded. "I want to know what's so damned valuable myself."

CHAPTER TWENTY-TWO

After rolling up the djinn's body in a bed sheet and stuffing it in a closet, I sat down in the building's study to examine Christopher's flash drive. The study was a pleasant-looking office filled with little pink trolls and a roll-top desk, which was incongruous with the fact that its former owner was an Vampire Nation commodore.

I was uncomfortable with Shannon's belief that we were safe in a house someone had just tried to murder us in, but there was no safe place in Nassau. I had to trust her judgment and see what was worth killing me for. Not that the Vampire Nation didn't have plenty of reasons already.

On the desk was Shannon's laptop, which was an Athena 9000 made by Pantheon Corp. It had the processing power of a supercomputer as well as mystical protections designed to prevent it from being hacked by anyone outside of the Red Room. Sticking in the flash drive, I found the contents of the folder were quantum-encrypted and had more defenses around them than the NSA or Division One. A single box appeared on the screen with a request for a password.

Unlike how Hollywood depicted hacking, it was impossible to get inside this sort of program without the code sign. I'd have one shot at guessing it before the flash drive's contents were deleted. I could *feel* the magical traps lying around it, ones designed to explode at the slightest tampering. I was getting tired of Christopher's tests.

"What sort of password would Christopher think only I would get," I muttered aloud, thinking of all the private jokes we shared. There was the name of the Hong Kong agent in Vegas we'd both been with, favorite movies, and countersigns we'd used on missions. In the end, it came down to what sort of man Christopher thought I was.

I typed in the word "PASSWORD," then hit enter. The screen faded away to the picture of Christopher's face. He was wearing the same clothes from the ski lodge, which made me think this message had been recorded right before he left for Aspen. The background was a digital electronic landscape, stretching to infinity.

"Password? Really?" Christopher said, staring. "That's how little you think of me?"

"What is the password?" I asked.

"Anything Derek Hawthorne types in," Christopher said. "It's safer that way."

I frowned. "So, is this you or some sort of interactive program?"

"An invention of my own. It's sort of a digital homunculus. It's my memories, personality, and beliefs but with no real will. It exists to answer your questions before deleting itself—leaving all of the information inside to use as you see fit."

"Like what was in the Bloodsword," I said.

"Yes," Christopher confirmed.

"Why not tell me this when we first talked?" I asked.

"I gave you the Bloodsword to give you leverage against Dracula. Adding my plans to it would result in him getting access to them if you decided to trade it back or lost it. Please, tell me you didn't kill anyone with it."

"A couple of dozen, it seems. Vampires, all of them."

Christopher's digital face scrunched up. "I see."

"The Vampire Nation is a clear and present threat to the world. I won't back down from them due to intimidation or because it's safe."

"I know, Derek. It makes you the perfect person to understand this information."

"Pardon?"

"The real me, the flesh and blood undead me, is mesmerized. All vampires since Dracula started enslaving his descendants are bent to his will. As a creation of magic, I'm not subject to the same mystical compulsions. Thus, I can look back on myself and say—I am brainwashed. It's why I need your help to stop me from destroying everything I hold dear, however unwittingly."

I wondered why the "other" Christopher in the Bloodsword reacted differently from this one. It had been more interested in guiding me to Nassau. "You're a machine evaluating yourself and now moving against the person you share the memories of. I find that creepy as fuck."

"Not a fan of artificial intelligence?" Christopher asked.

"I'm afraid Lucy will invent something that escapes into the internet and destroys us all. I'm not here to discuss things with a machine," I said.

"It's nevertheless true. Decades after your personality has been set in stone by the mesmerism, you become the person they try and make you into being—loyal, psychotic, and insane. This means that not all vampires are entirely responsible for their actions because of this mesmerism. The undead just need a small amount of blood to survive, and there's tens of thousands who deserve to be freed from their master's control rather than exterminated."

"War is not something that tends to show mercy." I wasn't about to reveal the Red Room's plans to go to war with the Vampire Nation.

"Total war is also an abomination. I say this as someone whose parents experienced the horrors of the Imperial Japanese," Christopher said.

"What have you got to show me?" I asked, looking at him straight in the eyes.

"Something that will change everything," Christopher said.

Christopher's digital face disappeared, and I was left with a terabyte of files to look over. There were videos, thousands of pages of documents, pictures, and confidential reports that the House had concealed not just from the agency at large, but also from me. Despite being a member of the Committee, I hadn't seen any of it. What I did see chilled my blood.

It took almost five hours to study the material enough to get a sense of it, and I would have to spend weeks reviewing it to grasp it all. Nevertheless, the material within was damning, and if it was a forgery, it was a very good forgery. There were several times I wished I could have consulted with Christopher's digital homunculus, but his words about it deleting itself appeared to be true. I regretted that, because there were still a lot of questions I wanted answers to.

I was writing down notes on a yellow pad when Shannon walked in, having changed into blue jeans and a white t-shirt. She was sipping a mug of coffee and looking at me with concern. "So, anything interesting?"

I stared at the screen before closing my eyes, giving them a chance to rest. "Yes. Division Zero."

Shannon snorted. "Division Zero is a myth. The kind of thing bored agents discuss because we're all a bunch of paranoid megalomaniacs."

"And sex addicts, don't forget that," I said, giving a half smile before frowning again. "It would seem Division Zero is not as mythical as people believe. It's one of the many products of Protocol Zero being put into effect—kind of obvious in hindsight."

"An entire division of the Red Room exists to study brainwashing?" I asked, having almost forgotten about the reason Christopher had involved me in all this Caribbean vampirates business.

"Yes. You know the CIA's psychic experiments?" Christopher asked.

"Project: Stargate?" Shannon suggested.

"Got it in one," Christopher said.

Project: Stargate was a program conducted by the CIA and DIA from the 1970s to 1995. Officially, the program was terminated after experts concluded it provided no useful data and its leaders were likely tampering with reports. The Red Room ran the project from behind the scenes, and any real psychics were shuffled off to the Black Room. The CIA still got their money's worth, as it provided actionable intelligence during the height of the Cold War. Division One had broken a lot of neutrality agreements to gain access to Washington funding, providing both actionable intelligence and mystical assistance to the United States during the Cold War. It was one of the reasons other Divisions hated us until I'd forced us all to work together and gave everyone a mutual target to hate.

"According to these documents, they stumbled onto how to duplicate vampire mesmerism just before Project: Stargate was shut down. Their first experiments were crude but capable of being non-mystical indoctrination techniques, the kinds cults and quack psychotherapists used to use. Combining the two, it became possible to completely change a person's loyalty. Given enough time, anyone could do a one-eighty on their beliefs. Not to mention psychic surgery."

"Psychic surgery?" Shannon asked.

"A psychic technique popularized in the Philippines and Spain before the Red Room denounced it as a fraud. Mostly because it was. Basically, it's literally conducting surgery with your mind and dissolving tumors as well as sealing injuries. Only one psychic in a hundred can do it. Andy Kaufman died because he relied on it to cure his cancer."

"Damn, I was hoping he'd faked his death. The Red Room practices this?"

"Division Zero's version is more like psychic neurosurgery combined with lobotomies. You dig a hole in someone's brain and fill it up with whatever you want. There are subtler uses too, including using these techniques to remove soldier's capacity for PTSD and their fear of monsters."

Shannon snorted. "Pfft! That sounds like a disaster waiting to happen."

"It's been obligatory for new recruits to the Black Room since 2001," I said.

Shannon stared. "What?"

"Remember those mandatory health spa trips they started enforcing last year? They use soft music and blinking lights to make sure we drink the House Kool-Aid."

Shannon clenched her fists. "Oh, those bastards."

"Eh, it didn't work on me or you, according to these documents. We're listed with an X on our ability to respond to the treatments. I'm not sure I disapprove, either. I saw a lot of people go into these treatment centers a complete wreck only to emerge with the ability to live normal lives."

"Except they were sent right back into combat thereafter."

She had a point. "Yeah, they were. Much like in World War 1, hospitals existed to patch up agents before putting them back into the field."

I pointed at the screen before me, showing a secret communication from the House in the late seventies. "The Project: Stargate research helped complete the House's ultimate goal of Protocol Zero—the destruction of all vampires everywhere."

"That doesn't sound *too* evil. Individuals aside, vampires are pretty bad."

"Protocol Ten was 'try to figure out how to kill all vampires with plague.' Protocol Eight was 'try and figure out how to prevent shape changers from being born', Protocol Seven was 'try and figure out how to prevent naturally occurring magic and how to induce it in test subjects.' Protocol Thirteen is 'make Pantheon Corp the largest corporation on Earth by starting wars', which is where Truman broke with them. They're not a good bunch of rules. I knew about most of them, but they concealed Zero from me. Probably because they were still doing it and it wasn't a money-sink like the others."

"We really need to stop making jokes about the House being the Illuminati because it's not funny anymore."

"No kidding," I said. "Division Zero has a giant research center devoted to this—called, appropriately enough, Camp Zero. Which, if you can't tell, shows these guys aren't very imaginative when it comes to naming."

"So there's a base somewhere where traitorous Red Room and House agents get sent to have their brains picked apart?"

I nodded. "Yep. Camp Zero is located a hundred and fifty miles away on an island black site. It's concealed from the rest of the world but has easy access to ships and helicopters carrying prisoners for quote-unquote treatment."

"Jesus Christ," Shannon said, appalled.

"It gets worse."

"Magical Guantanamo Bay gets worse?"

"Two and a half years ago, they managed to achieve consistent results for breaking not only agents with lingering loyalty to the Red Room, but also enemy agents. They developed a ninety-eight-percent-effective means of creating sleeper agents. Full-on *Manchurian Candidate* stuff where vampires, Bloodslaves, werewolves, humans, and so on could be made into unwitting pawns. They started inserting these agents throughout the Vampire Nation and its territories and have been using them to weaken them ever since."

"We're back to this being sorta bad."

"It's very bad. They've started wars, terrorist plots, and even financial crises to weaken the Vampire Nation's material resources. According to these reports, the vampires are a paper tiger now and in a perfect position to be eradicated. It just cost the lives of two hundred thousand people."

Shannon stared. "Wow."

"Mission accomplished," I said, disgusted. I looked at her mug of coffee. "May I?"

Shannon handed it over and I took a sip. "Knock yourself out. I added a little something extra. Blame the Irish in me."

"You're Scottish," I said, taking a drink. "My father is the Committee member supervising it."

Shannon just stared at me. "You can keep the coffee. Wow."

I took a long drink. I needed it. "Yeah, just when you think my opinion can't get any lower. I can kind of, maybe, see the justification for creating saboteurs with mind control. I don't approve of it, but it's no different than killing people. Doing it on your fellow agents, though, is unforgivable."

"Why didn't he order it done to Ashley, then?" Shannon asked.

"Excuse me?" I replied, confused.

"You said there's this place to send traitors to be brainwashed, and he runs it. Last year, your father told you he never believed for a second you'd kill Ashley. Hell, he's probably the person who sent Penny to meet you in the car."

"Are you *defending* my father?" I asked.

"Just confused," Shannon said.

I thought about what she was suggesting. "I don't know. The father I've come to know is very different from the one I grew up with, and all my family tells me he is. My Uncle Talbot described Nathan Hawthorne as one of the greatest heroes of

World War 2. Like a Pacific Theater version of Captain America. He was always a good father, supportive and nurturing. Then he ordered me to kill my fiancé, got two of my siblings killed and a third possessed, and has been neck-deep in the House's secret projects ever since before I joined the Committee."

"We're not exactly saints either. I don't mean to tell you how to live your life, but maybe you should give him the benefit of the doubt," Shannon said.

"Because he's my father?" I said, lightly mocking the idea.

"Because I don't want you getting yourself killed trying to do the right thing. I'd rather have you by my side, alive and corrupt, than try to take on the second-most powerful member of the Committee. Your dad or not."

"Says the woman on a mission from God." I meant that literally. Shannon had been directed by an Archangel to join the House. I still found that hard to believe.

"I'm a Christian existentialist. Nietzsche said, 'God is dead', but what he should have said was he gave us a mind to figure out what is righteous and what is wrong."

"I'm a Daoist because I know I may never have the answers, but I'm always looking for them."

"You're so sexy when you're philosophical," Shannon said, smirking. "So, what do you plan to do?"

"I need to break into Camp Zero and get proof the House is brainwashing its own agents."

"That seems like the opposite of not getting yourself killed."

I leaned back in my chair and crossed my arms. "There's nothing I can do about the war against the vampires that's coming up. Even if I believed Christopher's statement about the majority of them being mesmerized, I'm not sure I should do anything. There's a difference between killing normal people and those cursed with a disease that requires them to feed on the living. I can, however, put a serious wrench in the plans of the Committee to use brainwashing on the House's members. If I can get photographic evidence and distribute it to the House's members, they'll be forced to discontinue its use—perhaps on everyone."

"They'll kill you for that."

"They might. They'll have to catch me first." I paused. "I also need to see if I can secure Christopher's wife's freedom."

"You still want to help him with that? After all he's put you through?"

I snorted before saying sarcastically, "Not really. However, I'm just cursed with being a nice guy."

Shannon snorted.

"May I borrow your cellphone?"

"Sure." Shannon pulled it out and tossed it to me.

I pulled out a connection cord and attached it to the computer before dialing Penny's number.

This was going to be one awkward conversation.

CHAPTER TWENTY-THREE

The image that appeared on the computer was not of my sister, but of Lucy Danvers-Hawthorne. The White Room scientist was lying in bed with her eyes half shut and wearing a Hello Kitty shirt (Kitty having fangs and wearing goth clothing).

"Derek?" Lucy asked, looking half awake.

"It's three in the afternoon," I said, staring at her.

"Not in Paris, it isn't. I'm attending a conference hosted by your sister on mind-operated machinery."

"Which sister?" I asked, thinking about how many had joined the White Room.

"Hoshi," I asked.

"When we're about to go to war with the vampires?" I asked, offended. "Shouldn't you be preparing for DEFCON 1 or something? Hell, didn't I ask Penny to come here?"

"Yeah, but your guy never showed," Lucy said. "So she came back. Also, there were rumors you were on a killing spree so she assumed you had it under control."

I felt a headache coming on. "I see."

Shannon stepped behind me and waved. "Hi, Lucy."

"Hi," Lucy said, waving back. It was obvious she still wasn't awake yet.

"Could you—" I started to ask her to get my twin.

Lucy blinked, as if now aware of what was going on. "Derek? You're alive!"

"No kidding," I said. "I hadn't noticed."

"What?" I heard my sister's voice on the other side of the bed. "Derek?"

Penny bolted over the side of mattress and grabbed the side of the computer. My sister was wearing a red shirt with a black anarchy symbol on it. "What the hell, Derek? Where have you been?"

"Remember when we were sixteen playing Shadowrun and my Orc decker was possessed by a spirit of rage?" I quoted an old tabletop game session from back when I was a moody goth kid with no friends outside his family. As compared to a moody adult one with three.

Penny stared. "You've been on a rampage across Nassau, killing vampires?"

"Yeah," I said. "Pretty much."

Shannon rubbed the bridge of her nose. "Why on Earth am I stuck dating the world's only geek superspy?"

"He is, by far, not the only one," Lucy corrected. "I mean, look at Penny."

"I need your help to do something treasonous."

"Okay," Penny said, nodding.

"Well, that was easy," I said, taking a deep breath. I explained to her the situation.

Penny stared. "Wow, our world becomes more and more a dystopia every day."

I was about to make a Shannon and Molly Millions comparison, but I decided not to. There were too many pop culture references in this mission already. "So, will you help?"

"I said okay," Penny replied, shrugging. "The question is how we're going to be able to get inside this place."

"I have a few ideas," I said, thinking about Malcolm and wondering if he could bring backup.

Lucy, meanwhile, looked sick. "I can't believe the House would do something like this to us."

"You haven't been paying much attention, have you?" Shannon asked.

"Well, I know we do questionable things, but we're supposed to be doing it for the greater good. This . . . isn't."

I nodded, thinking about what I'd read. "Everyone's line for what is permissible and what's not is different. Altering a mind is not any less moral than killing someone. Likewise, the Committee has never considered its agents more than disposable tools for the enforcement of its agenda. We've always been expendable. This is just us being expendable in a different way."

"But you're on the Committee . . ." Lucy trailed off.

"I can't say I'm surprised," Penny said, her stare cold and unfeeling. "I've seen too many agents die and found out too much shit from you, Derek, to believe the Committee has any fond feelings for us. We need to expose this to the rest of the House before they end up micro-chipping our brains and having us singing show tunes while we hunt draugr."

"I hate draugr," Lucy said, grinding her teeth.

"Did Christopher include blueprints for the facility?" Shannon asked.

I nodded. "He did. He never got to visit it but found the original contractors who'd been mesmerized into forgetting they built it. He doesn't have any insight into who is guarding the place, but I suspect they'll use Sons of Mars private military contractors."

"Alec is heading them off now," Penny said, causing me to do a double take.

"How the hell . . ." I paused. "Listen, it doesn't matter. What matters is it's going to be well guarded, and stealth will be paramount."

"The best solution for this would be to get in, take pictures, and leave without discovery. From there, we can figure out a way to cover up our involvement in revealing it. Maybe blame it on Christopher," Shannon said, folding her arms.

"Cold, Shannon."

"So was setting you up to die," Shannon said.

She had a point there. "The best way I think we can get to the facility is with magic-resistant scuba gear, a fusion torch, and some chameleon pills. I'd like to be able to tap into their security feeds, but I'm not sure if we've got any equipment up to snuff given this seems to be top-of-the-line White Room surveillance."

Lucy snorted. "Please, like the White Room ever puts into use the best stuff. Everyone knows we hold back the best until we're done with the next generation."

"I wasn't aware. That seems like a very bad idea, and we're going to have a talk after this mission."

Lucy blanched. "Oops."

"I can get you all the equipment you need, as long as you agree to take me on the mission with you," Penny said, smiling.

"He's going to say no, you know," Shannon said, snorting.

"I don't care if he says no now. All that matters now is that he says yes," Penny said, confident.

"I feel like this conversation doesn't need me," I replied, looking between them.

"You'd be right," Penny replied. "You've tried to shut me out of this mission from the very beginning. This despite its dire importance to the House and the thousands of agents in the field who are going to get compromised if you don't find a way to prevent this war with the vamps."

I looked down at the keyboard. "I'm not sure anything I find at Camp Zero is going to make a difference, whether we go to war with the House or not. Christopher was our last chance at coming to a truce, and it turned out he wasn't in any position to bargain."

"I'm sorry," Shannon said. "I never would have arranged this meeting if I thought he couldn't be trusted. I just wanted . . . not to be the only good monster."

"You're not a monster," I said, wondering if preventing the war had ever even registered with Christopher. Probably not. This seemed more and more like it had been all a diversion in hopes of finding out what happened to his wife. "I want you here, Penny."

Penny stared. "What, really?"

I didn't want to tell her about Bloody Mary over teleconference. My ability to fool my sister was nonexistent, though, so I decided to come clean. "Yeah, I may have a slight demon problem."

"There's a sexy redheaded demon in his brain," Shannon said.

"Other than you?" Penny said.

"Oh, you tease," Shannon said.

I rolled my eyes. "I wasn't kidding about the possession bit, Penny. I've got it under control for now, but I have no idea how long that's going to last."

Penny's expression was even. "How bad is it?"

"Not Stephen bad, but she's powerful. I don't think she's strong enough to take me over. She could do so before when I was half dead, but I'm recovered now. I *think* she wants me to work with her voluntarily."

Penny wrinkled her brow. "Unusual behavior for a demon. They tend to go for the easy domination."

"Know many demons?" Shannon asked.

"Too many," Penny said, sighing. "Hazards of being a witch."

"I need you to meet me with the equipment today. We're running out of time," I said, biting my lip. "If we're going to war with the Vampire Nation soon, it's probable any captives they have will be destroyed."

"If they haven't already," Shannon said behind me.

She was right. "Yeah."

"Expect me soon," Penny said, nodding. "Do you want lethal or non-lethal weapons?"

"Penny!" Lucy said, shocked.

"Non-lethal," I said, not missing a beat. "I'm not interested in killing people on my own side, even if that's going to be a clue to who is spying on them."

"Suit yourself," Penny said, before turning her head. "Lucy, I'm going to need you to delete this conference from the record after we're done."

"Red Room conference calls are already impossible to decrypt except by me and six other people, but will do," Lucy said, staring at me. "Good luck, Derek. Don't get yourself killed trying to do the right thing. We don't have enough people doing that already."

My connection to Lucy and Penny evaporated, and I was left alone in the study with Shannon. We were taking a big step in terms of confronting the corruption at the heart of the House. The problem was it was very possible that doing so could end up getting us both killed—and all for nothing if we failed.

"You know, you don't have to support me through this." I stared at the blank screen.

"I'm going to pretend you didn't say that. It's better for us if I do."

"I just don't want you getting killed."

"As opposed to you doing it after your proclamation of eternal love."

"The timing is pretty awful, isn't it?"

"Men love proclaiming love before going off to war or certain death because they know it's going to make their girlfriend or object of affection feel guilty if they die. It's why so many girls cheat on their spouses during this time."

"That's . . . terrible."

"Hey, I just call 'em like I see 'em."

Getting up, I turned to face Shannon. "I'm not comfortable with the way this mission is leading. So far, it's been following someone else's trail of breadcrumbs, one after the other. I can't help but shake the feeling this is all a setup of some kind."

"Then don't go." Shannon shrugged. "No one's making you do anything."

"Aren't they? I can't leave this alone either. The Committee has been hiding things from me from the beginning. They're a reprehensible bunch of old wizards and witches who have as much respect for me as the Secretary of Education during wartime."

"There have been some pretty badass Secretaries of Education."

I gave a half smirk. Then I frowned. "The pieces don't fit yet. Christopher brings me a fake peace offering and sends me on the trail of Protocol Zero. Except Christopher has a flash drive full of information about it not a hundred and fifty miles from Nassau. Furthermore, Dracula was waiting for me halfway down the road to the airport. Christopher's mental homunculus says he's been brainwashed. Then there's the Bloodsword, which is an object Dracula should never have been willing to part with but is ready and willing to serve me."

"It does sound like a setup."

"I have a number of theories; the most prominent right now is this entire thing is an attempt to strike at the Red Room from the inside. The Wazir tried to get me on the Committee because he believed I'd serve as his catspaw against them."

"And we killed the Wazir. If you think Christopher or

Dracula are going to be using you, I'm guessing they didn't learn from his example."

"The confusing part is why now," I said, walking to the window and looking out through the shades.

"What do you mean?"

"It's been centuries since the last time the House and vampires fought a war against each other. The result of which, I remind you, was the destruction of every vampire in Europe. The House has bigger enemies to worry about than the undead, yet what they're describing here is total war with complete disregard for civilian casualties. Why does Division Zero want a war, and why are the vampires pushing back when they look hopelessly outmatched with this new alliance?"

"Search me," Penny said. "Politics aren't my strong suit. You're the devious mastermind."

"I'm actually pretty crap at this mastermind thing," I said, chuckling. "I'm good at unraveling the plots of others, but coming up with them? No, I'm a pretty clear point A to point B kind of guy."

I kept looking for a mastermind, and none of my suspects were matching up. Dracula might want to start a war with the House, but only if he'd win. Christopher didn't strike me as good enough to pull something off. He was close, but not quite talented enough to imagine something on this scale.

My father was capable of pulling something like this off, and the destruction of all vampires would benefit the House. However, my father never displayed any real desire to take the fight to the superhumans. He was a more "status quo is God" sort of individual, and anything that disrupted the supernatural balance of power was to be avoided.

Annabelle Jones. Bloody Mary's voice echoed in my mind. *You are missing the obvious.*

"Ah, you're back," I muttered aloud. "I was wondering how long it would take you to manifest again."

"Mary's returned? Good to know," Shannon said. "Wait, was she there when we were having sex?"

"No," I said.

Yes, Mary said in my head, her voice containing no trace of anger despite my earlier assault. *No need to lie, my love. It was an enjoyable experience. We should link minds, so I can participate next time. You'll find my style a bit baroque but quite pleasurable.*

"She mentioned Christopher's wife." I ignored Mary's innuendo.

You wished to find a devious mastermind, one capable of manipulating not just the House and the Vampire Nation but also its leaders—veteran Machiavellian manipulators like Dracula and your father. I say you need to look no further than Annabelle Jones. The woman who engineered the conflict that destroyed the vampires of Europe and came close to destroying her entire species. Bloody Mary seemed almost offended I hadn't figured it out for myself. *If you had given into my seductions, I would have presented you with the truth of this conspiracy upfront. She is the mastermind behind this, and you will find her at Camp Zero, working against her own as she did centuries ago.*

Given what I'd learned from Malcolm, it shouldn't have surprised me that Annabelle Jones was working with the Red Room against the Vampire Nation. That meant this entire mission was quixotic. Christopher had been chasing after the individuals who'd kidnapped his wife, only for her to be there voluntarily.

"Does Christopher know?" I asked.

No, Mary replied.

Fuck, I said, wondering what I was going to tell him.

The truth, I hope, Mary replied. *Of course, this doesn't mean you shouldn't go to Camp Zero.*

"Why? Christopher's wife is in no danger. I just need to track him down and tell him he got played," I said, shaking my head. "I can inform the rest of the Red Room about what I know without having to break into one of the most secure locations on the planet."

"You know, it's weird watching you have a one-sided conversation. Looking at you, one might be tempted to say you're crazy."

I looked at Shannon, biting back an acid response. She'd been joking, but this was not a funny situation. "I'm not Stephen. I can fight this."

Indeed, I half wondered why my reaction wasn't more severe. Most agents would have been freaking the hell out by the thought of being possessed. Normally, I would have been. Yet there was something almost comforting about Bloody Mary's presence. Something familiar. I couldn't put it into words.

Why? Bloody Mary replied. *Simple, Derek. Annabelle Jones isn't just maneuvering the Vampire Nation to be destroyed. She's manipulating the House, too. By tomorrow morning, your organization and family will be burning along with every vampire in the world.*

"And you couldn't have told me this earlier?"

You didn't ask.

CHAPTER TWENTY-FOUR

"How do you know this?" I said, sounding calmer than I was. Bloody Mary's statement that Annabelle Jones was going to destroy both the House and the Vampire Nation had my complete attention. Which was surprising since I'd intended to start tuning out my demonic friend.

I do not know, Bloody Mary said, her astral voice low. *I used the blood of the vampires you killed to work powerful divinations in order to find out the truth of what was vexing you. However, the truth has always been elusive to those who seek to plumb the future. I might have had more luck if you did the rituals instead of me through you. You have a hint of the Sight. Just a hint, at least before I enhanced your magical potential.*

"Show me what you saw," I said, tightening my fists. "Now."

As you wish, my love. The last words were playful, almost mocking. It was the first time she'd shown any annoyance at my earlier attack. Of course, given she was a demon, it might as well have been a promise of eternal vengeance. Little did I realize the vision she was about to show me was every bit of payback she'd ever need.

It came rushing like a flood into my brain, feeling every bit as horrific as Dracula's assault on my mind and then some. Pure white-hot agonizing pain forced me to my knees as my mind was opened up to pathways to the future man was never meant to travel.

I saw vampires descend like a plague of locusts into Division One, Division Two, and a hundred more of our bases. The identities of every single Red Room agent in the world were compromised and posted on the internet, vast rewards promised for their murder to any supernatural entity who could kill them. Hired murderers tracked down not just the House's personnel, but also their families and children.

Dhampir and blood slave mercenaries slaughtered children in their cribs after slitting the throats of their caretakers. Car bombs set by longstanding anti-Red Room terrorist organizations blew up supporters in Congress, British Parliament, the Russian oligarchy, and the Chinese Communist Party. Dozens of organizations were used as pawns by Dracula and his allies, turning the world's governments against us.

The Red Room fought back with everything it had but was too weakened by the initial assault. Its allies against the Vampire Nation turned against them as surely as they had the undead. In the end, the massive war destroyed the one thing the House was designed to protect. With its agents dead and its influenced crippled, no one was there to protect humanity from the Truth.

Knowledge of the supernatural leaked out into the media, and the world descended into chaos as everything the public thought they knew was revealed to be a lie. Those House members who were left were hunted down, arrested, put to trial, and executed. Penny, Lucy, Shannon, Alec, and Talbot all died before my eyes, killed by the so-called normal people we'd spent our life protecting. What was left after their deaths I couldn't see, because their fates blinded me to further visions.

I lay on the ground, holding my head and trying to force the pain from my mind. Every muscle in my body twitched while I struggled for breath. A cold sweat covered me. Shannon held my hand, sticking her steel hard fingers in my mouth to keep me from biting off my tongue.

You're welcome. Bloody Mary laughed. *Don't banish me again.*

"Derek," Shannon started to speak. "Are you—"

"No," I said, sitting up and coughing. "I'm not okay."

"I was going to ask in need of medical care. There's a hospital nearby."

I shook my head, coughing some more. "No hospital."

I squeezed Shannon's hand for comfort, making sure she was still alive. The things the mob had done to her had been unspeakable. But then again, they always were. Mankind lost fifty IQ points when they entered a crowd and gained ten pounds of viciousness in a five-pound bag.

As you can see, something bad is going to happen, Bloody Mary said, her voice flippant. *I'm not sure how the war with the vampires is going to lead to these events, but they will occur. You thought the vampires were going to lose badly. You were worried about genocide. In fact, you should have looked to your own house.*

I thought for a second. Climbing to my feet, I maneuvered my way back to the chair in front of the computer and plopped down. "I saw a vision of the House destroyed."

"Yeah, I guessed you saw something. How?" Shannon asked, filling her coffee mug with water from the nearby bathroom and handing it to me.

I took the mug and closed my eyes, trying to interpret the images I'd seen. "The House's greatest advantage has always been its secrecy. If any one of its enemies were to know its agents' identities and the location of its divisions, they'd be able to mount an endless series of attacks. Vampires can replace their numbers faster than we can replace our operatives. The thing is, they *don't* know who our agents are and where our bases are located. If they did, we wouldn't have a major advantage," I spoke aloud, slowly climbing to my feet. "What my vision showed was a compromise in our security."

"How bad a compromise?" Shannon said, helping me up. "Are we talking hacked files, a snitch, what?"

"Like if someone were able to kidnap my father and drain every bit of intelligence from his mind. There are a few other Committee members who know enough to engender that sort of apocalypse." I hesitated to use the word "apocalypse," but since it involved my family, I wasn't about to scrimp on the hyperbole.

"You think your father would be the target?"

"He's the only thing related to Division Zero that could cause such a reversal of the House's fortunes." I bit my lip. "The thing is, my father and the other Committee members have mental protections to prevent this sort of thing. I don't know a quarter of what he knows and the spells worked around my brain keep me from revealing any information."

"Even to Mary?" Shannon asked, raising an eyebrow.

Your secrets are as dark to me as Hell, Bloody Mary replied. *Of course, I would say that, wouldn't I?*

"I don't believe Mary has access to the House's secrets. Just my memories. The details are designed to be fuzzy to anyone but me. I also have a ten-conditioning level. I'm the last person in the Committee they'd be able to crack, and everyone else is damn near impossible as is."

Shannon's eyes widened. "Ten? Did your father do electroshock therapy on you growing up?"

"Why do people keep assuming I was abused as a child?"

"Because it would explain a lot."

I rolled my eyes. "My point stands. If Dracula or the Vampire Nation had access to my knowledge, they'd already be assaulting the House. He's not the sort of being who'd wait."

Shannon nodded. "I'll take your word for that. However, they're researching mind control there. Do you think Dracula thinks the House's own tech can break a Committee member?"

I paused, dominos falling in my head as everything started to fit together. "So just so we're clear. You think Dracula is going to attack Camp Zero to get at my father and the brainwashing tech there, so they can destroy the Red Room. All the while, the Vampire Nation is getting hammered by the House and its allies. Which has all been arranged by Christopher's girlfriend?"

"No, but your theory sounds about right." Shannon paused, taking a second to parse my statement. "*If* we believe Bloody Mary, Christopher, and our own unfounded guesses. If."

I took a sip of water down my parched throat. "The sad fact is I'm inclined to do just that. I trust Mary after a fashion."

Shannon looked at me sideways.

"Don't ask me why." I drank down the remainder of the mug's contents. "Well, there are two people on Earth who can verify my theory."

"Which are?"

I didn't answer but turned back to the computer. "How good are the rerouting systems on this?"

"Excellent. I always work with the best," Shannon said. "Why?"

I typed in a number on the computer's cellphone link-up I'd

seen on a file for "Major Enemies of the Red Room." I'd never seen any reason to dial it until now.

Seconds later, Dracula's image popped on the screen. He was sitting in the back of a limousine with Minka and Elizabeth beside him. Both women were wearing goth attire, while Dracula had changed into leather pants and a silk shirt.

Shannon's eyes widened.

That was unexpected, Bloody Mary said. *Albeit an excellent way to cut the Gordian Knot.*

Dracula was not easily surprised. However, I could see the tips of his eyebrows raise. "Fascinating. Do you have a desire to die, Cleaver? If so, I can grant you this wish. I lost a number of my men on that plane. Plus, I loved my jet. Tsk-tsk-tsk. How naughty of you to destroy it."

"In the words of Alexander Hamilton to Aaron Burr on the day of their duel, fuck you," I said, giving him the finger.

Childish? Yes. Fun? Quite.

"How very droll. What, may I ask, has driven you to contact me? Have you decided mortal life has no lasting appeal for you, and you've come to beg forgiveness for all the vampires you've murdered?"

I was betting a lot on a hunch, but I had Dracula's number now both figuratively and literally. "I think you're the guy behind Christopher's every action. You gave him the Bloodsword, mesmerized him into seeking me out, and have been following me to Protocol Zero so you can get at it through the front door. You assumed the Bloodsword would possess me and then I'd take out Nathan Hawthorne and deliver him to you along with all of Protocol Zero's research. Oh, I bet you wanted me to take out Annabelle Jones too."

"That is the most ludicrous—" Elizabeth started to say.

Dracula began to clap. "Oh, Derek, you are almost as good an agent as your father. In another lifetime, you might have beaten me."

"I find your statement to be the most insulting thing I've ever heard." I said, growling. "I am twice the agent he is."

"Sir…" Elizabeth trailed off. It was obvious she was stunned by the pronouncement. Dracula had turned on Ms. Jones.

Dracula chuckled. "I don't know why you are still surprised. You know Annabelle was a cannon waiting to fire. The sole reason I allowed her back was because I respected her violence and could manipulate her through you. I thought I could do it one better by giving her an ideal lover in Christopher, one shaped through mesmerism to be my spy on her activities. It took a few tweaks but was easy enough to accomplish."

I narrowed my eyes. "That's why he tried to kill me. You fried his brain."

"Oh, my dear Derek, you overestimate me. I suspect anyone who has known you for more than five minutes will want to kill you."

"It's true, but he grows on you. Like an inescapable fungus of death," Shannon said. "Hi, Dracula. Remember last time we met?"

"I'm sorry, do I know you?" Dracula said, feigning disinterest.

Shannon's look could have killed.

"Don't let him play you," I said, frowning. "I suppose that's all I wanted you to know. Goodbye."

"I don't think so," Dracula said, staring at me. "Bloody Mary, do be a dear and kill him for me."

A second passed.

I stared. "Still here."

Dracula frowned. "Well, that was unexpected. You are proving more interesting than anticipated, Cleaver. I am going to kill your friend, your family, and your organization. I do recognize you, Shannon, and I can assure you your end will be just as painful. The thing I'm torn about is which one of you I'll torture in front of their love—"

I turned off the computer.

"You hung up on Dracula?" Shannon asked, smiling.

"I did," I said cheerfully. "So, what did you do to him?"

Shannon's eyes took on a dangerous glint. "After I turned against my father, Dracula tried to recruit me into his little harem of brainwashed slaves. I tore off his head."

"A bit extreme."

"Some men won't take no for an answer."

I nodded. "Anyway, impressive. Not many supernaturals can kill an Old One."

"I'd fed a lot before doing it," Shannon said, looking down. "But yeah, I'm strong when I tap into my rage. The hate makes me powerful."

"That's not . . . ominous."

"You're the one who insists I'm not a monster."

Mary? I thought toward her.

Yes? Mary asked.

You were silent when Dracula ordered my death. I am grateful you didn't do it, though, I said.

You're welcome, Mary replied, sounding almost bored.

Yes, I was wondering if you'd been sent to win me over before maneuvering me to kidnap my father, I suggested.

Bloody Mary's voice became low and seductive. *Such may have been Dracula's plan, but it was not mine.*

Interesting, I said. *I suppose that's your definition of a trustworthy act.*

Isn't it yours? Bloody Mary asked.

I wasn't sure how to respond, so I went with my usual response. *I don't trust anyone.*

You can lie to yourself but not to me, lover, Bloody Mary said. *Trust comes easily to you and with great passion. The only person you never give a chance is yourself.*

We'll talk about this later, I said.

"He's going to try and live up to his promise to kill everyone we know," Shannon said. "He's a bad enemy to have."

"He was always my enemy," I said, deciding I'd have to find a permanent way of putting him down. "Do you think Dracula was telling the truth when he admitted to the plan I described? My instincts say yes, but I can't rely on them one hundred percent."

"I think Dracula is a card-carrying villain who would confess to anything he did and anything he hasn't done because he wants people to think he's the biggest, baddest, and meanest mother-sucker on the planet," I said, trying to sound less than impressed.

"Is he?" Shannon asked.

"He's close," I admitted.

"The problem is, getting my theory's confirmation means Dracula's plan is thwarted," I said.

"And that's a bad thing?" Shannon asked.

"It means he knows where Camp Zero is located. He's not going to hold off on attacking the place because his main plan has fallen through. In fact, I'm pretty sure he's going to launch one as soon as he can get one prepped."

Shannon stared. "Yeah, that seems probable. So, what are we going to do?"

I grimaced. "It means we're going to have to adjust our plans. Penny and Lucy are going to be ticked about it, especially if she's paying for the equipment out of pocket, but we need to warn Camp Zero's personnel."

"Are you sure you want to? These are brainwashing renegade operatives," Shannon said.

"Not to mention whatever the hell they're doing to supernaturals," I reminded her.

"Yeah, that too," Shannon said.

I thought about the casualty figures I'd read from Camp Zero's operations. There was also a list of names of people who'd been confirmed as going to Camp Zero and never returning— well into the hundreds, and that was just the identified. They were possibly still alive. I couldn't let them die in Dracula's attack. Unlikely as it could be, shutting down Camp Zero might mean innocent supernaturals being freed too. Then there was Bloody Mary's vision. It was too harsh to ignore. I had to stop it if I could.

Your trust means a great deal because I know the depths of emotion behind it, Mary cooed in my head. *I may betray you some day, but I promise you it'll be for good reason.*

Err, thanks, I said before speaking aloud to Shannon. "I don't like it any more than you do, but if it's a choice between evils, then better the Devil you know. I think it might be a good idea to keep the team on the side, though. Nothing prevents me from warning the House about an upcoming attack on their most hidden black site and breaking into it."

"Except common sense," Shannon said.

"I've never been blessed with an abundance of that quality," I said.

Shannon snorted. "Tell me about it."

"Are you up for following me on this?"

"I said I'd follow you anywhere, Derek. My feelings haven't changed in the past six hours." Shannon's sincerity touched me.

"Just checking," I said.

"Well stop," Shannon said.

I thought about my options and wondered if this was my destiny, to always be caught up in events too large to affect. I felt like the proverbial rat in a maze, moving from one corner to the next trying to figure out which way was the exit. Somehow, Dracula's manipulations and the House's secrecy had resulted in my protecting something I despised.

"So, what's the plan?"

"Get Malcolm onboard, contact my father, and take out Christopher's wife. I doubt Christopher will appreciate it, but my partner would have wanted me to put him down versus keeping him as an eternal pawn of the undead."

"Just like that."

"Just like that," I said, resolved. "In fact, warning the House about Dracula means they're less likely to suspect me when I blow the lid wide open on Protocol Zero. Are you up for breaking into the world's most secure location while I provide a distraction?"

Shannon smirked. "Why, Mister Councilman, I do believe I am."

CHAPTER TWENTY-FIVE

I had to contact both Malcolm and Nathan Hawthorne but having already dealt with one psychopath today in Dracula, I decided to call my werewolf friend first. Changing into my one suit of clothing, I took Shannon's phone and headed out past the back yard to the beach before dialing the number Malcolm had given me.

"Midnight Tech Support, how can I help you?" A voice lacking much of Malcolm's usual inflections answered the phone.

"Malcolm?" I asked, surprised at his lack of an accent.

"Oh, hey D." Malcolm's accent returned in force. "You still alive?"

"So far."

"Good to know. The Pact be celebrating the death of so many vampires. My pack is coming into town and we be going on a hunt. Kill some of the Mister Fangs, stick their heads on poles, the usual. Be good fun, yo."

"How would you like a chance to do some real damage to the Vampire Nation?"

"I'm listening."

"It's a long story." I was committing treason by revealing sensitive House information to an agent of a hostile foreign power, but as Richard Nixon said, it wasn't a crime when the president did it. Besides, how could I be expected to keep operational security about a facility I hadn't even been briefed on? So I gave Malcolm a stripped-down version of what Christopher had told me.

Malcolm was silent for a minute before responding. "Damn. You really are Che."

"Can I be Simón Bolívar instead? Because I'm not comfortable with the Guevara comparison."

"The Red Room be running a concentration camp and you tell me. That be crossing some lines."

"Technically, it's more a re-education camp, but we're splitting hairs. I'm going to try and shut it down, and I was curious if I could have your help."

I could hear the unease in Malcolm's voice. "This way above my pay grade."

"It also requires a warrior."

The tone of his voice became sharper. "No werewolf ever be tame, yo. We are a race of warriors. All of us be willing to lay down our lives for Mother Moon and Lord Sky."

I made it a point to do some research on shape-shifter mythology. "I want to break in, take some pictures, and get out. If Dracula attacks in the meantime, I'll try and release the prisoners as well as sabotage the place."

I didn't tell him I'd also try and help any House personnel to escape. I was between a rock and a hard place when it came to helping them in the expected attack. I wanted to see Camp Zero brought down, but I didn't want Dracula just to massacre everyone, either. Blame Black Room training, but I'd been taught not to abandon anyone to the monsters unless it was absolutely necessary.

"Sounds like you need an army."

"Or a few werewolves."

Malcolm's hesitation returned. "You know, D, if I was a suspicious man I'd say that you were going to use us to provide security and then cover all this up. That after all this, there won't be no prison there anymore."

Malcolm's paranoia was working against me. "If I was going to do that, why would I tell you about the place you had no idea existed thus far?"

Malcolm was silent.

"Yeah, that's what I thought." I sat down on a tuft of grass overlooking the beach's sand. "In fact, I'm hoping you guys will take proof of all this to the Pact."

"We be readying for war against the Vampire Nation. I

found that out today. The House be our allies."

I chose my next words carefully. "This war will not go a direction any of us want. I can't tell you how I know that, but believe me, it's true. I don't want to start a war with the Pact either. I just want to destroy this Camp Zero place and keep things at status quo."

"That may not be an option, D. If there be Pact personnel in those cages you describe, people will want blood."

"Then we'll pay reparations. Weirgild, whatever. I'll do what I can to bring about peace."

"Peace is what happens between war."

I sighed. "Do I have your help or not?"

Malcolm's next words made this very difficult. "I can name you Pactfriend and brother to my pack. You and everyone on your team will be immune. However, if we get there and things go south, I'll kill House folk to protect my people."

I'd seen what werewolf claws could do to human flesh. A team of US Marines, despite being armed with orihalcum weapons, had ended up slaughtered facing a single one of their kind. The thought of condemning fellow House personnel to that was sickening. "If things go south, I promise I'll fight beside you against my fellows."

Malcolm made a "hmph" noise. "I'll bring my people around. I just hope you don't get burned by this."

"I'm already on fire. A little more gasoline won't make a difference." I gave him the address of my current location and hung up.

"Are you sure it's wise trusting a werewolf?" Penny's voice spoke behind me.

I did a double take and turned around. My sister was standing there, now dressed in blue jeans and a jean jacket with blue ribbons tied in her hair. In her right hand was a large hand-carved walking stick that bore a resemblance to the legendary Staff of Hiawatha, an item Penny had once wielded.

Seeing her, I got up and wrapped her in an embrace. I wasn't the most touchy-feely sort of guy, but having my twin in my arms, I felt as if heavy chains were falling off my back. The possession, the flashbacks, Christopher, and all of it didn't feel like such a burden anymore. I had my other half with me.

The hug went on a little too long and Penny started patting my back. "Okay, not a stuffed animal here. You can let go."

"No," I said, continuing to hug her.

"I can curse you," my sister said. "You'll be giving presentations to the Committee with a blue tongue."

Reluctantly, I let go. "You have no idea the week I've been having."

"You're possessed. I'm pretty sure I do." Penny placed her hand on my head. "Okay, hold still."

"What are you going to do?"

"I'm going to blow the uppity spirit back to hell," Penny said, tightening her grip on her staff. "Beware, this is going to hurt—a lot."

No! Bloody Mary cried out.

I took Penny's hand by the wrist. "I'd like to hold off on the exorcism for a bit if you don't mind."

Penny stared at me. "Are you insane?"

Her look told me she was wondering if I was already under the influence of Bloody Mary, which I might well have been. "I'm actually being pragmatic. I've fallen out of a plane at several thousand feet and survived. I've fought an entire team of dhampir and avoided getting killed. I'm also on Dracula's personal hit list. The dem—Mary—has proven most useful."

"Mary." Penny looked at me skeptical. "It has a name now?"

I don't like her, Mary said. *She is prejudiced against Hell.*

I almost rolled my eyes at that. "She's made an oath that possessing isn't her goal. I don't intend for her to be a permanent resident, but since the Bloodsword is so important to Dracula, I need every advantage I can get."

If you don't want me in your mind, you can bind me to a body of some kind, Bloody Mary said. *I have always wanted my own form.*

Fat chance of that, I snapped back.

"You realize that's exactly what you'd say if you were mind controlled, right?" Penny said, looking like she was ready to knock me out and drag me to a priest.

"Check my mind," I said. "You know me better than anyone."

"Yes, which is why I'm worried." Penny placed her hand on my forehead.

Penny made a grunting noise, and then I felt a hot flash from her hand. She gritted her teeth and I could feel her presence moving through my mind, searching through my memories and examining my decisions. It was one of the techniques my father, possibly the greatest mind-manipulator on Earth, had taught her.

I expected the process to take only a few seconds, but Penny spent several minutes searching through my head. I was getting irritated by the whole thing by the time she stopped.

Frowning, Penny said, "She's deep in your subconscious, but the areas of your mind related to free will, secrets of the House, and other vital points are unaffected."

"That's what I said." In truth, I was relieved to find out I wasn't being manipulated. There was a difference between having faith and possessing proof.

"It's not normal," Penny pointed out. "Demons don't play nice with mortals. They possess you, use you up, and then jump into the next body. Throw in the fact that you're able to use the Bloodsword and it sounds like someone is setting you up."

"Excuse me?"

"Dracula was a holy warrior until he was turned into a tool of Tiamat-Abaddon. Watch yourself."

"I'm pretty sure Dracula was a monster the moment he was released from Turkish slavery. He wasn't corrupted to Hell's service; he chose it."

Penny shrugged. "Fine. This is all because you're badass and don't have to be afraid of the demon inside your head. You're using her, she's not using you, and everything is going to work out just fine."

"Thank you."

"That was sarcasm."

"No kidding."

I thought of the Bloodsword and the rush I'd gotten using it to slice through Black Squadron and the vampires on Dracula's jet. I could also, if I thought hard, catch glimpses of the other vampires I'd killed. The power I possessed with the weapon was amazing. It was enough to do the work of a dozen agents and, unlike the One Ring, could be used for good.

At least that's what I kept telling myself.

Power is an intoxicant no matter what form you choose, Bloody Mary said. *It is a lie we tell children that they should not seek it. Knowledge, influence, and wealth are all forms of it. Only those who have it are truly happy.*

I decided I would get Mary removed when this was done. *You oversold your case, Mary.*

Have I? Mary asked. *I think you'll agree with me soon enough.*

"How did you get here, anyway?" I said, looking at Penny. "Paris is hours away. And I thought you'd be bringing equipment."

Penny gestured with the side of her head to a fishing boat that hadn't been there before. I realized it was covered in more disguise and stealth charms than anything I'd seen.

"All the stuff you asked, and more is onboard," Penny said, smiling. "Division Four had a bunch of these and the French Chief was willing to hand it over without question. One of the benefits of being related to two Committee members, I guess."

"Yes, but how did you get here with it?"

Penny looked uncomfortable. "I kind of made a pact with an astral entity to fold space."

Teleportation was one of the few mystical powers regular humans couldn't do. The power was possible but required levels of energy that simply weren't available on the material plane. Instead, it required a being of the astral plane to serve as a bridge between two points of space.

Thought was the one infinite thing in the universe, and as beings of such, they were capable of being in two places at once. The metaphysics were complex but doable. My chief concern was that Penny was illustrating just the sort of haphazard acting before thinking I was prone to. Astral entities, be they gods, demons, or squid-tentacle monsters, were not the sort of people you made deals with causally. Dammit, only I could be an idiot for my twin!

I stared at her. "And you're calling me out about the Bloody Mary thing."

"A one-time deal! It won't come back to haunt me!"

"Right."

I put my hands-on Penny's shoulders. "Well, I'm glad you're here."

"We're family. Why wouldn't I be?"

I took a deep breath. *I don't suppose, Mary, you saw anything that might happen to us on this mission?*

Your sister is a warrior, Bloody Mary said. *Someday, in the future, she will fall. I do not speak of prophecy, for I have seen no images of her death but the one we seek to avert. I am simply speaking of an eventuality of all who live by violence. Eventually, it claims you. This is as true for you as for her.*

I regretted asking her. *I make my own destiny. I'm not going to let my sister get killed on this mission or any others.*

Destiny is the sum of our choices, Bloody Mary said. *We cannot change who we are. Only pain, sorrow, and love can.*

I wasn't going to let my twin die. I'd find a way to stop it. "It doesn't matter. Give me a tour of the boat. Malcolm and his company should be arriving soon."

"Who is Malcolm?"

"You'll see."

CHAPTER TWENTY-SIX

I spent the next hour and a half looking over the interior of the fishing boat. Penny had assembled all of equipment I'd requested and then some. There were guns, jamming equipment, body armor, diving equipment, explosives, and a few mystical items I had no idea as to the purpose of.

I spent most of that time hearing Penny's explanations and soaking up the fact that we were about to go against the House. The rest of my time had been spent sending a coded transmission to my father's private line, requesting a meeting.

I had questions and intended to get my answers from the source. Nathan hadn't responded yet, so Penny and I were in the boat's hold, surrounded by lockers full of weapons and machinery I only had the vaguest idea how to operate. This was the sort of vehicle for a highly trained team of six rather than the makeshift crew I'd assembled. I was pondering this when there was a knocking on the wooden door above us.

"Yes?" I asked, holding an M100, the latest in assault rifles.

"Our furry guests have arrived," Shannon's voice said on the other side.

I opened the door for her and noticed she'd changed into a pair of shorts and t-shirt, altering her features so she was now a black-haired girl with Eurasian features. A pair of sunglasses rested on the bridge of her nose.

"Nice disguise," I said, handing her the M100. "But you should go less tourist and more embittered local."

"I'll see what I can do," Shannon said, inspecting the assault rifle before looking at Penny. "We're going to have to do something about your favorite Scream Queen, though."

"I can clean up and look like one of the straights," Penny

said, snapping her fingers. "With just a gesture, people will see whatever I want them to."

Shannon was unimpressed. "I'm more worried about what cameras will pick up. We can't leave any visual evidence we were there."

"I've been on missions before, thank you," Penny said, taking a "better than thou" tone. "Are you sure we can trust the werewolves?"

"You know we can hear you down there," Malcolm's voice trailed from the deck above.

"Yes, we can," I said, more for Malcolm's benefit than Penny's. "I wouldn't bring them on this mission if they didn't have my complete trust."

They didn't, but beggars couldn't be choosers.

"You know we could be spending the rest of our lives on the run," Shannon said, reminding me of what we all knew.

"Well, then, at least it will be short," I said, giving Shannon a quick kiss on the lips. "Now let's go meet our allies for this bit of treason esoterrorism."

Walking up the fishing boat's steps, I came across to the wooden dock and saw six figures waiting there. The first was Malcolm, wearing a long leather coat over a t-shirt depicting a cartoon coyote underneath an anvil. He stood over the other five like a titan, all the other ones hovering around him like the Secret Service did the president. He was their leader, without a doubt. They were also worried about his safety.

The other five werewolves were a collection of Bahamian locals with African features and punk attire. One looked like Wesley Snipes with electric-blue dyed hair, another had a face-full of piercings, two were female identical twins with half-shaved hair, and the fifth had an undead rocker tattoo on his face. All of them were dressed similarly to Malcolm, complete with the coyote t-shirts. It made them look like a mix between a street gang and a bowling team.

"Meet the Dead Coyotes," Malcolm said. "We're a war pack."

I waved. "Nice to meet you all."

The last time I'd met with a werewolf pack, I'd been leading three squadrons of Marines and two teams of senior agents armed with grenade launchers. We'd lost half of our personnel and managed to triumph only because our witch forced them into human form. To this day, I wasn't even certain what we'd been fighting over.

The one with the face full of piercings looked disgusted. "We're not here because we want to be. All of us think Malcolm is making a terrible mistake getting involved with the Illuminati." He made a weird hand gesture, and it took me a second to realize it was a ward against the Evil Eye.

"Well, I didn't invite him to the torch-lit ceremonies where we worship Cthulhu and plot world domination through rap music, but there's still time," I said, looking among them. I couldn't believe they took the rumors about us seriously.

All of them stared daggers at me, except for Malcolm. They weren't big fans of sarcasm, it seemed.

"You should have held off on revealing the rituals to worship Cthulhu," Penny said, leaning up to whisper in my ear.

"Yeah, you could have started with how the Scottish Rite controls Baskin and Robbins," Shannon said, looking unimpressed with the group. "No one suspects the true purpose of Rocky Road is fiendish."

"Guys, now's not the time," I said, realizing we had to walk on eggshells with these guys. Malcolm was their leader, but they weren't fans of his decision to ally with me. In retrospect, it had been a miracle they'd showed up at all.

The man with the piercings growled, revealing dog-like canines. "You're mocking us."

I bit my tongue before I said something I regretted.

Shannon didn't. "No, that's just a joke. You'll know when we're mocking you."

I started counting the moments down before this turned into a free-for-all. Shannon could take down a transformed werewolf and so could Penny. I, now that I had the Bloodsword, could do the same. There were six werewolves here, one of whom was my friend, which meant inciting an attack was tantamount to suicide. I needed to calm the situation down and reign in the snark.

Which was a new experience for me.

C. T. Phipps

"Down, Shadow," Malcolm raised his right hand. "I owe Derek Hawthorne my life and he's killed many vampires. He is a worthy ally."

"He's a member of the Committee," Shadow said, snapping back. "His kind are as bad as the Fangs or worse."

I agreed with Shadow but wasn't going to bring that up right now for obvious reasons.

"Is this going to be a problem, Malcolm? Because I can do this without you," I said, lying through my teeth. I needed muscle on this trip in case things went south. Even six werewolves might not be enough to guarantee success.

"My people have been fighting the vampires for centuries," Malcolm said, all trace of his unusual vernacular gone. In its place was a deep and throaty Nassau accent, tinged with sorrow and sadness. "I have known thirty-six wolves, lions, and crows who have given their lives trying to break the hold of the Vampire Nation. My many-times-removed grandmother was the werewolf who killed Benjamen Horningold after his turn into one of the undead, and my father died trying to kill the vampire Joshua, whom we call Silverblade."

I thought about the muscular black vampire on Dracula's jet. "I had a chance to kill him earlier this week, but I failed. I'm sorry I didn't kill him."

"Like you could succeed where we have failed," Shadow said, taking my every word in the worst possible way.

Yeah, to be honest, I could. "That's not what I meant."

"Then what did you mean, Committee-man?" one of the twins asked.

"Yes, what?" the other twin said.

"Night, Day, I will brook no disrespect," Malcolm said. "Am I your leader or not?"

"You are," all the pack said at once, with little enthusiasm. "Our claws are yours, Pack Lord."

"Then shut the hell up and let me handle this," Malcolm snapped at them.

They all fell silent.

I smiled. I liked his style.

"So, say we all," Shannon said, under her breath.

"Night and Day?" Penny asked, looking between them. "Are those like your werewolf names?"

"Hacker handles," Malcolm said, smiling. "We met on the internet, yo."

"That must be very useful against the Vampire Nation," I said, trying to get our meeting back on track.

"And the Committee," Malcolm said, mollifying his pack's hostility. "Today, we are allies and perhaps tomorrow as well."

"I accept that," I said, hoping that would be the end of it. "Have you informed your group about what we're doing?"

"Breaking into Alcatraz, taking pictures, getting out. Killing anyone who tries to mess with us. That about it?" Malcolm said, looking at me.

"Yeah, that's it," I said.

"Dracula may attack soon," Penny said, looking between them. "In which case, do you know whom to attack?"

"Fangs and everyone who attacks us," Shadow said. "That right?"

"Two for two," I said.

"If worse comes to worse, I'll take you guys into the Otherworld and we'll escape that way," Penny said, providing a viable exit strategy. "I only have enough power for one use, though, so we'll have to use this fishing boat to get in."

"Shapechangers know the Otherworld," Day said, looking straight at Penny. "Don't worry about us."

"I'll be leading the mission." Shannon looked between them. "Malcolm, you can command your people, but we need a clear chain of command here."

The Dead Coyotes looked uncomfortable with Shannon's decision, exchanging glances that could only be described as predatory.

"I thought I would handle my people and you yours, or at least you would be in charge, D."

"Is something wrong with my leadership?" Shannon asked, adjusting her glasses.

"You're a lilin." Shadow, it seemed, was the blunt one. "We kill lilin."

"So do I." Shannon's voice brooked no disagreement.

"I think Shannon's the best one for straight-up infiltration and will be able to find an egress easier than I can," I said, honestly appraising our abilities. "It's my hope I can find a more direct route into the building."

"More direct, how?" Malcolm asked.

"I'm hoping they'll let me in," I answered, giving a confident smile.

They didn't look impressed.

Before I got to say anything else, I heard the Heavy's "Short Change Hero" play on my cellphone. Pulling it out, I checked it and saw the words: I'M HERE. Looking up above my head, I saw a helicopter approaching in the distance. My father, rather than communicate over the phone, had chosen to come here directly.

Great.

"Who is that?" Shadow said, following my gaze. "You better not have betrayed us, Committee-man."

"Shadow, I swear, another word and I will beat you so hard your aunt will be cursing me for a month," Malcolm said, following us both. "Not that I disagree with the sentiment. I don't recall a helicopter in your description, D."

"It's just the final piece to the puzzle," I said, walking to the edge of the boat and stepping out on the dock. "Are you willing to follow Shannon's lead?"

"A debt is a debt," Malcolm said. "I'm as anxious to get it repaid as you are to discharge it."

"Then do so," I said, looking between them. "It's a long ride to the island, and you guys better get started on it. I'll either catch up with you or find an alternative means of reaching the island."

"How will we communicate?" Penny asked.

I lifted my cellphone. "Lucy will be doing a lot of erasing this week."

Penny nodded. "Dad will understand once you explain the situation to him. He'll be an ally."

"Yeah, sure," I said, shaking my head. "That's what I expect to happen."

I turned around and started walking back to the house. I

gave my odds at about fifty-fifty for walking away from this meeting alive.

I was about to confront Nathan Hawthorne, the most powerful wizard in the world, about the evil he'd allowed to fester in the heart of the House.

CHAPTER TWENTY-SEVEN

A Hades-720 unmarked black helicopter landed in the middle of the house's back yard. Hades choppers were yet another fine product of the Pantheon Corporation and invisible to damn near all forms of surveillance. I suspected if I removed my Ring of Veritas, I wouldn't even be able to see it.

Nathan Hawthorne, looking as young as he had when I was born, stepped out of the back of the vehicle wearing a Panama hat and a white suit with a black tie. I was tempted to make a *Fantasy Island* reference, but my snark levels were running low. A pair of sunglasses rested on his face, and he looked relaxed for a man I'd discovered was running an underground prison specializing in mind control.

I did note one thing, though. He was carrying a glyph-covered walking stick tipped with a gold Chinese dragon on the end. It was an enhancer, which meant my father was prepared to be attacked. Dramatic overkill, since he was already one of the most powerful wizards on Earth.

"Greetings, Derek!" my father said, waving to his pilot. She was an attractive short-haired blonde woman in her mid-forties. The helicopter shut down its rotating blades as my father walked up to face me. "What does the prodigal son want from me this time?"

"Prodigal would mean I've returned," I said, wrinkling my nose. "Which I never intend to do."

"No, you just come to me whenever you need a favor," Nathan said.

"I don't put my personal distaste for you over the world."

"You realize I never intended for you to kill Ashley," Nathan said.

"The fact you didn't bother to tell me says everything it needs to about our relationship," I said.

"Would you like to know where she is now?" Nathan asked, leaning on his walking stick as if making a point.

"Also, that you'd say something like that. A real father would never blackmail his son."

"I would never blackmail you. This is extortion."

I hated when my father made jokes, especially when they were funny. "I'm not here about that."

Ashley was better off without me. It broke my heart to acknowledge it, which made me even angrier.

"I need to talk to you," I said, forcing down my distaste.

"So, I gathered."

"I'm glad to hear it. Wave hi to Nancy." Nathan gestured with his oft hand to the pilot.

"Hi, Nancy," I said, waving to her. She couldn't hear me, so I said, "Must you try and make me like your mistresses?"

"Your mother left me, Derek. As for mistresses, the laws of men prevent me from marrying them all. That doesn't mean you shouldn't treat the mothers of your siblings with respect."

I decided to nip this conversation in the bud. "Camp Zero is in danger."

My father stood very still. "How do you know about Camp Zero?"

"Dracula is going to attack it. Christopher had huge numbers of files on its layout, prisoners, and practices. I doubt he's scratched the surface, but he's clearly been investigating for some time. I wouldn't be surprised if there are several leaks."

My father put down his walking stick and removed his sunglasses. "You know, Derek, the Committee would find it a lot easier to trust you if not for the fact that you seem to make it a habit of getting priceless intelligence from our worst enemies."

"I thought I was *on* the Committee."

"You're no longer a pawn in the chess board of life, Derek, but that doesn't make you a king. You're more like a rook, bashing through things in straight lines. You have to earn the respect of your fellow Committee members."

"I would worry about their respect more if they weren't some of the evilest men on Earth."

"They are," my father said, surprising me. "They are, without a doubt, the most ruthless, ambitious, and intelligent monsters on Earth. From the kleptocracy dictatorships of Africa to the United States' current predominate position, they shape global politics to suit their whims. Dracula is on their level. Therefore you need their respect, so you can convince them to do things your way with a minimum of crushing the little guy."

"Which *giving them mind control* helps avoid," I said, trying not to growl. The whole situation with Camp Zero was insane.

"I sabotaged thirty years of research with Project: Stargate, making sure will-manipulating psychic powers seemed unusable by the House. Mind control has existed as an objective of rulers since the first cave men figured out threatening to bash in their neighbor's skull was a good way of getting what you want. You're lucky I slowed the progress of the technology as long as I did. Eventually, though, someone was going to figure it out. Which they did."

I was confused. I hadn't suspected Nathan to support my position. "So, you're saying you don't approve of Protocol Zero?"

"I find it one of the most repulsive operations the House has ever conceived of, which is saying something. Mind control is an abomination. Without free will there is functionally no difference between the living and the dead. Using it against vampires just opens the door to using it against humans—which they did, starting with our own agents. I got on board hoping to ride herd but failed."

I closed my eyes, shaking my head. "Why wasn't I informed of this? Why was I kept in the dark about all these agents sabotaging the Vampire Nation?"

"Because, Derek, you're the friendly face of the Committee. The next generation everyone trusts. You went out of your way to repudiate dozens of our most unpopular projects and divisions, all which made people think we'd stopped them. When . . . someone . . . cracked the code for manipulating minds and giving regular humans the power of mesmerism, it represented a fantastic change in the balance of power. The best

I could do was try and aim it. They could have used it in far more disturbing ways than targeting the vampire's infrastructure."

I made a mental note of his refusal to say who had cracked the code. "All of my negotiations were in bad faith, then? There was never any chance of peace between humans and vampires, was there?"

"Why would you want there to be? You said it yourself, the human race is someday going to wake up and discover the Truth. When the supernatural goes public, I don't care how many romantic vampire books exist, the undead are going to be a serious cause for concern. You can't really put a spin on eating people. If we take them off the board, we might arrange a more peaceful awakening."

"No matter how many people are killed in the crossfire."

"If you're referring to the war in the Middle East and terror attacks we sponsored to break the Vampire Nation's economic power, it was the *least* likely to result in millions of deaths. Collateral damage happens every year. Just how many people do you think have died because the House suppresses healing magic? The estimate would stagger you."

I guessed the number to be in the billions. "I don't know you."

"Wake up! It is better than the alternative. Human society exists because people don't think there's a monster under the bed. They're going to pull out their flashlights and find out the truth, but maybe we can keep them from screaming themselves to death. That's the only option here, Derek, and mesmerism is just another tool to do that."

I looked at him. "Do you really believe that?"

My father stopped, right before he was going to say something else. "No, I don't. It's the problem of being a spy. You sometimes forget which are the lies you're telling for the House and which you're telling yourself. The House has and will misuse this power and now that it's proven to work, they're going to use it more."

"Can't you oppose its use on moral grounds?"

Nathan raised an eyebrow.

"Okay, stupid question."

Nathan Hawthorne reached over and put his hand on my shoulder. "Are you familiar with Eric Arthur Blair's true story?"

"Who?"

"Also known as George Orwell. He was the author of *Animal Farm, 1984,* and *The Lion and the Unicorn.*"

"You could have just said George Orwell," I said, looking around.

"Did you know the CIA purchased the rights to his books after his death and misused funds to create pro-West, anti-communist movies based on his work?"

"I recall hearing about it."

"Did I ever tell you I was one of those CIA agents?" my father said, looking sick to his stomach. "I did it under one of my cover identities."

He hadn't told me. "I thought you liked communists. Mao gave you pandas and almost as many medals as the Allies did."

My father looked at me as if he were speaking to a small child. "It's difficult enough taking you seriously as a Committee member without you acting like a petulant child. I fought with the Red Army against the Japanese and made many friends. When I returned to China after the war, I saw those very same friends do unspeakable things to the people we fought for. I bit my tongue and worked to bring peace between the West and those same people because it was the best way for us all to not end up living on a nuclear dust ball. Can I finish my damn story?"

I was surprised at my father's vehemence. "All right."

"The Red Room had him killed."

I blinked. "Excuse me?"

"Orwell was already sick with tuberculosis so it was a pointless gesture, yet they smothered him in his hospital bed. Division Two believed he had insider knowledge of the Red Room. That his vision of a world of tortured drones serving underneath an all-powerful secret organization that edited the thoughts of its citizens was a reference to us."

"Was it?"

My father shrugged his shoulders. "It doesn't matter. The House has existed since ancient Babylon, and every government of the world has influenced us while the reverse is also true. Wherever there are methods of control and coercion, you'll find our fingerprints on it, and whenever someone comes up with a new method, we'll adopt it. Technology and magic are the tools of the system to dominate the world, not because they are evil, but because humanity's rulers are."

"Wow, I think you hate the House more than I do," I said.

My father ignored my words. "Division Two intended to suppress his work and let it fade from memory, but I found myself touched by its fundamental bleakness. I argued that it deserved a place in the public consciousness and kept it circulating. I'm the one who wrote the original movie adaptation's ending where Winston and Julia die shouting for Big Brother's downfall."

I wasn't sure why Nathan was telling me all this. "Okay, so you mutilated a classic work of dystopian fiction by giving it a cheesy generic ending. What does this have to do with anything?"

"My son, I want you to look around here. Take in what the Red Room is doing and what they will be able to accomplish. Your arrival here is more than the work of chance. It is destiny. You told me Dracula is going to attack to warn me. I think it's an opportunity. I want you to help me destroy Division Zero. Eradicate all of its records and salt the Earth so there's no remnant to rebuild from."

I furrowed my brow, looking sidewise at him.

"What are you doing?" Nathan asked.

"I'm trying to disbelieve the illusion of my father in front of me. Because there's no way you're him. Are you crazy?"

Nathan reached into the inside of his suit and pulled out his wallet. "Derek, I'm going to make a bet. One hundred dollars American that you were already planning to arrange a team to find out everything about Division Zero, so you could distribute the truth to the House in hopes of ruining the Committee's ability to use mind control—at least against its members."

I looked at his wallet. "Keep your money."

"I thought so. It won't work. The Chairman and his cronies would order you killed for betraying their trust. Then they'd have my other children killed as a lesson to me. Not that I'd

C. T. Phipps

allow it. No, I'd try and stop them and die horribly."

"Aren't you a bundle of joy?"

"I fought in World War 2. I saw what the Imperialists did, which their descendants deny to this day. I have seen what American military policy does on the ground, surrounded by corpses. This is the stuff humans do, my son. The monsters go one step further. Whether they be wizards or supernaturals. Joy doesn't enter into it."

"I have hope we can do better." I crossed my arms. "Us as a species, whether we have fangs or not."

"We've both killed three figures worth of individuals with our own two hands. Hope is a luxury you should have discarded long ago because we can choose the lesser evil, but not the greater good. That option left us when we became part of the oppressors."

"Maybe you read *1984* a little too thoroughly."

"Says the man who used to be obsessed with William Gibson."

"I turned to Tolkien when I hit twenty."

"If Dracula is going to attack Camp Zero, now might be a chance to strike at the resources. Your team, whomever it's composed of, can move in and eliminate the records of the facility. We'll then blame it on Dracula. I can provide you where we back up the research, the location of the physical records, and those individuals who'll have to die."

"You ruthless bastard."

"I'm sorry, did you think stopping a world-changing technological development was going to involve yarn and kittens? When one is faced with an implacable enemy, one needs to use force. Even if it means killing people on your side."

I stood there silent, then said, "All right."

Nathan seemed surprised. "I'm pleased you've made the mature decision."

"There's nothing mature about any of this. I'm just so sick of this mission, I want it done."

"Including the demon in your head?"

"I'll deal with it," I said calmly.

Nathan gave a half smile. "Then here's a word of advice.

Demons desire to be dominated. They require a master and the more powerful, the better. She will betray you for Dracula if he is stronger, and the reverse is also true."

Bloody Mary hissed in my mind.

"Thanks for the tip." I removed my ring, which had inexplicably returned to my hand, and put it once more into my pocket. "You're holding something back. You mentioned the person who cracked the so-called code of mesmerism twice in pretty oblique terms. Who is it?"

"She is a complication. One I leave you to decide how to solve."

"Still pretty damn evasive here. Who is it?" I was expecting it was one of his mistresses.

"It's your sister. She's the overseer of Protocol Zero's research."

CHAPTER TWENTY-EIGHT

It was times like this I hated how interwoven the families of the House had become. "My sister? Are you fucking kidding me?"

Nathan picked up his walking stick off the ground and held it under his left shoulder. "I don't find much humor in the matter, so no."

"Which sister? Hoshi?" I didn't believe for a second it was Penny.

"Rebecca," Nathan said.

I tried to reconcile that in my head. "The girl I used to take trick-or-treating around the mansion because it's the size of a small city?"

"Yes, my third eldest daughter. Your sister by another mother. The one I smuggled in two more pandas for the sixth birthday."

I still couldn't believe it. My next words were just absent-minded mutterings. "You need to stop doing that. I'm pretty sure that's bad for them as a species."

"You loved our panda collection growing up."

"That was before I knew what endangered meant," I said, taking a deep breath. "What the hell is Rebecca doing overseeing a gulag?"

"I believe that's my fault. I never recognized Rebecca's ambition or drive to prove herself worthy of the family name. With so many siblings and a father on the Committee, she was compelled to try and stand out as a scientist. She was working on healing shattered minds suffering from PTSD and magic-inspired psychosis when she changed."

"Changed?"

Nathan nodded. "At some point she did a study of how Bloodslaves were controlled by their masters to ignore even the most traumatizing atrocities. Getting a team to capture some of their kind, she dissected their brains and figured out how mesmerism worked. Rebecca submitted her results to the Chairman himself and got herself a big fat promotion."

"Dissected?" I asked for clarification. Most vampires turned to ash when they died, at least if they were a few years old.

"Vivisection would be a better term, but vampires aren't alive," Nathan said. "It's easy to think of the moral sacrifices we make as hard, but for others, they are eager and ready to do so. Rebecca believed breaking the Hippocratic Oath and other medical ethics was a way of demonstrating she was ready to serve at a higher level of the House's ranks."

"And she was right," I said, looking out onto the ocean waves behind us.

"I suppose she was."

I paused for a second. "I'm not going to kill my sister."

"I never wanted you to. Accursed is the kinslayer, for he is one of the few damned to hell without hope of forgiveness."

"Is that why you refuse to sign off on Stephen's execution?"

"Rebecca isn't Stephen. She's a scientist, first and foremost. What she's doing is evil, but perhaps she can be dissuaded from it."

"Have you tried?"

"Yes, and I failed. She thinks this is her chance to make a mark on history. Her chance at immortality. You're much more personable than I am, though. Also, I suspect you're capable of finding alternative means of removing the knowledge from her mind."

"Alternative?"

"Figure something out. Just don't tell me the details."

"How courageous of you."

Nathan looked contemptuously at me. "You have no idea the sacrifices I've made for you and the rest of the world. We need to move carefully if we want to stop the Red Room from being able to turn freedom into a joke. Other people have tried to stop our organization in the past, but unless you want to end up like the Kennedy brothers, we need to move swiftly as well as intelligently."

"You told me the Kennedy assassinations weren't the Red Room's doing," I said, realizing I was living in a world where it was entirely possible they had been killed by my allies. That was the problem of being a paranoid lunatic when you worked for an all-powerful conspiracy—everything insane seemed suddenly reasonable.

"No, they were both killed by lone gunmen. But my point still stands," Nathan said, teasing me with conspiracy theory like the Professor did. "You need to eliminate Camp Zero's backup drives at the main server by injecting a worm of some kind. I suggest uploading Red Room's many off-site virus programs. Dracula's attack will kill most of the scientists, but you need to make sure that the research in Rebecca's head is destroyed. There's a physical set of files in the lower levels. Those also must be destroyed. The entire building is monitored, so you'll have to disable the security camera systems lest they discover your involvement. I can provide the spells to prevent divination from determining your complicity. Oh, and you need to time this with Dracula's attack, so you may have to be there for a while."

"Is that all?" I asked.

"You've done far more complicated missions."

He was right. I needed to get over the feeling I was betraying my cause, even if I was. "All right. I'll communicate with my . . . group . . . and convey the details."

"The less I know, the better."

"I think we're a little past the point of plausible deniability."

"Very well. Contact your people. I'll give you a lift."

"A lift?" I asked.

"You're a member of the Committee. There's nothing preventing you from visiting one of our black sites. You might even gain the respect of other high-ranking officials for figuring out we were lying to you this entire time. Although they probably hoped you'd figure it out sooner."

"Everything is a criticism with you."

"Says the man who has all but accused me of child murder and worse."

"Give me ten minutes, then we'll head to Camp Zero."

My father nodded.

Ten minutes later, I'd made all the necessary arrangements. Shannon and I communicated with text that she said Penny had arrived. They were short, businesslike texts, unworthy of repetition. If either of us died, they were poor last words to speak to one another, but I couldn't bring myself to say anything meaningful. There was just too much going on and I couldn't sort it out in my head. Stepping into my father's helicopter, Nancy took us off the ground.

My father and I were left alone in the leather seats of the cabin as the transport traveled across the ocean. The two of us sat across from one another, silent, staring at one another for a long time. The trip convinced me of a fact I didn't want to face: that I was on the same path Nathan had walked before my birth. He'd spent his entire life trying to do good using the House's resources just to get sucked deeper into the lies, murder, and manipulation.

The Hades-class choppers were a prime example of how much the House was hurting the world. This vehicle could probably travel a thousand miles on a test tube of gasoline, yet there were wars being fought over oil. Some of them at the instigation of the House. I believed the ends justified the means, but how many times could I use that excuse before it became a self-serving delusion?

Was I past that point already?

"Nathan . . . Dad, what would happen if the Truth came out?" I felt a kinship to the old man I hadn't felt in years.

Nathan didn't respond for a minute, knowing what I was thinking. "Don't go down this road, Derek."

"It's my road to walk."

"Your mother left me because she thought differently."

"You never said why she left." I stared at him. "I assumed it was . . . dragon stuff."

"Dragon stuff?" My father raised an eyebrow.

"I was six when I started wondering about it. I stopped caring around puberty."

I'd never known Song Hawthorne except the descriptions

given by my uncle and father. She'd left when I was a toddler, long before any impression could be made. I had photos, recordings, and even interviews from the Red Room's World War 2 records, but nothing that told me anything substantial. Penny had gone to look for her when I was just a junior agent and didn't return for a year.

I never asked her what she found, just knew Penny met with my mother. Whatever she'd found had given her peace regarding their relationship, but I wanted no part of Song's excuses. It had been the origin of one of my few fights with Penny, my twin not understanding why I didn't want to hear all about it. I'd done my best to force my mother from my mind ever since. I didn't want to care who Song was because she didn't care enough about me to stay.

My father got a thoughtful look on his face before leaning on his walking stick as he sat down. "Your mother was one of the greatest warriors who ever lived. For thousands of years, she fought against everyone from the Mongols to the Imperialists. When we fell in love, she saw the best in me and that I could change the world as it entered the next magical age."

I didn't care what he had to say about her, but he clearly needed to talk about it. "What happened?"

"She saw I would have a choice to change the world. To define whether it would be an age of light or continue as it was— ruled by the House, ruled by secrets, ruled by lies. I had a choice to work with her to bring down the Committee and reveal the Truth or join it and make sure the world stayed the same. I chose the latter."

That put a new spin on her actions. I thought of Ashley before dismissing the comparison. "Why did you?"

My father stared at the floor, his shoulders slumping and his eyes deadened. "When my first family was killed by a wereshark, I grew to hate shapechangers with a passion you wouldn't believe. I wanted to make the supernatural world pay for their deaths, and the Committee gave me the weapons to do so. If not for your mother and Talbot, I would have killed hundreds of the Pact. Thousands if I could. Talbot and Song reminded me the supernatural species were just people like any other."

"I know something about revenge on an entire race."

My father looked at me, surprised. "Yes, I suppose you do. In time, my anger subsided and I realized the Committee was less a shield and more a straightjacket for society. I should have realized it long before, but the lies we tell ourselves are comforting ones."

"You haven't answered my question."

"You and Penelope changed everything. For both myself and your mother. For Song, who is one of the last spirit dragons alive, your birth was a herald to better things. For me, you were a sign I had something to lose again. Spartacus and his cohorts led seventy thousand slaves in an uprising that had morality, right, and justice on its side. It was a war that ended with them slaughtered and all six thousand captives crucified. The system can't be beaten. You can only do a little steering."

"How much steering have you been able to do?" I asked.

Nathan looked deep into my eyes. "Very little."

"But you think it's better than the alternative."

"The world would be different, which requires change," My father said. "Change can sometimes occur peacefully, but more often, it is a destructive process. The arrival of Cortez, the World Wars, the destruction of our Iroquois ancestors by the English who became our ancestors, and the Norse Ragnarok all changed the world. The revelation of the Truth would dwarf all of these and kill millions."

"It might save billions of lives in the long run."

"Such is the kind of justification for those who would make decisions for the world. We would not be able to fool humanity into thinking it's alone in the universe if not for their desire to believe it. You might want to open the world up to the Truth, help them escape Plato's cave, but in the end, they'll stone you as a madman."

I was surprised to discover I didn't believe that anymore. Somehow, somewhere, I'd lost my faith in the House and the belief that it was better to keep the Truth. I didn't care if the world would change because of what was found out.

The world wasn't what it could be.

The question was, what did I do about it now? I was in the same position I was when Ashley departed from the House.

There was no place on Earth I could hide, and fighting was another form of suicide. Yet I didn't want to continue to live like this. Joining the Committee was a mistake. In the words of Orwell, "The creatures outside looked from pig to man, and from man to pig, and from pig to man again; but already it was impossible to say which was which."

I didn't want to be a pig.

I was a man.

My father surprised me by reading my expression. "Choose your path, Derek. However, don't forget the people who will be affected by your choices."

The helicopter started to descend and I caught a glimpse of the island below. It was a tiny thing, barely more than a couple of miles, but beautiful. In its heart, I saw a large chemical plant, or at least that's what it looked like from above.

There were massive ball-shaped chambers, smokestacks, and an electronic tram around the place like the kind in Disney World. No smoke came from the smoke stacks, though, and I saw dozens of armed guards moving around the place. There were probably hundreds total.

"Nice disguise," I said, looking out the window. "A prison shaped like a factory. I should have realized from the plans."

"The panopticon design exists in all of those globes. Prisoners watching prisoners in a circle that allows no privacy," my father said, looking with me. "I don't know how many humans have been brought to this place over the years. Not nearly as many as the supernaturals. Most used to have merciful death awaiting them. Now, they aren't so lucky."

"How has it been kept a secret so long?"

"When no one asks questions, no one gets answers."

The helicopter touched ground on a helicopter pad in the middle of a square series of pipes that covered everything around us and led to a pair of metal doors surrounded by reinforced concrete. Once on the ground, I saw the pipes disguised unmanned gunnery emplacements that followed the helicopter via motion detection sensors.

"Yeah, that's not foreboding," I said, staring at the machine guns.

"I can assure you, you're entered into the face recognition software as a person they're not to shoot automatically."

"Which is so comforting."

"Machines only do what you tell them to do, not what they or you want. I find them singularly refreshing by comparison to people, who are evil and weak."

"And you wonder why I lost the faith."

"God forgives all but kinslaying, apostasy, and despair. This world is a form of hell, which is why bad things happen to good people, but we escape it upon death. Until then, the only thing you can do is mitigate the damage."

"I don't believe that."

"That's what worries me," Nathan said, opening the door of the helicopter for me to step out. "I've already contacted Rebecca telepathically and told her of your coming. She'll give you a tour of the facility. You can plan your next move from there. I'll make my own arrangements on the side."

"Are you sure you trust me with this?" I said, looking at the pilot's chair and wondering if we could trust my father's mistress. Obviously, Nathan Hawthorne trusted Nancy to freely talk treason in her presence.

Unless he had a spell guarding our conversation, which he probably did. Shaking my head, I stepped out and started walking to the concrete doors, which opened as I approached.

"I don't trust you at all, my son. You do whatever you think is right, regardless of who it hurts. It's why I've always been proud. Do you have a gun?"

"Is this the best place to ask?" I asked. "This is heavily monitored."

"And we're both members of the Committee. Answer the question," Nathan said.

I lifted my empty hands into the air. "Been relying on magic, fists, and swordplay for the past few days."

"This is not one of your video games." Nathan rolled his eyes. He unbuttoned his jacket and revealed a holster inside. Unstrapping it, he handed it over to me. "Take mine."

I took out the gun to look at it. It was a long RC-82, capable of three-burst round shots in an instant as well as using all manner of specialized ammunition. The thing was much heavier than my Pantheon .50 and wouldn't absorb the recoil the same way. Still, I was glad to have it.

"Great, the perfect weapon if I'm going to kill gangsters in Detroit," I muttered, putting a round in the chamber and running a brief check on the weapon. It was immaculately well-maintained.

"Don't look a gift horse in the mouth," Nathan said. "There's a reason guns replaced the old ways of fighting."

I strapped on the holster and hid it under my jacket. "Thanks."

"Don't die," Nathan said, closing the helicopter door before its engine started up again.

CHAPTER TWENTY-NINE

A s I passed through those big metal doors, it occurred to me I might be walking to my death.

The likelihood of Nathan Hawthorne sending me to my death was about one in five. I tended to believe him when he claimed he was appalled by the experiments going on here at Camp Zero and never intended half of the horrible things I'd known him to have done. There was just enough niggling doubt as to his intentions, though, that a part of me was afraid.

Seconds after I passed through the doors, I found myself in a long, pipe-filled corridor with concrete walls. The House's symbol was painted on the wall in the space between two rows of pipes. It consisted of a circle with a Masonic square and compass over a shield with a stylized H in front of it.

Passing through the H was a pair of crossed wands with the words *Condemnant quod non intellegunt* written underneath them. Translated from Latin, this phrase meant, "They condemn what they do not understand." I felt this was the most hypocritical phrase possible, since people didn't understand because the House kept them ignorant.

Coming down the hallway, dressed in black helmets with mirror visors and heavy black body armor, were a squadron of Sons of Mars mercenaries. Each was sporting a variant of the M100.

Less than a year ago, the private military contractors had assisted Cassandra in her attempted coup. The ringleaders had been punished, but the majority had been promoted for their efforts. The group had expanded into a massive military juggernaut with paychecks twice as lucrative. It was now the largest PMC on the planet, surpassing G4S and Hellfire Limited.

In this world, money trumped ideals.

This surprises you? Mary said in my head. *I would have thought it would be an accepted fact of your life.*

I'm always hoping the world will surprise me.

Then you'll always be disappointed.

The leader of the squadron got real close, so close I could see my reflection in his visor. "You're not on the authorized list of personnel, Councilman."

He said the word like he was cursing. I wondered what I'd done to the man to get him to dislike me. Given my previous associations with the Sons of Mars, I suspected I'd killed some of his friends. Oops.

"I was cleared for entrance by the other Councilman Hawthorne, soldier," I said, keeping my voice civil. I didn't want to antagonize him, mostly because I suspected his buddies would rally to his defense. The last thing I needed was a gang of thugs riding my ass when I was trying to sabotage this place.

"Oh, for crying out loud," a feminine voice said from the back of the hall. I couldn't see the source past the soldiers. "Did they teach you nothing about protocol wherever you trained?"

"The Marines, ma'am."

"Well, Semper Fi and get out of my fucking way," the woman said, and I realized it was Rebecca.

The squadron of mercenaries shared looks and parted to different sides of the hall, exposing a five-foot-four woman with brown hair in a topknot, chubby cheeks, a pair of spectacles, and a white dress shirt over black slacks. She had a lanyard around her neck and a clipboard under her arm. It was Rebecca Hawthorne all right, looking as sweet and pleasant as when I'd last seen her at the Division One New Year's Eve Party.

Standing beside Rebecca, at about four-foot even, was an albino naked figure with an overlarge head. The being had no visible sex organs and only four fingers. It was a member of the Grey species, a genetically engineered fairy-human hybrid created by the White Room in the late fifties. Known as "living computers," they were responsible for much of the UFO hysteria of the time. Today, they were almost extinct, the House having discontinued the experiments that created them after having successfully pushed humanity forward in the space race.

He, too, was wearing a lanyard.

"Derek! How wonderful for you to visit!" Rebecca said, smiling like it was Christmas. "You have no idea how long I've been waiting for you to come to Camp Zero."

"Uh, yeah," I said, totally not expecting things to have gone this way.

"Voot verrp veerp," the Grey said.

"Well, of course he's nervous!" Rebecca said, like she was talking to someone speaking English. "It's not every day someone gets brought into one of the inner secrets of the House. Even when one is a member of the Committee."

"Yes, that's it. You're right," I said, looking between them. Clearly, the Grey was empathic, but thankfully, not telepathic. Otherwise, this whole plan was dead in the water before it began.

Don't worry, Derek, Bloody Mary said. *I'll protect your precious thoughts.*

Thank you, I thought back. *That's very reassuring.*

You're welcome, Bloody Mary replied.

I was being sarcastic, I said.

When are you not sarcastic? Bloody Mary asked.

She had a point. Holding out my arms, I said, "It's good to see you, Rebecca."

Rebecca hugged me back, making this whole plan to betray her and destroy her operation more awkward. "You have no idea how worried I was about you. I'd heard you'd disappeared for a week."

"Well, I was just doing one of my off-the-grid self-imposed missions," I said, half-telling the truth.

"Ah, like the time you rescued your partner in North Korea. The one who got gored by a unicorn."

"Yes, Winston." Poor Winston, it turned out, had been the least troublesome of my partners.

Rebecca broke our embrace and started taking me by the hand down the hall. "Harold, do me a favor and get a report ready on the past year's activities for our guest. We have a great deal to discuss and I think it'll be best for my brother to be informed."

"Veep veep voo." The Grey blinked, its eyelids being on its side of its blackish orbs. The Grey proceeded to walk away, casting me an unpleasant look as he did so. He didn't trust me.

Which was the right attitude.

"Vaap!" The Grey called back at me.

"Don't use that kind of language." Rebecca shook a finger at the Grey before he vanished into a side door.

"You understand him?" I asked.

"He's my familiar."

I wondered how Rebecca had managed to create a bond with a sentient being. To do so, she'd have to have a dominant and superior view of her associate. You could turn pets into familiars, but to do so to a fellow being was tantamount to slavery, especially since familiars only lived as long as their masters.

"Impressive," I said, pulling my arm free. "I'm not just here for a tour, Becky."

"Oh?"

I decided I couldn't leave Rebecca unprepared, even if I thought what was going on here was evil beyond measure. "I believe the location of Camp Zero has been compromised. Dracula is going to attack soon and in force."

Rebecca looked like I'd told her it was probably going to rain tonight. "I'll raise our security level to Fuchsia and tell the guards to have everyone ready."

"Fuchsia?"

"I get to choose the colors and red-alert is passé."

"I think you should evacuate the facility." Abandoning it would also give me a chance to destroy their research and find some other way to stop Rebecca's plan. Gods and immortals forbid, a nonviolent solution to all this.

Rebecca snorted. "I'm not afraid of vampires."

"You should be."

"Says the so-called Cleaver."

"So-called is right. Only luck and circumstance has kept me alive in my encounters with the undead."

Rebecca pulled out a Hermes cellphone and typed in a short message before putting it back in her pocket. Seconds later, a series of yellow police lights in the ceiling started spinning as a siren played in the ground. The Sons of Mars mercenaries behind us jogged past us to take position elsewhere in the disguised prison facility.

"Yellow lights?" I asked.

"Fuchsia lights are harder to find than you think. I want to show you something."

"All right."

As I followed my sister, we passed through another set of metal doors and walked up a set of concrete stairs to another pair of doorways leading to one of the gigantic metal balls outside. The doors opened after Rebecca's lanyard was scanned with a laser-sight, and the two of us passed into a chamber that was hard to describe.

If I had to pick my words for evoking the sense of feeling the place invoked, I'd say it was like being in the interior of the Death Star combined with an asylum. The walls of the vast chamber were filled with thousands of clear transparent steel cells arranged on top of one another, covering the entirety of the ball's interior and forming a weird stadium-like grid around us.

Rising through the middle of the chamber was a central pillar containing a dozen elevators, which led to a staggering series of catwalks that allowed the prisoners to be attended to. At the top of this thirty-six-story geodesic sphere, twice as large as the one at Epcot Center, was a square-shaped control center that loomed over all this like a throne. You couldn't hear the Fuchsia alarm inside. Instead, pop music was playing in the background. Right now, it was "Justified and Ancient" by the KLF.

Not all the prison cells were occupied, but I was stunned to see just how many of them were. There were at least a thousand prisoners, including quite a few that were inhuman. I saw rakshasas, djinn, shape-shifters, vampires, boggarts, and hybrids of every sort. I'd known this place had been in operation for years, but I had no idea it was anywhere near this expansive. The Red Room must have been kidnapping dozens of people a month to achieve these sorts of results, and I'd never heard a whisper of this place outside of rumor.

Rebecca pulled out her clipboard and took a pen from it,

using it to point to different sections of the chamber. "The lower levels house those who are still being processed but the mid-levels are those we've managed to render compliant. The top levels are the best, though, because those are the ones we're able to put into the field."

"Put in the field?" I said, bewildered. The House must have spent a billion dollars on this place.

"Oh yes, secrecy is a paramount concern and our chief priority has always been figuring out how to create super-powered agents who could serve us in the field."

"Which you've been doing for a while."

"Oh yes, for almost a year now. The secrecy of the supernaturals has contributed to our work as they don't question when one of their lesser members disappears. The violence inherent in the system guarantees they just blame one of the other factions. Mostly, we've just been using them to acquire new members of our society. I foresee Division Zero someday becoming equal to the other branches of the House. A Purple Room, if you will, delivering superpowered soldiers to fight for human rights."

"How many humans are being . . . treated here?"

Rebecca paused to think about that. "Oh, hundreds. I'm sorry to say it's easy to overestimate their value. Dozens have died on the missions we've prepared for them. I don't supervise that part, but the project leaders warned me it was probable."

I reevaluated my earlier conclusions and decided my sister was quite probably insane. I walked over to the first level of cells. Many of these prisoners were in pain, tortured, but their screams were muted by the soundproof interiors of their cells. Instead, all I could hear was the pleasant tones of the Eurhythmics "Sex Crime," which had just started playing.

"How . . . do you justify this?" I gestured to the hallway of identical transparent steel cells around me.

Rebecca Hawthorne clutched her clipboard tight and frowned, ignoring the horrific nature of our surroundings. "It's my life's work. This is the place we're making incredible strides in the field of behavior modification and correctional procedure."

One of the Red Room's slang terms was newspeak. It was what agents used to refer to any outlet (government, corporate, or otherwise) that used buzzwords to try and cover up the actual substance of what they were doing. I had to wonder if my kid sister thought her actions were justified or was trying to convince herself. The background music pointed to the former, or to a lack of self-awareness bordering on the absurd.

"I can't say I'm not intrigued," I lied, realizing I didn't want to tip her off. To cover my disgust, I looked to my side. There, through a glass wall, I saw a room where a man was tied up in a ward-covered straight jacket. Hundreds of spiders were covering his body and face, crawling up and down his body. Bad mistake. Biting my lip, I pondered what I was going to say next. I didn't suffer from arachnophobia, but I suspected he did, by the look of sheer terror on his face. What was weird was he didn't scream, just contorted in disturbing ways. "Though some might find your methods unconventional."

Rebecca frowned. "The processing for breaking down psyches here is crude. It's brute force technique designed to reduce a subject to a neutral mental state, so they can be reprogrammed for Red Room service."

"Elsewhere you change behavior with lollipops and stuffed animals?" I couldn't help but ask.

Rebecca didn't seem to hear my reproach. "More so than you think. If allowed a proper time period, soft techniques can convince a subject they're willingly abandoning their past principles and embracing a new lifestyle. There's no one more dedicated to a new religion than a fresh convert, and the zeal displayed by some of the subjects I've treated is beyond compare. One carried a surgically implanted bomb to assassinate John Ross the Red Slaver."

I tried to hold back my disgust. How could she be proud she'd created a suicide bomber? "I want to speak with our father."

Rebecca glared. "He's not in charge here."

It was defensive, almost petulant, which wasn't what I expected.

"He's not?"

Rebecca puffed up her chest in pride. "No, he's not. I was chosen by the Chairman of the Committee to head up this project when I was nineteen. I was placed in charge of a lot of older agents who'd been working this facility for decades and who were using outdated methods. Many were cruel and abusive too. You wouldn't have been believed what sort of abuses were going on here before I cleaned the place up."

Keeping a straight face, I slipped into full "agent mode" and abandoned my love for my sibling to get as much information as possible. "There's a difference between abuse for a subject's own good versus something done for an torturer's own sadism."

"Exactly," Rebecca said.

I'd used that line when talking with torturers. "So, when did our father become involved?"

Rebecca looked peevish, like Nathan was interfering in her first real job. "He was involved in the original Project: Stargate research because of his powers influencing people. All very crude, half-assed, and very unscientific. He left when he became head of Division One and didn't become re-involved until my success with Ruthford."

"Wait, Osama Bin Vampire is here?"

"That description is crude and disrespectful."

"Sorry."

"John Ruthford was captured two years ago during a routine operation that lucked out. He proved to be resistant to enhanced interrogation—"

I gritted my teeth, hating that euphemism.

"That was when I applied my own techniques and proved I wasn't just theory. Within six months, he had shared every bit of actionable data on the Vampire Nation and his sub-organization within it. From there, we've been using him to send transmissions to his followers and play various factions against one another."

I thought about the missile strike against Ruthford's estate. It was a complete waste and pointless. He hadn't been an actual terrorist threat to the Red Room for years.

"We've even let him go on unsupervised trips to the outside world now." Rebecca started walking down the hall.

I followed her. "Annabelle Jones? Christopher's wife? She's here now?"

I walked in a circle, passing several other cells, these containing prisoners who had IVs attached to their arms and looked drugged to the gills. One of them, a black woman, was drawing on the ground with crayons. I shuddered to imagine what my sister had put her through and what they were going to do with her next.

Rebecca nodded. "Oh yes, upstairs."

"I need to speak with her now," I said, deciding I had to kill someone.

"Certainly," Rebecca said, smiling.

CHAPTER THIRTY

I'd done some questionable things in my time, but the sheer depravity and lack of respect for free will on display was a new level of evil for me. Worse than the Wazir turning a bunch of school kids into cannibalistic draugr. It put the final nail in the coffin for any loyalty I might have still felt for the Red Room and its masters. The House had created a facility to turn people into objects—and not just one or two, but on a mass scale.

There were two other geodesic domes here, probably containing other prison facilities they planned to fill up. How many thousands more people did they intend to brainwash? Were they going to do this to the public at large? Did the future hold nothing but brainwashed slaves?

Literally, the only thing preventing me from killing Rebecca Hawthorne right then was the fact that she was my sister. I wanted to believe she'd been put through a process like the ones being conducted here. As horrifying as the torture on display was, it would be better she be a victim of it than a perpetrator.

Is torture so much worse than murder? Is brainwashing? Bloody Mary asked, curious.

"Yes," I whispered, following Rebecca to the elevators. "Are you sure Annabelle can be trusted?"

"We've had no reason to doubt her intentions, but we've been careful to take appropriate precautions. For centuries, she's been a source of the Vampire Nation's movements and behaviors. Dracula did clue in to Annabelle's partnership with Division Zero, so we extracted her about a month ago. She's been helping with our efforts against high-value targets, under supervision, while we make plans to retrieve her husband."

I mulled that one over. "I think he's using Christopher as

a weapon to get close to her. He's uncovered vast amounts of information about your base. If you have any weaknesses, Christopher has found them."

"I find that very hard to believe."

I struggled not to roll my eyes as we arrived at the elevators and Rebecca called one down. It was the problem with many White Room operatives. They were so intelligent in other areas they had difficulty understanding when something horrible was going to happen.

Christopher's experience with Red Room operations had allowed him to find out a staggering amount of intelligence about Division Zero. Whether he'd done it by tapping phones, research, or mesmerism didn't matter. The fact was, he'd found out damn near everything about this deranged project.

There was no protecting this place, and I needed to convince my sister of it. Whether or not she was insane, I wasn't going to abandon her to Dracula's wrath. He'd been quite clear in his plans for my family.

"I'm a member of the Committee. Our father is a member of the Committee. Both of us say for you to go. Which means that you need to. It's the chain of command. When we tug the chain, you get pulled."

Rebecca looked as if I was talking crazy. "I'm going to have to clear this with the Chairman—"

"And he'll back us up," I lied, staring at her. I had no idea what the Chairman would say, but he'd just as likely order the place to defend itself to the last man. The man who headed the Committee was not squeamish about sacrificing lives to preserve his agenda.

"Fine. I'll make evacuation orders once we get to the central observation platform. We'll be set back months, but I suppose the net value in lives saved will be worth it," Rebecca said, relenting. The elevator arrived, its doors opening, and the two of us stepped in. "I think you're being paranoid, though. This is one of the most secure facilities in the House. It's not like Dracula is going to drop a bomb on us."

"He might," I said, watching the doors close on us.

She sighed. "Very well, I suppose we should take appropriate precautions. I've not gotten as far as I have in the White Room by being reckless. We can set ourselves up at the beta-site. The Committee has never been more enthusiastic about our work, and with the upcoming war with the Vampire Nation, there's no chance they won't approve all the additional upgrades I want installed."

Great, they were prepared for an evacuation. I knew this was too easy. "I'm glad to hear that."

"Funny how none of this ever landed on my desk. I think I should have been brought up to speed the moment I ascended to the Committee. I agree. The other members chose to censor your information access after you shut down so many long-standing projects. I thought it was unnecessary given you've always been a die-hard patriot to the cause of human advancement. Not to mention a veteran soldier of the war against the supernatural, strange girlfriends aside. I welcome your presence here because your lack of approval has always bothered me."

I took a deep breath, unsure how to proceed. It was hopeless trying to convince her how wrong this all was, but I had to try. Hypocritical or not, I felt I had to convince her some lines shouldn't be crossed. "I confess to . . . ambivalence over certain details. May I ask what the endgame is here? What does Protocol Zero accomplish in the long run?"

"You mean aside from providing valuable field assets? Turning countless monsters into weapons against other monsters?" Rebecca asked like my question was the most ridiculous thing in the world.

"Yes," I said, not hesitating.

Rebecca seemed surprised by my directness. "Oh, well, I suppose I have given the matter little thought. I think it's time the House started taking the next step. Are you familiar with the concept of memes?"

Memes were an idea created by biologist and prominent atheist Richard Dawkins. He claimed that cultures propagated their ideas the same way couples propagated their genes. You passed down your views from one generation to the next, influencing those around you. Doctor Dawkins believed a lot of the world's troubles were due to our inability to separate good memes from the bad.

"Yes, and I'm unimpressed. Richard Dawkins isn't the first man to come up with the idea of cultural ideals having a life cycle of their own. The Catholic Church did a pretty extensive analysis of good and evil for irony points."

"I don't believe in good or evil, Derek, just beneficial and harmful behaviors. I think with my research, we can start tackling the harmful behaviors of the world."

"You want to start applying your research outside to the rest of the world?" I somehow managed to contain my horror. Who did this to her? "Civilians?"

"I sense your skepticism. Think about how much change we can enact if we no longer must rely on wrong choices. We could start small, dealing with pedophiles and psychopaths, then go higher and deal with things like error. The House will become a guiding light to the world. We could bring about a new age of prosperity."

I wouldn't trust the House to mow my lawn without putting mines in it, let alone direct the fate of humanity. There was a reason the House stuck to containing the supernatural. When it tried to influence the regular world, things like the Black Sun and stock market crash of 1929 tended to result.

I tried to figure out how to reply without being condescending. "Yeah, and we could put 'This is your god' on money. Only you wouldn't be able to see without your special glasses." Okay, I failed. That was very condescending.

"That's a movie reference, isn't it?" Rebecca asked, staring at me as if I hadn't put down her suggestion.

"*They Live*," I said.

"Ah," Rebecca said, nodding. "I'll stream it."

I bit my lip. I didn't want to yell at my sister even if I thought she sounded like a lunatic. "I'm sorry, but I . . . don't approve. At all. I think altering people's decisions via coercive methods is, at best, reprehensible. At worst, I think it runs the risk of disrupting something precious within the human animal and causing it to . . . break. What you're proposing could drive humanity mad."

Rebecca shook her head, as if I were denying the existence of evolution or global warming. "You underestimate me, Derek. I'm not rushing into this half-cocked. This is a research center as well as a place of correction. People talk a great deal about free will, but what we think of as choice is a reaction to stimuli. What shapes our decision-making process is created by our parents, home nations, religions, neighbors, media exposure, and a thousand other people pouring a constant stream of data into our heads. Don't be fat, don't vote for the other guy, don't like Muslims, do like Christians, hate homosexuals, buy our product. It's an exhausting array of contradictory and nonsensical commands that every human being is overwhelmed by. Countless immoral views from sexual practices to war exist because bad data has accumulated. We can make a real difference by starting to edit the world's views on a large scale. Which, yes, will involve a lot of subliminal commands and low-scale mesmerism."

"All . . . right." I really had no idea what to say to that little rant.

"You understand, don't you?" Rebecca asked, realizing I'd been uncharacteristically silent.

"I think I do. At least, I'll give you the benefit of the doubt on this." If I'd said water was dry, I'd have been lying less.

"Thank you, Derek," Rebecca said, giving me another hug. "I've wanted to reveal this facility to the rest of the family for some time now. This is the future of the House and a chance for us to make changes to the entire world. We don't have to play peacemaker with the monsters anymore. We can take the fight directly to them. Hell, we can turn them all into assets against the worst of humanity. An army of supernatural killers purging the world of child molesters, war criminals, and worse. The sick can be separated from those who are willfully ignorant and the former cured while the latter are eliminated. Hell, we may not even need to eliminate the latter at all. We can just fix everybody."

There was no way I could continue letting this horrible place operate, but my options were limited to becoming the sort of esoterrorist I'd always opposed and sororicide (a.k.a. murdering your sister). Shannon, Malcolm, Penny, and whoever they brought were making their way here even as we spoke. All of them would be happy to help me bring this place collapsing down around Rebecca's ears, but I wasn't willing to make the call that needed to be made.

Rebecca needed either to die or to have her memory of her research erased. That was tantamount to torture, though, and torture of someone infinitely closer to me than the people she was abusing. For a man known by a wide variety of names, all meaning "Killer," I was a pussy cat when it came to my family.

I had no plans for dealing with what I'd found here. This was different from an operation designed to re-educate a small number of renegade operatives and sleeper agents. Camp Zero was a full-on military prison that represented a substantial investment for the House. Even if agents complained, it was just as probable the Committee would order a purge of dissenting elements versus shutting this monstrosity down. This was too valuable an asset to stop and might end up in every Division if I exposed it. A House that wanted to brainwash thousands of enemy species into loyal soldiers would not balk at a housecleaning of its own ranks.

Hell, there was no end of House personnel who'd approve of access to mesmerism and mind control techniques. If Rebecca's research was as far along as she claimed, it would open a new field of research for agents to specialize in. I was in the Manhattan Project of the mind, and the fate of free will on Earth was on the line.

The elevator door pinged and its doors opened. Rebecca straightened her shirt. "Oh well, it's time to meet with Miss Jones. Be on your best behavior, as we couldn't have completed this project without her."

Give me a sample of her blood and I'll do what must be done. Bloody Mary's voice was cold but firm.

I'm not going to let you kill my sister, I said.

I can do other things, Bloody Mary said. *Either way, though, she is a danger. Eviller than many of the monsters you have put down. I would know.*

She is what the House created, I said.

So are you, Bloody Mary said.

Following Rebecca, I took in Camp Zero's central observation room. It was a white room with hundreds of monitors, holographic read-outs, and a dozen Greys working in cooperation with White Room scientists. The screens cycled through images of torture before switching to monsters praying to posters of Rebecca or the House seal. I looked away, searching the room for Annabelle and finding her.

She was so obvious, I had to shake my head that I'd missed her in my first view. A woman in black mourning attire with a large hat and veil. Annabelle Jones was lovely, her features sculpted like an angel's, with long dark hair trailing down past her neck. The Elder vampire held an open parasol over her shoulder

Standing beside her was John Ruthford, six foot five, with a patrician face and perfectly combed blond hair. He was wearing a black shirt and slacks, which underscored the sheer power which radiated off him. Annabelle Jones was probably more powerful than Ruthford, but the terrorist had more of an obvious mystical presence.

Moving like she was floating, Annabelle turned and approached me, closing her parasol and turning it down like a walking stick. "Ah, Derek Hawthorne, so good to finally meet you. You're just in time."

I faked a smile. "Just in time for what?"

Annabelle stared at me with cold, unfeeling eyes underneath her veil. It was the gaze of a monster. A bipedal animal out for my blood. "For the end of Camp Zero."

CHAPTER THIRTY-ONE

Rebecca looked confused. "Excuse me?"

"I said Camp Zero is going to be destroyed." Annabelle practically purred. "And not a moment too soon. Really, I'm surprised Dracula waited this long. I suspect he wanted to make sure you were here, Mister Hawthorne. You've managed to irritate him more than any other mortal in the past century, if my contacts are correct."

The various people sitting at the controls around us continued to work without acknowledging what Annabelle said. They continued at their positions, oblivious to outside stimuli. This despite the fact the monitors showed images of huge cargo ships docking on the shores of the island, ropes coming over their side, and cranes off-loading huge metal containers.

We were being invaded. Annabelle curled her lip into a sneer, the contempt in it beyond measure. It was hard to imagine Christopher falling in love with such a woman, beauty aside, which made me wonder how much Dracula had altered his mind to achieve such a result. Was their entire relationship a lie? I hoped so. Otherwise he would hold it against me when I cut her head off.

"You heard what I said," Annabelle said. "The sun sets on the House this day, and none too soon for their most Frankensteinian creation."

"Actually, I'm quite fond of Frankenstein's Monster. He helped raise me," I said, watching the workers shut down all of the automated defenses before turning off the alerts. Camp Zero's metal doorways opened, leaving the invasion path wide open.

"You have the staff here mesmerized," I said, making an observation. "Even the Greys."

Annabelle's voice was entrancing to listen to, like music. "Indeed, Mister Hawthorne. I was the one who gave hints and clues to Christopher, so he could pass them along to Dracula. Now, an army of the dead and half-living will descend upon this place and a bloody war will be fought."

"You won't be able to release the prisoners," Rebecca said, shaking her head. "Only I can."

"A matter of little concern," Annabelle said. "I have no wish to minimize the casualties the Vampire Nation's forces will suffer."

Annabelle folded up her parasol and raised her veil, revealing a woman whose beauty made me weak in the knees. I took a deep breath and pushed away my awe, remembering she was my enemy. Annabelle was an Elder vampire, which meant anyone who wasn't conditioned to level six or higher was helpless before her gaze.

I narrowed my eyes, forcing away my awe at her looks. She was disgusting, and I should remember that. "What is your game, then? Dracula's attack here will destroy this place, but the House has the Vampire Nation by the balls. The House's forces hopelessly outnumber anything the Council of Ancients can bring to bear."

"Good," Annabelle said, smiling her bright red lips. They contrasted sharply against her marble-like skin. "I've wanted the destruction of the vampire race for centuries. Yet even the Hebrew God betrayed me in the end. The House is every bit as evil as those I have long desired the destruction of. Which is why Camp Zero is such a perfect tool to bring against them both. The Vampire Nation will lose this war, but it will carry stories of the horrors here, and proof of the House's perfidy, to all corners of the globe. The House can defeat one of the great supernatural nations, but it cannot defeat them all. When the Truth comes out, the world you believe in will burn."

"Why would you do this? We trusted you and gave you purpose. We were going to build a better world." Rebecca's reaction surprised me.

Annabelle looked at Rebecca sideways. "My dear, your definition of a better world and mine are quite different. I was going to mesmerize you, but difficult as that would have been, it proved unnecessary. Your unchanged mind is more horrific than any creature I could have turned you into."

"So, you led Dracula here. A lot of vampires die, but they bring word of Protocol Zero to the rest of the world. Anarchy reigns?" I asked, raising an eyebrow. "All for revenge?"

Annabelle shook her head. "Revenge is far from what motivates me. Hate for a lost loved one lasts only a short while, it turns out. At least, for the immortal. No, Mister Hawthorne, this isn't about revenge. This is about the realization that there's something fundamentally wrong with the world and doing something about it."

"Even if millions die," I observed, remembering my vision.

Annabelle wrinkled her nose. "Millions die every year. It is the process of life. Billions will be able to live because of what I am doing."

"What about Christopher?" I asked, surprised I cared more about him than all the House agents who were going to die in a few minutes. "He scoured the world for you. Stole the Bloodsword. Betrayed the Vampire Nation to me. He loves you. This entire sordid business is because he wanted to rescue you from some deep, dark hole he thought you were being held in."

"Christopher fell in love with me because he was made to," Annabelle said. "Dracula controls his minions by giving them what they desire most. Freedom from conscience. Lovers amongst the damned. Wealth. Power. For a time, it was enough to distract me from my beliefs, but Christopher was never anything more than a means to an end—for both me and the Warlord."

"Mother, may I?" Ruthford said, seething during our conversation. Gone was the earlier display of a serene brainwashed figure. In its place was a wild animal containing unimaginable rage, every inch of his body radiating fury.

"Of course, John," Annabelle said, pulling her parasol down from my chest. "Enjoy yourself."

Ruthford then sped around the room, barely visible to the naked eye. The necks of scientists, Greys, monitors, and security guards broke or were torn in two. The vampire terrorist slaughtered everyone inside the control chamber with a furious speed, killing dozens in a span of seconds. It was unnatural, since even the most psychotic vampire would stop to feed with so much blood spilled. Instead, Ruthford's actions were that of a madman driven to kill.

Not a hungry monster.

I was tempted to go for my gun or the Bloodsword to try and stop him, but a number of factors kept me from moving. One, he was doing the dirty work I needed to do. The people here had to die to shut down Camp Zero. If I tried to stop Ruthford, Annabelle would be able to kill me before I could draw my weapon. I needed to wait for the right moment and hope Bloody Mary had my back.

Always, Bloody Mary said, her voice amused. *Even when I'm trying to kill you.*

"You broke his conditioning," Rebecca said, narrowing her eyes. "How?"

Annabelle let out a short laugh. "Ha! That is what you're concerned about when you see a massacre of your coworkers and friends?"

"They can be replaced," Rebecca said. "How?"

I did a double take, looking at my sister like she was a different person.

Annabelle seemed amused by Rebecca's question. "Your torture and mind games are capable of breaking most beings, but the bond between a vampire and his creator is not so easily dashed aside. It took centuries for me to overcome my loyalty to Dracula."

On the monitors, I saw the attack had begun. Bloodslaves, draugr, dhampirs, and vampires were descending on Camp Zero. The mindless undead were there to soak up bullets and intimidate the living while the humans thinned their ranks. The vampires and their half-human offspring then descended on any survivors.

We were in it deep now.

"So why are you keeping us alive?" I asked the obvious question. I had a sneaking suspicion it was vanity. When you reached a certain age as an immortal parasite, you had to take life's pleasures where you got them.

"To give you an ounce of the suffering you have inflicted upon the world with your service to the Illuminated ones. Both as their minion and a member of their Council of False Kings," Annabelle said as a blood-soaked John Ruthford appeared beside her.

Annabelle lifted her right hand and I felt agonizing pain across my body. Like Dracula, Annabelle was a blood magician and possessed the same sorts of powers he'd used to incapacitate me before.

"Scream for me," Annabelle said. "I'll get your father and family eventually. Ruthford, when they cry out, kill them both."

Ruthford grinned, his fangs shining. "With pleasure."

Falling to my knees, I felt Bloody Mary protect me from the worst of the pain, and my hand moved for the Bloodsword.

Right before Rebecca hissed, "You forgot, Annabelle, I am a psychic surgeon."

Rebecca raised her right palm in front of not Annabelle but Ruthford and closed it. The vampire terrorist exploded like a popped balloon, showering all of us in gore. Annabelle's spell was disrupted right before I pulled the Bloodsword free and slashed off the Elder vampire's arms, both exploding into ash as they were separated from her body.

Annabelle hissed, and a shower of blood appeared from her wounds before forming into new arms, a display of mystical power I'd never seen before. She knocked the Bloodsword from my hands before grabbing me by the shoulders and throwing me across the room. I slammed against a set of monitors and rolled across the ground.

Time seemed to slow down as Annabelle moved to kill Rebecca. I reached into my jacket and pulled out my RC-82 before firing it several times into Annabelle's back. The orihalcum bullets struck into the vampire's heart but didn't kill her. Instead, she turned around and transformed into a hideous cloud of black smoke. The smoke seemed to possess features, the faces of screaming children and men visible in its back. It was one of the most hideous things I'd ever seen.

I fired repeatedly, but my bullets did nothing to harm it. Each

254 C. T. Phipps

was soaked up in the smoke, which melted a set of computers it passed through. I had one chance and cast down my gun before grabbing the ring in my pocket. The smoke enveloped me only for me to lash out with the darkness I had in my soul. The shadow magic Bloody Mary had taught me flew freely this time and with ease in every direction.

The smoke screamed.

The toxic black mist around me exploded, scattering in every direction. I saw horrifying images of draugr, pirates, Pantheon Corp towers, myself, and Dracula as Annabelle's magic collided with mine. Several control panels caught fire and a sprinkler system started pouring water down on our heads.

There was no sign of Annabelle. I stumbled over, collapsing from the exertion. I found it small comfort that my evil was greater than Annabelle's. I felt a brief kinship with the woman in that moment but knew at heart she was a victim lashing out—and I was a predator.

"Derek, are you okay?" Rebecca asked, confused. She looked dazed from her sudden and brutal victory over Ruthford.

Impressive. Mary's voice spoke in my head. *Shadow magic is an art you have great talent for. Your control is poor, though. You've filled your body with more black magic than I've seen anyone survive. You should see a doctor about that.*

Is Annabelle gone? I asked, surprised how relieved I was by my demon's survival. I didn't bother to entertain her request. I wasn't that far gone, yet.

I doubt it. Like Dracula, you must break one's connection with Tiamat-Abaddon to slay one such as her, Bloody Mary said. *Are you willing to wrestle with Hell's ruler for that?*

Yeah, I am, I said.

Interesting, Bloody Mary said.

"I'm fine, Rebecca. We just need to get this place's defenses back on," I replied, climbing to my feet and wiping the gore off my body.

"Agreed," Rebecca said. "Camp Zero is too important to lose."

I shook my head, ready to strangle her. Instead, I picked up my gun off the ground. I was down to a half clip.

Rebecca stumbled forward, passing several corpses along the way. She slumped over one of the control panels and batted away a blood-soaked lock of hair before starting to type away at a keyboard. Several small holographic icons appeared, which she moved around like she was on the set of a science fiction film.

"How long will it take to get this place back and running?" I asked, looking down at the ground.

"We can't," Rebecca said, sighing. "They've locked me out of the security protocols. It was a mistake to trust Ruthford with so much."

"You think?" I deadpanned.

"No time for recriminations," Rebecca said. "I've got important things to do."

"Like?"

"I'm dumping the research data and destroying the intranet backups on site. We can't have our information falling into the hands of vampires. It would turn their superstition-driven knowledge of mesmerism into a grand science," Rebecca said, pulling out a magitech-enhanced flash drive from the side. She then tossed it to me. "You need to protect this research with your life. There's over a thousand terabytes inside."

I caught it. Getting her data was proving surprisingly easy. "What about off-site backups?"

"We had two server farms, but they were destroyed by terrorist attacks. I love our father, but the security he provided both was shit. Most of the surviving research is hard copy below, and we'll have to blow that as well."

I tried not to smile. "I understand."

My joy left me as Rebecca turned and inputted another code. The room's ceiling lights turned an eerie shade of red as the alarms blaring were far more menacing than the earlier fuchsia alert siren.

All across the room, the holograms and screens showed the prison cells filling with a thick white smoke. The prisoners banged against the side of the walls, thrashed on the ground, or simply ignored the smoke as they mindlessly rocked themselves.

The living amongst them started violently retching, throwing up, while the undead acted like they were having a seizure.

Soon, they were still.

"Rebecca, what have you done?" I asked, staring in horror.

"Purple Alert," Rebecca said, breathing hard. "We can't have any of the subjects escape. Orihalcum dust mixed with sarin. What a waste."

"Of subjects?"

"What else?" Rebecca said, looking nonplussed.

I looked to one of the monitors, which listed a figure of 1,031 casualties. A tiny number when compared to the seven billion across the world. Yet it was an extraordinary amount of lost time and memories. Some of them had undoubtedly deserved to die, yes, but not all. Not all.

I made my choice.

My sister was a monster.

I hunted monsters.

"Tell me, Rebecca, would you put Shannon through all this if you got your hands on her?"

Rebecca looked up, confused. She turned her head and then the rest of her body to face me, crossing her arms. Her expression told me she was less than interested in the contents of my question, as if I were wasting her time. "Derek, don't be sentimental."

"You're right. I shouldn't be."

I lifted up my gun and shot her in the chest.

My hand shook after the act.

Rebecca looked confused, sliding against the control panel behind her. A large red circle grew around her chest area, my gun having shot her just to the side of the heart. The wound was fatal, but it would take a few minutes for her to die.

So I shot her in the head.

I looked down at her body. My damnation was sealed, but hadn't it been a long time ago? "What a waste."

I dropped the flash drive on the ground and smashed it to pieces with my foot.

CHAPTER THIRTY-TWO

I stared at Rebecca's corpse for a long time. Long enough for the sprinkler system to stop pouring water. I didn't know what the proper time was to stop. What was the right length of time to look at your sister's corpse when there was a crisis? How long did you subtract or add when you were the one who pulled the trigger? Looking up to the damaged controls and monitors around me, I couldn't deny we were in the middle of a crisis. The Vampire Nation's forces had already penetrated Camp Zero and looked like they were overwhelming the guards present.

I still had a job to do and that wasn't changing. I needed to find the backups for Rebecca's research and destroy them. Then I needed to get off this hellhole and figure out a way to make sure the House was prepared for whatever attacks happened next.

This isn't your responsibility, Bloody Mary said. *You don't have to be the one who serves as your brother's keeper.*

I'm already Cain, I said, looking over at Rebecca's corpse again. *Don't try and talk to me in Biblical parable.*

She deserved to die, Bloody Mary said.

So did I, I said.

Heading to one of the few remaining functioning control panels, I tried to draw up a schematic of the building. Along the way, I heard comm traffic from the scientists and guardsmen being slaughtered by Dracula's forces. It was a warzone out there, and they'd been crippled before combat had even begun. Humans versus monsters, and logic told me both needed to be taken down. Emotionally, though, I was on the side of the humans.

Accessing the security feeds, I lifted a headset off a corpse and put it on. "Camp Zero security, this is Committee member Hawthorne. What is your status?"

A flurry of responses filled my headset as I heard gunfire, screams, calm voices, and the sounds of war. Over half of Camp Zero's military forces were dead and almost as many in terms of personnel. No one had any idea how many hostiles were attacking, what direction they were coming from, or who was in the most danger. The fog of war was on the side of the Vampire Nation and it was killing everyone here.

Calling up images from all of the security cameras spread around Camp Zero, I did my best to try and direct the defenders. That, I could help with. "Team C, reinforce Team B in block 17. Teams A and D are destroyed, ignore any calls from them for reinforcement. Team G, I need you to take a collection of C4 to block four and blow up the file collections there. This is high priority. Team Y, prepare for assault from the southwest corridor. You've got incoming hostiles. Everyone else, hold your positions and dig in until we can get an organized evacuation going."

A series of affirmatives answered me before I also checked the rest of the systems to see if I could get any of the camp's defenses working again. Annabelle and Ruthford had done a number on the interior security systems. I wasn't a hacker, either, so I couldn't get the majority of them back online.

What I *could* do was shut the metal doors on several of Dracula's goons. It wouldn't do much in the long run, especially given that I saw they'd already infiltrated Camp Zero's armory, but it would give the defending forces some breathing room.

"Derek?" Shannon's voice spoke in my earpiece.

"Shannon?"

"No, it's the Easter Bunny. We're on the island's southern tip. Nathan sent us a blind spot to bring our boat in. All hell has broken loose."

"No kidding."

Penny spoke as well. "There's a hidden set of docks here. A bunch of the janitorial staff and some soldiers accompanying them are trying to flee here. I torched a set of draugr led by some sort of kennel master. The vampires are using them like dogs to sniff out the living. What do you want us to do with the survivors?"

"Is Malcolm with you?" I asked.

There was a sound like a microphone being grabbed. "You think we run away like yapping dogs? You don't know us, yo."

"I was worried you'd go on a rampage."

"That's better, D. There's dignity in that."

"He arrived with a pack of his brothers. Six very beefy black werewolf-looking dudes. The guards are rather freaked out by them. I had to turn their guns into salamanders to keep a firefight from breaking out," Penny spoke.

"Can you do that?" I tried to imagine what she was saying.

"Okay, I just made them jam, but it was cooler sounding my way. What do you want us to do with the survivors?"

It occurred to me Nathan Hawthorne would have wanted me to let them die. I didn't take orders from my father, though. "I'm going to inform the rest of the security any werewolves they see are on our side. I don't see any shape-shifters amongst Dracula's people anyway. Try and keep the survivors secure and I'm going to try and get an evacuation going."

"Are you sure that's wise?" Penny asked. "We're here to shut this place down."

I looked over at Rebecca. "I've taken care of the problem. Once we get the evacuation going, I'll radio the American government to bomb this place to the Stone Age. With any luck, Dracula will get caught in the explosion."

"That won't do you any good," Christopher's voice said behind me. "Because you'll already be dead."

"Oh sh—"

For the second time in half an hour, I found myself being thrown across the room. This time, I was able to manipulate my body's ki to harden my muscles and avoid getting my entire back bruised when I hit the wall. My gun, however, flew out of my hands. It hit the wall, discharging a bullet through a nearby window before clattering to the ground several feet away.

Christopher stood there, his business suit replaced with an all-black, form-fitting Phantom-suit like the kind Sons of Mars mercenaries had used to infiltrate Division One last year. On Christopher, it reminded me of a ninja's attire, which amused me since they were about the one thing I'd never fought before.

There were numerous blood splatters on Christopher's clothes, and I had to wonder how many people he'd killed on his way inside. Given he had both the natural stealth abilities of a vampire and the invisibility provided by the Phantom-suit, I no longer questioned how he'd gotten most of his information. He'd probably been walking the corridors of Camp Zero for weeks.

I also noticed Christopher had a silencer-equipped RC-214 in his right hand, which meant he was fully capable of killing me without touching me. Not that I could put up much of a fight right now. The events of the past twenty minutes had exhausted me, and I wasn't in the right headspace for doing battle with my ex-partner.

Coughing, my lungs inexplicably feeling tight, I covered my mouth. Pulling it away, I saw it was soaked in blood. Looking up to Christopher, I said, "So, that's how it's going to be? Forget all the David and Jonathan stuff. You're just going to kill me."

Christopher didn't aim his RC-214 at me. Instead, he just kept it facing the ground. "It would appear I'm not in control of my actions."

"Yeah, your AI doppelganger told me you were mind controlled."

Christopher smiled. "You have no idea how much effort it took to make sure I could make it free of Dracula's control. My entire life as a vampire, I have thought I was acting with free will. Yet now, here, I realize everything was a lie."

I thought of my relationship to the Red Room. "There's a lot of that going around."

Christopher aimed the RC-214 up at my head then jerked it to one side, shooting one of the damaged control panels. "I am capable of resisting to a limited extent. Dracula's orders were quite clear, though. Since you went off script, I am to kill you."

I didn't go for the Bloodsword or the gun on the ground. I could have drawn both to my hands. Instead, I just looked at my ex-partner. The person who'd helped Ashley get to freedom. "There's been a huge number of double, triple, and quadruple crosses around here. Dracula was playing you to get to me, Annabelle was playing you to get to Dracula, Nathan was playing Rebecca, I was playing Rebecca, and all of us were playing each other."

"Amazing how all of this has come to a head because you're immune to being mind controlled." Christopher aimed his gun at my head again. This time, he jerked it at the last second and fired above me.

"I wouldn't give myself too much credit. Ashley did something to my brain to protect me from mind-readers. It's possible she supercharged my resistance while she was at it."

"Always humble. You will not be pushed, filed, stamped, indexed, briefed, debriefed, or numbered," Christopher quoted *The Prisoner*. "Your life is your own. Whether it is because of your own will or a gift of love doesn't matter. The fact is you have a freedom I have never so envied."

"You can fight this, Chris."

"I'm trying to, believe me," Christopher said, starting to advance, the gun in his hand pointed at my heart. "Yet Dracula has been fine-tuning my mind for years. He's my sire, I'm sorry to say. I never had a chance to disobey him."

"You can do this."

"This isn't the movies, Derek. This place is a temple to what torture, mind control, and oppression can do to a mind. I am unable to resist the orders he's given me and every second I try, my will goes weaker. You need to kill me, my friend."

"I *can't*."

Bloody tears started to fall from his eyes as he stood over my body, his finger on the trigger. "What's worse is I know my feelings for Annabelle were a lie. That the desperate overwhelming need for her and worry was all implanted in my head. That she was never in any danger."

I hoped, against all reason, Annabelle was dead because she was not worth my friend's pain. I wanted to lie to my friend, tell him she had loved him all along. That the Vampire Nation was worth saving or Dracula hadn't played him like a Stradivarius. It was all a lie, though, and what I wanted to hear about the Red Room.

"Shannon and I still love you."

His finger twitched on the trigger.

I moved to one side, right before the gun went off. Christopher jerked back and I jumped up, delivering a brutal right blow to his jaw before punching another and flipping the vampire over into the electrical consoles nearby.

You need to kill him, Bloody Mary said.

Dracula's the one pulling the strings here, not him. I clenched my teeth, unable to see another way to stop him.

He wants you to kill him. Mary sounded desperate. End his suffering.

Shut up! I said.

I could make you. Mary snapped.

No, you can't, I said.

White-hot rage started to fill me, my blood boiling with hatred as everything turned around me. The Bloodsword flew to my hands and an overwhelming urge to kill Christopher, to save my life and the lives of any of his future victims, drowned out everything. I wanted to chop him up and seize his power for my own. But I didn't.

This was still Christopher. Someone who I'd known for years and counted as my friend and brother-in-arms. I'd given myself to the bloodlust throughout this quest, but that had been against the vampires who'd taken him from me. I would not kill my friend, not for Dracula, not for Mary, and not for myself. I am free.

Somehow, I willed my sword to fall from my hands and the sensation of astonishment from Mary couldn't be measured. The blade clattered against the ground while Christopher advanced, oblivious to the struggle that had just occurred.

Don't let yourself be killed, Mary begged. It was so uncharacteristic, I had no words to answer her.

Christopher rose from the ruined devices, electrical current swirling around his body, into his eyes, and through his fingertips. Vampirism hadn't taken away his proficiency with electromancy, it seemed. Indeed, he fed off the power, and all of the monitors and machines went dead around me.

Lifting his right hand, he aimed it at a fuse box and a stream of electricity flew from it into his palm. "The sad part is, I feel the same way. But we're not allowed to feel. We are just pawns in the game. Move here, move there. Love isn't part of what we're allowed to feel."

I ducked to the ground as he threw a bolt of lightning over my head. If he'd really been aiming, I'd be dead, but he wasn't. He was going through the motions of trying to kill me, perhaps even trying to work up the resolve to do so. That gave me time to save his life. To figure out a way to break him free from Dracula's mesmerism.

Ducking behind a corridor, I said, "That's what Dracula wants you to think. What the Committee does. They can only control us with our consent."

"Do you think I want this?!" Christopher shouted, his fangs bearing and his visage contorting into something hideous. All around me, the remaining undamaged controls sparked and caught fire. This time, the sprinkler system didn't put out the flames, letting the fire continue to grow.

I shouted, wondering if there was some sort of mystical hoodoo I could do to fix him. Mind-magic was an untapped field for me. Even if I could, I had no idea of the hows. Instead, I relied on words. "We freed Ashley together. We can free you!"

"Ashley is still dominated by the Red Room, Derek. I spoke to her last month. She's the head of the Network, spending her life in a futile attempt to cast down the organization that ruined her life. She's still defined by the system, dominated by it, and unable to escape."

I processed what he'd said. "Christopher, I can help you."

Christopher appeared behind me, grabbing me. Before I could respond, I felt an arc of electricity run through me. It was like being tasered, and my entire body went into a seizure that disabled me.

"No, you can't," Christopher said, biting me on the side of the neck.

Despite my lengthy experience with the undead, I had never been bitten before. I'd spoken to many victims, and they tended to describe a feeling of incandescent ecstasy. What I felt, instead, was nightmarish pain and agony.

It was like a series of saw blades being jammed into my neck and pressing down deep into my jugular. I moved my hands up to try and press my thumbs against Christopher's eyes as I felt gulps of blood enter his mouth. But try as I might, I couldn't get enough force up to make him stop drinking.

Why does it always fall to me to do the dirty work? Bloody Mary's voice was bored and disinterested.

But I could hear a trace of fear.

I felt Mary's presence pass from my body through the blood Christopher was drinking. The medium of exchange left me feeling woozy and confused, the vampire dropping me to the ground like a sack of potatoes. I moved my hand to the wound and it sealed over. The magic felt cleaner and more potent inside me. Without Bloody Mary's presence, draining much of my power to feed herself, I had a strength that I couldn't believe.

So, I straightened my legs before jumping and kicking Christopher in the face, smashing him into the elevators across the room. Christopher retched, choking on my blood. I ran and slammed him up against the wall before punching him hard in the chest, then smashing him across the jaw. Grabbing his wrist, I threw him on the ground and placed my foot on his neck.

"Breaking this won't kill you. It will, however, stop you from trying to do the same to me."

Christopher didn't respond, lying still. His was a ruined mass of gore, regenerating but at a glacially slow pace.

I took a deep breath, placing my hands on my knees. "Please don't jump up in a few seconds when I lower my guard. 'Cause I can't deal with that slasher movie bullshit right now."

I felt a presence leave his body, shimmering as the lights flickered above our heads. The blood of my sister and a dozen other corpses started pouring from their mouths, eyes, and wounds before forming into a puddle. From the puddle started to emerge a feminine pair of hands which then began to claw the ground in front of her. The top of a redheaded woman climbed out of the puddle, revealing the naked figure of Bloody Mary.

She was alive.

CHAPTER THIRTY-THREE

A ll around me was fire, the heat from the burning consoles wafting across my face as the air started to fill with smoke. A suitable atmosphere for the "Aphrodite rising from the waves" scene playing out before me. Bloody Mary herself was not covered in blood, but arose from it like sea-foam.

An incarnate demon.

Incarnates were amongst the most dangerous of all demons. They were physical manifestations of beings composed of thought. As such, they were not bound by things like the laws of physics or biology. It all made sense now. The blood sacrifices I'd been doing left and right had been feeding Bloody Mary's power. The power you got from killing a human was nothing compared to what you got from killing a vampire. I'd been so focused on getting what I wanted from the Bloodsword, I'd never bothered to think just what the hell Mary was getting in return.

Now I knew. Life.

I was surprisingly calm, and instead of doing something rash like shooting her or attacking, I walked to a nearby fire extinguisher on the wall. Picking it up, I began putting out the electrical fires surrounding me so I didn't suffocate or burn to death. If Mary wanted to kill me, there was precious little I could do about it right now. I'd bet everything on the Bloodsword, and now it was turning against me.

"I can still hear your thoughts, Derek," Bloody Mary said, frowning. "Really, I'm disappointed. You still think I'm going to betray you? Have I not demonstrated I am on your side?"

"I'm not what you'd call a trusting sort," I said, spraying the last of the flames out. "One of my closest friends just tried to kill me."

"Not willingly."

"This is the Grand High Cathedral of Not Willing."

"Not one of your better quips."

"I'm running low. Sorry."

Bloody Mary flicked her fingers and the shadows around the room swirled around her, covering her body and transforming into a magician's attire. She had a red top hat with a Queen of Hearts in the ribbon, the top half of a tuxedo, and the bottom half of bikini briefs over a set of high heels. Her makeup was thick and pasty with extra blush, giving her the look of a sexy harlequin.

"Matter from nothing," I said, staring at her. "Impressive."

"As a spirit, I am not as limited as a mortal minion."

"I can't say I approve of the body, though. Fun house chic isn't a fetish of mine."

Mary smiled at me. "Liar."

She had me there. "What do you want?"

Mary strode over to me, placing her arms around my waist and staring up into my eyes. "To kill Dracula."

"You don't have to—" I started to say before she placed a passionate kiss on my lips, biting my lip at the end to draw blood.

I pulled away, licking the inside of my lip. "I don't think that's going to help."

"Yet, you'd be mine if it helped you kill Dracula?"

"Yes."

She smiled. "I'm insulted. Yet in time, you will come to love me as I have come to love you. As will others you love. Kill Dracula for me, Derek Hawthorne, and I will provide you with the power to be an archwizard."

"No."

"No?" Bloody Mary asked, surprised.

"A. Dracula is immortal. So, killing him is like waiting for him to respawn in an online shooter, and B, I've got bigger things to worry about."

Bloody Mary wrinkled her brow. "What could be more important than murder?"

It was a bad thing that made me smile, right? "Christopher.

I need to figure out how the hell to fix him."

I wasn't sure Christopher could be fixed. There was no magical cure to mesmerism and even if, somehow, Dracula did die, then all of the damage he'd done to people's minds wouldn't magically fix itself. My father was a master mentalist but even with all he owed me, I doubt I could convince him to help.

Bloody Mary chuckled. "What if I could solve both your problems?"

I had a creeping sensation of dread, but also hope. "You'd think I'd know better than to get myself further involved here."

She smiled. "You are simply enjoying someone who accepts you for who you are."

"I have Shannon for that."

"I could teach Shannon to accept who she is as well. We would make a wonderful trio."

"I'll bear that in mind if I need a gang of killers."

"You *always* need a gang—"

"How can you help Christopher?"

"Promise to kill Dracula for me and I will give Christopher back his free will. I will also show you how to kill him permanently."

"You mean kill Dracula forever, right?" Exact wording was important when you were making a deal with a demon.

"Yes."

I knew I was being tricked here, but I didn't care. "Agreed." I'd have agreed to anything to save Christopher.

Bloody Mary gave me another kiss on the lips. "Excellent."

The demon turned around and walked to Christopher's side, placing her hand to his forehead. Her body collapsed into blood and the blood soaked into Christopher's skin, disappearing. My fallen comrade thrashed on the ground, looking like he was being eaten alive. He opened his mouth to scream but no sound escaped his lips.

Then he fell still.

Christopher's mouth again opened, slowly this time, and a bloody red mist poured out, reforming into Mary. She was still wearing her peculiar costume.

"It is done." Mary said, conjuring a plastic magic wand like the kind you bought at costume shops.

I decided to believe her. "How do I kill Dracula for good?"

"Break his contract with Tiamat-Abaddon."

I glared at her. "I already knew that."

"But you do not comprehend," Bloody Mary said, smiling. "A contract between a god and a mortal is like any other magical spell. It can be dispelled with sufficient application of magical force."

"You want me to just wave my hand." I did so for emphasis. "Then, poof, Dracula is vulnerable?"

"It will require much more effort than that, but yes, that's more or less what you have to do."

"Uh-huh."

Bloody Mary made her wand disappear and put her hands on her shapely hips. "I have not given you all the magical power you could ever need for you to fail, lover. Believe me, you have enough power to kill the Warlord."

I stared at my hand, wondering if it were true. "Is that what this all about? You want someone to kill Dracula?"

"Is it so hard to believe someone loves you unconditionally?" Bloody Mary asked. "That they wish to help you because you are an avatar of war?"

"You need to look up the word 'unconditionally' in the dictionary. I'm not going to change to be your professional warrior."

"Oh, dearest Derek, I don't want you to change at all because you already are."

Bloody Mary vanished into a swirl of blood while I felt the pressure from my brain release. She was gone.

For now.

I didn't have time to think about that. There were other things on my mind, like the fact that I was in a war zone with the people I cared about most. "Christopher . . ." I said, stumbling over to his side.

Christopher then hissed, his fangs extending. I jolted back, but he didn't go for my throat. Instead, he rolled over and began retching again. Clearing his throat, Christopher's face returned to normal. "Derek, your blood tastes *terrible*."

Lifting my pistol to his head, I said, "Remember that the next time you decide you want to snack on me. What do you feel like?"

Christopher rubbed his forehead. "Like killing Dracula. Sleeping with Shannon. Sleeping in general."

I narrowed my eyes. "Are you trying to get me to stake you?"

"I'm just being honest." He looked up at me for several seconds. "Okay, I don't feel like killing you."

"Will wonders never cease."

"What did you do?" Christopher asked, looking at me.

"What I always do. What I had to."

Christopher climbed to his feet and ran his fingers through his hair. "It's like I've been asleep for years. Everything is sharper now. I remember what's happened in the past but it's just . . . nonsensical. My past reasoning makes no sense."

"Because you were brainwashed."

Christopher looked up. "I've killed, Derek."

"Join the club."

"Innocents. Men, women, and—"

"Don't tell me anything you don't want me to know."

His hands shook as he looked down at them. "I'm still a vampire. I smell your blood and want to taste it. All the corpses here smell delicious, too. It's ... disgusting. I can hear the gunfire and the death. They sound like music."

I moved my pistol toward his heart. "I can end it if you want."

"After all the effort you went through to not kill me?"

"You weren't yourself before." I didn't want to hurt Christopher, not when he was finally back. *Really* here for the first time. If he didn't want to be a vampire, I respected that. I'd help him die if he desired it.

Gods help us all.

Christopher took several breaths, even though he no longer needed oxygen. "I want to live. I want to rend flesh. I want to help people. I want to kill Dracula. I don't want to kill innocents. I have a whirlwind in my head now."

"You're still a vampire. That's not going to change."

"No shit." Christopher looked up, meeting my gaze. "Thank you."

"You're welcome." I lowered my gun. "Don't try and kill me again. Next time, I might not be so nice."

"I won't," Christopher said, feeling his fangs. "There's no chance the House would take me back, is there?"

"Would you want to rejoin them?" I asked, imagining him as a vampire agent in service of those he'd betrayed, however unwittingly. No, I couldn't picture it. They might use a defecting vampire, but they'd never trust someone who'd served the Red Room once only to become an agent of another power.

Christopher looked around the ruined control room. "No way in hell. This place is insane. That doesn't mean I'm not in the mood to kick some ass."

I looked out one of the control room's windows to the gas-filled prison cells below. "I know what you mean. There's a war coming. One I can't stop. You need to keep your head low during it, unless you want to be killed."

"I have friends who'd be willing to help me set up a new life. Ones without fangs. I don't suppose you can replicate whatever you did to me. There's plenty of my kind out there who'd be decent people if they weren't mind controlled out the ears."

"Sorry, I think this is a one-time deal." I walked over to the Bloodsword and picked it up, sheathing it in my coat again.

"Pity. There are people out there who know something about breaking vampire mesmerism. Maybe I can help others of my kind break free."

"Will you help me kill Dracula first?" I asked, wondering if it was really possible to kill the Warlord forever.

"Tiamat-Abaddon herself couldn't keep me away."

Before I could say anything else, the elevators behind me pinged and revealed someone was coming up. Taking position in front of them, Christopher picked up his gun and aimed it beside me. It felt like we were partners again, two against the world.

"Don't shoot until you know they're unfriendly."

"Are there any friendlies here?"

"More than you'd think."

My statement proved to be accurate, as the doors opened to reveal Malcolm, Penny, Shannon, Shadow and the twins, Night and Day—all wearing wetsuits covered in stolen Kevlar. They were sporting stolen assault rifles and bandoliers of grenades. The other three werewolves were missing. From Malcolm's somber look, it wasn't that difficult to believe they'd suffered casualties getting here.

"Christopher?" Shannon said, looking at him then me.

"Hey, Red," Christopher said. "I owe your boyfriend one."

"Damn straight you do," I said.

Shannon tossed down her gun and embraced him.

I looked between the two of them. "A lesser man might be jealous."

They kissed.

"Don't be," Shannon said, giving Christopher another hug.

Penny didn't pay attention. "Derek, we've got a serious pro—oh my god, Rebecca."

Penny ran to the side of our fallen sister and took her by the arm. She clutched her to her chest and held her.

"What happened?" Penny asked, her voice shaking.

I thought of all the times my sister had looked after Rebecca, babysitting or helping her study for the Black Room.

"I'll tell you later," I said, closing my eyes. "Malcolm, what's the situation down there?'

I ignored the fact that I'd told them to stay put. Clearly, Shannon had chosen to defy my order.

Not that I was in any position to point fingers.

"Stone and Hyperion were killed by the Silverblade," Malcolm said, looking cold. "Shannon managed to hold him as we enacted our blood-price, though. We left Cobalt behind to guard the survivors we've rescued. He's unlikely to kill them all. How many shapechangers died here?"

"A lot," I said, staring at him. "They're dead now or will be soon."

Malcolm looked at Rebecca, then me, putting the pieces together in his head. His next words said everything that needed to be said. "I'll tell the Council you took care of this. That should be enough."

"Who's that?" Night asked, pointing at Christopher, still holding Shannon.

"A friend," I said. "Despite how he's holding my girl."

Shannon glared at me.

"Great, now we have a Fang in the gang," Shadow said. "This just keeps getting better and better."

"Thank you," I said, smiling. "I try. Now, we can do one of two things. We can slip quietly away or—"

"Dracula's downstairs," Christopher interrupted, breaking from Shannon. "Derek knows how to kill him. Forever."

"You heard all that?" I did a double take.

"I am a spy," Christopher said, shrugging.

Shannon walked back to me. "Then I guess we know where we're going next."

I looked at Malcolm and Penny.

Penny rose from Rebecca's corpse. "I'm in."

Malcolm looked at his remaining pack. "I have lost two good friends today. They will torment me in the afterlife forever if I don't make their deaths count."

I slapped my hands together and rubbed. "Okay, time to get Hammer Horror on his ass then.

CHAPTER THIRTY-FOUR

Camp Zero was being sacked.

That was the only word for it as my group moved from the prison to the barracks of Camp Zero. It was one of the bloodiest warzones I'd seen in my life, and I'd seen dozens. Despite my attempts to help the defenders put up a fight, we'd passed numerous bodies that had been raped, drained of blood, torn apart, or some combination thereof.

The victims of the draugr were especially hideous. The ghoul-like creatures didn't restrict themselves to drinking the blood of their victims but devoured them whole. Several times, we'd come across people being eaten alive. Lacking proper medical care and having no magic, there was nothing to do but put a bullet in the head of the dying after finishing off their attackers.

The mayhem of the vampires wasn't limited to slaughter. It was surreal, but even though this place was a prison, the vampires were trying to loot its contents. There were firefights among them, duels with swords, and even battles with their bare-handed claws.

When they couldn't come across living victims, they trashed whatever equipment or furniture they could find. Their history as pirates was not so distant a memory, it seemed. Either that, or the undead made it a point to recruit psychotic criminals.

Whatever the case, the defeat of Camp Zero's forces made it easier to sneak around through the place, and the extra gunfire when we ambushed the small groups that remained didn't hurt. They were too busy enjoying their "victory" to note that there were still living soldiers moving around the base, and there was no sign of organization to their horde. A few vampires had radios, but they weren't all that interested in using them.

I was taking point, having searched several dead guards for appropriate body armor and weapons. Christopher was at my side, using his status as a well-known vampire to get a few of them to lower their guard. Penny was in the middle, the perfect position to aid us with her magic, while the werewolves and Shannon followed up the rear. The whole thing felt like one of the video games I often kicked back with, only a lot more serious.

Surprise was on our side, and by the time we started nearing where Christopher indicated Dracula was, we'd eliminated almost twenty attackers without any of them being able to call for help. The werewolves were uncomfortable using firearms versus their claws, but I was trying to keep us inconspicuous.

We were nearing the end of the barracks and coming to a tunnel that led to one of the other "balls" when Christopher pointed to an open doorway, beside which a V in a circle was drawn in blood on the wall.

"We're getting close to Dracula." Christopher also looked nervous, as if all the blood around us was testing his patience.

"How close?" I asked, having relied on their connection to get us this far.

"Very close." Christopher looked away from a headless corpse nearby. "Close enough that he'll start picking up my presence soon, even if he's not looking for it."

"That's . . . not good."

"It might be," Christopher corrected. "With any luck, he thinks you're dead and I'm coming to report back in."

"How the hell did he know where I was, anyway?"

Christopher glanced sideways at me. "I've kind of been following you since the incident at the blood slave safe house."

"Wait, what?"

Malcolm, standing behind him, added, "What?"

"I was there with Skull Squadron," Christopher said, staring down at his feet. "When they fucked things up, I went invisible. The bit with the Chevrolet was *hilarious*, by the way. Sorry about sending the djinn after you."

"You better be sorry about it," Shannon said, growling. She

was a mixture of emotions about Christopher's return, and I was going to have to talk about where we stood on this. A part of me felt hypocritical feeling jealous, given our earlier conversation and my attraction to Bloody Mary, especially since Christopher was on our side.

Probably.

"Any chance your Phantom-suit will help with Dracula?" I asked.

"I doubt it," Christopher said. "Everything I can do, he can do better, and several times, no less. That includes seeing through technological illusions like this new House tech can do."

"I am not afraid of Dracula," Malcolm said, puffing up his chest.

"You should be," Christopher said. "You got yourself killed by a bunch of dhampir. He's a whole new ballgame."

"They had assault rifles," Malcolm snapped.

"So will Dracula's men. They're psychopaths, not stupid." Christopher glared at the werewolf. Since he'd joined the group, the already palpable tension had gotten worse. It was just the promise of bigger game in Dracula that kept them from tearing into each other.

"You were killed, Pack Lord?" Shadow asked.

"It is unimportant," Malcolm said, looking away.

Shadow growled, turning from him.

I snapped my fingers, drawing everyone's attention to me. "I don't suppose anyone has any suggestions for getting Dracula alone when we get to him? Even with all of the army spread through this place, he's going to have guards."

"Challenge him to a duel," Christopher said. "He'll be honor-bound to accept."

"Really?"

"Fuck no. What do you think this is, a movie?" Christopher shook his head. "We may be in a better position to ambush him than you might think, though. Black Squadron was part of his personal entourage, and a bunch of others didn't survive the destruction of Dracula's jet. Besides, any vampire who guards him is ornamental. He's the real threat."

"How tough are we talking here?" I asked, wondering at our chances.

"Remember the Lord of Chains?" Christopher said, bringing up the fallen demigod who represented Haiti's history of slavery.

"The one who ended up dying because we had a chain gun on the back of a car and LAW rockets?"

"Those would be very helpful right now," Christopher said. "He's got the power of an archwizard and a body that has absorbed the strength of thousands of dead. About the only thing we've got going for us is that you have the Bloodsword and its demon."

"Yeah," I said, not bothering to inform him that Mary had decided to take a hike.

Signaling for everyone to follow, we headed through the door and found ourselves descending into the basement level of Camp Zero. All along the wall, there were pictures of the staff celebrating various milestones and holidays. It was hard to reconcile their cruel, almost inhuman experiments with the images of people giving each other hugs or celebrating Christmas.

Then again, I was an assassin approaching three hundred kills. For close to a decade and a half, I'd killed and killed for the House. When I started, they told me all of my victims were evil and produced evidence to support that claim. Later, I stopped asking. Had Camp Zero started that way, or were the researchers here untroubled by such worries?

I knew people who were loving parents and spouses yet were willing to do unspeakable things to supernatural beings. They just didn't count as people to them. One agent I'd sanctioned, my first kill in fact, had gone on a killing spree because she'd discovered her husband had latent fairy blood. Her first victim had been her son upon his manifesting Redcap traits.

Comparing the monstrous acts performed by the staff and the vampires, it was hard not to draw the conclusion that neither humans nor supernaturals were the "real monsters." No, the evidence said both were, and we were far more similar than we gave ourselves credit for. Gods help us all.

We turned around a corner and the interior of the hallway

started to stink of blood. It was a smell, along with ripe, open intestines, that was unmistakable. The smell was more concentrated here than in the rest of the Camp, though, and there were indistinct hideous animal noises coming from down the hall.

I made a "shh" gesture before advancing, Christopher falling a step behind. Looking back, I saw his fangs were out, and he looked like he was trying desperately to concentrate. It was hard to imagine what he'd gone through these past few years.

I'd always assumed vampires had some natural instinct or sociopathic tendency that allowed them to do the things they did. If mesmerism was the reason vampires were capable of killing humans for food, then I'd done Christopher as much a disservice as a favor by freeing him of his conditioning.

"Do we need to fall back?" I mouthed.

Christopher shook his head and waved me forward, pulling out his pistol and lifting it above his head. Unlike the rest of us, he didn't use an assault rifle. That was because with his "new and improved" reflexes, headshots were never a problem— even against targets as fast as him. He was like a sniper with a handgun.

I nodded and mouthed, "All right."

Moving around the corner, I saw something from a horror film. As if the rest of the nightmare wasn't bad enough, a hallway of carnage greeted us. A dozen draugr were crouched over the dead, feasting on arms, legs, and even heads they'd cracked open to get the brains inside.

Draugr were hideous things, existing in the uncanny valley between human and corpse, their faces sunken in and their skin stretched tight against their skulls. These were older examples of their kind, so their noses had rotted off and bat-like patagia had formed between their arms and bodies.

Their ears had also expanded, becoming large circular things that stretched out. The draugr were a mixture of races but their skin had lost all pigment, becoming albino-white. They didn't bother with clothes, moving around naked on the ground amongst the filth and gore.

Yet as bad as the draugr were, it was the pair of dhampir at the end of the hall who were the worst. A man and a woman in working-class sailor's attire, the pair were surveying the draugr and looking *bored* during the process. The woman was rocking back and forth on her feet and it took me a second to realize she was listening to an iPod.

I told myself I was shooting them first for strategic purposes, but as they noticed me, I pulled down the trigger for other reasons. I wanted them to die. The insides of their chests exploded as I fired the M90 into both of their ribcages. The bullets inside the gun were exploding orihalcum rounds, doubly dangerous to monsters but with twice as much recoil.

The draugr all looked up at once, their gore-filled mouths dripping as they sensed new prey. I fell to my knees and started firing upwards, Penny lifting her staff up and sending the first six flying backward. Christopher fired at them, rapidly sending shot after shot into their sides, but the others came up behind them. The draugr ran up the sides of the walls and crawled on the ceiling, leaping with inhuman speed and unspeakable hunger.

Thankfully, we had hungry and fast predators of our own. The other attacking draugr were smashed from the air by three huge grey-furred wolves that tore into them. I kept firing over their heads into the draugr while Christopher and Shannon shot over my head. The ringing in my ears was tremendous as draugr heads exploded and others fell down.

Several seconds later, there were a lot more corpses spread across the ground. The draugr were dismembered, torn to shreds and being feasted on the same way they had done to others. It was no less unsettling when being done by my allies.

Getting up, I felt my right ear. The ringing inside both ears was terrible. "This is why I try and wear earplugs before combat."

"Please . . ." The female dhampir was still alive, my bullets having missed her heart. She stretched her hand out, a last-ditch attempt to save her life.

Christopher strode through the blood and werewolf butchery to kneel beside her and stick his fangs into her neck.

I looked away as he tore away the last few moments of the woman's life, sucking on the wound.

"Okay, that's disgusting." Penny covered her mouth and nose. The stench of carnage around us was overwhelming.

I was used to it.

"Come on, we don't have much time," I said, imagining what would happen once Dracula's makeshift army finished their revelry and started regrouping.

Shannon said, "Why would Dracula even create draugr?"

"Pretty damn intimidating, aren't they?" I asked, watching the Dead Coyotes shift back to their human forms, clothing intact. "I bet he keeps pits of these things and tosses prisoners down them like it's the fifteenth century."

Christopher broke away from the corpse he'd drained. "He does."

I'd been kidding. "Okay, how far are we from him?"

"He's right down the hall," Christopher said, getting up. His face was blank, empty of emotion. "We're almost done."

"Good," Shannon said, looking at the corpses. "I want a piece of him every bit as much as the next person."

"If the next person is me, you really don't," Christopher said, walking forward. He paid no attention to formation and moved like a zombie. I had no idea if it was because this was his first feeding since being free or if it had to do with Dracula's presence. Either way, I reluctantly followed him and everyone else moved to do the same, our shoes sloshing in the crimson mire underneath us.

The group proceeded down yet another hallway, this one opening to a large warehouse filled with dozens of metal shipping crates, racks of equipment, scaffolding, and ramps leading up to garage entrances. It was too large to properly secure, and crossing the area would put us in danger of being ambushed. The place was huge, easily the size of a football stadium. A reminder of how big this place really was.

Christopher pointed to the end of the warehouse, which had a yellow door beside yet another garage door entrance. "There."

I didn't like this. "Christopher, are you sure you're okay?"

"I feel his presence. It's all-encompassing. Like a black hole that wants to suck me back in."

Shannon raised her gun behind his back, her face a mix of emotions. All of them tortured.

I shook my head at her.

She nodded.

"Are you going to be okay?"

"I'm never going to be okay again, but you can tell Shannon to lower her gun. I'm not going to turn on you."

"I already did."

Christopher gave a short laugh. "You were too trusting, then."

"Why?"

"We've been made." Christopher looked up.

Looking up, I saw on the ceiling were nine more vampires. These were different from the rest of them. They were wearing stealth suits like Christopher but had disengaged their invisibility and were aiming laser-sight sniper rifles at our chests. One of them fell to the ground, landing on her feet before removing a mask to reveal the face of Elizabeth Cambridge.

"Why does this keep happening to me?" I muttered, raising my hand to keep everyone from doing something stupid.

Christopher didn't move, his eyes resting squarely on Elizabeth Cambridge. "Probably because you're the only person stupid enough to try and kill Dracula."

"Point taken."

CHAPTER THIRTY-FIVE

Seconds passed.

Elizabeth Cambridge stared at us, her gaze every bit as cold at Annabelle's, yet she gave no order for her soldiers to fire. The leader of Black Squadron was holding her assassins back, for reasons I could only guess. I was hoping it was because the pirate was going to join us, but such good fortune rarely existed in my life.

"Let me guess, you don't want to kill us," I said, keeping my hands raised in the air. "Glad to hear it. I knew you'd turn around."

"You are very wrong, Mister Hawthorne. I want to kill a great deal." Elizabeth Cambridge kept her eyes focused on me, ignoring the others. "With the slightest movement of my hand, my new Black Squadron will avenge their lost comrades."

Despite her words, she still hadn't given the command to fire, and I had to capitalize on her hesitation. If there were any doubts in her mind, I needed to make use of them. "The Vampire Nation doesn't take prisoners unless it intends to turn them. I can assure you, all of my people are ready to die before letting that happen. Christopher, certainly, knows it is a fate worse than death. Given I suspect you'd rather not spend eternity with me, you must have another reason to hold back."

"I need answers," Elizabeth said, determined.

Looking to my sides, I saw both Shannon and Penny were ready to fight. I shook my head. Violence wasn't the answer right now. No matter how bad our situation was, trying to get out of it when they had us dead to rights would be suicide.

Malcolm and his pack retreated into the shadows behind us, ready to use us as shields—a tactical choice I didn't begrudge them as long as they didn't start shooting.

"Answers you will have," I said, wondering what she wanted to know.

"I no longer feel Annabelle's presence. She might be regenerating, or she might be lost to the void. Who has killed her?"

Well, crap. Answering that question wasn't going to help our situation.

Christopher interrupted before I could. "Who has killed her is an answer you already know. *Dracula* is responsible for her demise. He has led us to ruin, Elizabeth. Even you, his most loyal disciple, must realize this. This attack has achieved us nothing."

"It has killed hundreds of House warriors." Elizabeth started to walk to us. "That alone justifies this attack."

"This place was the product of Annabelle's mind," Christopher said, stretching out his arms and gesturing to the building around us. "We cannot win a war with the Committee and its allies. Annabelle designed it that way. She hasn't been well for a very long time."

I leaned over and whispered. "Can we avoid bringing up her role in all this? I don't think that's going to win her over."

"Trust me. I know my wife's best friend," Christopher said, not bothering to look at me. "The truth is best."

"Annabelle gave you everything." Elizabeth sneered. "You should have died in New York. It would have spared the Vampire Nation much."

"Annabelle is dead, but not by our hands," Christopher lied. "Dracula's people tore her apart. She was never anything more than a pawn to him. We have a method to destroy the Warlord. Help us."

Elizabeth's eyes became dangerous. "I will kill you first for your treason. Then I will kill your partners."

"No, you won't," Christopher said, gazing into her eyes. His voice took on an authority that radiated outward like that of an ancient Roman orator. There was something hypnotic about it, calling one to listen. "You will leave us alone and take your men away. You are better than being Dracula's pawn. You are a woman who once ruled the high seas and a devoted leader to your crew. Protect them from both Dracula and the House. Take them away from this place. That way, Annabelle's sacrifice won't be in vain."

"I see." Elizabeth Cambridge seemed confused, then shook her head. She leapt into the air as the soldiers under her command scattered to the four corners of the warehouse and disappeared. Our way was clear to Dracula's location.

I watched them leave in stunned silence. "Wow, I can't believe that worked. I guess words really are mightier than guns."

"They aren't." Christopher said, a disgusted look on his face. "Dracula has abused, misused, and tormented his offspring for centuries. It was easy to use those emotions and Elizabeth's love for Annabelle to assist in my mesmerizing her."

"Wait, what?" Shannon asked, looking at Christopher.

"Awesome," Penny said, her voice taking on a cruel edge.

"Whatever works," Malcolm said, laughing. "I never thought I would be grateful to a Mister Fang."

Christopher looked away. "It seems nobody possesses willpower that can't be compromised."

I wanted to comfort my friend, but we didn't have time for that. "You did what you had to do. We need to get a move on."

"I understand."

I started walking forward to the yellow door at the end of the warehouse.

Christopher followed in step behind me. "I suppose we can take some small comfort in the fact that I never would have been able to succeed in persuading her if that wasn't what she really wanted to do, anyway."

Shannon looked past. "I know a lot about mind control and in the end, it's all about breaking someone. She's probably free for the first time in her life."

Everyone else followed, not saying another word. The Dead Coyotes assumed their wolf forms again. I could feel Shannon do the same, gaining muscle mass and growing an inch taller than I. Even Penny began drawing mystical energy into herself from her surroundings, filling the air with a sense of power.

As for me? All I had was the Bloodsword, the blood magic and obscuromancy Mary had given me, a gun not designed to kill beings of Dracula's power, plus a little kung fu. In a very real way, I was the weak link, yet Mary thought I had the ability to stop Dracula forever. I wondered if this was all some sort of trap, but if it was, it was a hell of a lot of effort to go to for what amounted to a schoolyard prank.

I pushed aside my doubts and focused on the task at hand. Modulating my breathing, I felt myself calm and become more focused. We reached the yellow door and I looked at it as if it might spontaneously pour forth a host of demons. Reaching to the door handle, I pushed it forward and stepped inside.

To Hell on Earth.

Dracula had converted the inside, once a simple storage area, into a throne room of the damned. On sharpened lead pipes stabbed into the concrete were fifty or sixty corpses, stabbed through the stomach and left to dribble blood to the ground. The Impaler was resting on an antique wooden throne he must have brought with him, looking bored as a trio of heads were mounted on makeshift spears behind him. I recognized two of them as prominent White Room scientists, probably individuals who'd helped run the place with Rebecca.

All of the walls in this abattoir were covered in the sort of glyphs Mary had drawn on the inside of my hotel room. The ground was covered in blood, the smell overpowering, and I saw Christopher tremble in awe of it as he walked in behind me. It wasn't just blood having this effect, though, but the power that circled around us. Dracula hadn't just killed these people; he'd tortured so he could harness the energy released at the moment of death. It was great power he'd used to sanctify this place as a wizard's focus. The room was a blood magician's chamber like no other.

Which meant we were screwed. Well, screwed-er. There was no backing down now, and we still had the small advantage that Dracula didn't know just how much Mary had taught me. Small advantage as that was.

Dracula didn't move, though he clearly saw us. Instead, he just gave a lazy blink of his eyes as if our arrival was the most natural thing in the world. "I have danced this dance so many times in the past that it no longer amuses me. Still, you have arrived as I knew you would. I'm almost disappointed. I'd hoped you'd be smarter than to throw your lives away."

"I had some Castlevania jokes prepared, but it'd be pretty tasteless to say them now," I said, looking at the horror show around me. "What do you even get out of this?"

"Power," Dracula intoned as if speaking some great insight instead of a stock supervillain answer. "Once I loved art, science, and women, but the blood is now all that matters. It gives me life and influence as well as a fleeting reminder of the joy I once took in the heat of battle."

Shadow moved in front of me, growling at Dracula.

Dracula didn't seem to notice, instead turning his focus on Christopher. "And you. Have you turned against me so quickly? Did you have the strength to resist my power, or did they somehow break you free? I think the latter, because you were never as strong as you thought you were."

"I no longer fear your jests or jibes," Christopher said, his voice low and cold. "I am free from your control. Now and forever."

"My control was all that kept you sane. You vomited your first three drinks of blood," Dracula said, pointing at his head. "Our race would have long since destroyed itself by suicide or starvation if not for the commands by their elders to ignore their conscience."

"Maybe that should tell you something," Penny said, lifting her staff as if preparing to shoot a fireball. Hell, for all I knew, she was. "We've come to put you down."

Malcolm and his pack advanced, encircling Dracula's throne. Shannon transformed fully into a lilin, a creature both beautiful and alien to look upon. I, on the other hand, tossed down my gun and removed the Bloodsword from its sheath. I didn't raise it yet, though. Conventional weapons had proven useless against Dracula in the past, even with orihalcum ammunition. Somehow, he'd immunized himself to it.

Dracula's lip curled into a sneer. "You have no idea how many I have slaughtered over the years seeking to claim my life.

Thousands. Tens of thousands. Bands just like yours, confident in their righteousness but weak in power."

I remained calm, keeping my breathing steady. "As I recall, quite a few succeeded. You come back from the dead. You're immortal, not invincible."

Dracula rose from his throne. "Then let us end this drama."

Stretching out his hands, he drew from the power of the room's sanctification and threw it at us. All my group fell to its knees, feeling the exact same attack he'd used on me in the jet. Penny tried to hold it back but couldn't, her power dissipating in the overwhelming agony. It was enough to kill us all instantly, but he was going to torture us to death. The problem was, he wasn't the only blood magician around anymore, and I absorbed the energy into myself. One moment we were all dying, and the next I felt like a Greek god.

"How the hell did you do that?" Penny shouted.

"No idea!" I lied, lifting the Bloodsword.

Bruce Lee taught it was better to move with your opponent than against him, utilizing his strength rather than fighting it. Somehow, I doubted he meant this, but feeling the blood magic flow into my body, I hurled the agony back at Dracula and sent the Warlord flying backwards across the room.

The Dead Coyotes launched themselves at Dracula while he struggled to get up. Despite their massive strength and speed, the vampire threw them around like rag dolls. Snouts, arms, and legs were broken as he fought like a madman. Conjuring a set of three-inch long claws made of bones, Dracula slashed open Malcolm's chest and impaled Shadow in the stomach. They weren't lethal wounds for werewolves, but the injuries tore the fight out of them.

The distraction allowed Shannon to grab him from behind as Christopher joined her, grappling with the monster. With her staff in hand, Penny unleashed a bolt of glowing white energy that struck Dracula in the chest. The Warlord hissed as his skin burst out into hideous burns all over his body.

This gave me the opening to run forward and ram the Bloodsword straight through Dracula's black heart. Reality wasn't like fiction, and it didn't function as a wooden stake as on so many shows, reducing Dracula to ash. It didn't even immobilize him. Instead, it just seemed to really tick him off.

"You are not getting away!" I shouted, trying to regain my momentum as I twisted the blade. The pain I inflicted on Dracula made me stronger, gave me a rush of joy and adrenaline that almost blinded me to the fact that I was in mortal peril.

Dracula responded by kicking me into a concrete pillar, the Bloodsword still buried in his chest. The impact of my body against the pillar shattered bones and left me coughing blood, even as I drew on the blood around me to knit my bones and repair my body.

Dracula did the same. He threw Christopher across the room with one hand and turned to fight Shannon hand to hand. Penny threw lightning, fire, ice, and more into the ancient monster, but none of it seemed to do any good. Every blow she struck, he healed within moments.

That was when the entire room started to shake.

"What the Devil?" Dracula shouted, lifting up Shannon with both hands and throwing her against the wall. Shannon's wings proved more than ornamental, though, and she managed to slow her velocity to a crawl. Hovering in the air, flapping her wings only once every few seconds, Shannon prepared for another attack—ignoring the fact that something big was happening outside.

Pieces of the ceiling started falling down as explosions sounded above our heads.

"Oh, Count von Count." I laughed, getting up, healed of my wounds. The blood magic was coursing through me as it was through Dracula, and I was ready to rip out his heart with my teeth. "Did I mention I told Councilman Hawthorne about your attack? He's probably brought the entire American Navy to bomb this place to oblivion."

"He would not harm his two eldest children," Dracula said, drawing the Bloodsword out of his body.

"Man, you don't know my father at all, do you?" I said, running up at him.

Dracula swung his sword to cut my head off at a speed no ordinary human could match, but I ducked under it and grabbed the weapon with my left hand. It cut deeply into my palm. As my blood was absorbed, I used it to concentrate on the magic within this place. I felt powerful, more powerful than I'd ever felt in my life, and I was willing to bet a living human being would always be stronger than a walking corpse when wielding blood magic.

Dracula grabbed me by the right side of my face and started squeezing with his free hand. Only the hardening of my muscles with magic kept me from being crushed like a grape, and only barely so. I looked at him with my left eye. Despite it not being one of my artificial eye's functions, I could see all the various weavings of magic through the Elder vampire's body.

I could see how the stolen ki moved through his veins to sustain his undead existence, how part of his energy went to Tiamat-Abaddon, and how dark energy from hell poured forth into Dracula from their connection.

I had him.

Knowing more about martial arts than the vampire who'd spent the past few centuries butchering rather than waging war, I broke his wrist with one movement of my hand. I turned around the Bloodsword and plunged it into his neck. Behind him, Shannon had gouged her claws into his back and with Christopher's help, ripped out his spine.

"Go ahead, Cleaver," Dracula said, his mouth leaking blackish blood. He let go of my face, content to die and return. "I'll come back. I'll kill your family, your lovers, your friends, and everyone you hold dear. I'll start with those you brought today. It will be centuries before the misery stops."

"Not this time."

I covered my right hand in the shadowy energy as I continued to hold the Bloodsword by the left. It allowed me to reach into the monster's chest and grab him by the heart. Dracula screamed as I grasped not just the withered blackish organ but his very soul. From there, I drew all of the hellish power that sustained him into my hand. I wanted to break his connection to the Lord of the Damned and end his cursed existence forever.

The horror that filled me as I touched the spiritual and

physical embodiment of evil was beyond mere words. I wasn't a great believer in justice, good, or fairness, but I understood in that moment what their pure opposite was. All of Dracula's crimes across five hundred years of life filled my mind, uncountable murdered innocents and slaughtered armies. He'd given me a taste of it earlier, but this was everything. Every death, mutilation, and torture he'd inflicted on a world he hated. Yet in his soul, I felt the metaphysical chains that bound him to these planes, and in my hand—I dissolved them.

The metaphysical doorway to hell, which meant he'd always be able to return after death, slammed shut. Dracula screamed, looking at me in confusion, then started choking. He looked more disoriented than anything, the events far different from any of his previous battles against mortals. Dracula's body disintegrated into shadows, which retreated before the ceiling lights above our head.

If Dracula had anything left of his humanity, it was sent screaming back into the cycle. God, Death, or the ghosts of his victims would keep him from resurrecting this time. Hell, eternal prison of those damned by all other gods, was no refuge. One might even say his fate was worse than damnation. I couldn't say what lay for him instead. Oblivion? Torture? Eradication of all evil within his spirit? These were metaphysical questions I didn't care about. All I knew for certain was he was gone and it felt good.

I was left holding nothing, my hand covered in horrific burns. I couldn't feel anything inside it because every nerve ending had been destroyed by the terrible power I'd absorbed. Closing my eyes, I cut off the flow of ki to my hand before falling to my knees, my face contorted in agony. In the back of my mind, I felt another doorway to hell open.

From the door, I heard a single sentence. The voice was like a choir of ten thousand damned souls. "Impressive."

The doorway shut and my mind emptied of all thought, too much having happened to process.

The rest of my party, horribly wounded and battered, looked on in a mixture of relief and shock. Both emotions vanished as more explosions caused more pieces of the stone above our heads to fall. The building was coming down on us, and I wasn't certain we could escape in time.

This was when I slumped over, unconscious.

CHAPTER THIRTY-SIX

This time, there was only blackness. I heard explosions, shouts, cries, and recriminations, but nothing roused me from the darkness I was surrounded by. It was surprisingly peaceful, the emptiness. I wondered if I was in Hell, damned to spend however many lifetimes here until I reincarnated as someone better.

My father had always raised us to believe hell wasn't a suffering place. The God he believed in was not the sort to condemn souls to endless torture, but instead leave them alone with their sin. I decided not. I didn't believe in that sort of Hell. As merciful and pleasant a prison as God or the Jade Emperor may create, the damned would make it a suffering place. After all, look what humans had done to the Earth, and that was including the good ones.

Time passed, and I realized I wasn't dead by the sound of music penetrating my ears. It took a second for me to identify the song as "Diamond Dogs" by David Bowie. Not something you'd expect to hear when coming out of a coma.

Fluttering my eyes, I realized I was in the Division One-controlled Saint Magnus's hospital in downtown Washington, DC. I'd spent enough time over the years to recognize it by sight. I had an IV in my left arm, several monitors and cords attached to my right arm (which I couldn't feel), and a pair of tubes stuck in my nose. There was also a catheter stuck in me and my immediate reaction was to get it out.

Instead, I lay there, taking in my surroundings. The room was almost completely white, even the furniture, and had a single wooden door leading to the outside while the bathroom entrance was covered in a glass one. There was an absurd amount of equipment in the room, enough that I felt like I was in a spaceship rather than a medical bay.

At the end of my bed was my father, reading *The Return of the King* out loud. He was sitting at my bedside wearing casual attire and looking like the caring father I didn't want him to be. The image of Rebecca flashed across my mind and I knew we could never reconcile now. He'd sent me to kill someone I'd loved for a second time.

And worst of all, this time I'd done it.

"You know, I've read that book a few hundred times," I said.

My father didn't react to my awakening with surprise. "I was hoping the sound of something familiar would awaken you sooner. I'd like to point out I started with *The Hobbit*."

"How long have I been out?" I asked, my voice dry.

My father handed over a juice box. I found I couldn't lift my right hand, so I took it with my left, taking a drink of strawberry lemonade.

"A little more than two weeks," Nathan said, looking distressed. "You've had numerous surgeries since then, complete with magical healing. No expense spared, but even then, it was touch and go. Your insides were pretty ravaged by black magic. I don't suppose you know anything about that?"

I knew the question was rhetorical. "Must be an aftereffect of my fight with Dracula."

"Yes, first the Wazir and now Dracula. You're becoming quite the legendary hero, my son. It's almost enough to make the Committee overlook all your indiscretions. The Vampire Nation remnant has failed in all of its attempts to bring the Warlord back to life, which indicates he's not coming back."

"I didn't kill either alone. What do you mean, remnant?"

"The Vampire Nation is finished. Like the Nazis after World War 2 or the Knights Templar, they have been crushed by the weight of history."

"Or your armies," I said, not believing his confident statement. Dracula had been their war leader but the rest of the Council of Ancients was still alive. Indeed, Dracula may have been weighing them down since he'd always been a proponent of living apart from humans.

"Just so," Nathan said, closing the book in front of him. "The war had no greater call to arms than the Vampire Nation's heinous attack on a civilian chemical plant in broad daylight with the entire US Navy witnessing it."

"Which is not, at all, what happened."

"The Pact, the Caliphate, Catholic Church, and other allies all believe it. Those who suspect otherwise have no reason to doubt our version of events."

"The Dead Coyotes—" I started to speak.

"Remember something different." Nathan said, waving his hand as if hypnotizing me. "Don't worry, we released them back to the Pact with no injury save to their memories. The pack refused medals, so I arranged for a wire transfer in the effect of six figures. I understand Malcolm is using his share to build a school."

"And Christopher?"

"Your pet vampire donated six pints of blood, which we filtered and used to keep you stabilized through the process of recovery. He then disappeared before he could be brought up on charges and exterminated. Almost like someone left him in an unlocked interrogation room, near the exit."

"Thank you."

"I didn't say it was me. It will be a difficult world for him to survive in now that the Vampire Nation is destroyed and scattered. Like most dictatorships, it was controlled by Dracula's cult of personality. With him gone, they are doubly pressed to survive our assassinations."

"I'd like to see files on the war."

Nathan shook his head. "Sit, rest, and recover. There's nothing you can do. You must learn to choose your battles. The Committee suspects you were behind Rebecca's death but will not press the issue. Tend to your wounds and protect those you love from recrimination."

"How bad are my wounds?"

"Your right arm under the elbow is artificial," Nathan said. My eyes widened.

"Lucy called in specialists from around the world and helped incorporate the magitech to make it appear indistinguishable from a regular one," Nathan said. "Full *Empire Strikes Back* technology. This device will be harder to adjust to than your false eye, though, and the technology is less proven. You will suffer pain in it from time to time and will never be able to use magic through it again. I can't say what effect it'll have on your shooting."

I stared at my arm. "Great, I'm becoming more machine now than man."

"Speaking as someone who has lived through a great number of American wars, I request you don't make comparisons of prosthetics to Lord Vader. Far too many good and decent men lack access to devices like the one you now sport—another failure of the House system."

"Sorry. Pain always puts me in the mood to quote *Star Wars*."

Nathan snorted. "Then it's a wonder you aren't quoting it all the time. You should consider retiring from field work. You were too old for it before you became one of the most powerful men in the world."

"I'll never involve myself in a case again," I lied.

I never wanted to involve myself in anything House-related again, but there was nothing I could do about that. No one left the House unless it was in a body bag, and they'd probably send out assassins after Christopher once they'd given him a sufficient head start. He was right that I'd probably no longer be doing missions on the ground, but I couldn't just flick off my instincts like a light switch.

"I'll believe it when I see it." Nathan took back the juice box.

"Anything else I should know?"

"We did a complete neurological and mental scan of your brain after doing three separate exorcisms. There's no sign of the Bloodsword's demon. I wrote down there were indications she was using a low-level mind control to influence you into trusting her, but there were none. Why, for the love of God, were you working with that thing?"

"I dunno," I said. "I guess because Mary saved my life."

Nathan looked annoyed. "Well, promise me you won't get involved with any more black magic. The sorcery you worked almost killed you and would have given enough time. The sole reason you're not riddled with cancer is Hoshi's nanites."

"What does the family think happened to Rebecca?" I asked, looking away.

"You missed the funeral. I gave a moving speech about her sacrificing her life for the House. Penny knows the truth but would never betray your confidence. Everyone else thinks she was researching medicine."

"I wanted to find another way—"

"Rebecca is the sixth child I've lost and the second I fear for the soul of." Nathan stood up from his chair. "If you decide to continue studying the paths of sorcery, Derek, I suggest you do not pursue the path of longevity as I have. It wears on the soul."

I asked him one final question. "What happened to the Bloodsword?"

"If I had your gift for quips, I'd say it was being researched by top men. In truth, though, I have no idea."

"No idea?"

Nathan walked to the door before turning to me and nodding. "It disappeared soon after our researchers acquired it. Lucy is beside herself. In my mind, I suspect it will show up whenever your friendly neighborhood demon wants you to have it again."

"Great," I said, taking deep breath. "When do I get discharged?"

"You just emerged from a coma. Trust me, we're all aware of how tough you are."

I didn't want to spend any more time here. "I've been in a coma twice before. The White Room had me wakened from them within hours and sent back into the field."

Nathan frowned. "A few days but, given your body-control abilities, you might be able to leave any time you want. I wouldn't recommend it, though."

"Goodbye, Nathan."

Nathan departed, leaving me alone in the room. I looked to my right arm and stared at it, willing it to move. It didn't make any grinding noises like in a science fiction movie, but looked and felt like an ordinary arm.

I moved my fingers several times and wondered why they

hadn't tried a transplant or tissue growth like they did in Europe. Was I incompatible, or did Lucy just trust technology over flesh when trying to patch me back up?

I was wiggling my fingers when I saw Shannon pop her head in. She was wearing a round white hat and a red-threaded anachronistic nineteenth-century suit. I had to blink a few times to make sure I wasn't seeing things. In her right hand was an umbrella.

"You're awake?" Shannon said, walking in.

"Why are you dressed like you just stepped off a stagecoach?" I asked, staring at her.

"Wetwork waits for no one. My current mission is at a steampunk convention."

"And I missed it?" I asked, feigning horror.

"There's still a couple of days," Shannon said, looking at my new arm. "How's the wrist action, Tin Man?"

"So far so good, but it feels heavier than my regular arm. I'll have to try it out on delicate tasks," I said, lacing my words with innuendo.

Shannon snorted. "Just make sure you have complete control before you bring that thing anywhere near me."

"Will do," I said.

Shannon walked over to my side, put down her umbrella and looked at me. "I want to hug you, but I'm not sure how to get around all these wires."

"I'll have a nurse remove them," I said, annoyed by my surroundings. I needed to get away from all this. The House, the conspiracies, the lies, and the murder. You couldn't leave the Committee, but maybe they'd let me take a leave of absence. "I want to check out within the hour."

"Are you sure that's wise?" Shannon looked even more concerned than Nathan.

"Better than waiting here in a prone state until the Committee decides my handling of the Camp Zero situation was suspicious," I said, shifting in the bed. "Though I suppose if they were going to kill me they would have just let me die."

"No one wants you to die," Shannon said, placing her hand on my right hand. I felt the warmth of her hand against my artificial skin. I had to commend Lucy's work. "Everyone in the House is talking about your heroic defeat of Dracula."

"How a vampire, three werewolves, a witch, and a lilin helped me kill him with black magic?" I asked.

"Sounds like a video game, doesn't it?" Shannon joked.

"A little," I admitted.

Shannon smiled coyly. "Yeah, that's why they edited it into a more sanitized story. I think it involves rescuing me from being kidnapped since I'm a helpless damsel in distress."

I snorted.

A dark look came over my face. "Shannon, there's something you need to know. My sister, Rebecca—"

"I figured it out."

"Do you still want to be with a kinslayer?"

"I'm an ex-serial killing Satanist and you're asking me if I want to be with you after you killed your psycho sister."

I stared at her. "Yes?"

"The warrior-poet-assassin thing is usually pretty hot, but drop the angst, Derek. We have enough trouble in our lives worrying about things we need to without you angsting about someone who doesn't deserve it."

I didn't respond.

Shannon leaned over and gave me a kiss on the lips. "You've got another couple of visitors outside."

"You brought a meal for us to enjoy?"

Shannon raised an eyebrow. "Really, Derek? You've had your entire body completely bit to shit and you're thinking about a threesome?"

"You're a succubus, Shannon. It's entirely your fault. Besides, I want to see if this new hand works as well as I'm hoping."

"That's not creepy."

"I need my hands for two things."

"Shooting and eating?"

I smirked at her.

Shannon poked me in the shoulder, which hurt a bit more than would have been comfortable for sex, even if it were possible in a hospital where we were undoubtedly being watched by all manner of the House's security.

"I really think you should take these two." Shannon pulled away.

The smile ran away from my face. "Oh?"

Shannon nodded. "I'll talk to you afterward."

Now I was curious. "Send them in."

Shannon walked to the door and waved to someone outside of my sight, leading to my uncle Ben Talbot coming in. Ben stood well over six feet in height with broad shoulders and over three hundred pounds of muscle. His face was riddled with scars, and I knew the rest of his body was equally covered in them. Ben was the real-life inspiration for Mary Shelley's *Frankenstein*.

A century before Shannon, he'd been the House's first supernatural agent and had a storied career spanning decades, against everything from demons to Ghost Hitler. Today, he was wearing an extra-large Hawaiian shirt and a pair of baggy beige cargo shorts with flip-flops. A pair of mirror sunglasses rested on his nose.

It was a ridiculous look, but one that was entirely him. Behind him, Christopher entered the room. It was insane—suicidally so, really. The House was extremely good at detecting supernatural infiltrators, and we were now at war with the Vampire Nation (what was left of it).

He was at least dressed differently. He'd adopted a brown overcoat over a blue sweater with a scarf. Christopher was even wearing blue jeans, which was a sharp contrast to the richly dressed man who had greeted me at the ski lodge. Christopher looked more like himself now, but that couldn't change the fact that he still was a vampire and always would be.

At least, until he was killed.

"Hey," I said, wondering what had managed to bring him out of retirement. "A vampire, succubus, and Frankenstein walk into a hospital bed to visit a cyborg blood mage."

Shannon rolled her eyes.

Christopher looked to Shannon. "Shannon, if you don't mind, could you give us a couple of minutes alone?"

"Sure." Shannon departed, shutting the door behind her.

"This feels foreboding," I said, looking between my guests. "How the hell did you two meet?"

"Hard work on his part," Talbot said, putting his hands together. "I met him during my vacation in Hawaii. He couldn't get in touch with you after the events on Nassau so he wanted to use me as an intermediary."

"He shouldn't be here," I muttered.

"No shit he shouldn't be," Talbot said. "However, he is."

"Okay, but if this turns into a secret plot to kidnap me and drag me off to some hostile nation—"

"That'll be Thursday," Christopher said.

"Point taken."

Christopher looked over his shoulder, as if worried Red Room agents would burst in at any second. "We need to talk."

"Do we?" I said, looking at my artificial arm and flexing the fingers. "Dracula is permanently dead, Protocol Zero is no more, the Vampire Nation has taken a serious hit and probably will lose this war without revealing the Truth, plus your wife is dead along with my sister, but it's okay because they were both assholes. Am I missing anything?"

"The House set you up."

"Did it?" I asked, not at all surprised.

Christopher explained his theory. "The only reason you didn't have layers upon layers of security at Aspen, that Dracula was able to pick you up, and that I was even able to get a meeting with you is because the rest of the Committee wants you gone."

I sighed. "Christopher, if the Committee wanted me dead, I'd be dead. The only reason I'm alive is Nathan."

"That's what he wants you to think. I think your father is the one who wants you dead."

I stared at him. "No."

Talbot looked away, giving more credence to the theory than I was comfortable with. He'd once been my father's best friend.

Christopher sighed. "You've changed the game board. Twice. The Emerald Eye and Vampire Nation are both collapsing. The House was weakened both times, but it's going to grow in power now. That's going to give you security in your position. The other Committee members may not see you as an equal, but you're going to be their hatchet man from now on. The Dragon they use to guard their treasure."

"I was always their killer."

"Perhaps." Christopher closed his eyes. "But maybe you can be more. I've been in contact with Ashley. Close contact."

I stared at him, then looked at Talbot. "Can we talk? Freely, I mean."

"For another few minutes," Talbot replied. "I've got every possible amulet and ward for keeping this conversation quiet active."

I nodded. "…how is she?"

"That's the thing," Christopher said, staring. "I contacted her as soon as my free will was restored. I felt I owed it to you to try and get you back in touch with her. I thought maybe I owed you something for all you've done for me. You deserve a chance at a normal life away from this hellhole. I thought maybe we could fake your death and find you a nice hidey-hole off the grid."

I admitted, that sounded attractive. "And?"

"The Committee found her. They know about everything you did for her and are holding her prisoner."

My mouth went dry. "Help me get her back."

"I will," Christopher said.

It was time to end my association with the House.

ABOUT THE AUTHOR

C.T. Phipps is a lifelong student of horror, science fiction, and fantasy. An avid tabletop gamer, he discovered this passion led him to write and turned him into a lifelong geek. He is a regular blogger and also a reviewer for The Bookie Monster.

BIBLIOGRAPHY

The Rules of Supervillainy (Supervillainy Saga #1)
The Games of Supervillainy (Supervillainy Saga #2)
The Secrets of Supervillainy (Supervillainy Saga #3)
The Kingdom of Supervillany (Supervillainy Saga #4)
The Tournament of Supervillany (Supervillainy Saga #5)
The Future of Supervillainy (Supervillainy Saga #6)
I Was a Teenage Weredeer (The Bright Falls Mysteries, Book 1)
An American Weredeer in Michigan (The Bright Falls Mysteries, Book 2)
Esoterrorism (Red Room, Vol. 1)
Eldritch Ops (Red Room, Vol. 2)
Agent G: Infiltrator (Agent G, Vol. 1)
Agent G: Saboteur (Agent G, Vol. 2)
Agent G: Assassin (Agent G, Vol. 3)
Cthulhu Armageddon (Cthulhu Armageddon, Vol. 1)
The Tower of Zhaal (Cthulhu Armageddon, Vol. 2)
Lucifer's Star (Lucifer's Star, Vol. 1)
Lucifer's Nebula (Lucifer's Star, Vol. 2)
Straight Outta Fangton (Straight Outta Fangton, Vol. 1)
100 Miles and Vampin' (Straight Outta Fangton, Vol. 2)
Wraith Knight (Wraith Knight, Vol. 1)
Wraith Lord (Wraith Knight, Vol. 2)

Curious about other Crossroad Press books?
Stop by our site:
http://store.crossroadpress.com
We offer quality writing
in digital, audio, and print formats.